THE EARLY WORK OF PHILIP K. DICK

VOLUME TWO:

BREAKFAST AT TWILIGHT & OTHER STORIES

THE EARLY WORK OF
PHILIP
K. DICK

VOLUME TWO:
BREAKFAST AT TWILIGHT
& OTHER STORIES

SERIES EDITOR:
GREGG RICKMAN

PRIME BOOKS

THE EARLY WORK OF PHILIP K. DICK

VOLUME TWO:
BREAKFAST AT TWILIGHT & OTHER STORIES

———

Interior design and typesetting by
Linduna [www.linduna.com]

Prime Books
www.prime-books.com

ISBN: 978-1-60701-203-0

TABLE OF CONTENTS

———

INTRODUCTION
BY GREGG RICKMAN

Philip K. Dick (1928-1982) is now universally considered one of the great science fiction writers of the 20th century. In his own time recognition came slower, and grudgingly. Discussing with amazement how good he found Dick's first novel, *Solar Lottery*, in 1955, author and critic Damon Knight referred to him as "that short story writer who for the past five years or so has been popping up all over—in one year, 1953, he published twenty-seven stories—with a sort of unobtrusive and chameleon-like competence." His early mentor Anthony Boucher, editor of *The Magazine of Fantasy and Science Fiction,* noted with amusement how his stories fit their intended markets, no matter how different: "The editors of *Whizzing Star Patrol* and of the *Quaint Quality Quarterly* are in complete agreement upon Mr. Dick as a singularly satisfactory contributor."

Dick actually published 31 stories in 1953, and 28 in 1954. Thirteen that he wrote in this period are published here. But rather than see Dick's prolific output in his early years as a science fiction writer as a cause for criticism, it should be celebrated. Dick, who had made his debut in the July 1952 issue of the downmarket *Planet Stories* (but had made his first sale to Boucher's quaint quality monthly *F&SF*) was finding his way as a writer, exploring different themes, testing his strengths. The first story by Philip K. Dick included in this book, "Survey Team," reached his agents at the Scott Meredith Literary Agency on April 3, 1953; the last, the novella "A World of Talent," reached the agency on June 4 of the following year. The meticulous records kept by the sub-agents who handled his work at SMLA are a marvelous guide as to just what Dick wrote and when. And Dick's fiction of these months comprises a panoramic portrait of America and the world during some of the chilliest days of the Cold War.

Genial war hero Dwight David Eisenhower took office as president on January 20, 1953. Dick would satirize Ike's grinning banality in his 1955 story "The Mold of Yancy" (published 1958), but the president's good nature was but a charming façade. The first months of the Eisenhower Administration, during which the stories in this book were written, were marked by stern Secretary of State John Foster Dulles' confrontational stance with the Soviet Union. The Secretary's brother Allan Dulles chaired the Central Intelligence Agency, involved in 1953-54 with the overthrow of two foreign governments, in Iran and Guatemala. Senator Joseph McCarthy and his highly publicized crusade against a vast communist conspiracy dominated an uncritical news media. Other highly placed officials such as Vice President Richard Nixon and FBI Director J. Edgar Hoover were also famous for their stern anti-Communism. Hoover personally oversaw his agency's close surveillance of many American citizens suspected of being (or knowing) subversives. A purge of suspected Communist sympathizers from federal and state jobs, from schools, and from the media continued.

Berkeley, California, home of the University of California, was considered a liberal hotbed at the time. The Federal Bureau of Investigation regularly photographed the radicals who spoke at UC Berkeley's Sather Gate. Philip Dick's wife Kleo (a part-time student) attended these rallies out of interest. Sometime in 1952 the Bureau sent two agents to interview her and her husband, seeking information and asking if they wanted to become informers. "It was never anything we seriously considered," she told me in a 1985 interview. It was in this period that Dick himself, in his telling, was questioned a number of times by FBI agents, one of whom in particular befriending the author and helping him to learn to drive.

According to Kleo, and to his other friends of the time, Dick's politics were liberal and anti-communist. He played by his own account a double game, writing his friend Sandra Meisel in 1979: "The climate of reactionary terror was still very much with us... , The FBI still visited me several times a month to see how and what I was doing. (I was learning to drive, and I used to get them to ride with me while I practiced ... I figured if a traffic cop stopped me, the presence of two FBI men would save me from a ticket.)"

Outwardly conformist in his private life, Dick's writing questioned many of his era's assumptions. "The Hanging Stranger" (which reached the Scott Meredith agency on May 4, 1953, and was published by *Science Fiction Adventures* in its December issue) encapsulates the fearful paranoia of the time very succinctly. Ed Loyce, owner of a TV sales and repair store, notices a man dangling from a lamppost. He panics, and panics again at the fact that no one wants to pay any attention to it. While the story evolves into an aliens-taking-over-the-Earth story, it's no less political for that.

The CIA's overthrow of democratic governments in Iran and Nicaragua, and the contempt these overthrows revealed for the aspirations of those nation's peoples, is critically addressed by Dick's writing. "Tony and the Beetles," included here, foresees an end to inevitable human expansion across the universe. Its anti-imperialist message echoes the work of other authors critical of European or American assumptions about pleasant relationships between colonized and colonizers. The naïve boy Tony learns the hard way that his native friends don't want to play with him anymore—the lesson of better-known works like Orwell's *Burmese Days* or Greene's *The Ugly American,* a lesson the U.S. would go on to learn again in Vietnam and more recently Iraq.

"What are you, a goddamn beetle-lover?" asks the dad in "Tony and the Beetles." Dick's interest in trying to understand foreign cultures extends to trying to comprehend the minds of robots (as in "The Last of the Masters") and of people living in other times, like the "Middle Twentieth Century" denizens historian George Miller emulates in "Exhibit Piece."

1953 also saw the death of Soviet dictator Joseph Stalin in March, civilian revolts against the communist government of East Germany in June, and the end of the four years of the Korean War in a bloody stalemate in July. Dick references the East German revolt (quickly and brutally repressed) in a one-line comment in "The Last of the Masters" (which reached the agency a month after the revolt had run its course, on July 15, 1953) about how the worldwide marches which led to the end of all governments (and the destruction of all the world's A-bombs) had "started in East Germany." In harsh reality, atomic bombs continued to proliferate. The U.S. exploded its first hydrogen bomb, 450 times more powerful than the atomic bomb dropped on Nagasaki, on Nov. 1, 1952. A further advance came with the first thermonuclear device, exploded at Bikini Atoll in the South Pacific on March 1, 1954. The Soviets, meanwhile, developed and exploded their own advanced nuclear weapons in 1953-55.

In 1950 physicist Leo Szilard had proposed the concept of a cobalt bomb, suggesting that its intense radiation and long half-life could destroy all life on earth. At the end of "Exhibit Piece," as 22nd century historian George Miller settles down to relax after successfully escaping to the 1950s, his idyll is destroyed when he opens his newspaper to read

RUSSIA REVEALS COBALT BOMB
TOTAL WORLD DESTRUCTION AHEAD

How does one react to this terror? In a 1955 essay, "Pessimism in Science Fiction," Dick argued that an sf writer "is not merely inclined to act out the Cassandra role; he is absolutely obliged to," and stories like "Exhibit Piece" and its time-traveling mirror image "Breakfast at Twilight" live up to that demand. The end of "Breakfast at Twilight" is practically a call to arms, albeit a passive one: "I should have had it looked at. Before it was too late."

It follows that as an escape from these looming nightmares that many Dick protagonists retreat into worlds of their own. Both George Miller in "Exhibit Piece," and Bors the robot in "The Last of the Masters" construct "an accurate and detailed reproduction of a society two centuries gone," to quote the latter story. Both entities are accused of "breaking up mentally," for construction of their "model universe" amounts to "A hell of a job. Trying to shut out the real world."

In "Exhibit Piece" World Directorate official Edwin Carnap, who attempts to coax George Miller out of the 1950s-style home that Miller has taken refuge in, is most likely named after the logical positivist philosopher Rudolf Carnap (1891-1970). Carnap was best known for attempting to abolish the study of metaphysics from serious philosophical discussion. Dick's Carnap accuses Miller of rationalizing his psychotic "delusions into a logical system." Dick would famously undergo intense religious experiences in the 1960s and 1970s, but his fiction indicates he was seriously contemplating the great questions of metaphysics in 1953.

Metaphysics are indeed one way out. But Dick, in 1953-54, endorses western technology over Eastern mysticism in "The Turning Wheel." "The Last of the Masters" expresses sympathy for both the Anarchist League, which had brought down all governments worldwide, and the robot-created private world which has secretly kept a technological society going. In "Survey Team" Dick employs the device of humanity, after a world war, taking refuge in subterranean tunnels, "working and sleeping and dying without seeing the sun." Dick will rework this device many times, notably *The Penultimate Truth* (1964). Humanity's life underground gives rise in this story to mutant children, "wan faced pseudo mutants with eyes like blind fish." Dick several times in his 1953 fiction expands on the idea of war-produced mutants, notably in the deeply disturbing "The Crawlers."

Philip Dick told me in 1981 that his early stories comprised "the most conventional science fiction imaginable. It all starts off with looking through the vid screen. 'Captain! Look through the vid screen! I believe I see a strange object!' "

Dick was too hard on himself. The closest story in this collection to this model is a space fantasy, "Strange Eden." The story does indeed seem conventional in its first paragraph, as a space captain surveys a promising new world. But as early as the second paragraph Dick reveals Captain Johnson as weak and cowardly ("He blinked nervously"). His brave second in command, meanwhile, is an oaf whose cupidity dooms him. Already in this early story Dick undercuts the standard models of heroic space captains and noble explorers—a model that was later taken up and institutionalized in TV and cinema, as in the many incarnations of *Star Trek*.

Dick also dissented from the mainstream of science fiction with his treatment of "psionics," the extrasensory powers of precognition, telepathy, telekinesis and others that were very much in vogue in the 1950s. The possibility that these powers existed was taken quite seriously at the time; even Rudolf Carnap had some books on the subject in his library. Dick told me in 1981:

> The definition of science fiction in those days, in the mid-'50s, was just incredibly limited. There was all this "psi" stuff that John W. Campbell (editor of one of the field's leading magazines, *Astounding*) was promoting, and it had gotten to the point where he said that psionics was the necessary premise for science fiction stories . . . Now that is really narrowing the field down.
>
> Campbell said that you not only have to write about psionics, but the psis have to be in charge and they have to be good. They can neither be marginal nor can they be negative.

It was Philip K. Dick who broke with this, brilliantly, in the concluding novella of this volume. "A World of Talent" is a breakthrough work for the field. His Psis are hard-bitten survivalists, manipulating the world around them for their benefit. His story, further, brings into play the concept of "anti-talents," individuals who can block precogs, telepaths, etc. from reading them. "Consider the various Psi talents as survival weapons," says Dick's hero. "Consider telepathic ability as evolving for the defense of an organism. It puts the Telepath head and shoulders above his enemies. Is this going to continue? Don't these things usually balance out?" Anti-talents evolve to balance what would otherwise be unchallenged power. Dick's subtle reading of the checks and balances implicit in his field's imaginative constructs already marked him off as ahead of his field—as early as 1953. Dick himself used checks and balances in his own life, riding with FBI agents as a precaution against being pulled over by the local police.

As we have seen, many of Dick's most appealing characters, like the autistic boy Manfred Steiner in *Martian Time-Slip* (1964) live in worlds of their own. Tim Purcell, the eight-year-old boy of "A World of Talent," anticipates Manfred in his special abilities. He suffers, as he is not in phase with the rest of the world. "Try to hold an objective orientation," his father tells him gently, urging him to step back from his disconcerting obsessions. The sympathetic anti-talent Patricia Ann Connley (so different from her equally dark haired girl namesake, Pat Conley, in *Ubik*) comments on Tim's strangeness. "He takes his alternate world so seriously. Not a pleasant world, I guess. Too many responsibilities."

Fantasy stories were Dick's first love. "Strange Eden" openly references Greek mythology. The ultimate early expression of one of his great themes, the complete psychological possession of one person by another entity, comes in the brilliant "Upon the Dull Earth." Dick's acclaimed later work on these themes—notably the demonic *The Three Stigmata of Palmer Eldritch* (1965)—is prefigured here, in the tragedy of Silvia Everett.

One well-known sf author suggested that the contemporary vogue for Philip Dick will pass as we leave the 20th century and its specific issues— like the Cold War—behind. Others suggest instead that Dick was a postmodernist *avant la lettre* and that his best work still speaks to our fragmented, dissociated selves in this post-2001 age of surveillance, paranoia and the commodification of everything. Such critics cite acclaimed work like *Ubik* (1969), with its frustrated nonentity of a protagonist (with the silicon-sounding moniker of "Joe Chip") scrounging for enough small change to pay his surly, AI-laden door to open. I would go further, and point, as a demonstration of this author's continuing relevance, not to this volume's best stories, but to a relatively minor work, a humorous tale Dick himself later disowned. "Sales Pitch," with its inescapable din of commercials, strangely anticipates today's unceasing digital cable, or the unending news cycles of the internet:

> "All the news while it's news," a metallic voice dinned at him. "Have a retinal vid-screen installed in your least used eye. Keep in touch with the world; don't wait for out-of-date hourly summaries."

The story's ultimate demonic device that cannot be shut off, the fasrad, "is always ready to answer any theoretical or factual inquiry," rendering it the Google or Wikipedia of Dick's imagination. The true sign of its ill nature, though, is the caveat the fasrad instantly adds: "Anything not metaphysical."

For in the face of looming destruction, metaphysics will come to offer Philip Dick the most likely way out.

Gregg Rickman
Berkeley, California
May, 2008

Works Cited

Philip K. Dick, "Pessimism in Science Fiction," *Oblique* 6 (1955), rpt. in Lawrence Sutin, ed., *The Shifting Realities of Philip K. Dick* (New York: Pantheon, 1995)

Damon Knight, *In Search of Wonder* (Second edition, Chicago: Advent, 1967)

Gregg Rickman, *Philip K. Dick: In His Own Words* (Long Beach, CA: Fragments West/The Valentine Press, 1984; second ed., 1989)

Gregg Rickman, *To the High Castle, Philip K. Dick: A Life 1928-1962* (Long Beach, CA: Fragments West/The Valentine Press, 1989)

BREAKFAST AT TWILIGHT

"Dad?" Earl asked, hurrying out of the bathroom, "you going to drive us to school today?"

Tim McLean poured himself a second cup of coffee. "You kids can walk for a change. The car's in the garage."

Judy pouted. "It's raining."

"No it isn't," Virginia corrected her sister. She drew the shade back. "It's all foggy, but it isn't raining."

"Let me look." Mary McLean dried her hands and came over from the sink. "What an odd day. Is that fog? It looks more like smoke. I can't make out a thing. What did the weatherman say?"

"I couldn't get anything on the radio," Earl said. "Nothing but static."

Tim stirred angrily. "That darn thing on the blink again? Seems like I just had it fixed." He got up and moved sleepily over to the radio. He fiddled idly with the dials. The three children hurried back and forth, getting ready for school. "Strange," Tim said.

"I'm going," Earl opened the front door.

"Wait for your sisters," Mary ordered absently.

"I'm ready," Virginia said. "Do I look all right?"

"You look fine," Mary said, kissing her.

"I'll call the radio repair place from the office," Tim said.

He broke off. Earl stood at the kitchen door, pale and silent, his eyes wide with terror.

"What is it?"

"I—I came back."

"What is it? Are you sick?"

"I can't go to school."

They stared at him. "What is wrong?" Tim grabbed his son's arm. "Why can't you go to school?"

"They—they won't let me."

"*Who?*"

"The soldiers." It came tumbling out with a rush. "They're all over. Soldiers and guns. And they're coming here."

"Coming? Coming here?" Tim echoed, dazed.

"They're coming here and they're going to—" Earl broke off, terrified. From the front porch came the sound of heavy boots. A crash. Splintering wood. Voices.

"Good Lord," Mary gasped. "What is it, Tim?"

Tim entered the living room, his heart laboring painfully. Three men stood inside the door. Men in gray-green uniforms, weighted with guns and complex tangles of equipment. Tubes and hoses. Meters on thick cords. Boxes and leather straps and antennas. Elaborate masks locked over their heads. Behind the masks Tim saw tired, whisker-stubbled faces, red-rimmed eyes that gazed at him in brutal displeasure.

One of the soldiers jerked up his gun, aiming at McLean's middle. Tim peered at it dumbly. *The gun.* Long and thin. Like a needle. Attached to a coil of tubes.

"What in the name of—" he began, but the soldier cut him off savagely.

"Who are you?" His voice was harsh, guttural. "What are you doing here?" He pushed his mask aside. His skin was dirty. Cuts and pocks lined his sallow flesh. His teeth were broken and missing.

"Answer!" a second soldier demanded. "What are you doing here?"

"Show your blue card," the third said. "Let's see your Sector number." His eyes strayed to the children and Mary standing mutely at the dining room door. His mouth fell open.

"*A woman!*"

The three soldiers gazed in disbelief.

"What the hell is this?" the first demanded. "How long has this woman been here?"

Tim found his voice. "She's my wife. What is this? What—"

"Your *wife*?" They were incredulous.

"My wife and children. For God's sake—"

"Your wife? And you'd bring her here? You must be out of your head!"

"He's got ash sickness," one said. He lowered his gun and strode across the living room to Mary. "Come on, sister. You're coming with us."

Tim lunged.

A wall of force hit him. He sprawled, clouds of darkness rolling around him. His ears sang. His head throbbed. Everything receded. Dimly, he was aware of shapes moving. Voices. The room. He concentrated.

The soldiers were herding the children back. One of them grabbed Mary by the arm. He tore her dress away, ripping it from her shoulders. "Gee," he snarled. "He'd bring her here, and she's not even strung!"

"Take her along."

"OK, Captain." The soldier dragged Mary toward the front door. "We'll do what we can with her."

"The kids." The captain waved the other soldier over with the children. "Take them along. I don't get it. No masks. No cards. How'd this house miss getting hit? Last night was the worst in months!"

Tim struggled painfully to his feet. His mouth was bleeding. His vision blurred. He hung on tight to the wall. "Look," he muttered. "For God's sake—"

The captain was staring into the kitchen. "Is that—is that *food*?" He advanced slowly through the dining room. "Look!"

The other soldiers came after him, Mary and the children forgotten. They stood around the table, amazed.

"Look at it!"

"Coffee." One grabbed up the pot and drank it greedily down. He choked, black coffee dripping down his tunic. "Hot. Jeeze. Hot coffee."

"Cream!" Another soldier tore open the refrigerator. "Look. Milk. Eggs. Butter. Meat." His voice broke. "It's full of food."

The captain disappeared into the pantry. He came out, lugging a case of canned peas. "Get the rest. Get it all. We'll load it in the snake."

He dropped the case on the table with a crash. Watching Tim intently, he fumbled in his dirty tunic until he found a cigarette. He lit it slowly, not taking his eyes from Tim. "All right," he said. "Let's hear what you have to say."

Tim's mouth opened and closed. No words came. His mind was blank. Dead. He couldn't think.

"This food. Where'd you get it? And these things." The captain waved around the kitchen. "Dishes. Furniture. How come this house hasn't been hit? How did you survive last night's attack?"

"I—" Tim gasped.

The captain came toward him ominously. "The woman. And the kids. All of you. What are you doing here?" His voice was hard. "You better be able to explain, mister. You better be able to explain what you're doing here—or we'll have to burn the whole damn lot of you."

Tim sat down at the table. He took a deep, shuddering breath, trying to focus his mind. His body ached. He rubbed blood from his mouth, conscious of a broken molar and bits of loose tooth. He got out a handkerchief and spat the bits into it. His hands were shaking.

"Come on," the captain said.

Mary and the children slipped into the room. Judy was crying.

Virginia's face was blank with shock. Earl stared wide-eyed at the soldiers, his face white.

"Tim," Mary said, putting her hand on his arm. "Are you all right?"

Tim nodded. "I'm all right."

Mary pulled her dress around her. "Tim, they can't get away with it. Somebody'll come. The mailman. The neighbors. They can't just—"

"Shut up," the captain snapped. His eyes flickered oddly. "The mailman? What are you talking about?" He held out his hand. "Let's see your yellow slip, sister."

"Yellow slip?" Mary faltered.

The captain rubbed his jaw. "No yellow slip. No masks. No cards."

"They're geeps," a soldier said.

"Maybe. And maybe not."

"They're geeps, Captain. We better burn 'em. We can't take any chances."

"There's something funny going on here," the captain said. He plucked at his neck, lifting up a small box on a cord. "I'm getting a police here."

"A police?" A shiver moved through the soldiers. "Wait, Captain. We can handle this. Don't get a police. He'll put us on 4 and then we'll never—"

The captain spoke into the box. "Give me Web B."

Tim looked up at Mary. "Listen, honey. I—"

"Shut up." A soldier prodded him. Tim lapsed into silence.

The box squawked. "Web B."

"Can you spare a police? We've run into something strange. Group of five. Man, woman, three kids. No masks, no cards, the woman not strung, dwelling completely intact. Furniture, fixtures, about two hundred pounds of food."

The box hesitated. "All right. Police on the way. Stay there. Don't let them escape."

"I won't." The captain dropped the box back in his shirt. "A polic will be here any minute. Meanwhile, let's get the food loaded."

From outside came a deep thundering roar. It shook the house, rattling the dishes in the cupboard.

"Jeez," a soldier said. "That was close."

"I hope the screens hold until nightfall." The captain grabbed up the case of canned peas. "Get the rest. We want it loaded before the polic comes."

The two soldiers filled their arms and followed him through the house, out the front door. Their voice diminished as they strode down the path.

Tim got to his feet. "Stay here," he said thickly.

"What are you doing?" Mary asked nervously.

"Maybe I can get out." He ran to the back door and unlatched it, hands shaking. He pulled the door wide and stepped out on the back porch. "I don't see any of them. If we can only . . . "

He stopped.

Around him gray clouds blew. Gray ash, billowing as far as he could see. Dim shapes were visible. Broken shapes, silent and unmoving in the grayness.

Ruins.

Ruined buildings. Heaps of rubble. Debris everywhere. He walked slowly down the back steps. The concrete walk ended abruptly. Beyond it, slag and heaps of rubble were strewn. Nothing else. Nothing as far as the eye could see.

Nothing stirred. Nothing moved. In the gray silence there was no life. No motion. Only the clouds of drifting ash. The slag and the endless heaps.

The city was gone. The buildings were destroyed. Nothing remained. No people. No life. Jagged walls, empty and gaping. A few dark weeds growing among the debris. Tim bent down, touching a weed. Rough, thick stalk. And the slag. It was a metal slag. Melted metal. He straightened up—

"Come back inside," a crisp voice said.

He turned numbly. A man stood on the porch, behind him, hands on his hips. A small man, hollow-cheeked. Eyes small and bright, like two black coals. He wore a uniform different from the soldiers'. His mask was pushed back, away from his face. His skin was yellow, faintly luminous, clinging to his cheekbones. A sick face, ravaged by fever and fatigue.

"Who are you?" Tim said.

"Douglas. Political Commissioner Douglas."

"You're—you're the police," Tim said.

"That's right. Now come inside. I expect to hear some answers from you. I have quite a few questions.

"The first thing I want to know," Commissioner Douglas said, "is how this house escaped destruction."

Tim and Mary and the children sat together on the couch, silent and unmoving, faces blank with shock.

"Well?" Douglas demanded.

Tim found his voice. "Look," he said. "I don't know. I don't know anything. We woke up this morning like every other morning. We dressed and ate breakfast—"

"It was foggy out," Virginia said, "We looked out and saw the fog."

"And the radio wouldn't work," Earl said.

"The radio?" Douglas's thin face twisted. "There haven't been any audio signals in months. Except for government purposes. This house. All of you. I don't understand. If you were geeps—"

"Geeps. What does that mean?" Mary murmured.

"Soviet general-purpose troops."

"Then the war has begun."

"North America was attacked two years ago," Douglas said. "In 1978."

Tim sagged. "1978. Then this is 1980." He reached suddenly into his pocket. He pulled out his wallet and tossed it to Douglas. "Look in there."

Douglas opened the wallet suspiciously. "Why?"

"The library card. The parcel receipts. Look at the dates." Tim turned to Mary. "I'm beginning to understand now. I had an idea when I saw the ruins."

"Are we winning?" Earl piped.

Douglas studied Tim's wallet intently. "Very interesting. These are all old. Seven and eight years." His eyes flickered. "What are you trying to say? That you came from the past? That you're time travelers?"

The captain came back inside. "The snake is all loaded, sir."

Douglas nodded curtly. "All right. You can take off with your patrol."

The captain glanced at Tim. "Will you be—"

"I'll handle them."

The captain saluted. "Fine, sir." He quickly disappeared through the door. Outside, he and his men climbed aboard a long thin truck, like a pipe mounted on treads. With a faint hum the truck leaped forward.

In a moment only gray clouds and the dim outline of ruined buildings remained.

Douglas paced back and forth, examining the living room, the wallpaper, the light fixture and chairs. He picked up some magazines and thumbed through them. "From the past. But not far in the past."

"Seven years?"

"Could it be? I suppose. A lot of things have happened in the last few months. Time travel." Douglas grinned ironically. "You picked a bad spot, McLean. You should have gone farther on."

"I didn't pick it. It just happened."

"You must have done *something*."

Tim shook his head. "No. Nothing. We got up. And we were—here."

Douglas was deep in thought. "Here. Seven years in the future. Moved forward through time. We know nothing about time travel.

No work has been done with it. There seem to be evident military possibilities."

"How did the war begin?" Mary asked faintly.

"Begin? It didn't begin. You remember. There was war seven years ago."

"The real war. This."

"There wasn't any point when it became—this. We fought in Korea. We fought in China. In Germany and Yugoslavia and Iran. It spread, farther and farther. Finally the bombs were falling here. It came like the plague. The war *grew*. It didn't begin." Abruptly he put his notebook away. "A report on you would be suspect. They might think that I had the ash sickness."

"What's that?" Virginia asked.

"Radioactive particles in the air. Carried to the brain. Causes insanity. Everybody has a touch of it, even with the masks."

"I'd sure like to know who's winning," Earl repeated. "What was that outside? That truck. Was it rocket propelled?"

"The snake? No. Turbines. Boring snout. Cuts through the debris."

"Seven years," Mary said. "So much has changed. It doesn't seem possible."

"So much?" Douglas shrugged. "I suppose so. I remember what I was doing seven years ago. I was still in school. Learning. I had an apartment and a car. I went out dancing. I bought a TV set. But these things were there. The twilight. This. Only I didn't know. None of us knew. But they were there."

"You're a Political Commissioner?" Tim asked.

"I supervise the troops. Watch for political deviation. In a total war we have to keep people under constant surveillance. One Commie down in the Webs could wreck the whole business. We can't take chances."

Tim nodded. "Yes. It was there. The twilight. Only we didn't understand it."

Douglas examined the books in the bookcase. "I'll take a couple of these along. I haven't seen fiction in months. Most of it disappeared. Burned back in '77."

"Burned?"

Douglas helped himself. "Shakespeare. Milton. Dryden. I'll take the old stuff. It's safer. None of the Steinbeck and Dos Passos. Even a police can get in trouble. If you stay here, you better get rid of *that*." He tapped a volume of Dostoevski, *The Brothers Karamazov.*

"If we stay! What else can we do?"

"You want to stay?"

"No," Mary said quietly.

Douglas shot her a quick glance. "No, I suppose not. If you stay you'll be separated, of course. Children to the Canadian Relocation Centers. Women are situated down in the undersurface factory-labor camps. Men are automatically a part of Military."

"Like those there who left," Tim said.

"Unless you can qualify for the id block."

"What's that?"

"Industrial Designing and Technology. What training have you had? Anything along scientific lines?"

"No. Accounting."

Douglas shrugged. "Well, you'll be given a standard test. If your IQ is high enough you could go in the Political Service. We use a lot of men." He paused thoughtfully, his arms loaded with books. "You better go back, McLean. You'll have trouble getting accustomed to this. I'd go back, if I could. But I can't."

"Back?" Mary echoed. "How?"

"The way you came."

"We just came."

Douglas halted at the front door. "Last night was the worst rom attack so far. They hit this whole area."

"Rom?"

"Robot operated missiles. The Soviets are systematically destroying continental America, mile by mile. Roms are cheap. They make them by the million and fire them off. The whole process is automatic. Robot factories turn them out and fire them at us. Last night they came over here—waves of them. This morning the patrol came in and found nothing. Except you, of course."

Tim nodded slowly. "I'm beginning to see."

"The concentrated energy must have tipped some unstable time fault. Like a rock fault. We're always starting earthquakes. But a *time quake* . . . Interesting. That's what happened, I think. The release of energy, the destruction of matter, sucked your house into the future. Carried the house seven years ahead. This street, everything here, this very spot, was pulverized. Your house, seven years back, was caught in the undertow. The blast must have lashed back through time."

"Sucked into the future," Tim said. "During the night. While we were asleep."

Douglas watched him carefully. "Tonight," he said, "there will be another rom attack. It should finish off what is left." He looked at his watch. "It is now four in the afternoon. The attack will begin in a few hours. You should be undersurface. Nothing will survive up here. I can take you down with me, if you want. But if you want to take a chance, if you want to stay here—"

"You think it might tip us back?"

"Maybe. I don't know. It's a gamble. It might tip you back to your own time, or it might not. If not—"

"If not we wouldn't have a chance of survival."

Douglas flicked out a pocket map and spread it open on the couch. "A patrol will remain in this area another half-hour. If you decide to come undersurface with us, go down the street this way." He traced a line on the map. "To this open field here. The patrol is a Political unit. They'll take you the rest of the way down. You think you can find the field?"

"I think so," Tim said, looking at the map. His lips twisted. "That open field used to be the grammar school my kids went to. That's where they were going when the troops stopped them. Just a little while ago."

"Seven years ago," Douglas corrected. He snapped the map shut and restored it to his pocket. He pulled his mask down and moved out the front door onto the porch. "Maybe I'll see you again. Maybe not. It's your decision. You'll have to decide one way or the other. In any case—good luck."

He turned and walked briskly from the house.

"Dad," Earl shouted, "are you going in the Army? Are you going to wear a mask and shoot one of those guns?" His eyes sparkled with excitement. "Are you going to drive a *snake*?"

Tim McLean squatted down and pulled his son to him. "You want that? *You want to stay here*? If I'm going to wear a mask and shoot one of those guns we can't go back."

Earl looked doubtful. "Couldn't we go back later?"

Tim shook his head. "Afraid not. We've got to decide now, whether we're going back or not."

"You heard Mr. Douglas," Virginia said disgustedly. "The attack's going to start in a couple hours."

Tim got to his feet and paced back and forth. "If we stay in the house we'll get blown to bits. Let's face it. There's only a faint chance we'll be tipped back to our own time. A slim possibility—a long shot. Do we want to stay here with roms falling all around us, knowing any second it may be the end—hearing them come closer, hitting nearer—lying on the floor, waiting, listening—"

"Do you really want to go back?" Mary demanded.

"Of course, but the risk—"

"I'm not asking you about the risk. I'm asking you if you really want to go back. Maybe you want to stay here. Maybe Earl's right. You in a uniform and a mask, with one of those needle guns. Driving a snake."

"With you in a factory-labor camp! And the kids in a Government Relocation Center! How do you think that would be? What do you think they'd teach them? What do you think they'd grow up like? And believe . . . "

"They'd probably teach them to be very useful."

"Useful! To what? To themselves? To mankind? Or to the war effort . . . ?"

"They'd be alive," Mary said. "They'd be safe. This way, if we stay in the house, wait for the attack to come—"

"Sure," Tim grated. "They would be alive. Probably quite healthy. Well fed. Well clothed and cared for." He looked down at his children, his face hard. "They'd stay alive, all right. They'd live to grow up and become adults. But what kind of adults? You heard what he said! Book burnings in '77. What'll they be taught from? What kind of ideas are left, since '77? What kind of beliefs can they get from a Government Relocation Center? What kind of values will they have?"

"There's the id block," Mary suggested.

"Industrial Designing and Technology. For the bright ones. The clever ones with imagination. Busy slide rules and pencils. Drawing and planning and making discoveries. The girls could go into that. They could design the guns. Earl could go into the Political Service. He could make sure the guns were used. If any of the troops deviated, didn't want to shoot, Earl could report them and have them hauled off for reeducation. To have their political faith strengthened—in a world where those *with* brains design weapons and those *without* brains fire them."

"But they'd be alive," Mary repeated.

"You've got a strange idea of what being alive is! You call that alive? Maybe it is." Tim shook his head wearily. "Maybe you're right. Maybe we should go undersurface with Douglas. Stay in this world. Stay alive."

"I didn't say that," Mary said softly. "Tim, I had to find out if you *really* understood why it's worth it. Worth staying in the house, taking the chance we won't be tipped back."

"Then you want to take the chance?"

"Of course! We *have* to. We can't turn our children over to them—to the Relocation Center. To be taught how to hate and kill and destroy." Mary smiled up wanly. "Anyhow, they've always gone to the Jefferson School. And here, in this world, it's only an open field."

"Are we going back?" Judy piped. She caught hold of Tim's sleeve imploringly "Are we going back now?"

Tim disengaged her arm. "Very soon, honey."

Mary opened the supply cupboards and rooted in them. "Everything's here. What did they take?"

"The case of canned peas. Everything we had in the refrigerator. And they smashed the front door."

"I'll bet we're beating them!" Earl shouted. He ran to the window and peered out. The sight of the rolling ash disappointed him. "I can't see anything! Just the fog!" He turned questioningly to Tim. "Is it always like this, here?"

"Yes," Tim answered.

Earl's face fell. "Just fog? Nothing else. Doesn't the sun shine ever?"

"I'll fix some coffee," Mary said.

"Good." Tim went into the bathroom and examined himself in the mirror. His mouth was cut, caked with dried blood. His head ached. He felt sick at his stomach.

"It doesn't seem possible," Mary said, as they sat down at the kitchen table.

Tim sipped his coffee. "No. It doesn't." Where he sat he could see out the window. The clouds of ash. The dim, jagged outline of ruined buildings.

"Is the man coming back?" Judy piped. "He was all thin and funny-looking. He isn't coming back, is he?"

Tim looked at his watch. It read ten o'clock. He reset it, moving the hands to four-fifteen. "Douglas said it would begin at nightfall. That won't be long."

"Then we're really staying in the house," Mary said.

"That's right."

"Even though there's only a little chance?"

"Even though there's only a little chance we'll get back. Are you glad?"

"I'm glad," Mary said, her eyes bright. "It's worth it, Tim. You know it is. Anything's worth it, any chance. *To get back*. And something else. We'll all be here together. . . . We can't be—broken up. Separated."

Tim poured himself more coffee. "We might as well make ourselves comfortable. We have maybe three hours to wait. We might as well try to enjoy them."

At six-thirty the first rom fell. They felt the shock, a deep rolling wave of force that lapped over the house.

Judy came running in from the dining room, face white with fear. "Daddy! What is it?"

"Nothing. Don't worry."

"Come on back," Virginia called impatiently. "It's your turn." They were playing Monopoly.

Earl leaped to his feet. "I want to see." He ran excitedly to the window. "I can see where it hit!"

Tim lifted the shade and looked out. Far off, in the distance, a white glare burned fitfully. A towering column of luminous smoke rose from it.

A second shudder vibrated through the house. A dish crashed from the shelf, into the sink.

It was almost dark outside. Except for the two spots of white Tim could make out nothing. The clouds of ash were lost in the gloom. The ash and the ragged remains of buildings.

"That was closer," Mary said.

A third rom fell. In the living room windows burst, showering glass across the rug.

"We better get back," Tim said.

"Where?"

"Down in the basement. Come on." Tim unlocked the basement door and they trooped nervously downstairs.

"Food," Mary said. "We better bring the food that's left."

"Good idea. You kids go on down. We'll come along in a minute."

"I can carry something," Earl said.

"Go on down." The fourth rom hit, farther off than the last. "And stay away from the window."

"I'll move something over the window," Earl said. "The big piece of plywood we used for my train."

"Good idea." Tim and Mary returned to the kitchen. "Food. Dishes. What else?"

"Books." Mary looked nervously around. "I don't know. Nothing else. Come on."

A shattering roar drowned out her words. The kitchen window gave, showering glass over them. The dishes over the sink tumbled down in a torrent of breaking china. Tim grabbed Mary and pulled her down.

From the broken window rolling clouds of ominous gray drifted into the room. The evening air stank, a sour, rotten smell. Tim shuddered.

"Forget the food. Let's get back down."

"But—"

"Forget it." He grabbed her and pulled her down the basement stairs. They tumbled in a heap, Tim slamming the door after them.

"Where's the food?" Virginia demanded.

Tim wiped his forehead shakily. "Forget it. We won't need it."

"Help me," Earl gasped. Tim helped him move the sheet of plywood over the window above the laundry tubs. The basement was cold and silent. The cement floor under them was faintly moist.

Two roms struck at once. Tim was hurled to the floor. The concrete hit him and he grunted. For a moment blackness swirled around him. Then he was on his knees, groping his way up.

"Everybody all right?" he muttered.

"I'm all right," Mary said. Judy began to whimper. Earl was feeling his way across the room.

"I'm all right," Virginia said. "I guess."

The lights flickered and dimmed. Abruptly they went out. The basement was pitch-black.

"Well," Tim said. "There they go."

"I have my flashlight," Earl winked the flashlight on. "How's that?"

"Fine," Tim said.

More roms hit. The ground leaped under them, bucking and heaving. A wave of force shuddering the whole house.

"We better lie down," Mary said.

"Yes. Lie down." Tim stretched himself out awkwardly. A few bits of plaster rained down around them.

"When will it stop?" Earl asked uneasily.

"Soon," Tim said.

"Then we'll be back?"

"Yes. We'll be back."

The next blast hit them almost at once. Tim felt the concrete rise under him. It grew, swelling higher and higher. He was going up. He shut his eyes, holding on tight. Higher and higher he went, carried up by the ballooning concrete. Around him beams and timbers cracked. Plaster poured down. He could hear glass breaking. And a long way off, the licking crackles of fire.

"Tim," Mary's voice came faintly.

"Yes."

"We're not going to—to make it."

"I don't know."

"We're not. I can tell."

"Maybe not." He grunted in pain as a board struck his back, settling over him. Boards and plaster, covering him, burying him. He could smell the sour smell, the night air and ash. It drifted and rolled into the cellar, through the broken window.

"Daddy," Judy's voice came faintly.

"What?"

"Aren't we going back?"

He opened his mouth to answer. A shattering roar cut his words off. He jerked, tossed by the blast. Everything was moving around him. A vast wind tugged at him, a hot wind, licking at him, gnawing at him. He held on tight. The wind pulled, dragging him with it. He cried out as it seared his hands and face.

"Mary—"

Then silence. Only blackness and silence.

Cars.

Cars were stopping nearby. Then voices. And the noise of footsteps. Tim stirred, pushing the boards from him. He struggled to his feet.

"Mary." He looked around. "We're back."

The basement was in ruins. The walls were broken and sagging. Great gaping holes showed a green line of grass beyond. A concrete walk. The small rose garden. The white stucco house next door.

Lines of telephone poles Roofs. Houses. The city. As it had always been. Every morning.

"We're back!" Wild joy leaped through him. *Back*. Safe. It was over. Tim pushed quickly through the debris of his ruined house. "Mary, are you all right?"

"Here." Mary sat up, plaster dust raining from her. She was white all over, her hair, her skin, her clothing. Her face was cut and scratched. Her dress was torn. "Are we really back?"

"Mr. McLean! You all right?"

A blue-clad policeman leaped down into the cellar. Behind him two white-clad figures jumped. A group of neighbors collected outside, peering anxiously to see.

"I'm OK," Tim said. He helped Judy and Virginia up. "I think we're all OK."

"What happened?" The policeman pushed boards aside, coming over. "A bomb? Some kind of a bomb?"

"The house is a shambles," one of the white-clad interns said. "You sure nobody's hurt?"

"We were down here. In the basement."

"You all right, Tim?" Mrs. Hendricks called, stepping down gingerly into the cellar.

"What happened?" Frank Foley shouted. He leaped down with a crash. "God, Tim! What the hell were you doing?"

The two white-clad interns poked suspiciously around the ruins. "You're lucky, mister. Damn lucky. There's nothing left upstairs."

Foley came over beside Tim. "Damn it man! I *told* you to have that hot water heater looked at!"

"What?" Tim muttered.

"The hot water heater! I told you there was something wrong with the cut-off. It must've kept heating up, not turned off . . . ." Foley winked nervously. "But I won't say anything, Tim. The insurance. You can count on me."

Tim opened his mouth. But the words didn't come. What could he say?—No, it wasn't a defective hot water heater that I forgot to have repaired. No, it wasn't a faulty connection in the stove. It wasn't any of those things. It wasn't a leaky gas line, it wasn't a plugged furnace, it wasn't a pressure cooker we forgot to turn off.

It's war. Total war. And not just war for me. For my family. For my house.

It's for your house, too. Your house and my house and all the houses. Here and in the next block, in the next town, the next state and country and continent. The whole world, like this. Shambles and ruins. Fog and dank weeds growing in the rusting slag. War for all of us. For everybody crowding down into the basement, white-faced, frightened, somehow sensing something terrible.

And when it really came, when the five years were up, there'd be no escape. No going back, tipping back into the past, away from it. When it came for them all, it would have them for eternity; there would be no one climbing back out, as he had.

Mary was watching him. The policeman, the neighbors, the white-clad interns—all of them were watching him. Waiting for him to explain. To tell them what it was.

"Was it the hot water heater?" Mrs. Hendricks asked timidly. "That was it, wasn't it, Tim? Things like that do happen. You can't be sure . . . "

"Maybe it was home brew," a neighbor suggested, in a feeble attempt at humor. "Was that it?"

He couldn't tell them. They wouldn't understand, because they didn't want to understand. They didn't want to know. They needed reassurance. He could see it in their eyes. Pitiful, pathetic fear. They sensed something terrible—and they were afraid. They were searching his face, seeking his help. Words of comfort. Words to banish their fear.

"Yeah," Tim said heavily. "It was the hot water heater."

"I thought so!" Foley breathed. A sigh of relief swept through them all. Murmurs, shaky laughs. Nods, grins.

"I should have got it fixed," Tim went on. "I should have had it looked at a long time ago. Before it got in such bad shape." Tim looked around at the circle of anxious people, hanging on his words. "I should have had it looked at. Before it was too late."

SURVEY TEAM

Halloway came up through six miles of ash to see how the rocket looked in landing. He emerged from the lead-shielded bore and joined Young, crouching down with a small knot of surface troops.

The surface of the planet was dark and silent. The air stung his nose. It smelled foul. Halloway shivered uneasily. "Where the hell are we?"

A soldier pointed into the blackness. "The mountains are over there. See them? The Rockies, and this is Colorado."

Colorado . . . The old name awakened vague emotion in Halloway. He fingered his blast rifle. "When will it get here?" he asked. Far off, against the horizon, he could see the Enemy's green and yellow signal flares. And an occasional flash of fission white.

"Any time now. It's mechanically controlled all the way, piloted by robot. When it comes it really comes."

An Enemy mine burst a few dozen miles away. For a brief instant the landscape was outlined in jagged lightning. Halloway and the troops dropped to the ground automatically. He caught the dead burned smell of the surface of Earth as it was now, thirty years after the war began.

It was a lot different from the way he remembered it when he was a kid in California. He could remember the valley country, grape orchards and walnuts and lemons. Smudge pots under the orange trees. Green mountains and sky the color of a woman's eyes. And the fresh smell of the soil . . .

That was all gone now. Nothing remained but gray ash pulverized with the white stones of buildings. Once a city had been in this spot. He could see the yawning cavities of cellars, filled now with slag, dried rivers of rust that had once been buildings. Rubble strewn everywhere, aimlessly . . .

The mine flare faded out and the blackness settled back. They got cautiously to their feet. "Quite a sight," a soldier murmured.

"It was a lot different before," Halloway said.

"Was it? I was born undersurface."

"In those days we grew our food right in the ground, on the surface. In the soil. Not in underground tanks. We—"

Halloway broke off. A great rushing sound filled the air suddenly, cutting off his words. An immense shape roared past them in the blackness, struck someplace close, and shook the earth.

"The rocket!" a soldier shouted. They all began running, Halloway lumbering awkwardly along.

"Good news, I hope," Young said, close by him.

"I hope, too," Halloway gasped. "Mars is our last chance. If this doesn't work we're finished. The report on Venus was negative; nothing there but lava and steam."

❖ ❖ ❖

Later they examined the rocket from Mars.

"It'll do," Young murmured.

"You're sure?" Director Davidson asked tensely. "Once we get there we can't come running back."

"We're sure." Halloway tossed the spools across the desk to Davidson. "Examine them yourself. The air on Mars will be thin, and dry. The gravity is much weaker than ours. But we'll be able to live there, which is more than you can say for this God-forsaken Earth."

Davidson picked up the spools. The unblinking recessed lights gleamed down on the metal desk, the metal walls and floor of the office. Hidden machinery wheezed in the walls, maintaining the air and temperature. "I'll have to rely on you experts, of course. If some vital factor is not taken into account—"

"Naturally, it's a gamble," Young said. "We can't be sure of all factors at this distance." He tapped the spools. "Mechanical samples and photos. Robots creeping around, doing the best they can. We're lucky to have *anything* to go on."

"There's no radiation at least," Halloway said. "We can count on that. But Mars will be dry and dusty and cold. It's a long way out. Weak sun. Deserts and wrinkled hills."

"Mars is old," Young agreed.

"It was cooled a long time ago. Look at it this way: We have eight planets, excluding Earth. Pluto to Jupiter is *out*. No chance of survival there. Mercury is nothing but liquid metal. Venus is still volcano and steam—pre-Cambrian. That's seven of the eight. Mars is the only possibility *a priori*."

"In other words," Davidson said slowly, "Mars *has* to be okay because there's nothing else for us to try."

"We could stay here. Live on here in the undersurface systems like gophers."

"We could not last more than another year. You've seen the recent psych graphs."

They had. The tension index was up. Men weren't made to live in metal tunnels, living on tank-grown food, working and sleeping and dying without seeing the sun.

It was the children they were really thinking about. Kids that had never been up to the surface. Wan-faced pseudo mutants with eyes like blind fish. A generation born in the subterranean world. The tension index was up because men were seeing their children alter and meld in with a world of tunnels and slimy darkness and dripping luminous rocks.

"Then it's agreed?" Young said.

Davidson searched the faces of the two technicians. "Maybe we could reclaim the surface, revive Earth again, renew its soil. It hasn't really gone that far, has it?"

"No chance," Young said flatly. "Even if we could work an arrangement with the Enemy there'll be particles in suspension for another fifty years. Earth will be too hot for life the rest of this century. *And we can't wait.*"

"All right," Davidson said. "I'll authorize the survey team. We'll risk that, at least. You want to go? Be the first humans to land on Mars?"

"You bet," Halloway said grimly. "It's in our contract that I go."

❖ ❖ ❖

The red globe that was Mars grew steadily larger. In the control room Young and van Ecker, the navigator, watched it intently.

"We'll have to bail," van Ecker said. "No chance of landing at this velocity."

Young was nervous. "That's all right for us, but how about the first load of settlers? We can't expect women and children to jump."

"By then we'll know more." Van Ecker nodded and Captain Mason sounded the emergency alarm. Throughout the ship relay bells clanged ominously. The ship throbbed with scampering feet as crew members grabbed their jump-suits and hurried to the hatches.

"Mars," Captain Mason murmured, still at the viewscreen. "Not like Luna. This is the real thing."

Young and Halloway moved toward the hatch. "We better get going."

Mars was swelling rapidly. An ugly bleak globe, dull red. Halloway fitted on his jump helmet. Van Ecker came behind him.

Mason remained in the control cabin. "I'll follow," he said, "after the crew's out."

The hatch slid back and they moved out onto the jump shelf. The crew were already beginning to leap.

"Too bad to waste a ship," Young said.

"Can't be helped." Van Ecker clamped his helmet on and jumped. His brake-units sent him spinning upward, rising like a balloon into the blackness above them. Young and Halloway followed. Below them the ship plunged on, downward toward the surface of Mars. In the sky tiny luminous dots drifted—the crew members.

"I've been thinking," Halloway said into his helmet speaker.

"What about?" Young's voice came in his earphones.

"Davidson was talking about overlooking some vital factor. There is one we haven't considered."

"What's that?"

"The Martians."

"Good God!" van Ecker chimed in. Halloway could see him drifting off to his right, settling slowly toward the planet below. "You think there *are* Martians?"

"It's possible. Mars will sustain life. If we can live there other complex forms could exist, too."

"We'll know soon enough," Young said.

Van Ecker laughed. "Maybe they trapped one of our robot rockets. Maybe they're expecting us."

Halloway was silent. It was too close to be funny. The red planet was growing rapidly. He could see white spots at the poles. A few hazy blue-green ribbons that had once been called *canals*. Was there a civilization down there, an organized culture waiting for them, as they drifted slowly down? He groped at his pack until his fingers closed over the butt of his pistol.

"Better get your guns out," he said.

"If there's a Martian defense system waiting for us we won't have a chance," Young said. "Mars cooled millions of years ahead of Earth. It's a cinch they'll be so advanced we won't even be—"

"Too late now," Mason's voice came faintly. "You experts should have thought of that before."

"Where are you?" Halloway demanded.

"Drifting below you. The ship is empty. Should strike any moment. I got all the equipment out, attached it to automatic jump units."

A faint flash of light exploded briefly below, winked out. The ship, striking the surface . . .

"I'm almost down," Mason said nervously. "I'll be the first . . . "

❖❖❖

Mars had ceased to be a globe. Now it was a great red dish, a vast plain of dull rust spread out beneath them. They fell slowly, silently, toward it. Mountains became visible. Narrow trickles of water that were rivers. A vague checker-board pattern that might have been fields and pastures . . .

Halloway gripped his pistol tightly. His brake-units shrieked as the air thickened. He was almost down. A muffled *crunch* sounded abruptly in his earphones.

"Mason!" Young shouted.

"I'm down," Mason's voice came faintly.

"You all right?"

"Knocked the wind out of me. But I'm all right."

"How does it look?" Halloway demanded.

For a moment there was silence. Then: "Good God!" Mason gasped. "A *city!*"

"A city?" Young yelled. "What kind? What's it like?"

"Can you see them?" van Ecker shouted. "What are they like? Are there a lot of them?"

They could hear Mason breathing. His breath rasped hoarsely in their phones. "No," he gasped at last. "No sign of life. No activity. The city is—it looks deserted."

"*Deserted?*"

"Ruins. Nothing but ruins. Miles of wrecked columns and walls and rusting scaffolding."

"Thank God," Young breathed. "They must have died out. We're safe. They must have evolved and finished their cycle a long time ago."

"Did they leave us anything?" Fear clutched at Halloway. "Is there anything left for *us?*" He clawed wildly at his brake-units, struggling frantically to hurry his descent. "Is it all gone?"

"You think they used up everything?" Young said. "You think they exhausted all the—"

"I can't tell." Mason's weak voice came, tinged with uneasiness. "It looks bad. Big pits. Mining pits. I can't tell, but it looks bad . . . "

Halloway struggled desperately with his brake-units.

The planet was a shambles.

"Good God," Young mumbled. He sat down on a broken column and wiped his face. "Not a damn thing left. Nothing."

❖ ❖ ❖

Around them the crew were setting up emergency defense units. The communications team was assembling a battery-driven transmitter. A bore team was drilling for water. Other teams were scouting around, looking for food.

"There won't be any signs of life," Halloway said. He waved at the endless expanse of debris and rust. "They're gone, finished a long time ago."

"I don't understand," Mason muttered. "How could they wreck a whole planet?"

"We wrecked Earth in thirty years."

"Not this way. They've *used* Mars up. Used up everything. Nothing left. Nothing at all. It's one vast scrap-heap."

Shakily Halloway tried to light a cigarette. The match burned feebly, then sputtered out. He felt light and dopey. His heart throbbed heavily. The distant sun beat down, pale and small. Mars was a cold, a lonely dead world.

Halloway said, "They must have had a hell of a time, watching their cities rot away. No water or minerals, finally no soil." He picked up a handful of dry sand, let it trickle through his fingers.

"Transmitter working," a crew member said.

Mason got to his feet and lumbered awkwardly over to the transmitter. "I'll tell Davidson what we've found." He bent over the microphone.

Young looked across at Halloway. "Well, I guess we're stuck. How long will our supplies carry us?"

"Couple of months."

"And then—" Young snapped his fingers. "Like the Martians." He squinted at the long corroded wall of a ruined house. "I wonder what they were like."

"A semantics team is probing the ruins. Maybe they'll turn up something."

Beyond the ruined city stretched out what had once been an industrial area. Fields of twisted installations, towers and pipes and machinery. Sand-covered and partly rusted. The surface of the land was pocked with great gaping sores. Yawning pits where scoops had once dredged. Entrances of underground mines. Mars was honey-combed. Termite-ridden. A whole race had burrowed and dug in trying to stay alive. The Martians had sucked Mars dry, then fled it.

"A graveyard," Young said. "Well, they got what they deserved."

"You blame them? What should they have done? Perished a few thousand years sooner and left their planet in better shape?"

"They could have left us *something*," Young said stubbornly. "Maybe we can dig up their bones and boil them. I'd like to get my hands on one of them long enough to—"

A pair of crewmen came hurrying across the sand. "Look at these!"

They carried armloads of metal tubes, glittering cylinders heaped up in piles. "Look what we found buried!"

Halloway roused himself. "What is it?"

"Records. Written documents. Get these to the semantics team!" Carmichael spilled his armload at Halloway's feet. "And this isn't all. We found something else—installations."

"Installations? What kind?"

"Rocket launchers. Old towers, rusty as hell. There are fields of them on the other side of the town." Carmichael wiped perspiration from his red face. "They didn't die, Halloway. They took off. They used up this place, then left."

Doctor Judde and Young pored over the gleaming tubes. "It's coming," Judde murmured, absorbed in the shifting pattern undulating across the scanner.

"Can you make anything out?" Halloway asked tensely.

"They left, all right. Took off. The whole lot of them."

Young turned to Halloway. "What do you think of that? So they didn't die out."

"Can't you tell where they went?"

Judde shook his head. "Some planet their scout ships located. Ideal climate and temperature." He pushed the scanner aside. "In their last period the whole Martian civilization was oriented around this escape planet. Big project, moving a society lock, stock and barrel. It took them three or four hundred years to get everything of value off Mars and on its way to the other planet."

"How did the operation come out?"

"Not so good. The planet was beautiful. But they had to adapt. Apparently they didn't anticipate all the problems arising from colonization on a strange planet." Judde indicated a cylinder. "The colonies deteriorated rapidly. Couldn't keep the traditions and techniques going. The society broke apart. Then came war, barbarism."

"Then their migration was a failure." Halloway pondered. "Maybe it can't be done. Maybe it's impossible."

"Not a failure," Judde corrected. "They lived, at least. This place was no good any more. Better to live as savages on a strange world than stay here and die. So they say, on these cylinders."

"Come along," Young said to Halloway. The two men stepped outside the semantics hut. It was night. The sky was littered with glowing stars. The two moons had risen. They glimmered coldly, two dead eyes in the chilly sky.

"This place won't do," Young stated. "We can't migrate here. That's settled."

Halloway eyed him. "What's on your mind?"

"This was the last of the nine planets. We tested every one of them." Young's face was alive with emotion. "None of them will support life. All of them are lethal or useless, like this rubbish heap. The whole damn solar system is out."

"So?"

"We'll have to leave the solar system."

"And go where? *How?*"

Young pointed toward the Martian ruins, to the city and the rusted, bent rows of towers. "Where *they* went. They found a place to go. An untouched world outside the solar system. And they developed some kind of outer-space drive to get them there."

"You mean—"

"Follow them. This solar system is dead. But outside, someplace in some other system, they found an escape world. And they were able to get there."

"We'd have to fight with them if we land on their planet. They won't want to share it."

Young spat angrily on the sand. "Their colonies deteriorated. Remember? Broke down into barbarism. We can handle them. We've got everything in the way of war weapons—weapons that can wipe a planet clean."

"We don't want to do that."

"What *do* we want to do? Tell Davidson we're stuck on Terra?

Let the human race turn into underground moles? Blind crawling things . . . ”

“If we follow the Martians we’ll be competing for their world. They found it; the damn thing belongs to them, not us. And maybe we can’t work out their drive. Maybe the schematics are lost.”

Judde emerged from the semantics hut. “I’ve some more information. The whole story is here. Details on the escape planet. Fauna and flora. Studies of its gravity, air density, mineral possessions, soil layer, climate, temperature—everything.”

“How about their drive?”

“Breakdown on that, too. Everything.” Judde was shaking with excitement. “I have an idea. Let’s get the designs team on these drive schematics and see if they can duplicate it. If they can, we could follow the Martians. We could sort of *share* their planet with them.”

“See?” Young said to Halloway. “Davidson will say the same thing. It’s obvious.”

Halloway turned and walked off.

“What’s wrong with him?” Judde asked.

“Nothing. He’ll get over it.” Young scratched out a quick message on a piece of paper. “Have this transmitted to Davidson back on Terra.”

Judde peered at the message. He whistled. “You’re telling him about the Martian migration. And about the escape planet.”

“We want to get started. It’ll take a long time to get things under way.”

“Will Halloway come around?”

“He’ll come around,” Young said. “Don’t worry about him.”

❖ ❖ ❖

Halloway gazed up at the towers. The leaning, sagging towers from which the Martian transports had been launched thousands of years before.

Nothing stirred. No sign of life. The whole dried-up planet was dead.

Halloway wandered among the towers. The beam from his helmet cut a white path in front of him. Ruins, heaps of rusting metal. Bales of wire and building material. Parts of uncompleted equipment. Half-buried construction sections sticking up from the sand.

He came to a raised platform and mounted the ladder cautiously. He found himself in an observation mount, surrounded by the remains of dials and meters. A telescopic sight stuck up, rusted in place, frozen tight.

"Hey," a voice came from below. "Who's up there?"

"Halloway."

"God, you scared me." Carmichael slid his blast rifle away and climbed the ladder. "What are you doing?"

"Looking around."

Carmichael appeared beside him, puffing and red-faced. "Interesting, these towers. This was an automatic sighting station. Fixed the take-off for supply transports. The population was already gone." Carmichael slapped at the ruined control board. "These supply ships continued to take-off, loaded by machines and dispatched by machines, after all the Martians were gone."

"Lucky for them they had a place to go."

"Sure was. The minerals team says there's not a damn thing left here. Nothing but dead sand and rock and debris. Even the water's no good. They took everything of value."

"Judde says their escape world is pretty nice."

"Virgin." Carmichael smacked his fat lips. "Never touched. Trees and meadows and blue oceans. He showed me a scanner translation of a cylinder."

"Too bad we don't have a place like that to go. A virgin world for ourselves."

Carmichael was bent over the telescope. "This here sighted for them. When the escape planet swam into view a relay delivered a trigger charge to the control tower. The tower launched the ships. When the ships were gone a new flock came up into position." Carmichael began to polish the encrusted lenses of the telescope, wiping the accumulated rust and debris away. "Maybe we'll see their planet."

In the ancient lenses a vague luminous globe was swimming. Halloway could make it out, obscured by the filth of centuries, hidden behind a curtain of metallic particles and dirt.

Carmichael was down on his hands and knees, working with the focus mechanism. "See anything?" he demanded.

Halloway nodded. "Yeah."

Carmichael pushed him away. "Let me look." He squinted into the lens. "Aw, for God's sake!"

"What's wrong? Can't you see it?"

"I see it," Carmichael said, getting down on his hands and knees again. "The thing must have slipped. Or the time shift is too great. But this is supposed to adjust automatically. Of course, the gear box has been frozen for—"

"What's wrong?" Halloway demanded.

"That's Earth. Don't you recognize it?"

"Earth!"

Carmichael sneered with disgust. "This fool thing must be busted. I wanted to get a look at their dream planet. That's just old Terra, where we came from. All my work trying to fix this wreck up, and what do we see?"

❖ ❖ ❖

"*Earth!*" Halloway murmured. He had just finished telling Young about the telescope.

"I can't believe it," Young said. "But the description fitted Earth thousands of years ago . . . "

"How long ago did they take off?" Halloway asked.

"About six hundred thousand years ago," Judde said.

"And their colonies descended into barbarism on the new planet."

The four men were silent. They looked at each other, tight-lipped.

"We've destroyed two worlds," Halloway said at last. "Not one. Mars first. We finished up here, then we moved to Terra. And we destroyed Terra as systematically as we did Mars."

"A closed circle," Mason said. "We're back where we started. Back to reap the crop our ancestors sowed. They left Mars this way. Useless. And now we're back here poking around the ruins like ghouls."

"Shut up," Young snapped. He paced angrily back and forth. "I can't believe it."

"We're Martians. Descendants of the original stock that left here. We're back from the colonies. Back home." Mason's voice rose hysterically. "We're home again, where we belong!"

Judde pushed aside the scanner and got to his feet. "No doubt about it. I checked their analysis with our own archeological records. It fits. Their escape world was Terra, six hundred thousand years ago."

"What'll we tell Davidson?" Mason demanded. He giggled wildly. "We've found a perfect place. A world untouched by human hands. Still in the original cellophane wrapper."

Halloway moved to the door of the hut, stood gazing silently out. Judde joined him. "This is catastrophic. We're really stuck. What the hell are you looking at?"

Above them, the cold sky glittered. In the bleak light the barren plains of Mars stretched out, mile after mile of empty, wasted ruin.

"At that," Halloway said. "You know what it reminds me of?"

"A picnic site."

"Broken bottles and tin cans and wadded up plates. After the picnickers have left. Only, the picnickers are back. They're back—and they have to live in the mess they made."

"What'll we tell Davidson?" Mason demanded.

"I've already called him," Young said wearily. "I told him there was a planet, out of the solar system. Someplace we could go. The Martians had a drive."

"A drive." Judde pondered. "Those towers." His lips twisted. "Maybe they did have an outer space drive. Maybe it's worth going on with the translation."

They looked at each other.

"Tell Davidson we're going on," Halloway ordered. "We'll keep on until we find it. We're not staying on this God-forsaken junkyard." His gray eyes glowed. "We'll find it, yet. A virgin world. A world that's unspoiled."

"*Unspoiled*," Young echoed. "Nobody there ahead of us."

"We'll be the first," Judde muttered avidly.

"It's wrong!" Mason shouted. "Two are enough! Let's not destroy a third world!"

Nobody listened to him. Judde and Young and Halloway gazed up, faces eager, hands clenching and unclenching. As if they were already there. As if they were already holding onto the new world, clutching it with all their strength. Tearing it apart, atom by atom . . .

THE HANGING STRANGER

At five o'clock Ed Loyce washed up, tossed on his hat and coat, got his car out and headed across town toward his TV sales store. He was tired. His back and shoulders ached from digging dirt out of the basement and wheeling it into the back yard. But for a forty-year-old man he had done okay. Janet could get a new vase with the money he had saved; and he liked the idea of repairing the foundations himself.

It was getting dark. The setting sun cast long rays over the scurrying commuters, tired and grim-faced, women loaded down with bundles and packages, students, swarming home from the university, mixing with clerks and businessmen and drab secretaries. He stopped his Packard for a red light and then started it up again. The store had been open without him; he'd arrive just in time to spell the help for dinner, go over the records of the day, maybe even close a couple of sales himself. He drove slowly past the small square of green in the center of the street, the town park. There were no parking places in front of LOYCE TV SALES AND SERVICE. He cursed under his breath and swung the car in a U-turn. Again he passed the little square of green with its lonely drinking fountain and bench and single lamppost.

From the lamppost something was hanging. A shapeless dark bundle, swinging a little with the wind. Like a dummy of some sort.

Loyce rolled down his window and peered out. What the hell was it? A display of some kind? Sometimes the Chamber of Commerce put up displays in the square.

Again he made a U-turn and brought his car around. He passed the park and concentrated on the dark bundle. It wasn't a dummy. And if it was a display it was a strange kind. The hackles on his neck rose and he swallowed uneasily. Sweat slid out on his face and hands.

It was a body. A human body.

❖ ❖ ❖

"Look at it!" Loyce snapped. "Come on out here!"

Don Fergusson came slowly out of the store, buttoning his pin-stripe coat with dignity. "This is a big deal, Ed. I can't just leave the guy standing there."

"See it?" Ed pointed into the gathering gloom. The lamppost jutted up against the sky—the post and the bundle swinging from it. "There it is. How the hell long has it been there?" His voice rose excitedly. "What's wrong with everybody? They just walk on past!"

Don Fergusson lit a cigarette slowly. "Take it easy, old man. There must be a good reason, or it wouldn't be there."

"A reason! What kind of a reason?"

Fergusson shrugged. "Like the time the Traffic Safety Council put that wrecked Buick there. Some sort of civic thing. How would I know?"

Jack Potter from the shoe shop joined them. "What's up, boys?"

"There's a body hanging from the lamppost," Loyce said. "I'm going to call the cops."

"They must know about it," Potter said. "Or otherwise it wouldn't be there."

"I got to get back in." Fergusson headed back into the store. "Business before pleasure."

Loyce began to get hysterical. "You see it? You see it hanging there? A man's body! A dead man!"

"Sure, Ed. I saw it this afternoon when I went out for coffee."

"You mean it's been there all afternoon?"

"Sure. What's the matter?" Potter glanced at his watch. "Have to run. See you later, Ed."

Potter hurried off, joining the flow of people moving along the sidewalk. Men and women, passing by the park. A few glanced up curiously at the dark bundle—and then went on. Nobody stopped. Nobody paid any attention.

"I'm going nuts," Loyce whispered. He made his way to the curb and crossed out into traffic, among the cars. Horns honked angrily at him. He gained the curb and stepped up onto the little square of green.

The man had been middle-aged. His clothing was ripped and torn, a gray suit, splashed and caked with dried mud. A stranger. Loyce had never seen him before. Not a local man. His face was partly turned away, and in the evening wind he spun a little, turning gently, silently. His skin was gouged and cut. Red gashes, deep scratches of congealed blood. A pair of steel-rimmed glasses hung from one ear, dangling foolishly. His eyes bulged. His mouth was open, tongue thick and ugly blue.

"For Heaven's sake," Loyce muttered, sickened. He pushed down his nausea and made his way back to the sidewalk. He was shaking all over, with revulsion—and fear.

Why? Who was the man? Why was he hanging there? What did it mean?

And—why didn't anybody notice?

He bumped into a small man hurrying along the sidewalk. "Watch it!" the man grated. "Oh, it's you, Ed."

Ed nodded dazedly. "Hello, Jenkins."

"What's the matter?" The stationery clerk caught Ed's arm. "You look sick."

"The body. There in the park."

"Sure, Ed." Jenkins led him into the alcove of LOYCE TV SALES AND SERVICE. "Take it easy."

Margaret Henderson from the jewelry store joined them. "Something wrong?"

"Ed's not feeling well."

Loyce yanked himself free. "How can you stand here? Don't you see it? For God's sake—"

"What's he talking about?" Margaret asked nervously.

"The body!" Ed shouted. "The body hanging there!"

More people collected. "Is he sick? It's Ed Loyce. You okay, Ed?"

"The body!" Loyce screamed, struggling to get past them. Hands caught at him. He tore loose. "Let me go! The police! Get the police!"

"Ed—"

"Better get a doctor!"

"He must be sick."

"Or drunk."

Loyce fought his way through the people. He stumbled and half fell. Through a blur he saw rows of faces, curious, concerned, anxious. Men and women halting to see what the disturbance was. He fought past them toward his store. He could see Fergusson inside talking to a man, showing him an Emerson TV set. Pete Foley in the back at the service counter, setting up a new Philco. Loyce shouted at them frantically. His voice was lost in the roar of traffic and the murmuring around him.

"Do something!" he screamed. "Don't stand there! Do something! Something's wrong! Something's happened! Things are going on!"

The crowd melted respectfully for the two heavy-set cops moving efficiently toward Loyce.

❖❖❖

"Name?" the cop with the notebook murmured.

"Loyce." He mopped his forehead wearily. "Edward C. Loyce. Listen to me. Back there—"

"Address?" the cop demanded. The police car moved swiftly through traffic, shooting among the cars and buses. Loyce sagged against the seat, exhausted and confused. He took a deep shuddering breath.

"1368 Hurst Road."

"That's here in Pikeville?"

"That's right." Loyce pulled himself up with a violent effort. "Listen to me. Back there. In the square. Hanging from the lamppost—"

"Where were you today?" the cop behind the wheel demanded.

"Where?" Loyce echoed.

"You weren't in your shop, were you?"

"No." He shook his head. "No, I was home. Down in the basement."

"In the *basement?*"

"Digging. A new foundation. Getting out the dirt to pour a cement frame. Why? What has that to do with—"

"Was anybody else down there with you?"

"No. My wife was downtown. My kids were at school." Loyce looked from one heavy-set cop to the other. Hope flickered across his face, wild hope. "You mean because I was down there I missed—the explanation? I didn't get in on it? Like everybody else?"

After a pause the cop with the notebook said: "That's right. You missed the explanation."

"Then it's official? The body—it's *supposed* to be hanging there?"

"It's supposed to be hanging there. For everybody to see."

Ed Loyce grinned weakly. "Good Lord. I guess I sort of went off the deep end. I thought maybe something had happened. You know, something like the Ku Klux Klan. Some kind of violence. Communists or Fascists taking over." He wiped his face with his breast-pocket handkerchief, his hands shaking. "I'm glad to know it's on the level."

"It's on the level." The police car was getting near the Hall of Justice. The sun had set. The streets were gloomy and dark. The lights had not yet come on.

"I feel better," Loyce said. "I was pretty excited there, for a minute. I guess I got all stirred up. Now that I understand, there's no need to take me in, is there?"

The two cops said nothing.

"I should be back at my store. The boys haven't had dinner. I'm all right, now. No more trouble. Is there any need of—"

"This won't take long," the cop behind the wheel interrupted. "A short process. Only a few minutes."

"I hope it's short," Loyce muttered. The car slowed down for a stoplight. "I guess I sort of disturbed the peace. Funny, getting excited like that and—"

Loyce yanked the door open. He sprawled out into the street and rolled to his feet. Cars were moving all around him, gaining speed as the light changed. Loyce leaped onto the curb and raced among the people, burrowing into the swarming crowds. Behind him he heard sounds, shouts, people running.

They weren't cops. He had realized that right away. He knew every cop in Pikeville. A man couldn't own a store, operate a business in a small town for twenty-five years without getting to know all the cops.

They weren't cops—and there hadn't been any explanation. Potter, Fergusson, Jenkins, none of them knew why it was there. They didn't know—and they didn't care. *That* was the strange part.

Loyce ducked into a hardware store. He raced toward the back, past the startled clerks and customers, into the shipping room and through the back door. He tripped over a garbage can and ran up a flight of concrete steps. He climbed over a fence and jumped down on the other side, gasping and panting.

There was no sound behind him. He had got away.

He was at the entrance of an alley, dark and strewn with boards and ruined boxes and tires. He could see the street at the far end. A street light wavered and came on. Men and women. Stores. Neon signs. Cars.

And to his right—the police station.

He was close, terribly close. Past the loading platform of a grocery store rose the white concrete side of the Hall of Justice. Barred windows. The police antenna. A great concrete wall rising up in the darkness. A bad place for him to be near. He was too close. He had to keep moving, get farther away from them.

Them?

Loyce moved cautiously down the alley. Beyond the police station was the City Hall, the old-fashioned yellow structure of wood and gilded brass and broad cement steps. He could see the endless rows of offices, dark windows, the cedars and beds of flowers on each side of the entrance.

And—something else.

Above the City Hall was a patch of darkness, a cone of gloom denser than the surrounding night. A prism of black that spread out and was lost into the sky.

He listened. Good God, he could hear something. Something that made him struggle frantically to close his ears, his mind, to shut out the sound. A buzzing. A distant, muted hum like a great swarm of bees.

Loyce gazed up, rigid with horror. The splotch of darkness, hanging over the City Hall. Darkness so thick it seemed almost solid. *In the vortex something moved.* Flickering shapes. Things, descending from the sky, pausing momentarily above the City Hall, fluttering over it in a dense swarm and then dropping silently onto the roof.

Shapes. Fluttering shapes from the sky. From the crack of darkness that hung above him.

He was seeing—them.

❖ ❖ ❖

For a long time Loyce watched, crouched behind a sagging fence in a pool of scummy water.

They were landing. Coming down in groups, landing on the roof of the City Hall and disappearing inside. They had wings. Like giant insects of some kind. They flew and fluttered and came to rest—and then crawled crab-fashion, sideways, across the roof and into the building.

He was sickened. And fascinated. Cold night wind blew around him and he shuddered. He was tired, dazed with shock. On the front steps of the City Hall were men, standing here and there. Groups of men coming out of the building and halting for a moment before going on.

Were there more of them?

It didn't seem possible. What he saw descending from the black chasm weren't men. They were alien—from some other world, some other dimension. Sliding through this slit, this break in the shell of the universe. Entering through this gap, winged insects from another realm of being.

On the steps of the City Hall a group of men broke up. A few moved toward a waiting car. One of the remaining shapes started to re-enter the City Hall. It changed its mind and turned to follow the others.

Loyce closed his eyes in horror. His senses reeled. He hung on tight, clutching at the sagging fence. The shape, the man-shape, had abruptly fluttered up and flapped after the others. It flew to the side-walk and came to rest among them.

Pseudo-men. Imitation men. Insects with ability to disguise them-selves as men. Like other insects familiar to Earth. Protective color-ation. Mimicry.

Loyce pulled himself away. He got slowly to his feet. It was night. The alley was totally dark. But maybe they could see in the dark. Maybe darkness made no difference to them.

He left the alley cautiously and moved out onto the street. Men and women flowed past, but not so many, now. At the bus stops stood waiting groups. A huge bus lumbered along the street, its lights flashing in the evening gloom.

Loyce moved forward. He pushed his way among those waiting and when the bus halted he boarded it and took a seat in the rear, by the door. A moment later the bus moved into life and rumbled down the street.

Loyce relaxed a little. He studied the people around him. Dulled, tired faces. People going home from work. Quite ordinary faces. None of them paid any attention to him. All sat quietly, sunk down in their seats, jiggling with the motion of the bus.

The man sitting next to him unfolded a newspaper. He began to read the sports section, his lips moving. An ordinary man. Blue suit. Tie. A businessman, or a salesman. On his way home to his wife and family.

Across the aisle a young woman, perhaps twenty. Dark eyes and hair, a package on her lap. Nylons and heels. Red coat and white Angora sweater. Gazing absently ahead of her.

A high school boy in jeans and black jacket.

A great triple-chinned woman with an immense shopping bag loaded with packages and parcels. Her thick face dim with weariness.

Ordinary people. The kind that rode the bus every evening. Going home to their families. To dinner.

Going home—with their minds dead. Controlled, filmed over with the mask of an alien being that had appeared and taken possession of them, their town, their lives. Himself, too. Except that he happened to be deep in his cellar instead of in the store. Somehow, he had been overlooked. They had missed him. Their control wasn't perfect, foolproof.

Maybe there were others.

Hope flickered in Loyce. They weren't omnipotent. They had made a mistake, not got control of him. Their net, their field of control, had passed over him. He had emerged from his cellar as he had gone down. Apparently their power-zone was limited.

A few seats down the aisle a man was watching him. Loyce broke off his chain of thought. A slender man, with dark hair and a small mustache. Well-dressed, brown suit and shiny shoes. A book between his small hands. He was watching Loyce, studying him intently. He turned quickly away.

Loyce tensed. One of *them?* Or—another they had missed?

The man was watching him again. Small dark eyes, alive and clever. Shrewd. A man too shrewd for them—or one of the things itself, an alien insect from beyond.

The bus halted. An elderly man got on slowly and dropped his token into the box. He moved down the aisle and took a seat opposite Loyce.

The elderly man caught the sharp-eyed man's gaze. For a split second something passed between them.

A look rich with meaning.

Loyce got to his feet. The bus was moving. He ran to the door. One step down into the well. He yanked the emergency door release. The rubber door swung open.

"Hey!" the driver shouted, jamming on the brakes. "What the hell—?"

Loyce squirmed through. The bus was slowing down. Houses on all sides. A residential district, lawns and tall apartment buildings. Behind him, the bright-eyed man had leaped up. The elderly man was also on his feet. They were coming after him.

Loyce leaped. He hit the pavement with terrific force and rolled against the curb. Pain lapped over him. Pain and a vast tide of blackness. Desperately, he fought it off. He struggled to his knees and then slid down again. The bus had stopped. People were getting off.

Loyce groped around. His fingers closed over something. A rock, lying in the gutter. He crawled to his feet, grunting with pain. A shape loomed before him. A man, the bright-eyed man with the book.

Loyce kicked. The man gasped and fell. Loyce brought the rock down. The man screamed and tried to roll away. "*Stop!* For God's sake listen—"

He struck again. A hideous crunching sound. The man's voice cut off and dissolved in a bubbling wail. Loyce scrambled up and back. The others were there, now. All around him. He ran, awkwardly, down the sidewalk, up a driveway. None of them followed him. They had stopped and were bending over the inert body of the man with the book, the bright-eyed man who had come after him.

Had he made a mistake?

But it was too late to worry about that. He had to get out—away from them. Out of Pikeville, beyond the crack of darkness, the rent between their world and his.

❖ ❖ ❖

"Ed!" Janet Loyce backed away nervously. "What is it? What—"

Ed Loyce slammed the door behind him and came into the living room. "Pull down the shades. Quick."

Janet moved toward the window. "But—"

"Do as I say. Who else is here besides you?"

"Nobody. Just the twins. They're upstairs in their room. What's happened? You look so strange. Why are you home?"

Ed locked the front door. He prowled around the house, into the kitchen. From the drawer under the sink he slid out the big butcher knife and ran his finger along it. Sharp. Plenty sharp. He returned to the living room.

"Listen to me," he said. "I don't have much time. They know I escaped and they'll be looking for me."

"Escaped?" Janet's face twisted with bewilderment and fear. "Who?"

"The town has been taken over. They're in control. I've got it pretty well figured out. They started at the top, at the City Hall and police department. What they did with the *real* humans they—"

"What are you talking about?"

"We've been invaded. From some other universe, some other

dimension. They're insects. Mimicry. And more. Power to control minds. Your mind."

"My mind?"

"Their entrance is *here*, in Pikeville. They've taken over all of you. The whole town—except me. We're up against an incredibly powerful enemy, but they have their limitations. That's our hope. They're limited! They can make mistakes!"

Janet shook her head. "I don't understand, Ed. You must be insane."

"Insane? No. Just lucky. If I hadn't been down in the basement I'd be like all the rest of you." Loyce peered out the window. "But I can't stand here talking. Get your coat."

"My coat?"

"We're getting out of here. Out of Pikeville. We've got to get help. Fight this thing. They *can* be beaten. They're not infallible. It's going to be close—but we may make it if we hurry. Come on!" He grabbed her arm roughly. "Get your coat and call the twins. We're all leaving. Don't stop to pack. There's no time for that."

White-faced, his wife moved toward the closet and got down her coat. "Where are we going?"

Ed pulled open the desk drawer and spilled the contents out onto the floor. He grabbed up a road map and spread it open. "They'll have the highway covered, of course. But there's a back road. To Oak Grove. I got onto it once. It's practically abandoned. Maybe they'll forget about it."

"The old Ranch Road? Good Lord—it's completely closed. Nobody's supposed to drive over it."

"I know." Ed thrust the map grimly into his coat. "That's our best chance. Now call down the twins and let's get going. Your car is full of gas, isn't it?"

Janet was dazed.

"The Chevy? I had it filled up yesterday afternoon." Janet moved toward the stairs. "Ed, I—"

"Call the twins!" Ed unlocked the front door and peered out. Nothing stirred. No sign of life. All right so far.

"Come on downstairs," Janet called in a wavering voice. "We're—going out for a while."

"Now?" Tommy's voice came.

"Hurry up," Ed barked. "Get down here, both of you."

Tommy appeared at the top of the stairs. "I was doing my home-work. We're starting fractions. Miss Parker says if we don't get this done—"

"You can forget about fractions." Ed grabbed his son as he came down the stairs and propelled him toward the door. "Where's Jim?"

"He's coming."

Jim started slowly down the stairs. "What's up, Dad?"

"We're going for a ride."

"A ride? Where?"

Ed turned to Janet. "We'll leave the lights on. And the TV set. Go turn it on." He pushed her toward the set. "So they'll think we're still—"

He heard the buzz. And dropped instantly, the long butcher knife out. Sickened, he saw it coming down the stairs at him, wings a blur of motion as it aimed itself. It still bore a vague resemblance to Jimmy. It was small, a baby one. A brief glimpse—the thing hurtling at him, cold, multi-lensed inhuman eyes. Wings, body still clothed in yellow T-shirt and jeans, the mimic outline still stamped on it. A strange half-turn of its body as it reached him. What was it doing?

A stinger.

Loyce stabbed wildly at it. It retreated, buzzing frantically. Loyce rolled and crawled toward the door. Tommy and Janet stood still as statues, faces blank. Watching without expression. Loyce stabbed again. This time the knife connected. The thing shrieked and faltered. It bounced against the wall and fluttered down.

Something lapped through his mind. A wall of force, energy, an alien mind probing into him. He was suddenly paralyzed. The mind entered his own, touched against him briefly, shockingly. An utter alien presence, settling over him—and then it flickered out as the thing collapsed in a broken heap on the rug.

It was dead. He turned it over with his foot. It was an insect, a fly of some kind. Yellow T-shirt, jeans. His son Jimmy . . . He closed his mind tight. It was too late to think about that. Savagely he scooped up his knife and headed toward the door. Janet and Tommy stood stone-still, neither of them moving.

The car was out. He'd never get through. They'd be waiting for him. It was ten miles on foot. Ten long miles over rough ground, gulleys and open fields and hills of uncut forest. He'd have to go alone.

Loyce opened the door. For a brief second he looked back at his wife and son. Then he slammed the door behind him and raced down the porch steps.

A moment later he was on his way, hurrying swiftly through the darkness toward the edge of town.

❖ ❖ ❖

The early morning sunlight was blinding. Loyce halted, gasping for breath, swaying back and forth. Sweat ran down in his eyes. His clothing was torn, shredded by the brush and thorns through which he had crawled. Ten miles—on his hands and knees. Crawling, creeping through the night. His shoes were mud-caked. He was scratched and limping, utterly exhausted.

But ahead of him lay Oak Grove.

He took a deep breath and started down the hill. Twice he stumbled and fell, picking himself up and trudging on. His ears rang. Everything receded and wavered. But he was there. He had got out, away from Pikeville.

A farmer in a field gaped at him. From a house a young woman watched in wonder. Loyce reached the road and turned onto it. Ahead of him was a gasoline station and a drive-in. A couple of trucks, some chickens pecking in the dirt, a dog tied with a string.

The white-clad attendant watched suspiciously as he dragged himself up to the station. "Thank God." He caught hold of the wall. "I didn't think I was going to make it. They followed me most of the way. I could hear them buzzing. Buzzing and flitting around behind me."

"What happened?" the attendant demanded. "You in a wreck? A holdup?"

Loyce shook his head wearily. "They have the whole town. The City Hall and the police station. They hung a man from the lamp-post. That was the first thing I saw. They've got all the roads blocked. I saw them hovering over the cars coming in. About four this morning I got beyond them. I knew it right away. I could feel them leave. And then the sun came up."

The attendant licked his lip nervously. "You're out of your head. I better get a doctor."

"Get me into Oak Grove," Loyce gasped. He sank down on the gravel. "We've got to get started—cleaning them out. Got to get started right away."

❖ ❖ ❖

They kept a tape recorder going all the time he talked. When he had finished the Commissioner snapped off the recorder and got to his feet. He stood for a moment, deep in thought. Finally he got out his cigarettes and lit up slowly, a frown on his beefy face.

"You don't believe me," Loyce said.

The Commissioner offered him a cigarette. Loyce pushed it impatiently away. "Suit yourself." The Commissioner moved over to the window and stood for a time looking out at the town of Oak Grove. "I believe you," he said abruptly.

Loyce sagged. "Thank God."

"So you got away." The Commissioner shook his head. "You were down in your cellar instead of at work. A freak chance. One in a million."

Loyce sipped some of the black coffee they had brought him. "I have a theory," he murmured.

"What is it?"

"About them. Who they are. They take over one area at a time. Starting at the top—the highest level of authority. Working down from there in a widening circle. When they're firmly in control they go on to the next town. They spread, slowly, very gradually. I think it's been going on for a long time."

"A long time?"

"Thousands of years. I don't think it's new."

"Why do you say that?"

"When I was a kid . . . A picture they showed us in Bible League. A religious picture—an old print. The enemy gods, defeated by Jehovah. Moloch, Beelzebub, Moab, Baalin, Ashtaroth—"

"So?"

"They were all represented by figures." Loyce looked up at the Commissioner. "Beelzebub was represented as—a giant fly."

The Commissioner grunted. "An old struggle."

"They've been defeated. The Bible is an account of their defeats. They make gains—but finally they're defeated."

"Why defeated?"

"They can't get everyone. They didn't get me. And they never got the Hebrews. The Hebrews carried the message to the whole world. The realization of the danger. The two men on the bus. I think they understood. Had escaped, like I did." He clenched his fists. "I killed one of them. I made a mistake. I was afraid to take a chance."

The Commissioner nodded. "Yes, they undoubtedly had escaped, as you did. Freak accidents. But the rest of the town was firmly in control." He turned from the window, "Well, Mr. Loyce. You seem to have figured everything out."

"Not everything. The hanging man. The dead man hanging from

the lamppost. I don't understand that. *Why?* Why did they deliberately hang him there?"

"That would seem simple." The Commissioner smiled faintly. "*Bait.*"

Loyce stiffened. His heart stopped beating. "Bait? What do you mean?"

"To draw you out. Make you declare yourself. So they'd know who was under control—and who had escaped."

Loyce recoiled with horror. "Then they *expected* failures! They anticipated—" He broke off. "They were ready with a trap."

"And you showed yourself. You reacted. You made yourself known." The Commissioner abruptly moved toward the door. "Come along, Loyce. There's a lot to do. We must get moving. There's no time to waste."

Loyce started slowly to his feet, numbed. "And the man. *Who was the man?* I never saw him before. He wasn't a local man. He was a stranger. All muddy and dirty, his face cut, slashed—"

There was a strange look on the Commissioner's face as he answered, "Maybe," he said softly, "you'll understand that, too. Come along with me, Mr. Loyce." He held the door open, his eyes gleaming. Loyce caught a glimpse of the street in front of the police station. Policemen, a platform of some sort. A telephone pole—and a rope! "Right this way," the Commissioner said, smiling coldly.

❖ ❖ ❖

As the sun set, the vice-president of the Oak Grove Merchants' Bank came up out of the vault, threw the heavy time locks, put on his hat and coat, and hurried outside onto the sidewalk. Only a few people were there, hurrying home to dinner.

"Good night," the guard said, locking the door after him.

"Good night," Clarence Mason murmured. He started along the street toward his car. He was tired. He had been working all day down in the vault, examining the lay-out of the safety deposit boxes to see if there was room for another tier. He was glad to be finished.

At the corner he halted. The street lights had not yet come on. The street was dim. Everything was vague. He looked around—and froze.

From the telephone pole in front of the police station, something large and shapeless hung. It moved a little with the wind.

What the hell was it?

Mason approached it warily. He wanted to get home. He was tired and hungry. He thought of his wife, his kids, a hot meal on the dinner table. But there was something about the dark bundle, something ominous and ugly. The light was bad; he couldn't tell what it was. Yet it drew him on, made him move closer for a better look. The shapeless thing made him uneasy. He was frightened by it. Frightened—and fascinated.

And the strange part was that nobody else seemed to notice it.

THE EYES HAVE IT

It was quite by accident I discovered this incredible invasion of Earth by lifeforms from another planet. As yet, I haven't done anything about it; I can't think of anything to do. I wrote to the Government, and they sent back a pamphlet on the repair and maintenance of frame houses. Anyhow, the whole thing is known; I'm not the first to discover it. Maybe it's even under control.

I was sitting in my easy-chair, idly turning the pages of a paper-backed book someone had left on the bus, when I came across the reference that first put me on the trail. For a moment I didn't respond. It took some time for the full import to sink in. After I'd compre-hended, it seemed odd I hadn't noticed it right away.

The reference was clearly to a nonhuman species of incredible properties, not indigenous to Earth. A species, I hasten to point out, customarily masquerading as ordinary human beings. Their disguise, however, became transparent in the face of the following observations by the author. It was at once obvious the author knew everything. Knew everything—and was taking it in his stride. The line (and I tremble remembering it even now) read:

... *his eyes slowly roved about the room.*

Vague chills assailed me. I tried to picture the eyes. Did they roll like dimes? The passage indicated not; they seemed to move through the air, not over the surface. Rather rapidly, apparently. No one in the story was surprised. That's what tipped me off. No sign of amazement at such an outrageous thing. Later the matter was amplified.

. . . his eyes moved from person to person.

There it was in a nutshell. The eyes had clearly come apart from the rest of him and were on their own. My heart pounded and my breath choked in my windpipe. I had stumbled on an accidental mention of a totally unfamiliar race. Obviously non-Terrestrial. Yet, to the characters in the book, it was perfectly natural—which suggested they belonged to the same species.

And the author? A slow suspicion burned in my mind. The author was taking it rather *too easily* in his stride. Evidently, he felt this was quite a usual thing. He made absolutely no attempt to conceal this knowledge. The story continued:

. . . presently his eyes fastened on Julia.

Julia, being a lady, had at least the breeding to feel indignant. She is described as blushing and knitting her brows angrily. At this, I sighed with relief. They weren't *all* non-Terrestrials. The narrative continues:

. . . slowly, calmly, his eyes examined every inch of her.

Great Scott! But here the girl turned and stomped off and the matter ended. I lay back in my chair gasping with horror. My wife and family regarded me in wonder.

"What's wrong, dear?" my wife asked.

I couldn't tell her. Knowledge like this was too much for the ordinary run-of-the-mill person. I had to keep it to myself. "Nothing," I gasped. I leaped up, snatched the book, and hurried out of the room.

❖ ❖ ❖

In the garage, I continued reading. There was more. Trembling, I read the next revealing passage:

. . . he put his arm around Julia. Presently she asked him if he would remove his arm. He immediately did so, with a smile.

It's not said what was done with the arm after the fellow had removed it. Maybe it was left standing upright in the corner. Maybe it was thrown away. I don't care. In any case, the full meaning was there, staring me right in the face.

Here was a race of creatures capable of removing portions of their anatomy at will. Eyes, arms—and maybe more. Without batting an eyelash. My knowledge of biology came in handy, at this point. Obviously they were simple beings, unicellular, some sort of primitive single-celled things. Beings no more developed than starfish. Starfish can do the same thing, you know.

I read on. And came to this incredible revelation, tossed off coolly by the author without the faintest tremor:

. . . *outside the movie theater we split up. Part of us went inside, part over to the cafe for dinner.*

Binary fission, obviously. Splitting in half and forming two entities. Probably each lower half went to the cafe, it being farther, and the upper halves to the movies. I read on, hands shaking. I had really stumbled onto something here. My mind reeled as I made out this passage:

. . . *I'm afraid there's no doubt about it. Poor Bibney has lost his head again.*

Which was followed by:

. . . *and Bob says he has utterly no guts.*

Yet Bibney got around as well as the next person. The next person, however, was just as strange. He was soon described as:

. . . *totally lacking in brains.*

❖ ❖ ❖

There was no doubt of the thing in the next passage. Julia, whom I had thought to be the one normal person, reveals herself as also being an alien lifeform, similar to the rest:

. . . *quite deliberately, Julia had given her heart to the young man.*

It didn't relate what the final disposition of the organ was, but I didn't really care. It was evident Julia had gone right on living in her usual manner, like all the others in the book. Without heart, arms, eyes, brains, viscera, dividing up in two when the occasion demanded. Without a qualm.

. . . thereupon she gave him her hand.

I sickened. The rascal now had her hand, as well as her heart. I shudder to think what he's done with them, by this time.

. . . he took her arm.

Not content to wait, he had to start dismantling her on his own. Flushing crimson, I slammed the book shut and leaped to my feet. But not in time to escape one last reference to those carefree bits of anatomy whose travels had originally thrown me on the track:

. . . her eyes followed him all the way down the road and across the meadow.

I rushed from the garage and back inside the warm house, as if the accursed things were following *me*. My wife and children were playing Monopoly in the kitchen. I joined them and played with frantic fervor, brow feverish, teeth chattering.

I had had enough of the thing. I want to hear no more about it. Let them come on. Let them invade Earth. I don't want to get mixed up in it.

I have absolutely no stomach for it.

THE TURNING WHEEL

Bard Chai said thoughtfully, "Cults." He examined a tape-report grinding from the receptor. The receptor was rusty and unoiled; it whined piercingly and sent up an acrid wisp of smoke. Chai shut it off as its pitted surface began to heat ugly red. Presently he finished with the tape and tossed it with a heap of refuse jamming the mouth of a disposal slot.

"What about cults?" Bard Sung-wu asked faintly. He brought himself back with an effort, and forced a smile of interest on his plump olive-yellow face. "You were saying?"

"Any stable society is menaced by cults; our society is no exception." Chai rubbed his finely-tapered fingers together reflectively. "Certain lower strata are axiomatically dissatisfied Their hearts burn with envy of those the wheel has placed above them; in secret they form fanatic, rebellious bands. They meet in the dark of night; they insidiously express inversions of accepted norms; they delight in flaunting basic mores and customs."

"Ugh," Sung-wu agreed. "I mean," he explained quickly, "it seems incredible people could practice such fanatic and disgusting rites." He got nervously to his feet. "I must go, if it's permitted."

"Wait," snapped Chai. "You are familiar with the Detroit area?"

Uneasily, Sung-wu nodded. "Very slightly."

With characteristic vigor, Chai made his decision. "I'm sending you; investigate and make a blue-slip report. If this group is dangerous, the Holy Arm should know. It's of the worst elements—the Techno class." He made a wry face. "Caucasians, hulking, hairy things. We'll give you six months in Spain, on your return; you can poke over ruins of abandoned cities."

"Caucasians!" Sung-wu exclaimed, his face turning green. "But I haven't been well; please, if somebody else could go—"

"You, perhaps, hold to the Broken Feather theory?" Chai raised an eyebrow. "An amazing philologist, Broken Feather; I took partial instruction from him. He held, you know, the Caucasian to be descended of Neanderthal stock. Their extreme size, thick body hair, their general brutish cast, reveal an innate inability to comprehend anything but a purely animalistic horizontal; proselytism is a waste of time."

He affixed the younger man with a stern eye. "I wouldn't send you, if I didn't have unusual faith in your devotion."

Sung-wu fingered his beads miserably. "Elron be praised," he muttered; "you are too kind."

Sung-wu slid into a lift and was raised, amid great groans and whirrings and false stops, to the top level of the Central Chamber building. He hurried down a corridor dimly lit by occasional yellow bulbs. A moment later he approached the doors of the scanning offices and flashed his identification at the robot guard. "Is Bard Fei-p'ang within?" he inquired.

"Verily," the robot answered, stepping aside.

Sung-wu entered the offices, bypassed the rows of rusted, discarded machines, and entered the still-functioning wing. He located his brother-in-law, hunched over some graphs at one of the desks, laboriously copying material by hand. "Clearness be with you," Sung-wu murmured.

Fei-p'ang glanced up in annoyance. "I told you not to come again; if the Arm finds out I'm letting you use the scanner for a personal plot, they'll stretch me on the rack."

"Gently," Sung-wu murmured, his hand on his relation's shoulder. "This is the last time. I'm going away; one more look, a final look." His olive face took on a pleading, piteous cast. "The turn comes for me very soon; this will be our last conversation."

Sung-wu's piteous look hardened into cunning. "You wouldn't want it on your soul; no restitution will be possible at this late date."

Fei-p'ang snorted. "All right; but for Elron's sake, do it quickly."

Sung-wu hurried to the mother-scanner and seated himself in the rickety basket. He snapped on the controls, clamped his forehead to the viewpiece, inserted his identity tab, and set the space-time finger into motion. Slowly, reluctantly, the ancient mechanism coughed into life and began tracing his personal tab along the future track.

Sung-wu's hands shook; his body trembled; sweat dripped from his neck, as he saw himself scampering in miniature. *Poor Sung-wu*, he thought wretchedly. The mite of a thing hurried about its duties; this was but eight months hence. Harried and beset, it performed its tasks—and then, in a subsequent continuum, fell down and died.

Sung-wu removed his eyes from the viewpiece and waited for his pulse to slow. He could stand that part, watching the moment of death; it was what came next that was too jangling for him.

He breathed a silent prayer. Had he fasted enough? In the four-day purge and self-flagellation, he had used the whip with metal points, the heaviest possible. He had given away all his money; he had smashed a lovely vase his mother had left him, a treasured heirloom; he had rolled in the filth and mud in the center of town. Hundreds had seen him. Now, surely, all this was enough. But time was so short!

Faint courage stirring, he sat up and again put his eyes to the viewpiece. He was shaking with terror. What if it hadn't changed? What if his mortification weren't enough? He spun the controls, sending the finger tracing his time-track past the moment of death.

Sung-wu shrieked and scrambled back in horror. His future was the same, exactly the same; there had been no change at all. His guilt had been too great to be washed away in such short a time; it would take ages—and he didn't have ages.

He left the scanner and passed by his brother-in-law. "Thanks," he muttered shakily.

For once, a measure of compassion touched Fei-p'ang's efficient brown features. "Bad news? The next turn brings an unfortunate manifestation?"

"Bad scarcely describes it."

Fei-p'ang's pity turned to righteous rebuke. "Who do you have to blame but yourself?" he demanded sternly. "You know your conduct in this manifestation determines the next; if you look forward to a future life as a lower animal, it should make you glance over your behavior and repent your wrongs. The cosmic law that governs us is impartial. It is true justice: cause and effect; what you do determines what you next become—there can be no blame and no sorrow. There can be only understanding and repentance." His curiosity overcame him. "What is it? A snake? A squirrel?"

"It's no affair of yours," Sung-wu said, as he moved unhappily toward the exit doors.

"I'll look myself."

"Go ahead." Sung-wu pushed moodily out into the hall. He was dazed with despair: it hadn't changed; it was still the same.

In eight months he would die, stricken by one of the numerous plagues that swept over the inhabited parts of the world. He would become feverish, break out with red spots, turn and twist in an anguish of delirium. His bowels would drop out; his flesh would waste away; his eyes would roll up; and after an interminable time of suffering, he would die. His body would lie in a mass heap, with hundreds of others—a whole streetful of dead, to be carted away by one of the robot sweepers, happily immune. His mortal remains would be burned in a common rubbish incinerator at the outskirts of the city.

Meanwhile, the eternal spark, Sung-wu's divine soul, would hurry from this space-time manifestation to the next in order. But it would not rise; it would sink; he had watched its descent on the scanner many times. There was always the same hideous picture—a sight beyond endurance—of his soul, as it plummeted down like a stone, into one of the lowest continua, a sinkhole of a manifestation at the very bottom of the ladder.

He had sinned. In his youth, Sung-wu had got mixed up with a black-eyed wench with long flowing hair, a glittering waterfall down her back and shoulders. Inviting red lips, plump breasts, hips that undulated and beckoned unmistakably. She was the wife of a friend, from the Warrior class, but he had taken her as his mistress; he had been *certain* time remained to rectify his venality.

But he was wrong: the wheel was soon to turn for him. The plague—not enough time to fast and pray and do good works. He was determined to go down, straight down to a wallowing, foul-aired planet in a stinking red-sun system, an ancient pit of filth and decay and unending slime—a jungle world of the lowest type.

In it, he would be a shiny-winged fly, a great blue-bottomed, buzzing carrion-eater that hummed and guzzled and crawled through the rotting carcasses of great lizards, slain in combat.

From this swamp, this pest-ridden planet in a diseased, contaminated system, he would have to rise painfully to the endless rungs of the cosmic ladder he had already climbed. It had taken eons to climb this far, to the level of a human being on the planet Earth, in the bright yellow Sol system; now he would have to do it all over again.

❖ ❖ ❖

Chai beamed, "Elron be with you," as the corroded observation ship was checked by the robot crew, and finally okayed for limited flight. Sung-wu slowly entered the ship and seated himself at what remained of the controls. He waved listlessly, then slammed the lock and bolted it by hand.

As the ship limped into the late afternoon sky, he reluctantly consulted the reports and records Chai had transferred to him.

The Tinkerists were a small cult; they claimed only a few hundred members, all drawn from the Techno class, which was the most despised of the social castes. The Bards, of course, were at the top; they were the teachers of society, the holy men who guided man to clearness. Then the Poets; they turned into saga the great legends of Elron Hu, who lived (according to legend) in the hideous days of the Time of Madness. Below the Poets were the Artists; then the Musicians; then the Workers, who supervised the robot crews. After them the Businessmen, the Warriors, the Farmers, and finally, at the bottom, the Technos.

Most of the Technos were Caucasians—immense white-skinned things, incredibly hairy, like apes; their resemblance to the great apes was striking. Perhaps Broken Feather was right; perhaps they did have Neanderthal blood and were outside the possibility of clearness. Sung-wu had always considered himself an anti-racist; he disliked those who maintained the Caucasians were a race apart. Extremists believed eternal damage would result to the species if the Caucasians were allowed to intermarry.

In any case, the problem was academic; no decent, self-respecting woman of the higher classes—of Indian or Mongolian, or Bantu stock—would allow herself to be approached by a *Cauc*.

Below his ship, the barren countryside spread out, ugly and bleak. Great red spots that hadn't yet been overgrown, and slag surfaces were still visible—but by this time most ruins were covered by soil and crabgrass. He could see men and robots farming; villages, countless tiny brown circles in the green fields; occasional ruins of ancient cities—gaping sores like blind mouths, eternally open to the sky. They would never close, not now.

Ahead was the Detroit area, named, so it ran, for some now-forgotten spiritual leader. There were more villages, here. Off to his left, the leaden surface of a body of water, a lake of some kind. Beyond that—only Elron knew. No one went that far; there was no human life there, only wild animals and deformed things spawned from radiation infestation still lying heavy in the north.

He dropped his ship down. An open field lay to his right; a robot farmer was plowing with a metal hook welded to its waist, a section torn off some discarded machine. It stopped dragging the hook and gazed up in amazement, as Sung-wu landed the ship awkwardly and bumped to a halt.

"Clearness be with you," the robot rasped obediently, as Sung-wu climbed out.

Sung-wu gathered up his bundle of reports and papers and stuffed them in a briefcase. He snapped the ship's lock and hurried off toward the ruins of the city. The robot went back to dragging the rusty metal hook through the hard ground, its pitted body bent double with the strain, working slowly, silently, uncomplaining.

The little boy piped, "Whither, Bard?" as Sung-wu pushed wearily through the tangled debris and slag. He was a little black-faced Bantu, in red rags sewed and patched together. He ran alongside Sung-wu like a puppy, leaping and bounding and grinning white-teethed.

Sung-wu became immediately crafty; his intrigue with the black-haired girl had taught him elemental dodges and evasions. "My ship broke down," he answered cautiously; it was certainly common enough. "It was the last ship still in operation at our field."

The boy skipped and laughed and broke off bits of green weeds that grew along the trail. "I know somebody who can fix it," he cried carelessly.

Sung-wu's pulse-rate changed. "Oh?" he murmured, as if uninterested. "There are those around here who practice the questionable art of repairing."

The boy nodded solemnly.

"Technos?" Sung-wu pursued. "Are there many of them here, around these old ruins?"

More black-faced boys, and some little dark-eyed Bantu girls, came scampering through the slag and ruins. "What's the matter with your ship?" one hollered at Sung-wu. "Won't it run?"

They all ran and shouted around him, as he advanced slowly—an unusually wild bunch, completely undisciplined. They rolled and fought and tumbled and chased each other around madly.

"How many of you," Sung-wu demanded, "have taken your first instruction?"

There was a sudden uneasy silence. The children looked at each other guiltily; none of them answered.

"Good Elron!" Sung-wu exclaimed in horror. "Are you all untaught?"

Heads hung guiltily.

"How do you expect to phase yourselves with the cosmic will? How can you expect to know the divine plan? This is really too much!"

He pointed a plump finger at one of the boys. "Are you constantly preparing yourself for the life to come? Are you constantly purging and purifying yourself? Do you deny yourself meat, sex, entertainment, financial gain, education, leisure?"

But it was obvious; their unrestrained laughter and play proved they were still jangled, far from clear—And clearness is the only road by which a person can gain understanding of the eternal plan, the cosmic wheel which turns endlessly, for all living things.

"Butterflies!" Sung-wu snorted with disgust. "You are no better than the beasts and birds of the field, who take no heed of the morrow. You play and game for today, thinking tomorrow won't come. Like insects—"

But the thought of insects reminded him of the shiny-winged bluerumped fly, creeping over a rotting lizard carcass, and Sung-wu's stomach did a flip-flop; he forced it back in place and strode on, toward the line of villages emerging ahead.

Farmers were working the barren fields on all sides. A thin layer of soil over slag; a few limp wheat stalks waved, thin and emaciated. The ground was terrible, the worst he had seen. He could feel the metal under his feet; it was almost to the surface. Bent men and women watered their sickly crops with tin cans, old metal containers picked from the ruins. An ox was pulling a crude cart.

In another field, women were weeding by hand; all moved slowly, stupidly, victims of hookworms, from the soil. They were all barefoot. The children hadn't picked it up yet, but they soon would.

Sung-wu gazed up at the sky and gave thanks to Elron; here, suffering was unusually severe; trials of exceptional vividness lay on every hand. These men and women were being tempered in a hot crucible; their souls were probably purified to an astonishing degree. A baby lay in the shade, beside a half-dozing mother. Flies crawled over its eyes; its mother breathed heavily, hoarsely, her mouth open. An unhealthy flush discolored her brown cheeks. Her belly bulged; she was already pregnant again. Another eternal soul to be raised from a lower level. Her great breasts sagged and wobbled as she stirred in her sleep, spilling out over her dirty wraparound.

"Come here," Sung-wu called sharply to the gang of black-faced children who followed along after him. "I'm going to talk to you."

The children approached, eyes on the ground, and assembled in a silent circle around him. Sung-wu sat down, placed his briefcase beside him and folded his legs expertly under him in the traditional posture outlined by Elron in his seventh book of teaching.

"I will ask and you will answer," Sung-wu stated. "You know the basic catechisms?" He peered sharply around. "Who knows the basic catechisms?"

One or two hands went up. Most of the children looked away unhappily.

"First!" snapped Sung-wu. "*Who are you*? You are a minute fragment of the cosmic plan.

"Second! *What are you*? A mere speck in a system so vast as to be beyond comprehension.

"Third! *What is the way of life?* To fulfill what is required by the cosmic forces.

"Fourth! *Where are you?* On one step of the cosmic ladder.

"Fifth! *Where have you been?* Through endless steps; each turn of the wheel advances or depresses you.

"Sixth! *What determines your direction at the next turn?* Your conduct in this manifestation.

"Seventh! *What is right conduct?* Submitting yourself to the eternal forces, the cosmic elements that make up the divine plan.

"Eighth! *What is the significance of suffering?* To purify the soul.

"Ninth! *What is the significance of death?* To release the person from this manifestation, so he may rise to a new rung of the ladder.

"Tenth—"

But at that moment Sung-wu broke off. Two quasi-human shapes were approaching him. Immense white-skinned figures striding across the baked fields, between the sickly rows of wheat.

Technos—coming to meet him; his flesh crawled. Caucs. Their skin glittered pale and unhealthy, like nocturnal insects, dug from under rocks.

He rose to his feet, conquered his disgust, and prepared to greet them.

Sung-wu said, "Clearness!" He could smell them, a musky sheep smell, as they came to a halt in front of him. Two bucks, two immense sweating males, skin damp and sticky, with beards, and long disorderly hair. They wore sailcloth trousers and boots. With horror Sung-wu perceived a thick body-hair, on their chests, like woven mats—tufts in their armpits, on their arms, wrists, even the backs of their hands. Maybe Broken Feather was right; perhaps, in these great lumbering blond-haired beasts, the archaic Neanderthal stock—the false men—still survived. He could almost see the ape, peering from behind their blue eyes.

"Hi," the first Cauc said. After a moment he added reflectively, "My name's Jamison."

"Pete Ferris," the other grunted. Neither of them observed the customary deferences; Sung-wu winced but managed not to show it. Was it deliberate, a veiled insult, or perhaps mere ignorance? This was hard to tell; in lower classes there was, as Chai said, an ugly undercurrent of resentment and envy, and hostility.

"I'm making a routine survey," Sung-wu explained, "on birth and death rates in rural areas. I'll be here a few days. Is there some place I can stay? Some public inn or hostel?"

The two Cauc bucks were silent. "Why?" one of them demanded bluntly.

Sung-wu blinked. "Why? Why what?"

"Why are you making a survey? If you want any information we'll supply it."

Sung-wu was incredulous. "Do you know to whom you're talking? I'm a Bard! Why, you're ten classes down; how dare you—" He choked with rage. In these rural areas the Technos had utterly forgotten their place. What was ailing the local Bards? Were they letting the system break apart?

He shuddered violently at the thought of what it would mean if Technos and Farmers and Businessmen were allowed to intermingle—even intermarry, and eat, and drink, in the same places. The whole structure of society would collapse. If all were to ride the same carts, use the same outhouses; it passed belief. A sudden nightmare picture loomed up before Sung-wu, of Technos living and mating with women of the Bard and Poet classes. He visioned a horizontally-oriented society, all persons on the same level, with horror. It went against the very grain of the cosmos, against the divine plan; it was the Time of Madness all over again. He shuddered.

"Where is the Manager of this area?" he demanded. "Take me to him; I'll deal directly with him."

The two Caucs turned and headed back the way they had come, without a word. After a moment of fury, Sung-wu followed behind them.

They led him through withered fields and over barren, eroded hills on which nothing grew; the ruins increased. At the edge of the city, a line of meager villages had been set up; he saw leaning, rickety wood huts, and mud streets. From the villages a thick stench rose, the smell of offal and death.

Dogs lay sleeping under the huts; children poked and played in the filth and rotting debris. A few old people sat on porches, vacant-faced, eyes glazed and dull. Chickens pecked around, and he saw pigs and skinny cats—and the eternal rusting piles of metal, sometimes thirty feet high. Great towers of red slag were heaped up everywhere.

Beyond the villages were the ruins proper—endless miles of abandoned wreckage; skeletons of buildings; concrete walls; bathtubs and pipe; overturned wrecks that had been cars. All these were from the Time of Madness, the decade that had finally rung the curtain down on the sorriest interval in man's history. The five centuries of madness and jangledness were now known as the Age of Heresy, when man had gone against the divine plan and taken his destiny in his own hands.

They came to a larger hut, a two-story wood structure. The Caucs climbed a decaying flight of steps; boards creaked and gave ominously under their heavy boots. Sung-wu followed them nervously; they came out on a porch, a kind of open balcony.

On the balcony sat a man, an obese copper-skinned official in unbuttoned breeches, his shiny black hair pulled back and tied with a bone against his bulging red neck. His nose was large and prominent, his face, flat and wide, with many chins. He was drinking lime juice from a tin cup and gazing down at the mud street below. As the two Caucs appeared he rose slightly, a prodigious effort.

"This man," the Cauc named Jamison said, indicating Sung-wu, "wants to see you."

Sung-wu pushed angrily forward. "I am a Bard, from the Central Chamber; do you people recognize *this*?" He tore open his robe and flashed the symbol of the Holy Arm, gold worked to form a swathe of flaming red. "I insist you accord me proper treatment! I'm not here to be pushed around by any—"

He had said too much; Sung-wu forced his anger down and gripped his briefcase. The fat Indian was studying him calmly; the two Caucs had wandered to the far end of the balcony and were squatting down in the shade. They lit crude cigarettes and turned their backs.

"Do you permit this?" Sung-wu demanded, incredulous. "This—mingling?"

The Indian shrugged and sagged down even more in his chair. "Clearness be with you," he murmured; "will you join me?" His calm expression remained unchanged; he seemed not to have noticed. "Some lime juice? Or perhaps coffee? Lime juice is good for these." He tapped his mouth; his soft gums were lined with caked sores.

"Nothing for me," Sung-wu muttered grumpily, as he took a seat opposite the Indian; "I'm here on an official survey."

The Indian nodded faintly. "Oh?"

"Birth and death rates." Sung-wu hesitated, then leaned toward the Indian. "I insist you send those two Caucs away; what I have to say to you is private."

The Indian showed no change of expression; his broad face was utterly impassive. After a time he turned slightly. "Please go down to the street level," he ordered. "As you will."

The two Caucs got to their feet, grumbling, and pushed past the table, scowling and darting resentful glances at Sung-wu. One of them hawked and elaborately spat over the railing, an obvious insult.

"Insolence!" Sung-wu choked. "How can you allow it? Did you see them? By Elron, it's beyond belief!"

The Indian shrugged indifferently—and belched. "All men are brothers on the wheel. Didn't Elron Himself teach that, when He was on Earth?"

"Of course. But—"

"Are not even these men our brothers?"

"Naturally," Sung-wu answered haughtily, "but they must know their place; they're an insignificant class. In the rare event some object wants fixing, they're called; but in the last year I do not recall a single incident when it was deemed advisable to repair anything. The need of such a class diminishes yearly; eventually such a class and the elements composing it—"

"You perhaps advocate sterilization?" the Indian inquired, heavy-lidded and sly.

"I advocate *something*. The lower classes reproduce like rabbits; spawning all the time—much faster than we Bards. I always see some swollen-up Cauc woman, but hardly a single Bard is born these days; the lower classes must fornicate constantly."

"That's about all that's left them," the Indian murmured mildly. He sipped a little lime juice. "You should try to be more tolerant."

"Tolerant? I have nothing against them, as long as they—"

"It is said," the Indian continued softly, "that Elron Hu, Himself, was a Cauc."

Sung-wu spluttered indignantly and started to rejoin, but the hot words stuck fast in his mouth; down in the mud street something was coming.

Sung-wu demanded, "What is it?" He leaped up excitedly and hurried to the railing.

A slow procession was advancing with solemn step. As if at a signal, men and women poured from their rickety huts and excitedly lined the street to watch. Sung-wu was transfixed, as the procession neared; his senses reeled. More and more men and women were collecting each moment; there seemed to be hundreds of them. They were a dense, murmuring mob, packed tight, swaying back and forth, faces avid. An hysterical moan passed through them, a great wind that stirred them like leaves of a tree. They were a single collective whole, a vast primitive organism, held ecstatic and hypnotized by the approaching column.

The marchers wore a strange costume: white shirts, with the sleeves rolled up; dark gray trousers of an incredibly archaic design, and black shoes. All were dressed exactly alike. They formed a dazzling double line of white shirts, gray trousers, marching calmly and solemnly, faces up, nostrils flared, jaws stern. A glazed fanaticism stamped each man and woman, such a ruthless expression that Sung-wu shrank back in terror. On and on they came, figures of grim stone in their primordial white shirts and gray trousers, a frightening breath from the past. Their heels struck the ground in a dull, harsh beat that reverberated among the rickety huts. The dogs woke; the children began to wail. The chickens flew squawking.

"Elron!" Sung-wu cried. "What's happening?"

The marchers carried strange symbolic implements, ritualistic images with esoteric meaning that of necessity escaped Sung-wu. There were tubes and poles, and shiny webs of what looked like metal. *Metal*! But it was not rusty; it was shiny and bright. He was stunned; they looked—new.

The procession passed directly below. After the marchers came a huge rumbling cart. On it was mounted an obvious fertility symbol, a corkscrew-bore as long as a tree; it jutted from a square cube of gleaming steel; as the cart moved forward the bore lifted and fell.

After the cart came more marchers, also grim-faced, eyes glassy, loaded down with pipes and tubes and armfuls of glittering equipment. They passed on, and then the street was filled by surging throngs of awed men and women, who followed after them, utterly dazed. And then came children and barking dogs.

The last marcher carried a pennant that fluttered above her as she strode along, a tall pole, hugged tight to her chest. At the top, the bright pennant fluttered boldly. Sung-wu made its marking out, and for a moment consciousness left him. There it was, directly below; it had passed under his very nose, out in the open for all to see—unconcealed. The pennant had a great T emblazoned on it.

"They—" he began, but the obese Indian cut him off.

"The Tinkerists," he rumbled, and sipped his lime juice.

Sung-wu grabbed up his briefcase and scrambled toward the stairs. At the bottom, the two hulking Caucs were already moving into motion. The Indian signaled quickly to them. "Here!" They started grimly up, little blue eyes mean, red-rimmed and cold as stone; under their pelts their bulging muscles rippled.

Sung-wu fumbled in his cloak. His shiver-gun came out; he squeezed the release and directed it toward the two Caucs. But nothing happened; the gun had stopped functioning. He shook it wildly; flakes of rust and dried insulation fluttered from it. It was useless, worn out; he tossed it away and then, with the resolve of desperation, jumped through the railing.

He, and a torrent of rotten wood, cascaded to the street. He hit, rolled, struck his head against the corner of a hut, and shakily pulled himself to his feet.

He ran. Behind him, the two Caucs pushed after him through the throngs of men and women milling aimlessly along. Occasionally he glimpsed their white, perspiring faces. He turned a corner, raced between shabby huts, leaped over a sewage ditch, climbed heaps of sagging debris, slipped and rolled and at last lay gasping behind a tree, his briefcase still clutched.

The Caucs were nowhere in sight. He had evaded them; for the moment, he was safe.

He peered around. Which way was his ship? He shielded his eyes against the late-afternoon sun until he managed to make out its bent, tubular outline. It was far off to his right, barely visibly in the dying glare that hung gloomily across the sky. Sung-wu got unsteadily to his feet and began walking cautiously in that direction.

He was in a terrible spot; the whole region was pro-Tinkerist—even the Chamber-appointed Manager. And it wasn't along class lines; the cult had knifed to the top level. And it wasn't just Caucs, anymore; he couldn't count on Bantu or Mongolian or Indian, not in this area. An entire countryside was hostile, and lying in wait for him.

Elron, it was worse than the Arm had thought! No wonder they wanted a report. A whole area had swung over to a fanatic cult, a violent extremist group of heretics, teaching a most diabolical doctrine. He shuddered—and kept on, avoiding contact with the farmers in their fields, both human and robot. He increased his pace, as alarm and horror pushed him suddenly faster.

If the thing were to spread, if it were to hit a sizable portion of mankind, it might bring back the Time of Madness.

❖❖❖

The ship was taken. Three or four immense Caucs stood lounging around it, cigarettes dangling from their slack mouths, white-faced and hairy. Stunned, Sung-wu moved back down the hillside, prickles of despair numbing him. The ship was lost; they had got there ahead of him. What was he supposed to do now?

It was almost evening. He'd have to walk fifty miles through the darkness, over unfamiliar, hostile ground, to reach the next inhabited area. The sun was already beginning to set, the air turning cool; and in addition, he was sopping wet with filth and slimy water. He had slipped in the gloom and fallen in a sewage ditch.

He retraced his steps, mind blank. What could he do? He was helpless; his shiver-gun had been useless. He was alone, and there was no contact with the Arm. Tinkerists swarming on all sides; they'd probably gut him and sprinkle his blood over the crops—or worse.

He skirted a farm. In the fading twilight, a dim figure was working, a young woman. He eyed her cautiously, as he passed; she had her back to him. She was bending over, between rows of corn. What was she doing? Was she—good Elron!

He stumbled blindly across the field toward her, caution forgotten. "Young woman! *Stop*! In the name of Elron, stop at once!"

The girl straightened up. "Who are you?"

Breathless, Sung-wu arrived in front of her, gripping his battered briefcase and gasping. "Those are our *brothers*! How can you destroy them? They may be close relatives, recently deceased." He struck and knocked the jar from her hand; it hit the ground and the imprisoned beetles scurried off in all directions.

The girl's cheeks flushed with anger. "It took me an hour to collect those!"

"You were killing them! Crushing them!" He was speechless with horror. "I saw you!"

"Of course." The girl raised her black eyebrows. "They gnaw the corn."

"They're our brothers!" Sung-wu repeated wildly. "Of course they gnaw the corn; because of certain sins committed, the cosmic forces have—" He broke off, appalled. "Don't you *know*? You've never been told?"

The girl was perhaps sixteen. In the fading light she was a small, slender figure, the empty jar in one hand, a rock in the other. A tide of black hair tumbled down her neck. Her eyes were large and luminous; her lips full and deep red; her skin a smooth copper-brown—Polynesian, probably. He caught a glimpse of firm brown breasts as she bent to grab a beetle that had landed on its back. The sight made his pulse race; in a flash he was back three years.

"What's your name?" he asked, more kindly.

"Frija."

"How old are you?"

"Seventeen."

"I am a Bard; have you ever spoken to a Bard before?"

"No," the girl murmured. "I don't think so."

She was almost invisible in the darkness. Sung-wu could scarcely see her, but what he saw sent his heart into an agony of paroxysms; the same cloud of black hair, the same deep red lips. This girl was younger, of course—a mere child, and from the Farmer class, at that. But she had Liu's figure, and in time she'd ripen—probably in a matter of months.

Ageless, honeyed craft worked his vocal cords. "I have landed in this area to make a survey. Something has gone wrong with my ship and I must remain the night. I know no one here, however. My plight is such that—"

"Oh," Frija said, immediately sympathetic. "Why don't you stay with us, tonight? We have an extra room, now that my brother's away."

"Delighted," Sung-wu answered instantly. "Will you lead the way? I'll gladly repay you for your kindness." The girl moved off toward a vague shape looming up in the darkness. Sung-wu hurried quickly after her. "I find it incredible you haven't been instructed. This whole area has deteriorated beyond belief. What ways have you fallen in? We'll have to spend much time together; I can see that already. Not one of you even approaches clearness—you're jangled, every one of you."

"What does that mean?" Frija asked, as she stepped up on the porch and opened the door.

"Jangled?" Sung-wu blinked in amazement. "We *will* have to study much together." In his eagerness, he tripped on the top step, and barely managed to catch himself. "Perhaps you need complete instruction; it may be necessary to start from the very bottom. I can arrange a stay at the Holy Arm for you—under my protection, of course. Jangled means out of harmony with the cosmic elements. How can you live this way? My dear, you'll have to be brought back in line with the divine plan!"

"What plan is that?" She led him into a warm living room; a crackling fire burned in the grate. Two or three men sat around a rough wood table, an old man with long white hair and two younger men. A frail, withered old woman sat dozing in a rocker in the corner. In the kitchen, a buxom young woman was fixing the evening meal.

"Why, *the* plan!" Sung-wu answered, astounded. His eyes darted around. Suddenly his briefcase fell to the floor. "Caucs," he said.

They were all Caucasians, even Frija. She was deeply tanned; her skin was almost black; but she was a Cauc, nonetheless. He recalled: Caucs, in the sun, turned dark, sometimes even darker than Mongolians. The girl had tossed her work robe over a door hook; in her household shorts her thighs were as white as milk. And the old man and woman—

"This is my grandfather," Frija said, indicating the old man. "Benjamin Tinker."

❖ ❖ ❖

Under the watchful eyes of the two younger Tinkers, Sung-wu was washed and scrubbed, given clean clothes, and then fed. He ate only a little; he didn't feel very well.

"I can't understand it," he muttered, as he listlessly pushed his plate away. "The scanner at the Central Chamber said I had eight months left. The plague will—" He considered. "But it can always change. The scanner goes on prediction, not certainty; multiple possibilities; free will . . . Any overt act of sufficient significance—"

Ben Tinker laughed. "You want to stay alive?"

"Of course!" Sung-wu muttered indignantly.

They all laughed—even Frija, and the old woman in her shawl, snow-white hair and mild blue eyes. They were the first Cauc women he had ever seen. They weren't big and lumbering like the male Caucs; they didn't seem to have the same bestial characteristics. The two young Cauc bucks looked plenty tough, though; they and their father were poring over an elaborate series of papers and reports, spread out on the dinner table, among the empty plates.

"This area," Ben Tinker murmured. "Pipes should go here. And here. Water's the main need. Before the next crop goes in, we'll dump a few hundred pounds of artificial fertilizers and plow it in. The power plows should be ready, then."

"After that?" one of the tow-headed sons asked.

"Then spraying. If we don't have the nicotine sprays, we'll have to try the copper dusting again. I prefer the spray, but we're still behind on production. The bore has dug us up some good storage caverns, though. It ought to start picking up."

"And here," a son said, "there's going to be need of draining. A lot of mosquito breeding going on. We can try the oil, as we did over here. But I suggest the whole thing be filled in. We can use the dredge and scoop, if they're not tied up."

Sung-wu had taken this all in. Now he rose unsteadily to his feet, trembling with wrath. He pointed a shaking finger at the elder Tinker.

"You're—meddling!" he gasped.

They looked up. "Meddling?"

"With the plan! With the cosmic plan! Good Elron—you're interfering with the divine processes. Why—" He was staggered by a realization so alien it convulsed the very core of his being. "You're actually going to set back turns of the wheel."

"That," said old Ben Tinker, "is right."

Sung-wu sat down again, stunned. His mind refused to take it all in. "I don't understand; what'll happen? If you slow the wheel, if you disrupt the divine plan—"

"He's going to be a problem," Ben Tinker murmured thoughtfully. "If we kill him, the Arm will merely send another; they have hundreds like him. And if we don't kill him, if we send him back, he'll raise a hue and cry that'll bring the whole Chamber down here. It's too soon for this to happen. We're gaining support fast, but we need another few months."

Sweat stood out on Sung-wu's plump forehead. He wiped it away shakily. "If you kill me," he muttered, "you will sink down many rungs of the cosmic ladder. You have risen this far; why undo the work accomplished in endless ages past?"

Ben Tinker fixed one powerful blue eye on him. "My friend," he said slowly, "isn't it true one's next manifestation is determined by one's moral conduct in this?"

Sung-wu nodded. "Such is well-known."

"And what is right conduct?"

"Fulfilling the divine plan," Sung-wu responded immediately.

"Maybe our whole Movement in part of the plan," Ben Tinker said thoughtfully. "Maybe the cosmic forces *want* us to drain the swamps and kill the grasshoppers and inoculate the children; after all, the cosmic forces put us all here."

"If you kill me," Sung-wu wailed, "I'll be a carrion-eating fly. I *saw* it, a shiny-winged blue-rumped fly crawling over the carcass of a dead lizard—In a rotting, steaming jungle in a filthy cesspool of a planet." Tears came; he dabbed at them futilely. "In an out-of-the-way system, at the bottom of the ladder!"

Tinker was amused. "Why this?"

"I've sinned." Sung-wu sniffed and flushed. "I committed adultery."

"Can't you purge yourself?"

"There's no time!" His misery rose to wild despair. "My mind is *still* impure!" He indicated Frija, standing in the bedroom doorway, a supple white and tan shape in her household shorts. "I continue to think carnal thoughts; I can't rid myself. In eight months the plague will turn the wheel on me—and it'll be done! If I lived to be an old man, withered and toothless—no more appetite—" His plump body quivered in a frenzied convulsion. "There's no *time* to purge and atone. According to the scanner, I'm going to die a young man!"

After this torrent of words, Tinker was silent, deep in thought. "The plague," he said, at last. "What, exactly, are the symptoms?"

Sung-wu described them, his olive face turning to a sickly green. When he had finished, the three men looked significantly at each other.

Ben Tinker got to his feet. "Come along," he commanded briskly, taking the Bard by the arm. "I have something to show you. It is left from the old days. Sooner or later we'll advance enough to turn out our own, but right now we have only these remaining few. We have to keep them guarded and sealed."

"This is for a good cause," one of the sons said. "It's worth it." He caught his brother's eye and grinned.

❖❖❖

Bard Chai finished reading Sung-wu's blue-slip report; he tossed it suspiciously down and eyed the younger Bard. "You're sure? There's no further need of investigation?"

"The cult will wither away," Sung-wu murmured indifferently. "It lacks any real support; it's merely an escape valve, without intrinsic validity."

Chai wasn't convinced. He reread parts of the report again. "I suppose you're right; but we've heard so many—"

"Lies," Sung-wu said vaguely. "Rumors. Gossip. May I go?" He moved toward the door.

"Eager for your vacation?" Chai smiled understandingly. "I know how you feel. This report must have exhausted you. Rural areas, stagnant backwaters. We must prepare a better program of rural education. I'm convinced whole regions are in a jangled state. We've got to bring clearness to these people. It's our historic role; our class function."

"Verily," Sung-wu murmured, as he bowed his way out of the office and down the hall.

As he walked he fingered his beads thankfully. He breathed a silent prayer as his fingers moved over the surface of the little red pellets, shiny spheres that glowed freshly in place of the faded old—the gift of the Tinkerists. The beads would come in handy; he kept his hand on them tightly. Nothing must happen to them, in the next eight months. He had to watch them carefully, while he poked around the ruined cities of Spain—and finally came down with the plague.

He was the first Bard to wear a rosary of penicillin capsules.

THE LAST OF THE MASTERS

Consciousness collected around him. He returned with reluctance; the weight of centuries, an unbearable fatigue, lay over him. The ascent was painful. He would have shrieked if there were anything to shriek with. And anyhow, he was beginning to feel glad.

Eight thousand times he had crept back thus, with ever-increasing difficulty. Someday he wouldn't make it. Someday the black pool would remain. But not this day. He was still alive; above the aching pain and reluctance came joyful triumph.

"Good morning," a bright voice said. "Isn't it a nice day? I'll pull the curtains and you can look out."

He could see and hear. But he couldn't move. He lay quietly and allowed the various sensations of the room to pour in on him. Carpets, wallpaper, tables, lamps, pictures. Desk and vidscreen. Gleaming yellow sunlight streamed through the window. Blue sky. Distant hills. Fields, buildings, roads, factories. Workers and machines.

Peter Green was busily straightening things, his young face wreathed with smiles. "Lots to do today. Lots of people to see you. Bills to sign. Decisions to make. This is Saturday. There will be people coming in from the remote sectors. I hope the maintenance crew has done a good job." He added quickly, "They have, of course. I talked to Fowler on my way over here. Everything's fixed up fine."

The youth's pleasant tenor mixed with the bright sunlight. Sounds and sights, but nothing else. He could feel nothing. He tried to move his arm but nothing happened.

"Don't worry," Green said, catching his terror. "They'll soon be along with the rest. You'll be all right. You *have* to be. How could we survive without you?"

He relaxed. God knew, it had happened often enough before. Anger surged dully. Why couldn't they coordinate? Get it up all at once, not piecemeal. He'd have to change their schedule. Make them organize better.

Past the bright window a squat metal car chugged to a halt. Uniformed men piled out, gathered up heavy armloads of equipment, and hurried toward the main entrance of the building.

"Here they come," Green exclaimed with relief. "A little late, eh?"

"Another traffic tie-up," Fowler snorted, as he entered. "Something wrong with the signal system again. Outside flow got mixed up with the urban stuff; tied up on all sides. I wish you'd change the law."

Now there was motion all around him. The shapes of Fowler and McLean loomed, two giant moons abruptly ascendant. Professional faces that peered down at him anxiously. He was turned over on his side. Muffled conferences. Urgent whispers. The clank of tools.

"Here," Fowler muttered. "Now here. No, that's later. Be careful. Now run it up through here."

The work continued in taut silence. He was aware of their closeness. Dim outlines occasionally cut off his light. He was turned this way and that, thrown around like a sack of meal.

"Okay," Fowler said. "Tape it."

A long silence. He gazed dully at the wall, at the slightly-faded blue and pink wallpaper. An old design that showed a woman in hoopskirts, with a little parasol over her dainty shoulder. A frilly white blouse, tiny tips of shoes. An astoundingly clean puppy at her side.

Then he was turned back, to face upward. Five shapes groaned and strained over him. Their fingers flew, their muscles rippled under their shirts. At last they straightened up and retreated. Fowler wiped sweat from his face; they were all tense and bleary eyed.

"Go ahead," Fowler rasped. "Throw it."

Shock hit him. He gasped. His body arched, then settled slowly down.

His body. He could feel. He moved his arms experimentally. He touched his face, his shoulder, the wall. The wall was real and hard. All at once the world had become three-dimensional again.

Relief showed on Fowler's face. "Thank—God." He sagged wearily. "How do you feel?"

After a moment he answered, "All right."

Fowler sent the rest of the crew out. Green began dusting again, off in the corner. Fowler sat down on the edge of the bed and lit his pipe. "Now listen to me," he said. "I've got bad news. I'll give it to you the way you always want it, straight from the shoulder."

"What is it?" he demanded. He examined his fingers. He already knew.

There were dark circles under Fowler's eyes. He hadn't shaved. His square-jawed face was drawn and unhealthy. "We were up all night. Working on your motor system. We've got it jury-rigged, but it won't hold. Not more than another few months. The thing's climbing. The basic units can't be replaced. When they wear out they're gone. We can weld in relays and wiring, but we can't fix the five synapsis-coils. There were only a few men who could make those, and they've been dead two centuries. If the coils burn out—"

"Is there any deterioration in the synapsis-coils?" he interrupted.

"Not yet. Just motor areas. Arms, in particular. What's happening to your legs will happen to your arms and finally all your motor system. You'll be paralyzed by the end of the year. You'll be able to see, hear, and think. And broadcast. But that's all." He added, "Sorry, Bors. We're doing all we can."

"All right," Bors said. "You're excused. Thanks for telling me straight. I—guessed."

"Ready to go down? A lot of people with problems, today. They're stuck until you get there."

"Let's go." He focused his mind with an effort and turned his attention to the details of the day. "I want the heavy metals research program speeded. It's lagging, as usual. I may have to pull a number of men from related work and shift them to the generators. The water level will be dropping soon. I want to start feeding power along the lines while there's still power to feed. As soon as I turn my back everything starts falling apart."

Fowler signalled Green and he came quickly over. The two of them bent over Bors and, grunting, hoisted him up and carried him to the door. Down the corridor and outside.

They deposited him in the squat metal car, the new little service truck. Its polished surface was a startling contrast to his pitted, corroded hull, bent and splotched and eaten away. A dull, patina-covered machine of archaic steel and plastic that hummed faintly, rustily, as the men leaped in the front seat and raced the car out onto the main highway.

❖❖❖

Edward Tolby perspired, pushed his pack up higher, hunched over, tightened his gun belt, and cursed.

"Daddy," Silvia reproved. "Cut that."

Tolby spat furiously in the grass at the side of the road. He put his arm around his slim daughter. "Sorry, Silv. Nothing personal. The damn heat."

Mid-morning sun shimmered down on the dusty road. Clouds of dust rose and billowed around the three as they pushed slowly along. They were dead tired. Tolby's heavy face was flushed and sullen. An unlit cigarette dangled between his lips. His big, powerfully built body was hunched resentfully forward. His daughter's canvas shirt clung moistly to her arms and breasts. Moons of sweat darkened her back. Under her jeans her thigh muscles rippled wearily.

Robert Penn walked a little behind the two Tolby's, hands deep in his pockets, eyes on the road ahead. His mind was blank; he was half asleep from the double shot of hexobarb he had swallowed at the last League camp. And the heat lulled him. On each side of the road fields stretched out, pastures of grass and weeds, a few trees here and there. A tumbled-down farmhouse. The ancient rusting remains of a bomb shelter, two centuries old. Once, some dirty sheep.

"Sheep," Penn said. "They eat the grass too far down. It won't grow back."

"Now he's a farmer," Tolby said to his daughter.

"Daddy," Silvia snapped. "Stop being nasty."

"It's this heat. This damn heat." Tolby cursed again, loudly and futilely. "It's not worth it. For ten pinks I'd go back and tell them it was a lot of pig swill."

"Maybe it is, at that," Penn said mildly.

"All right, you go back," Tolby grunted. "You go back and tell them it's a lot of pig swill. They'll pin a medal on you. Maybe raise you up a grade."

Penn laughed. "Both of you shut up. There's some kind of town ahead."

Tolby's massive body straightened eagerly. "Where?" He shielded his eyes. "By God, he's right. A village. And it isn't a mirage. You see it, don't you?" His good humor returned and he rubbed his big hands together. "What say, Penn. A couple of beers, a few games of throw with some of the local peasants—maybe we can stay overnight." He licked his thick lips with anticipation. "Some of those village wenches, the kind that hang around the grog shops—"

"I know the kind you mean," Penn broke in. "The kind that are tired of doing nothing. Want to see the big commercial centers. Want to meet some guy that'll buy them mecho-stuff and take them places."

At the side of the road a farmer was watching them curiously. He had halted his horse and stood leaning on his crude plow, hat pushed back on his head.

"What's the name of this town?" Tolby yelled.

The farmer was silent a moment. He was an old man, thin and weathered. "This town?" he repeated.

"Yeah, the one ahead."

"That's a nice town." The farmer eyed the three of them. "You been through here before?"

"No, sir," Tolby said. "Never."

"Team break down?"

"No, we're on foot."

"How far you come?"

"About a hundred and fifty miles."

The farmer considered the heavy packs strapped on their backs. Their cleated hiking shoes. Dusty clothing and weary, sweat-streaked faces. Jeans and canvas shirts. Ironite walking staffs. "That's a long way," he said. "How far you going?"

"As far as we feel like it," Tolby answered. "Is there a place ahead we can stay? Hotel? Inn?"

"That town," the farmer said, "is Fairfax. It has a lumber mill, one of the best in the world. A couple of pottery works. A place where you can get clothes put together by machines. Regular mecho-clothing. A gun shop where they pour the best shot this side of the Rockies. And a bakery. Also there's an old doctor living there, and a lawyer. And some people with books to teach the kids. They came with t.b. They made a school house out of an old barn."

"How large a town?" Penn asked.

"Lot of people. More born all the time. Old folks die. Kids die. We had a fever last year. About a hundred kids died. Doctor said it came from the water hole. We shut the water hole down. Kids died anyhow. Doctor said it was the milk. Drove off half the cows. Not mine. I stood out there with my gun and I shot the first of them came to drive off my cow. Kids stopped dying as soon as fall came. I think it was the heat."

"Sure is hot," Tolby agreed.

"Yes, it gets hot around here. Water's pretty scarce." A crafty look slid across his old face. "You folks want a drink? The young lady looks pretty tired. Got some bottles of water down under the house. In the mud. Nice and cold." He hesitated. "Pink a glass."

Tolby laughed. "No, thanks."

"Two glasses a pink," the farmer said.

"Not interested," Penn said. He thumped his canteen and the three of them started on. "So long."

The farmer's face hardened. "Damn foreigners," he muttered. He turned angrily back to his plowing.

The town baked in silence. Flies buzzed and settled on the backs of stupefied horses, tied up at posts. A few cars were parked here and there. People moved listlessly along the sidewalks. Elderly lean-bodied men dozed on porches. Dogs and chickens slept in the shade under houses. The houses were small, wooden, chipped and peeling boards, leaning and angular—and old. Warped and split by age and heat. Dust lay over everything. A thick blanket of dry dust over the cracking houses and the dull-faced men and animals.

Two lank men approached them from an open doorway. "Who are you? What do you want?"

They stopped and got out their identification. The men examined the sealed-plastic cards. Photographs, fingerprints, data. Finally they handed them back.

"AL," one said. "You really from the Anarchist League?"

"That's right," Tolby said.

"Even the girl?" The men eyed Silvia with languid greed. "Tell you what. Let us have the girl a while and we'll skip the head tax."

"Don't kid me," Tolby grunted. "Since when does the League pay head tax or any other tax?" He pushed past them impatiently. "Where's the grog shop? I'm dying!"

A two-story white building was on their left. Men lounged on the porch, watching them vacantly. Penn headed toward it and the

Tolby's followed. A faded, peeling sign lettered across the front read: *Beer, Wine on Tap.*

"This is it," Penn said. He guided Silvia up the sagging steps, past the men, and inside. Tolby followed; he unstrapped his pack gratefully as he came.

The place was cool and dark. A few men and women were at the bar; the rest sat around tables. Some youths were playing throw in the back. A mechanical tune-maker wheezed and composed in the corner, a shabby, half-ruined machine only partially functioning. Behind the bar a primitive scene-shifter created and destroyed vague phantasmagoria: seascapes, mountain peaks, snowy valleys, great rolling hills, a nude woman that lingered and then dissolved into one vast breast. Dim, uncertain processions that no one noticed or looked at. The bar itself was an incredibly ancient sheet of transparent plastic, stained and chipped and yellow with age. Its n-grav coat had faded from one end; bricks now propped it up. The drink mixer had long since fallen apart. Only wine and beer were served. No living man knew how to mix the simplest drink.

Tolby moved up to the bar. "Beer," he said. "Three beers." Penn and Silvia sank down at a table and removed their packs, as the bartender served Tolby three mugs of thick, dark beer. He showed his card and carried the mugs over to the table.

The youths in the back had stopped playing. They were watching the three as they sipped their beer and unlaced their hiking boots. After a while one of them came slowly over.

"Say," he said. "You're from the League."

"That's right," Tolby murmured sleepily.

Everyone in the place was watching and listening. The youth sat down across from the three; his companions flocked excitedly around and took seats on all sides. The juveniles of the town. Bored, restless, dissatisfied. Their eyes took in the ironite staffs, the guns, the heavy metal-cleated boots. A murmured whisper rustled through them. They were about eighteen. Tanned, rangy.

"How do you get in?" one demanded bluntly.

"The League?" Tolby leaned back in his chair, found a match, and lit his cigarette. He unfastened his belt, belched loudly, and settled back contentedly. "You get in by examination."

"What do you have to know?"

Tolby shrugged. "About everything." He belched again and scratched thoughtfully at his chest, between two buttons. He was conscious of the ring of people around on all sides. A little old man with a beard and horn-rimmed glasses. At another table, a great tub of a man in a red shirt and blue-striped trousers, with a bulging stomach.

Youths. Farmers. A Negro in a dirty white shirt and trousers, a book under his arm. A hard-jawed blonde, hair in a net, red nails and high heels, tight yellow dress. Sitting with a gray-haired businessman in a dark brown suit. A tall young man holding hands with a young black-haired girl, huge eyes, in a soft white blouse and skirt, little slippers kicked under the table. Under the table her bare, tanned feet twisted; her slim body was bent forward with interest.

"You have to know," Tolby said, "how the League was formed. You have to know how we pulled down the governments that day. Pulled them down and destroyed them. Burned all the buildings. And all the records. Billions of microfilms and papers. Great bonfires that burned for weeks. And the swarms of little white things that poured out when we knocked the buildings over."

"You killed them?" the great tub of a man asked, lips twitching avidly.

"We let them go. They were harmless. They ran and hid. Under rocks." Tolby laughed. "Funny little scurrying things. Insects. Then we went in and gathered up all the records and equipment for making records. By God, we burned everything."

"And the robots," a youth said.

"Yeah, we smashed all the government robots. There weren't many of them. They were used only at high levels. When a lot of facts had to be integrated."

The youth's eyes bulged. "You saw them? You were there when they smashed the robots?"

Penn laughed. "Tolby means the League. That was two hundred years ago."

The youth grinned nervously. "Yeah. Tell us about the marches."

Tolby drained his mug and pushed it away. "I'm out of beer."

The mug was quickly refilled. He grunted his thanks and continued, voice deep and furry, dulled with fatigue. "The marches. That was really something, they say. All over the world, people getting up, throwing down what they were doing—"

"It started in East Germany," the hard-jawed blonde said. "The riots."

"Then it spread to Poland," the Negro put in shyly. "My grandfather used to tell me how everybody sat and listened to the television. His grandfather used to tell him. It spread to Czechoslovakia and then Austria and Roumania and Bulgaria. Then France. And Italy."

"France was first!" the little old man with beard and glasses cried violently. "They were without a government a whole month. The people saw they could live without a government!"

"The marches started it," the black-haired girl corrected. "That was the first time they started pulling down the government buildings. In East Germany and Poland. Big mobs of unorganized workers."

"Russia and America were the last," Tolby said. "When the march on Washington came there was close to twenty million of us. We were big in those days! They couldn't stop us when we finally moved."

"They shot a lot," the hard-faced blonde said.

"Sure. But the people kept coming. And yelling to the soldiers. 'Hey, Bill! Don't shoot!' 'Hey, Jack! It's me, Joe.' 'Don't shoot—we're your friends!' 'Don't kill us, join us!' And by God, after a while they did. They couldn't keep shooting their own people. They finally threw down their guns and got out of the way."

"And then you found the place," the little black-haired girl said breathlessly.

"Yeah. We found the place. *Six* places. Three in America. One in Britain. Two in Russia. It took us ten years to find the last place—and make sure it was the last place."

"What then?" the youth asked, bug-eyed.

"Then we busted every one of them." Tolby raised himself up, a massive man, beer mug clutched, heavy face flushed dark red. "Every damn A-bomb in the whole world."

❖ ❖ ❖

There was an uneasy silence.

"Yeah," the youth murmured. "You sure took care of those war people."

"Won't be any more of them," the great tub of a man said. "They're gone for good."

Tolby fingered his ironite staff. "Maybe so. And maybe not. There just might be a few of them left."

"What do you mean?" the tub of a man demanded.

Tolby raised his hard gray eyes. "It's time you people stopped kidding us. You know damn well what I mean. We've heard rumors. Someplace around this area there's a bunch of them. Hiding out."

Shocked disbelief, then anger hummed to a roar. "That's a lie!" the tub of a man shouted.

"Is it?"

The little man with beard and glasses leaped up. "There's nobody here has anything to do with governments! We're all good people!"

"You better watch your step," one of the youths said softly to Tolby. "People around here don't like to be accused."

Tolby got unsteadily to his feet, his ironite staff gripped. Penn got up beside him and they stood together. "If any of you knows something," Tolby said, "you better tell it. Right now."

"Nobody knows anything," the hard-faced blonde said. "You're talking to honest folks."

"That's so," the Negro said, nodding his head. "Nobody here's doing anything wrong."

"You saved our lives," the black-haired girl said. "If you hadn't pulled down the governments we'd all be dead in the war. Why should we hold back something?"

"That's true," the great tub of a man grumbled. "We wouldn't be alive if it wasn't for the League. You think we'd do anything against the League?"

"Come on," Silvia said to her father. "Let's go." She got to her feet and tossed Penn his pack.

Tolby grunted belligerently. Finally he took his own pack and hoisted it to his shoulder. The room was deathly silent. Everyone stood frozen, as the three gathered their things and moved toward the door.

The little dark-haired girl stopped them. "The next town is thirty miles from here," she said.

"The road's blocked," her tall companion explained. "Slides closed it years ago."

"Why don't you stay with us tonight? There's plenty of room at our place. You can rest up and get an early start tomorrow."

"We don't want to impose," Silvia murmured.

Tolby and Penn glanced at each other, then at the girl. "If you're sure you have plenty of room—"

The great tub of a man approached them. "Listen. I have ten yellow slips. I want to give them to the League. I sold my farm last year. I don't need any more slips; I'm living with my brother and his family." He pushed the slips at Tolby. "Here."

Tolby pushed them back. "Keep them."

"This way," the tall young man said, as they clattered down the sagging steps, into a sudden blinding curtain of heat and dust. "We have a car. Over this way. An old gasoline car. My dad fixed it so it burns oil."

"You should have taken the slips," Penn said to Tolby, as they got into the ancient, battered car. Flies buzzed around them. They could hardly breathe; the car was a furnace. Silvia fanned herself with a rolled-up paper. The black-haired girl unbuttoned her blouse.

"What do we need money for?" Tolby laughed good-naturedly. "I haven't paid for anything in my life. Neither have you."

The car sputtered and moved slowly forward, onto the road. It began to gain speed. Its motor banged and roared. Soon it was moving surprisingly fast.

'You saw them," Silvia said, over the racket. "They'd give us anything they had. We saved their lives." She waved at the fields, the farmers and their crude teams, the withered crops, the sagging old farmhouses. "They'd all be dead, if it hadn't been for the League." She smashed a fly peevishly. "They depend on us."

The black-haired girl turned toward them, as the car rushed along the decaying road. Sweat streaked her tanned skin. Her half-covered breasts trembled with the motion of the car. "I'm Laura Davis. Pete and I have an old farmhouse his dad gave us when we got married."

"You can have the whole downstairs," Pete said.

"There's no electricity, but we've got a big fireplace. It gets cold at night. It's hot in the day, but when the sun sets it gets terribly cold."

"We'll be all right," Penn murmured. The vibration of the car made him a little sick.

"Yes," the girl said, her black eyes flashing. Her crimson lips twisted. She leaned toward Penn intently, her small face strangely alight. "Yes, we'll take good care of you."

At that moment the car left the road.

Silvia shrieked. Tolby threw himself down, head between his knees, doubled up in a ball. A sudden curtain of green burst around Penn. Then a sickening emptiness, as the car plunged down. It struck with a roaring crash that blotted out everything. A single titanic cataclysm of fury that picked Penn up and flung his remains in every direction.

❖ ❖ ❖

"Put me down," Bors ordered. "On this railing for a moment before I go inside."

The crew lowered him onto the concrete surface and fastened magnetic grapples into place. Men and women hurried up the wide steps, in and out of the massive building that was Bors' main offices.

The sight from these steps pleased him. He liked to stop here and look around at his world. At the civilization he had carefully constructed. Each piece added painstakingly, scrupulously with infinite care, throughout the years.

It wasn't big. The mountains ringed it on all sides. The valley was a level bowl, surrounded by dark violet hills. Outside, beyond the hills, the regular world began. Parched fields. Blasted, poverty-stricken towns. Decayed roads. The remains of houses, tumbled-down farm buildings. Ruined cars and machinery. Dust-covered people creeping listlessly around in hand-made clothing, dull rags and tatters.

He had seen the outside. He knew what it was like. At the mountains the blank faces, the disease, the withered crops, the crude plows and ancient tools all ended here. Here, within the ring of hills, Bors had constructed an accurate and detailed reproduction of a society two centuries gone. The world as it had been in the old days. The time of governments. The time that had been pulled down by the Anarchist League.

Within his five synapsis-coils the plans, knowledge, information, blueprints of a whole world existed. In the two centuries he had carefully recreated that world, had made this miniature society that glittered and hummed on all sides of him. The roads, buildings, houses, industries of a dead world, all a fragment of the past, built with his hands, his own metal fingers and brain.

"Fowler," Bors said.

Fowler came over. He looked haggard. His eyes were red-rimmed and swollen. "What is it? You want to go inside?"

Overhead, the morning patrol thundered past. A string of black dots against the sunny, cloudless sky. Bors watched with satisfaction. "Quite a sight."

"Right on the nose," Fowler agreed, examining his wristwatch. To their right, a column of heavy tanks snaked along a highway between green fields. Their gun-snouts glittered. Behind them a column of foot soldiers marched, faces hidden behind bacteria masks.

"I'm thinking," Bors said, "that it may be unwise to trust Green any longer."

"Why the hell do you say that?"

"Every ten days I'm inactivated. So your crew can see what repairs are needed." Bors twisted restlessly. "For twelve hours I'm completely helpless. Green takes care of me. Sees nothing happens. But—"

"But what?"

"It occurs to me perhaps there'd be more safety in a squad of troops. It's too much of a temptation for one man, alone."

Fowler scowled. "I don't see that. How about me? I have charge of inspecting you. I could switch a few leads around. Send a load through your synapsis-coils. Blow them out."

Bors whirled wildly, then subsided. "True. You could do that." After a moment he demanded, "But what would you gain? You know I'm the only one who can keep all this together. I'm the only one who knows how to maintain a planned society, not a disorderly chaos! If it weren't for me, all this would collapse, and you'd have dust and ruins and weeds. The whole outside would come rushing in to take over!"

"Of course. So why worry about Green?"

Trucks of workers rumbled past. Loads of men in blue-green, sleeves rolled up, armloads of tools. A mining team, heading for the mountains.

"Take me inside," Bors said abruptly.

Fowler called McLean. They hoisted Bors and carried him past the throngs of people, into the building, down the corridor and to his office. Officials and technicians moved respectfully out of the way as the great pitted, corroded tank was carried past.

"All right," Bors said impatiently. "That's all. You can go."

Fowler and McLean left the luxurious office, with its lush carpets, furniture, drapes and rows of books. Bors was already bent over his desk, sorting through heaps of reports and papers.

Fowler shook his head, as they walked down the hall. "He won't last much longer."

"The motor system? Can't we reinforce the—"

"I don't mean that. He's breaking up mentally. He can't take the strain any longer."

"None of us can," McLean muttered.

"Running this thing is too much for him. Knowing it's all dependent on him. Knowing as soon as he turns his back or lets down it'll begin to come apart at the seams. A hell of a job, trying to shut out the real world. Keeping his model universe running."

"He's gone on a long time," McLean said.

Fowler brooded. "Sooner or later we're going to have to face the situation." Gloomily, he ran his fingers along the blade of a large screwdriver. "He's wearing out. Sooner or later somebody's going to have to step in. As he continues to decay . . . " He stuck the screwdriver back in his belt, with his pliers and hammer and soldering iron. "One crossed wire."

"What's that?"

Fowler laughed. "Now he's got me doing it. One crossed wire and—*poof.* But what then? That's the big question."

"Maybe," McLean said softly, "you and I can then get off this rat race. You and I and all the rest of us. And live like human beings."

"*Rat race,*" Fowler murmured. "Rats in a maze. Doing tricks. Performing chores thought up by somebody else."

McLean caught Fowler's eye. "By somebody of another species."

❖❖❖

Tolby struggled vaguely. Silence. A faint dripping close by. A beam pinned his body down. He was caught on all sides by the twisted wreck of the car. He was head down. The car was turned on its side. Off the road in a gully, wedged between two huge trees. Bent struts and smashed metal all around him. And bodies.

He pushed up with all his strength. The beam gave, and he managed to get to a sitting position. A tree branch had burst in the windshield. The black-haired girl, still turned toward the back seat, was impaled on it. The branch had driven through her spine, out her chest, and into the seat; she clutched at it with both hands, head limp, mouth half-open. The man beside her was also dead. His hands were gone; the windshield had burst around him. He lay in a heap among the remains of the dashboard and the bloody shine of his own internal organs.

Penn was dead. Neck snapped like a rotten broom handle. Tolby pushed his corpse aside and examined his daughter. Silvia didn't stir. He put his ear to her shirt and listened. She was alive. Her heart beat faintly. Her bosom rose and fell against his ear.

He wound a handkerchief around her arm, where the flesh was ripped open and oozing blood. She was badly cut and scratched; one leg was doubled under her, obviously broken. Her clothes were ripped, her hair matted with blood. But she was alive. He pushed the twisted door open and stumbled out. A fiery tongue of afternoon sunlight struck him and he winced. He began to ease her limp body out of the car, past the twisted door-frame.

A sound.

Tolby glanced up, rigid. Something was coming. A whirring insect that rapidly descended. He let go of Silvia, crouched, glanced around, then lumbered awkwardly down the gully. He slid and fell and rolled among the green vines and jagged gray boulders. His gun gripped, he lay gasping in the moist shadows, peering, upward.

The insect landed. A small air-ship, jet-driven. The sight stunned him. He had heard about jets, seen photographs of them. Been briefed and lectured in the history-indoctrination courses at the League Camps. But to *see* a jet!

Men swarmed out. Uniformed men who started from the road, down the side of the gully, bodies crouched warily as they approached the wrecked car. They lugged heavy rifles. They looked grim and experienced, as they tore the car doors open and scrambled in.

"One's gone," a voice drifted to him.

"Must be around somewhere."

"Look, this one's alive! This woman. Started to crawl out. The rest all dead."

Furious cursing. "Damn Laura! She should have leaped! The fanatic little fool!"

"Maybe she didn't have time. God's sake, the thing's all the way through her." Horror and shocked dismay. "We won't hardly be able to get her loose."

"Leave her." The officer directing things waved the men back out of the car. "Leave them all."

"How about this wounded one?"

The leader hesitated. "Kill her," he said finally. He snatched a rifle and raised the butt. "The rest of you fan out and try to get the other one. He's probably—"

Tolby fired, and the leader's body broke in half. The lower part sank down slowly; the upper dissolved in ashy fragments. Tolby turned and began to move in a slow circle, firing as he crawled. He got two more of them before the rest retreated in panic to their jet-powered insect and slammed the lock.

He had the element of surprise. Now that was gone. They had strength and numbers. He was doomed. Already, the insect was rising. They'd be able to spot him easily from above. But he had saved Silvia. That was something.

He stumbled down a dried-up creek bed. He ran aimlessly; he had no place to go. He didn't know the countryside, and he was on foot. He slipped on a stone and fell headlong. Pain and billowing darkness beat at him as he got unsteadily to his knees. His gun was gone, lost in the shrubbery. He spat broken teeth and blood. He peered wildly up at the blazing afternoon sky.

The insect was leaving. It hummed off toward the distant hills. It dwindled, became a black ball, a fly-speck, then disappeared.

Tolby waited a moment. Then he struggled up the side of the ravine to the wrecked car. They had gone to get help. They'd be back. Now was his only chance. If he could get Silvia out and down the road, into hiding. Maybe to a farmhouse. Back to town.

He reached the car and stood, dazed and stupefied. Three bodies remained, the two in the front seat, Penn in the back. But Silvia was gone.

They had taken her with them. Back where they came from. She had been dragged to the jet-driven insect; a trail of blood led from the car up the side of the gully to the highway.

With a violent shudder Tolby pulled himself together. He climbed into the car and pried loose Penn's gun from his belt. Silvia's ironite staff rested on the seat; he took that, too. Then he started off down the road, walking without haste, carefully, slowly.

An ironic thought plucked at his mind. He had found what they were after. The men in uniform. They were organized, responsible to a central authority. In a newly-assembled jet.

Beyond the hills was a government.

❖ ❖ ❖

"Sir," Green said. He smoothed his short blond hair anxiously, his young face twisting.

Technicians and experts and ordinary people in droves were everywhere. The offices buzzed and echoed with the business of the day. Green pushed through the crowd and to the desk where Bors sat, propped up by two magnetic frames.

"Sir," Green said. "Something's happened."

Bors looked up. He pushed a metal-foil slate away and laid down his stylus. His eye cells clicked and flickered; deep inside his battered trunk motor gears whined. "What is it?"

Green came close. There was something in his face, an expression Bors had never seen before. A look of fear and glassy determination. A glazed, fanatic cast, as if his flesh had hardened to rock. "Sir, scouts contacted a League team moving North. They met the team outside Fairfax. The incident took place directly beyond the first road block."

Bors said nothing. On all sides, officials, experts, farmers, workmen, industrial managers, soldiers, people of all kinds buzzed and murmured and pushed forward impatiently. Trying to get to Bors' desk. Loaded down with problems to be solved, situations to be explained. The pressing business of the day. Roads, factories, disease control. Repairs. Construction. Manufacture. Design. Planning. Urgent problems for Bors to consider and deal with. Problems that couldn't wait.

"Was the League team destroyed?" Bors said.

"One was killed. One was wounded and brought here." Green hesitated. "One escaped."

For a long time Bors was silent. Around him the people murmured and shuffled; he ignored them. All at once he pulled the vidscanner to him and snapped the circuit open. "One escaped? I don't like the sound of that."

"He shot three members of our scout unit. Including the leader. The others got frightened. They grabbed the injured girl and returned here."

Bors' massive head lifted. "They made a mistake. They should have located the one who escaped."

"This was the first time the situation—"

"I know," Bors said. "But it was an error. Better not to have touched them at all, than to have taken two and allowed the third to get away." He turned to the vidscanner. "Sound an emergency alert. Close down the factories. Arm the work crews and any male farmers capable of using weapons. Close every road. Remove the women and children to the undersurface shelters. Bring up the heavy guns and supplies. Suspend all non-military production and—" He considered. "Arrest everyone we're not sure of. On the C sheet. Have them shot." He snapped the scanner off.

"What'll happen?" Green demanded, shaken.

"The thing we've prepared for. Total war."

"We have weapons!" Green shouted excitedly. "In an hour there'll be ten thousand men ready to fight. We have jet-driven ships. Heavy artillery. Bombs. Bacteria pellets. What's the League? A lot of people with packs on their backs!"

"Yes," Bors said. "A lot of people with packs on their backs."

"How can they do anything? How can a bunch of anarchists organize? They have no structure, no control, no central power."

"They have the whole world. A billion people."

"*Individuals!* A club, not subject to law. Voluntary membership. We have disciplined organization. Every aspect of our economic life operates at maximum efficiency. We—you—have your thumb on everything. All you have to do is give the order. Set the machine in motion."

Bors nodded slowly. "It's true the anarchist can't coordinate. The League can't organize. It's a paradox. Government by anarchists . . . Antigovernment, actually. Instead of governing the world they tramp around to make sure no one else does."

"Dog in the manger."

"As you say, they're actually a voluntary club of totally unorganized individuals. Without law or central authority. They maintain no society—they can't govern. All they can do is interfere with anyone else who tries. Troublemakers. But—"

"But what?"

"It was this way before. Two centuries ago. They were unorganized. Unarmed. Vast mobs, without discipline or authority. Yet they pulled down all the governments. All over the world."

"We've got a whole army. All the roads are mined. Heavy guns. Bombs. Pellets. Every one of us is a soldier. We're an armed camp!"

Bors was deep in thought. "You say one of them is here? One of the League agents?"

"A young woman."

Bors signalled the nearby maintenance crew. "Take me to her. I want to talk to her in the time remaining."

❖ ❖ ❖

Silvia watched silently, as the uniformed men pushed and grunted their way into the room. They staggered over to the bed, pulled two chairs together, and carefully laid down their massive armload.

Quickly they snapped protective struts into place, locked the chairs together, threw magnetic grapples into operation, and then warily retreated.

"All right," the robot said. "You can go." The men left. Bors turned to face the woman on the bed.

"A machine," Silvia whispered, white-faced. "You're a machine."

Bors nodded slightly without speaking.

Silvia shifted uneasily on the bed. She was weak. One leg was in a transparent plastic cast. Her face was bandaged and her right arm ached and throbbed. Outside the window, the late afternoon sun sprinkled through the drapes. Flowers bloomed. Grass. Hedges. And beyond the hedges, buildings and factories.

For the last hour the sky had been filled with jet-driven ships. Great flocks that raced excitedly across the sky toward distant hills. Along the highway cars hurtled, dragging guns and heavy military equipment. Men were marching in close rank, rows of gray-clad soldiers, guns and helmets and bacteria masks. Endless lines of figures, identical in their uniforms, stamped from the same matrix.

"There are a lot of them," Bors said, indicating the marching men.

"Yes." Silvia watched a couple of soldiers hurry by the window. Youths with worried expressions on their smooth faces. Helmets bobbing at their waists. Long rifles. Canteens. Counters. Radiation shields. Bacteria masks wound awkwardly around their necks, ready to go into place. They were scared. Hardly more than kids. Others followed. A truck roared into life. The soldiers were swept off to join the others.

"They're going to fight," Bors said, "to defend their homes and factories."

"All this equipment. You manufacture it, don't you?"

"That's right. Our industrial organization is perfect. We're totally productive. Our society here is operated rationally. Scientifically. We're fully prepared to meet this emergency."

Suddenly Silvia realized what the emergency was. "The League! One of us must have got away." She pulled herself up. "Which of them? Penn or my father?"

"I don't know," the robot murmured indifferently.

Horror and disgust choked Silvia. "My God," she said softly. "You have no understanding of us. You run all this, and you're incapable of empathy. You're nothing but a mechanical computer. One of the old government integration robots."

"That's right. Two centuries old."

She was appalled. "And you've been alive all this time. We thought we destroyed all of you!"

"I was missed. I had been damaged. I wasn't in my place. I was in a truck, on my way out of Washington. I saw the mobs and escaped."

"Two hundred years ago. Legendary times. You actually saw the events they tell us about. The old days. The great marches. The day the governments fell."

"Yes. I saw it all. A group of us formed in Virginia. Experts, officials, skilled workmen. Later we came here. It was remote enough, off the beaten path."

"We heard rumors. A fragment . . . Still maintaining itself. But we didn't know where or how."

"I was fortunate," Bors said. "I escaped by a fluke. All the others were destroyed. It's taken a long time to organize what you see here. Fifteen miles from here is a ring of hills. This valley is a bowl—mountains on all sides. We've set up road blocks in the form of natural slides. Nobody comes here. Even in Fairfax, thirty miles off, they know nothing."

"That girl. Laura."

"Scouts. We keep scout teams in all inhabited regions within a hundred mile radius. As soon as you entered Fairfax, word was relayed to us. An air unit was dispatched. To avoid questions, we arranged to have you killed in an auto wreck. But one of you escaped."

Silvia shook her head, bewildered. "How?" she demanded. "How do you keep going? Don't the people revolt?" She struggled to a sitting position. "They must know what's happened everywhere else. How do you control them? They're going out now, in their uniforms. But—*will they fight? Can you count on them?*"

Bors answered slowly. "They trust me," he said. "I brought with me a vast amount of knowledge. Information and techniques lost to the rest of the world. Are jet-ships and vidscanners and power cables made anywhere else in the world? I retain all that knowledge. I have memory units, synapsis-coils. Because of me they have these things. Things you know only as dim memories, vague legends."

"What happens when you die?"

"I won't die! I'm eternal!"

"You're wearing out. You have to be carried around. And your right arm. you can hardly move it!" Silvia's voice was harsh, ruthless. "Your whole tank is pitted and rusty."

The robot whirred; for a moment he seemed unable to speak. "My knowledge remains," he grated finally. "I'll always be able to communicate. Fowler has arranged a broadcast system. Even when I talk—" He broke off. "Even then. Everything is under control. I've organized every aspect of the situation. I've maintained this system for two centuries. It's got to be kept going!"

Silvia lashed out. It happened in a split second. The boot of her cast caught the chairs on which the robot rested. She thrust violently with her foot and hands; the chairs teetered, hesitated—

"Fowler!" the robot screamed.

Silvia pushed with all her strength. Blinding agony seared through her leg; she bit her lip and threw her shoulder against the robot's pitted hulk. He waved his arms, whirred wildly, and then the two chairs slowly collapsed. The robot slid quietly from them, over on his back, his arms still waving helplessly.

Silvia dragged herself from the bed. She managed to pull herself to the window; her broken leg hung uselessly, a dead weight in its transparent plastic cast. The robot lay like some futile bug, arms waving, eye lens clicking, its rusty works whirring in fear and rage.

"Fowler!" it screamed again. "Help me!"

Silvia reached the window. She tugged at the locks; they were sealed. She grabbed up a lamp from the table and threw it against the glass. The glass burst around her, a shower of lethal fragments. She stumbled forward—and then the repair crew was pouring into the room.

Fowler gasped at the sight of the robot on its back. A strange expression crossed his face. "Look at him!"

"Help me!" the robot shrilled. "Help me!"

One of the men grabbed Silvia around the waist and lugged her back to the bed. She kicked and bit, sunk her nails into the man's cheek. He threw her on the bed, face down, and drew his pistol. "Stay there," he gasped.

The others were bent over the robot, getting him to an upright position.

"What happened?" Fowler said. He came over to the bed, his face twisting. "Did he fall?"

Silvia's eyes glowed with hatred and despair. "I pushed him over. I almost got there." Her chest heaved. "The window. But my leg—"

"Get me back to my quarters!" Bors cried.

The crew gathered him up and carried him down the hall, to his private office. A few moments later he was sitting shakily at his desk, his mechanism pounding wildly, surrounded by his papers and memoranda.

He forced down his panic and tried to resume his work. He had to keep going. His vidscreen was alive with activity. The whole system was in motion. He blankly watched a subcommander sending up a cloud of black dots, jet bombers that shot up like flies and headed quickly off.

The system had to be preserved. He repeated it again and again. He had to save it. Had to organize the people and make *them* save it. If the people didn't fight, wasn't everything doomed?

Fury and desperation overwhelmed him. The system couldn't preserve itself; it wasn't a thing apart, something that could be separated from the people who lived it. Actually it *was* the people. They were identical; when the people fought to preserve the system they were fighting to preserve nothing less than themselves.

They existed only as long as the system existed.

He caught sight of a marching column of white-faced troops, moving toward the hills. His ancient synapsis-coils radiated and shuddered uncertainly, then fell back into pattern. He was two centuries old. He had come into existence a long time ago, in a different world. That world had created him; through him that world still lived. As long as he existed, that world existed. In miniature, it still functioned. His model universe, his recreation. His rational, controlled world, in which each aspect was fully organized, fully analyzed and integrated.

He kept a rational, progressive world alive. A humming oasis of productivity on a dusty, parched planet of decay and silence.

Bors spread out his papers and went to work on the most pressing problem. The transformation from a peace-time economy to full military mobilization. Total military organization of every man, woman, child, piece of equipment and dyne of energy under his direction.

❖ ❖ ❖

Edward Tolby emerged cautiously. His clothes were torn and ragged. He had lost his pack, crawling through the brambles and vines. His face and hands were bleeding. He was utterly exhausted.

Below him lay a valley. A vast bowl. Fields, houses, highways. Factories. Equipment. Men.

He had been watching the men three hours. Endless streams of them, pouring from the valley into the hills, along the roads and paths. On foot, in trucks, in cars, armored tanks, weapons carriers. Overhead, in fast little jetfighters and great lumbering bombers. Gleaming ships that took up positions above the troops and prepared for battle.

Battle in the grand style. The two-centuries-old full-scale war that was supposed to have disappeared. But here it was, a vision from the past. He had seen this in the old tapes and records, used in the camp orientation courses. A ghost army resurrected to fight again. A vast host of men and guns, prepared to fight and die.

Tolby climbed down cautiously. At the foot of a slope of boulders a soldier had halted his motorcycle and was setting up a communications antenna and transmitter. Tolby circled, crouched, expertly approached him. A blond-haired youth, fumbling nervously with the wires and relays, licking his lips uneasily, glancing up and grabbing for his rifle at every sound

Tolby took a deep breath. The youth had turned his back; he was tracing a power circuit. It was now or never. With one stride Tolby stepped out, raised his pistol and fired. The clump of equipment and the soldier's rifle vanished.

"Don't make a sound," Tolby said. He peered around. No one had seen; the main line was half a mile to his right. The sun was setting.

Great shadows were falling over the hills. The fields were rapidly fading from brown-green to a deep violet. "Put your hands up over your head, clasp them, and get down on your knees."

The youth tumbled down in a frightened heap. "What are you going to do?" He saw the ironite staff, and the color left his face. "You're a League agent!"

"Shut up," Tolby ordered. "First, outline your system of responsibility. *Who's your superior?*"

The youth stuttered forth what he knew. Tolby listened intently. He was satisfied. The usual monolithic structure. Exactly what he wanted.

"At the top," he broke in. "At the top of the pillar. Who has ultimate responsibility?"

"Bors."

"Bors!" Tolby scowled. "That doesn't sound like a name. Sounds like—" He broke off, staggered. "We should have guessed! An old government robot. Still functioning."

The youth saw his chance. He leaped up and darted frantically away.

Tolby shot him above the left ear. The youth pitched over on his face and lay still. Tolby hurried to him and quickly pulled off his dark gray uniform. It was too small for him of course. But the motorcycle was just right. He'd seen tapes of them; he'd wanted one since he was a child. A fast little motorcycle to propel his weight around. Now he had it.

Half an hour later he was roaring down a smooth, broad highway toward the center of the valley and the buildings that rose against the dark sky. His headlights cut into the blackness; he still wobbled from side to side, but for all practical purposes he had the hang of it. He increased speed; the road shot by, trees and fields, haystacks, stalled farm equipment. All traffic was going against him, troops hurrying to the front.

The front. Lemmings going out into the ocean to drown. A thousand, ten thousand, metal-clad figures, armed and alert. Weighted down with guns and bombs and flame throwers and bacteria pellets.

There was only one hitch. No army opposed them. A mistake had been made. It took two sides to make a war, and only one had been resurrected.

A mile outside the concentration of buildings he pulled his motorcycle off the road and carefully hid it in a haystack. For a moment he considered leaving his ironite staff. Then he shrugged and grabbed it up, along with his pistol. He always carried his staff, it was the League symbol. It represented the walking Anarchists who patrolled the world on foot, the world's protection agency.

He loped through the darkness toward the outline ahead. There were fewer men here. He saw no women or children. Ahead, charged wire was set up. Troops crouched behind it, armed to the teeth. A searchlight moved back and forth across the road. Behind it, radar vanes loomed and behind them an ugly square of concrete. The great offices from which the government was run.

For a time he watched the searchlight. Finally he had its motion plotted. In its glare, the faces of the troops stood out, pale and drawn. Youths. They had never fought. This was their first encounter. They were terrified.

When the light was off him, he stood up and advanced toward the wire. Automatically, a breach was slid back for him. Two guards raised up and awkwardly crossed bayonets ahead of him.

"Show your papers!" one demanded. Young lieutenants. Boys, white-lipped, nervous. Playing soldier.

Pity and contempt made Tolby laugh harshly and push forward. "Get out of my way."

One anxiously flashed a pocket light. "Halt! What's the code-key for this watch?" He blocked Tolby's way with his bayonet, hands twisting convulsively.

Tolby reached in his pocket, pulled out his pistol, and as the searchlight started to swerve back, blasted the two guards. The bayonets clattered down and he dived forward. Yells and shapes rose on all sides. Anguished, terrified shouts. Random firing. The night was lit up, as he dashed and crouched, turned a corner past a supply warehouse, raced up a flight of stairs and into the massive building ahead.

He had to work fast. Gripping his ironite staff, he plunged down a gloomy corridor. His boots echoed. Men poured into the building behind him. Bolts of energy thundered past him; a whole section of the ceiling burst into ash and collapsed behind him.

He reached stairs and climbed rapidly. He came to the next floor and groped for the door handle. Something flickered behind him. He half-turned, his gun quickly up—

A stunning blow sent him sprawling. He crashed against the wall; his gun flew from his fingers. A shape bent over him, rifle gripped. "Who are you? What are you doing here?"

Not a soldier. A stubble-chinned man in stained shirt and rumpled trousers. Eyes puffy and red. A belt of tools, hammer, pliers, screw-driver, a soldering iron, around his waist.

Tolby raised himself up painfully. "If you didn't have that rifle—"

Fowler backed warily away. "Who are you? This floor is forbidden to troops of the line. You know this—" Then he saw the ironite staff. "By God," he said softly. "You're the one they didn't get." He laughed shakily. "You're the one who got away."

Tolby's fingers tightened around the staff, but Fowler reacted instantly. The snout of the rifle jerked up, on a line with Tolby's face.

"Be careful," Fowler warned. He turned slightly; soldiers were hurrying up the stairs, boots drumming, echoing shouts ringing. For a moment he hesitated, then waved his rifle toward the stairs ahead. "Up. Get going."

Toby blinked. "What—"

"Up!" The rifle snout jabbed into Tolby. "Hurry!"

Bewildered, Tolby hurried up the stairs, Fowler close behind him.

At the third floor Fowler pushed him roughly through the doorway, the snout of his rifle digging urgently into his back. He found himself in a corridor of doors. Endless offices.

"Keep going," Fowler snarled. "Down the hall. Hurry!"

Tolby hurried, his mind spinning. "What the hell are you—"

"I could never do it," Fowler gasped, close to his ear. "Not in a million years. But it's got to be done."

Tolby halted. "What is this?"

They faced each other defiantly, faces contorted, eyes blazing. "He's in there," Fowler snapped, indicating a door with his rifle. "You have one chance. Take it."

For a fraction of a second Tolby hesitated. Then he broke away. "Okay. I'll take it."

Fowler followed after him. "Be careful. Watch your step. There's a series of check points. Keep going straight, in all the way. As far as you can go. And for God's sake, hurry!"

His voice faded, as Tolby gained speed. He reached the door and tore it open.

Soldiers and officials ballooned. He threw himself against them; they sprawled and scattered. He scrambled on, as they struggled up and stupidly fumbled for their guns. Through another door, into an inner office, past a desk where a frightened girl sat, eyes wide, mouth open. Then a third door, into an alcove.

A wild-faced youth leaped up and snatched frantically for his pistol. Tolby was unarmed, trapped in the alcove. Figures already pushed against the door behind him. He gripped his ironite staff and backed away as the blond-haired fanatic fired blindly. The bolt burst a foot away; it flicked him with a tongue of heat.

"You dirty anarchist!" Green screamed. His face distorted, he fired again and again. "You murdering anarchist spy!"

Tolby hurled his ironite staff. He put all his strength in it; the staff leaped through the air in a whistling arc, straight at the youth's head. Green saw it coming and ducked. Agile and quick, he jumped away, grinning humorlessly. The staff crashed against the wall and rolled clanging to the floor.

"Your walking staff!" Green gasped and fired.

The bolt missed him on purpose. Green was playing games with him. Tolby bent down and groped frantically for the staff. He picked it up. Green watched, face rigid, eyes glittering. "Throw it again!" he snarled.

Tolby leaped. He took the youth by surprise. Green grunted, stumbled back from the impact, then suddenly fought with maniacal fury.

Tolby was heavier. But he was exhausted. He had crawled hours, beat his way through the mountains, walked endlessly. He was at the end of his strength. The car wreck, the days of walking. Green was in perfect shape. His wiry, agile body twisted away. His hands came up. Fingers dug into Tolby's windpipe; he kicked the youth in the groin. Green staggered back, convulsed and bent over with pain.

"All right," Green gasped, face ugly and dark. His hand fumbled with his pistol. The barrel came up.

Half of Green's head dissolved. His hands opened and his gun fell to the floor. His body stood for a moment, then settled down in a heap, like an empty suit of clothes.

Tolby caught a glimpse of a rifle snout pushed past him—and the man with the tool belt. The man waved him on frantically. "Hurry!"

Tolby raced down a carpeted hall, between two great flickering yellow lamps. A crowd of officials and soldiers stumbled uncertainly after him, shouting and firing at random. He tore open a thick oak door and halted.

He was in a luxurious chamber. Drapes, rich wallpaper. Lamps. Bookcases. A glimpse of the finery of the past. The wealth of the old days. Thick carpets. Warm radiant heat. A vidscreen. At the far end, a huge mahogany desk.

At the desk a figure sat. Working on heaps of papers and reports, piled masses of material. The figure contrasted starkly with the lushness of the furnishings. It was a great pitted, corroded tank of metal. Bent and greenish, patched and repaired. An ancient machine.

"Is that you, Fowler?" the robot demanded.

Tolby advanced, his ironite staff gripped.

The robot turned angrily. "Who is it? Get Green and carry me down into the shelter. One of the roadblocks has reported a League agent already—" The robot broke off. Its cold, mechanical eye lens bored up at the man. It clicked and whirred in uneasy astonishment. "I don't know you."

It saw the ironite staff.

"League agent," the robot said. "You're the one who got through." Comprehension came. "*The third one.* You came here. You didn't go back." Its metal fingers fumbled clumsily at the objects on the desk, then in the drawer. It found a gun and raised it awkwardly.

Tolby knocked the gun away; it clattered to the floor. "Run!" he shouted at the robot. "Start running!"

It remained. Tolby's staff came down. The fragile, complex brain-unit of the robot burst apart. Coils, wiring, relay fluid, spattered over his arms and hands. The robot shuddered. Its machinery thrashed. It half-rose from its chair, then swayed and toppled. It crashed full length on the floor, parts and gears rolling in all directions.

"Good God," Tolby said, suddenly seeing it for the first time. Shakily, he bent over its remains. "It was crippled."

Men were all around him. "He's killed Bors!" Shocked, dazed faces. "Bors is dead!"

Fowler came up slowly. "You got him, all right. There's nothing left now."

Tolby stood holding his ironite staff in his hands. "The poor blasted thing," he said softly. "Completely helpless. Sitting there and I came and killed him. He didn't have a chance."

❖❖❖

The building was bedlam. Soldiers and officials scurried crazily about, grief-stricken, hysterical. They bumped into each other, gathered in knots, shouted and gave meaningless orders.

Tolby pushed past them; nobody paid any attention to him. Fowler was gathering up the remains of the robot. Collecting the smashed pieces and bits. Tolby stopped beside him. Like Humpty-Dumpty, pulled down off his wall he'd never be back together, not now.

"Where's the woman?" he asked Fowler. "The League agent they brought in."

Fowler straightened up slowly. "I'll take you." He led Tolby down the packed, surging hall, to the hospital wing of the building.

Silvia sat up apprehensively as the two men entered the room. "What's going on?" She recognized her father. "Dad! Thank God! It was you who got out."

Tolby slammed the door against the chaos of sound hammering up and down the corridor. "How are you? How's your leg?"

"Mending. What happened?"

"I got him. The robot. He's dead."

For a moment the three of them were silent. Outside, in the halls, men ran frantically back and forth. Word had already leaked out. Troops gathered in huddled knots outside the building. Lost men, wandering away from their posts. Uncertain. Aimless.

"It's over," Fowler said.

Tolby nodded. "I know."

"They'll get tired of crouching in their foxholes," Fowler said. "They'll come filtering back. As soon as the news reaches them, they'll desert and throw away their equipment."

"Good," Tolby grunted. "The sooner the better." He touched Fowler's rifle. "You, too, I hope."

Silvia hesitated. "Do you think—"

"Think what?"

"Did we make a mistake?"

Tolby grinned wearily. "Hell of a time to think about that."

"He was doing what he thought was right. They built up their homes and factories. This whole area . . . They turn out a lot of goods. I've been watching through the window. It's made me think. They've done so much. Made so much."

"Made a lot of guns," Tolby said.

"We have guns, too. We kill and destroy. We have all the disadvantages and none of the advantages."

"We don't have war," Tolby answered quietly. "To defend this neat little organization there are ten thousand men up there in those hills. All waiting to fight. Waiting to drop their bombs and bacteria pellets, to keep this place running. But they won't. Pretty soon they'll give up and start to trickle back."

"This whole system will decay rapidly," Fowler said. "He was already losing his control. He couldn't keep the clock back much longer."

"Anyhow, it's done," Silvia murmured. "We did our job." She smiled a little. "Bors did his job and we did ours. But the times were against him and with us."

"That's right," Tolby agreed. "We did our job. And we'll never be sorry."

Fowler said nothing. He stood with his hands in his pockets, gazing silently out the window. His fingers were touching something. Three undamaged synapsis-coils. Intact memory elements from the dead robot, snatched from the scattered remains.

Just in case, he said to himself. *Just in case the times change.*

STRANGE EDEN

Captain Johnson was the first man out of the ship. He scanned the planet's great rolling forests, its miles of green that made your eyes ache. The sky overhead that was pure blue. Off beyond the trees lapped the edges of an ocean, about the same color as the sky, except for a bubbling surface of incredibly bright seaweed that darkened the blue almost to purple.

He had only four feet to go from the control board to the automatic hatch, and from there down the ramp to the soft black soil dug up by the jet blast and strewn everywhere, still steaming. He shaded his eyes against the golden sun, and then, after a moment, removed his glasses and polished them on his sleeve. He was a small man, thin and sallow-faced. He blinked nervously without his glasses and quickly fitted them back in place. He took a deep breath of the warm air, held it in his lungs, let it roll through his system, then reluctantly let it escape.

"Not bad," Brent rumbled, from the open hatch.

"If this place were closer to Terra there'd be empty beer cans and plastic plates strewn around. The trees would be gone. There'd be old jet motors in the water. The beaches would stink to high heaven. Terran Development would have a couple of million little plastic houses set up everywhere."

Brent grunted indifferently. He jumped down, a huge barrel-chested man, sleeves rolled up, arms dark and hairy.

"What's that over there? Some kind of trail?"

Captain Johnson uneasily got out a star chart and studied it. "No ship ever reported this area, before us. According to this chart the whole system's uninhabited."

Brent laughed. "Ever occur to you there might already be culture here? Non-Terran?"

Captain Johnson fingered his gun. He had never used it; this was the first time he had been assigned to an exploring survey outside the patrolled area of the galaxy. "Maybe we ought to take off. Actually, we don't have to map this place. We've mapped the three bigger planets, and this one isn't really required."

Brent strode across the damp ground, toward the trail. He squatted down and ran his hands over the broken grass. "Something comes along here. There's a rut worn in the soil." He gave a startled exclamation. "Footprints!"

"People?"

"Looks like some kind of animal. Large—maybe a big cat." Brent straightened up, his heavy face thoughtful. "Maybe we could get ourselves some fresh game. And if not, maybe a little sport."

Captain Johnson fluttered nervously. "How do we know what sort of defenses these animals have? Let's play it safe and stay in the ship. We can make the survey by air; the usual processes ought to be enough for a little place like this. I hate to stick around here." He shivered. "It gives me the creeps."

"The creeps?" Brent yawned and stretched, then started along the trail, toward the rolling miles of green forest. "I like it. A regular national park—complete with wildlife. You stay in the ship. I'll have a little fun."

❖❖❖

Brent moved cautiously through the dark woods, one hand on his gun. He was an old-time surveyor; he had wandered around plenty of remote places in his time, enough to know what he was doing. He halted from time to time, examining the trail and feeling the soil. The large prints continued and were joined by others. A whole group of animals had come along this way, several species, all large. Probably flocking to a water source. A stream or pool of some kind.

He climbed a rise—then abruptly crouched. Ahead of him an animal was curled up on a flat stone, eyes shut, obviously sleeping. Brent moved around in a wide circle, carefully keeping his face to the animal. It was a cat, all right. But not the kind of cat he had ever seen before. Something like a lion—but larger. As large as a Terran rhino. Long tawny fur, great pads, a tail like a twisted spare-rope. A few flies crawled over its flanks; muscles rippled and the flies darted off. Its mouth was slightly open; he could see gleaming white fangs that sparkled moistly in the sun. A vast pink tongue. It breathed heavily, slowly, snoring in its slumber.

Brent toyed with his r-pistol. As a sportsman he couldn't shoot it sleeping: he'd have to chuck a rock at it and wake it up. But as a man looking at a beast twice his weight, he was tempted to blast its heart out and lug the remains back to the ship. The head would look fine; the whole damn pelt would look fine. He could make up a nice story to go along with it—the thing dropping on him from a branch, or maybe springing out of a thicket, roaring and snarling.

He knelt down, rested his right elbow on his right knee, clasped the butt of his pistol with his left hand, closed one eye, and carefully aimed. He took a deep breath, steadied the gun, and released the safety catch.

As he began squeezing the trigger, two more of the great cats sauntered past him along the trail, nosed briefly at their sleeping relation, and continued on into the brush.

Feeling foolish, Brent lowered his gun. The two beasts had paid no attention to him. One had glanced his way slightly, but neither had paused or taken any notice. He got unsteadily to his feet, cold sweat breaking out on his forehead. Good God, if they had wanted they could have torn him apart. Crouching there with his back turned—

He'd have to be more careful. Not stop and stay in one place. Keep moving, or go back to the ship. No, he wouldn't go back to the ship. He still needed something to show pipsqueak Johnson. The little Captain was probably sitting nervously at the controls, wondering what had happened to him. Brent pushed carefully through the shrubs and regained the trail on the far side of the sleeping cat. He'd explore some more, find something worth bringing back, maybe camp the night in a sheltered spot. He had a pack of hard rations, and in an emergency he could raise Johnson with his throat transmitter.

He came out on a flat meadow. Flowers grew everywhere, yellow and red and violet blossoms; he strode rapidly through them. The planet was virgin—still in its primitive stage. No humans had come here; as Johnson said, in a while there'd be plastic plates and beer cans and rotting debris. Maybe he could take out a lease. Form a corporation and claim the whole damn thing. Then slowly subdivide, only to the best people. Promise them no commercialization; only the most exclusive homes. A garden retreat for wealthy Terrans who had plenty of leisure. Fishing and hunting: all the game they wanted. Completely tame, too. Unfamiliar with humans.

His scheme pleased him. As he came out of the meadow and plunged into dense trees, he considered how he'd raise the initial investment. He might have to cut others in on it; get somebody with plenty of loot to back him. They'd need good promotion and advertising; really push the thing good. Untouched planets were getting scarce; this might well be the last. If he missed this, it might be a long time before he had another chance to . . .

His thoughts died. His scheme collapsed. Dull resentment choked him and he came to an abrupt halt.

Ahead the trail broadened. The trees were farther apart; bright sunlight sifted down into the silent darkness of the ferns and bushes and flowers. On a little rise was a building. A stone house, with steps, a front porch, solid white walls like marble. A garden grew around it. Windows. A path. Smaller buildings in the back. All neat and pretty—and extremely modern-looking. A small fountain sprinkled blue water into a basin. A few birds moved around the gravel paths, pecking and scratching.

The planet was inhabited.

Brent approached warily. A wisp of gray smoke trailed out of the stone chimney. Behind the house were chicken pens, a cow-like thing dozing in the shade by its water trough. Other animals, some dog-like, and a group that might have been sheep. A regular little farm—but not like any farm he had seen. The buildings were of marble, or what looked like marble. And the animals were penned in by some kind of force-field. Everything was clean; in one corner a disposal tube sucked exhausted water and refuse into a half-buried tank.

He came to steps leading up to a back porch and, after a moment of thought, climbed them. He wasn't especially frightened. There was a serenity about the place, an orderly calm. It was hard to imagine any harm coming from it. He reached the door, hesitated, and then began looking for a knob.

There wasn't any knob. At his touch the door swung open. Feeling foolish, Brent entered. He found himself in a luxurious hall; recessed lights flickered on at the pressure of his boots on the thick carpets. Long glowing drapes hid the windows. Massive furniture—he peered into a room. Strange machines and objects. Pictures on the walls. Statues in the corners. He turned a corner and emerged into a large foyer. And still no one.

A huge animal, as large as a pony, moved out of a doorway, sniffed at him curiously, licked his wrist, and wandered off. He watched it go, heart in his mouth.

Tame. All the animals were tame. What kind of people had built this place? Panic stabbed at him. Maybe not people. Maybe some other race. Something alien, from beyond the galaxy. Maybe this was the frontier of an alien empire, some kind of advanced station.

While he was thinking about it, wondering if he should try to get out, run back to the ship, vid the cruiser station at Orion IX, there was a faint rustle behind him. He turned quickly, hand on his gun.

"Who—" he gasped. And froze.

A girl stood there, face calm, eyes large and dark, a cloudy black. She was tall, almost as tall as he, a little under six feet. Cascades of black hair spilled down her shoulders, down to her waist. She wore a glistening robe of some oddly-metallic material; countless facets glittered and sparkled and reflected the overhead lights. Her lips were deep red and full. Her arms were folded beneath her breasts; they stirred faintly as she breathed. Beside her stood the pony-like animal that had nosed him and gone on.

"Welcome, Mr. Brent," the girl said. She smiled at him; he caught a flash of her tiny white teeth. Her voice was gentle and lilting, remarkably pure. Abruptly she turned; her robe fluttered behind her as she passed through the doorway and into the room beyond. "Come along. I've been expecting you."

Brent entered cautiously. A man stood at the end of the long table, watching him with obvious dislike. He was huge, over six feet, broad shoulders and arms that rippled as he buttoned his cloak and moved toward the door. The table was covered with dishes and bowls of food; robot servants were clearing away the things silently. Obviously, the girl and man had been eating.

"This is my brother," the girl said, indicating the dark-faced giant. He bowed slightly to Brent, exchanged a few words with the girl in an unfamiliar, liquid tongue, and then abruptly departed. His footsteps died down the hall.

"I'm sorry," Brent muttered. "I didn't mean to bust in here and break up anything."

"Don't worry. He was going. Actually, we don't get along very well." The girl drew the drapes aside to reveal a wide window overlooking the forest. "You can watch him go. His ship is parked out there. See it?"

It took a moment for Brent to make out the ship. It blended into the scenery perfectly. Only when it abruptly shot upward at a ninety-degree angle did he realize it had been there all the time. He had walked within yards of it.

"He's quite a person," the girl said, letting the drapes fall back in place. "Are you hungry? Here, sit down and eat with me. Now that Aeetes is gone and I'm all alone."

Brent sat down cautiously. The food looked good. The dishes were some kind of semi-transparent metal. A robot set places in front of him, knives, forks, spoons, then waited to be instructed. The girl gave it orders in her strange liquid tongue. It promptly served Brent and retired.

He and the girl were alone. Brent began to eat greedily; the food was delicious. He tore the wings from a chicken-like fowl and gnawed at it expertly. He gulped down a tumbler of dark red wine, wiped his mouth on his sleeve, and attacked a bowl of ripe fruit. Vegetables, spiced meats, seafood, warm bread—he gobbled down everything with pleasure. The girl ate a few dainty bites; she watched him curiously, until finally he was finished and had pushed his empty dishes away.

"Where's your Captain?" she asked. "Didn't he come?"

"Johnson? He's back at the ship." Brent belched noisily. "How come you speak Terran? It's not your natural language. And how did you know there's somebody with me?"

The girl laughed, a tinkling musical peal. She wiped her slim hands on a napkin and drank from a dark red glass. "We watched you on the scanner. We were curious. This is the first time one of your ships has penetrated this far. We wondered what your intentions were."

"You didn't learn Terran by watching our ship on a scanner."

"No. I learned your language from people of your race. That was a long time ago. I've spoken your language as long as I can remember."

Brent was baffled. "But you said our ship was the first to come here."

The girl laughed. "True. But we've often visited your little world. We know all about it. It's a stop-over point when we travel in that direction. I've been there many times—not for a while, but in the old days when I traveled more."

A strange chill settled over Brent. "Who are you people? Where are you from?"

"I don't know where we're from originally," the girl answered. "Our civilization is all over the universe, by now. It probably started from one place, back in legendary times. By now it's practically everywhere."

"Why haven't we run into your people before?"

The girl smiled and continued eating. "Didn't you hear what I said? You *have* met us. Often. We've even brought Terrans here. I remember one time very clearly, a few thousand years ago—"

"How long are your years?" Brent demanded.

"We don't have years." The girl's dark eyes bored into him, luminous with amusement. "I mean *Terran* years."

It took a minute for the full impact to hit him. "Thousand years," he murmured. "You've been alive a thousand years?"

"Eleven thousand," the girl answered simply. She nodded, and a robot cleared away the dishes. She leaned back in her chair, yawned, stretched like a small, lithe cat, then abruptly sprang to her feet. "Come on. We've finished eating. I'll show you my house."

Brent scrambled up and hurried after her, his confidence shattered. "You're immortal, aren't you?" He moved between her and the door, breathing rapidly, heavy face flushed. "You don't age."

"Age? No, of course not."

Brent managed to find words. "You're gods."

The girl smiled up at him, dark eyes flashing merrily. "Not really. You have just about everything we have—almost as much knowledge, science, culture. Eventually you'll catch up with us. We're an old race.

Millions of years ago our scientists succeeded in slowing down the processes of decay; since then we've ceased to die."

"Then your race stays constant. None die, none are born."

The girl pushed past him, through the doorway and down the hall. "Oh, people are born all the time. Our race grows and expands." She halted at a doorway. "We haven't given up any of our pleasures." She eyed Brent thoughtfully, his shoulders, arms, his dark hair, heavy face. "We're about like you, except that we're eternal. You'll probably solve that, too, sometime."

"You've moved among us?" Brent demanded. He was beginning to understand. "Then all those old religions and myths were true. Gods. Miracles. You've had contact with us, given us things. Done things for us." He followed her wonderingly into the room.

"Yes. I suppose we've done things for you. As we pass through." The girl moved about the room, letting down massive drapes. Soft darkness fell over the couches and bookcases and statues. "Do you play chess?"

"Chess?"

"It's our national game. We introduced it to some of your Brahmin ancestors." Disappointment showed on her sharp little face. "You don't play? Too bad. What do you do? What about your companion? He looked as if his intellectual capacity was greater than yours. Does he play chess? Maybe you ought to go back and get him."

"I don't think so," Brent said. He moved toward her. "As far as I know he doesn't do anything." He reached out and caught her by the arm. The girl pulled away, astonished. Brent gathered her up in his big arms and drew her tight against him. "I don't think we need him," he said.

He kissed her on the mouth. Her red lips were warm and sweet; she gasped and fought wildly. He could feel her slim body struggling against him. A cloud of fragrant scent billowed from her dark hair. She tore at him with her sharp nails, breasts heaving violently. He let go and she slid away, wary and bright-eyed, breathing quickly, body tense, drawing her luminous robe about her.

"I could kill you," she whispered. She touched her jeweled belt. "You don't understand, do you?"

Brent came forward. "You probably can. But I bet you won't."

She backed away from him. "Don't be a fool." Her red lips twisted and a smile flickered briefly. "You're brave. But not very smart. Still, that's not such a bad combination in a man. Stupid and brave." Agilely, she avoided his grasp and slipped out of his reach. "You're in good physical shape, too. How do you manage it aboard that little ship?"

"Quarterly fitness courses," Brent answered. He moved between her and the door. "You must get pretty damn bored here, all by yourself. After the first few thousand years it must get trying."

"I find things to do," she said. "Don't come any closer to me. As much as I admire your daring, it's only fair to warn you that—"

Brent grabbed her. She fought wildly; he pinned her hands together behind her back with one paw, arched her body taut, and kissed her half-parted lips. She sank her tiny white teeth into him; he grunted and jerked away. She was laughing, black eyes dancing, as she struggled. Her breath came rapidly, cheeks flushed, half-covered breasts quivering, body twisting like a trapped animal. He caught her around the waist and grabbed her up in his arms.

A wave of force hit him.

He dropped her; she landed easily on her feet and danced back. Brent was doubled up, face gray with agony. Cold sweat stood out on his neck and hands. He sank down on a couch and closed his eyes, muscles knotted, body writhing with pain.

"Sorry," the girl said. She moved around the room, ignoring him, "It's your own fault—I told you to be careful. Maybe you better get out of here. Back to your little ship. I don't want anything to happen to you. It's against our policy to kill Terrans."

"What—was that?"

"Nothing much. A form of repulsion, I suppose. This belt was constructed on one of our industrial planets; it protects me but I don't know the operational principle."

Brent manage to get to his feet. "You're pretty tough for a little girl."

"A little girl? I'm pretty *old* for a little girl. I was old before you were born. I was old before your people had rocket ships. I was old before you knew how to weave clothing and write your thoughts down with symbols. I've watched your race advance and fall back into barbarism and advance again. Endless nations and empires. I was alive when the Egyptians first began spreading out into Asia Minor. I saw the city builders of the Tigris Valley begin putting up their brick houses. I saw the Assyrian war chariots roll out to fight. I and my friends visited Greece and Rome and Minos and Lydia and the great kingdoms of the red-skinned Indians. We were gods to the ancients, saints to the Christians. We come and go. As your people advanced we came less often. We have other way-stations; yours isn't the only stop-over point."

Brent was silent. Color was beginning to come back to his face. The girl had thrown herself down on one of the soft couches; she leaned back against a pillow and gazed up at him calmly, one arm outstretched, the other across her lap. Her long legs were tucked under her, tiny feet pressed together. She looked like a small, contented kitten resting after a game. It was hard for him to believe what she had told him. But his body still ached; he had felt a minute portion of her power-field, and it had almost killed him. That was something to think about.

"Well?" the girl asked, presently. "What are you going to do? It's getting late. I think you ought to go back to your ship. Your Captain will be wondering what happened to you."

Brent moved over to the window and drew aside the heavy drapes. The sun had set. Darkness was settling over the forests outside. Stars had already begun to come out, tiny dots of white in the thickening violet. A distant line of hills jutted up black and ominous.

"I can contact him," Brent said. He tapped at his neck. "In case of emergency. Tell him I'm all right."

"*Are you all right?* You shouldn't be here. You think you know what you're doing? You think you can handle me." She raised herself up slightly and tossed her black hair back over her shoulders. "I can see what's going on in your mind. I'm so much like a girl you had an affair with, a young brunette you used to wrap around your finger—and boast about to your companions."

Brent flushed. "You're a telepath. You should have told me."

"A partial telepath. All I need. Toss me your cigarettes. We don't have such things."

Brent fumbled in his pocket, got his pack out and tossed it to her. She lit up and inhaled gratefully. A cloud of gray smoke drifted around her; it mixed with the darkening shadows of the room. The corners dissolved into gloom. She became an indistinct shape, curled up on the couch, the glowing cigarette between her dark red lips.

"I'm not afraid," Brent said.

"No, you're not. You're not a coward. If you were as smart as you are brave—but then I guess you wouldn't be brave. I admire your bravery, stupid as it is. Man has a lot of courage. Even though it's based on ignorance, it's impressive." After a moment, she said, "Come over here and sit with me."

"What do I have to be worried about?" Brent asked after a while. "If you don't turn on that damn belt, I'll be all right."

In the darkness, the girl stirred. "There's more than that." She sat up a little, arranged her hair, pulled a pillow behind her head. "You see, we're of totally different races. My race is millions of years advanced over yours. Contact with us—close contact—is lethal. Not to us, of course. To you. You can't be with me and remain a human being."

"What do you mean?"

"You'll undergo changes. Evolutionary changes. There's pull which we exert. We're fully charged; close contact with us will exert influence on the cells of your body. Those animals outside. They've evolved slightly; they're no longer wild beasts. They're able to understand simple commands and follow basic routines. As yet, they have no language. With such low animals it's a long process; and my contact with them hasn't really been close. But with you—"

"I see."

"We're not supposed to let humans near us. Aeetes cleared out of here. I'm too lazy to go—I don't especially care. I'm not mature and responsible, I suppose." She smiled slightly. "And my kind of close contact is a little closer than most."

Brent could barely make out her slim form in the darkness. She lay back against the pillows, lips parted, arms folded beneath her breasts, head tilted back. She was lovely. The most beautiful woman he had ever seen. After a moment he leaned toward her. This time she didn't move away. He kissed her gently. Then he put his arms around her slender body and drew her tight against him. Her robe rustled. Her soft hair brushed against him, warm and fragrant.

"It's worth it," he said.

"You're sure? You can't turn back, once it's begun. Do you understand? You won't be human any more. You'll have evolved. Along lines your race will take millions of years from now. You'll be an outcast, a forerunner of things to come. Without companions."

"I'll stay." He caressed her cheek, her hair, her neck. He could feel the blood pulsing beneath the downy skin; a rapid pounding in the hollow of her throat. She was breathing rapidly; her breasts rose and fell against him. "If you'll let me."

"Yes," she murmured. "I'll let you. If it's what you really want. But don't blame me." A half-sad, half-mischievous smile flitted across her sharp features; her dark eyes sparkled. "Promise you won't blame me? It's happened before—I hate people to reproach me. I always say never again. No matter what."

"Has it happened before?"

The girl laughed, softly and close to his ear. She kissed him warmly and hugged him hard against her. "In eleven thousand years," she whispered, "it's happened quite often."

❖ ❖ ❖

Captain Johnson had a bad night. He tried to raise Brent on the emergency com, but there was no response. Only faint static and a distant echo of a vid program from Orion X. Jazz music and sugary commercials.

The sounds of civilization reminded him that they had to keep moving. Twenty-four hours was all the time allotted to this planet, smallest of its system.

"Damn," he muttered. He fixed a pot of coffee and checked his wristwatch. Then he got out of the ship and wandered around in the early-morning sunlight. The sun was beginning to come up. The air turned from dark violet to gray. It was cold as hell. He shivered and stamped his feet and watched some small bird-like things fly down to peck around the bushes.

He was just beginning to think of notifying Orion XI when he saw her.

She walked quickly toward the ship. Tall and slim in a heavy fur jacket, her arms buried in the deep pelt. Johnson stood rooted to the spot, dumbfounded. He was too astonished even to touch his gun. His mouth fell open as the girl halted a little way off, tossed her dark hair back, blew a cloud of silvery breath at him and then said, "I'm sorry you had a bad night. It's my fault. I should have sent him right back."

Captain Johnson's mouth opened and shut. "Who are you?" he managed finally. Fear seized him. "Where's Brent? What happened?"

"He'll be along." She turned back toward the forest and made a sign. "I think you'd better leave, now. He wants to stay here and that is best—for he's changed. He'll be happy in my forest with the other—men. It's strange how all you humans come out exactly alike. Your race is moving along an unusual path. It might be worth our while to study you, sometime. It must have something to do with your low esthetic plateau. You seem to have an innate vulgarity, which eventually will dominate you."

From out of the woods came a strange shape. For a moment, Captain Johnson thought his eyes were playing tricks on him. He blinked, squinted, then grunted in disbelief. Here, on this remote planet—but there was no mistake. It was definitely an immense cat-like beast that came slowly and miserably out of the woods after the girl.

The girl moved away, then halted to wave to the beast, who whined wretchedly around the ship.

Johnson stared at the animal and felt a sudden fear. Instinctively he knew that Brent was not coming back to the ship. Something had happened on this strange planet—that girl . . .

Johnson slammed the airlock shut and hurried to the control panel. He had to get back to the nearest base and make a report. This called for an elaborate investigation.

As the rockets blasted Johnson glanced through the viewplate. He saw the animal shaking a huge paw futilely in the air after the departing ship.

Johnson shuddered. That was too much like a man's angry gesture . . .

TONY AND THE BEETLES

Reddish-yellow sunlight filtered through the thick quartz windows into the sleep-compartment. Tony Rossi yawned, stirred a little, then opened his black eyes and sat up quickly. With one motion he tossed the covers back and slid to the warm metal floor. He clicked off his alarm clock and hurried to the closet.

It looked like a nice day. The landscape outside was motionless, undisturbed by winds or dust-shift. The boy's heart pounded excitedly. He pulled his trousers on, zipped up the reinforced mesh, struggled into his heavy canvas shirt, and then sat down onto the edge of the cot to tug on his boots. He closed the seams around their tops and then did the same with his gloves. Next he adjusted the pressure on his pump unit and strapped it between his shoulder blades. He grabbed his helmet from the dresser, and he was ready for the day.

In the dining-compartment his mother and father had finished breakfast. Their voices drifted to him as he clattered down the ramp. A disturbed murmur; he paused to listen. What were they talking about? Had he done something wrong, again?

And then he caught it. Behind their voices was another voice. Static and crackling pops. The all-system audio signal from Rigel IV. They had it turned up full blast; the dull thunder of the monitor's voice boomed loudly. The war. Always the war. He sighed, and stepped out into the dining-compartment.

"Morning," his father muttered.

"Good morning, dear," his mother said absently. She sat with her head turned to one side, wrinkles of concentration webbing her forehead. Her thin lips were drawn together in a tight line of concern. His father had pushed his dirty dishes back and was smoking, elbows on the table, dark hairy arms bare and muscular. He was scowling, intent on the jumbled roar from the speaker above the sink.

"How's it going?" Tony asked. He slid into his chair and reached automatically for the ersatz grapefruit. "Any news from Orion?"

Neither of them answered. They didn't hear him. He began to eat his grapefruit. Outside, beyond the little metal and plastic housing unit, sounds of activity grew. Shouts and muffled crashes, as rural merchants and their trucks rumbled along the highway toward Karnet. The reddish daylight swelled; Betelgeuse was rising quietly and majestically.

"Nice day," Tony said. "No flux wind. I think I'll go down to the n-quarter awhile. We're building a neat spaceport, a model, of course, but we've been able to get enough materials to lay out strips for—"

With a savage snarl his father reached out and struck. The audio roar immediately died. "I knew it!" He got up and moved angrily away from the table. "I told them it would happen. They shouldn't have moved so soon. Should have built up Class A supply bases, first."

"Isn't our main fleet moving in from Bellatrix?" Tony's mother fluttered anxiously. "According to last night's summary the worse that can happen is Orion IX and X will be dumped."

Joseph Rossi laughed harshly. "The hell with last night's summary. They know as well as I do what's happening."

"What's happening?" Tony echoed, as he pushed aside his grapefruit and began to ladle out dry cereal. "Are we losing the battle?"

"Yes!" His father's lips twisted. "Earthmen, losing to—to *beetles*. I told them. But they couldn't wait. My God, there's ten good years left in this system. Why'd they have to push on? Everybody knew Orion would be tough. The whole damn beetle fleet's strung out around there. Waiting for us. And we have to barge right in."

"But nobody ever thought beetles would fight," Leah Rossi protested mildly. "Everybody thought they'd just fire a few blasts and then—"

"They *have* to fight! Orion's the last jump-off. If they don't fight here, where the hell can they fight?" Rossi swore savagely. "Of course they're fighting. We have all their planets except the inner Orion string—not that they're worth much, but it's the principle of the thing. If we'd built up strong supply bases, we could have broken up the beetle fleet and really clobbered it."

"Don't say 'beetle'," Tony murmured, as he finished his cereal. "They're Pas-udeti, same as here. The word 'beetle' comes from Betelgeuse. An Arabian word we invented ourselves."

Joe Rossi's mouth opened and closed. "What are you, a goddamn beetle-lover?"

"Joe," Leah snapped. "For heaven's sake."

Rossi moved toward the door. "If I was ten years younger I'd be out there. I'd really show those shiny-shelled insects what the hell they're up against. Them and their junky beat-up old hulks. Converted freighters!" His eyes blazed. "When I think of them shooting down Terran cruisers with *our* boys in them—"

"Orion's their system," Tony murmured.

"*Their* system! When the hell did you get to be an authority on space law? Why, I ought to—" He broke off, choked with rage. "My own kid," he muttered. "One more crack out of you today and I'll hang one on you you'll feel the rest of the week."

Tony pushed his chair back. "I won't be around today. I'm going into Karnet, with my EEP."

"Yeah, to play with beetles!"

Tony said nothing. He was already sliding his helmet in place and snapping the clamps tight. As he pushed through the back door, into the lock membrane, he unscrewed his oxygen tap and set the tank filter into action. An automatic response, conditioned by a lifetime spent on a colony planet in an alien system.

❖ ❖ ❖

A faint flux wind caught at him and swept yellow-red dust around his boots. Sunlight glittered from the metal roof of his family's housing unit, one of endless rows of squat boxes set in the sandy slope, protected by the line of ore-refining installations against the horizon. He made an impatient signal, and from the storage shed his EEP came gliding out, catching the sunlight on its chrome trim.

"We're going down into Karnet," Tony said, unconsciously slipping into the Pas dialect. "Hurry up!"

The EEP took up its position behind him, and he started briskly down the slope, over the shifting sand, toward the road. There were quite a few traders out, today. It was a good day for the market; only a fourth of the year was fit for travel. Betelgeuse was an erratic and undependable sun, not at all like Sol (according to the edutapes fed to Tony four hours a day, six days a week—he had never seen Sol himself).

He reached the noisy road. Pas-udeti were everywhere. Whole groups of them, with their primitive combustion-driven trucks, battered and filthy, motors grinding protestingly. He waved at the trucks as they pushed past him. After a moment one slowed down. It was piled with *tis*, bundled heaps of gray vegetables, dried and prepared for the table. A staple of the Pas-udeti diet. Behind the wheel lounged a dark-faced elderly Pas, one arm over the open window, a rolled leaf between his lips. He was like all other Pas-udeti: lank and hard-shelled, encased in a brittle sheath in which he lived and died.

"You want a ride?" the Pas murmured—required protocol when an Earthman on foot was encountered.

"Is there room for my EEP?"

The Pas made a careless motion with his claw. "It can run behind."

Sardonic amusement touched his ugly old face. "If it gets to Karnet we'll sell it for scrap. We can use a few condensers and relay tubing. We're short of electronic maintenance stuff."

"I know," Tony said solemnly, as he climbed into the cabin of the truck. "It's all been sent to the big repair base at Orion I. For your warfleet."

Amusement vanished from the leathery face. "Yes, the warfleet." He turned away and started up the truck again. In the back, Tony's EEP had scrambled up on the load of *tis* and was gripping precariously with its magnetic lines.

Tony noticed the Pas-udeti's sudden change of expression, and he was puzzled. He started to speak to him—but now he noticed unusual quietness among the other Pas, in the other trucks, behind and in front of his own. The war, of course. It had swept through this system a century ago; these people had been left behind. Now all eyes were on Orion, on the battle between the Terran warfleet and the Pas-udeti collection of armed freighters.

"Is it true," Tony asked carefully, "that you're winning?"

The elderly Pas grunted. "We hear rumors."

Tony considered. "My father says Terra went ahead too fast. He says we should have consolidated. We didn't assemble adequate supply bases. He used to be an officer, when he was younger. He was with the fleet for two years."

The Pas was silent a moment. "It's true," he said at last, "that when you're so far from home, supply is a great problem. We, on the other hand, don't have that. We have no distances to cover."

"Do you know anybody fighting?"

"I have distant relatives." The answer was vague; the Pas obviously didn't want to talk about it.

"Have you ever seen your warfleet?"

"Not as it exists now. When this system was defeated most of our units were wiped out. Remnants limped to Orion and joined the Orion fleet."

"Your relatives were with the remnants?"

"That's right."

"Then you were alive when this planet was taken?"

"Why do you ask?" The old Pas quivered violently. "What business is it of yours?"

Tony leaned out and watched the walls and buildings of Karnet grow ahead of them. Karnet was an old city. It had stood thousands of years. The Pas-udeti civilization was stable; it had reached a certain point of technocratic development and then leveled off. The Pas had intersystem ships that had carried people and freight between planets in the days before the Terran Confederation. They had combustion-driven cars, audiophones, a power network of a magnetic type. Their plumbing was satisfactory and their medicine was highly advanced. They had art forms, emotional and exciting. They had a vague religion.

"Who do you think will win the battle?" Tony asked.

"I don't know." With a sudden jerk the old Pas brought the truck to a crashing halt. "This is as far as I go. Please get out and take your EEP with you."

Tony faltered in surprise. "But aren't you going—?"

"No farther!"

Tony pushed the door open. He was vaguely uneasy; there was a hard, fixed expression on the leathery face, and the old creature's voice had a sharp edge he had never heard before. "Thanks," he murmured. He hopped down into the red dust and signaled his EEP. It released it magnetic lines, and instantly the truck started up with a roar, passing on inside the city.

Tony watched it go, still dazed. The hot dust lapped at his ankles; he automatically moved his feet and slapped at his trousers. A truck honked, and his EEP quickly moved him from the road, up to the level pedestrian ramp. Pas-udeti in swarms moved by, endless lines of rural people hurrying into Karnet on their daily business. A massive public bus had stopped by the gate and was letting off passengers.

Male and female Pas. And children. They laughed and shouted; the sounds of their voices blended with the low hum of the city.

"Going in?" a sharp Pas-udeti voice sounded close behind him. "Keep moving—you're blocking the ramp."

It was a young female, with a heavy armload clutched in her claws. Tony felt embarrassed; female Pas had a certain telepathic ability, part of their sexual makeup. It was effective on Earthmen at close range.

"Here," she said. "Give me a hand."

Tony nodded his head, and the EEP accepted the female's heavy armload. "I'm visiting the city," Tony said, as they moved with the crowd toward the gates. "I got a ride most of the way, but the driver let me off out here."

"You're from the settlement?"

"Yes."

She eyed him critically. "You've always lived here, haven't you?"

"I was born here. My family came here from Earth four years before I was born. My father was an officer in the fleet. He earned an Emigration Priority."

"So you've never seen your own planet. How old are you?"

"Ten years. Terran."

"You shouldn't have asked the driver so many questions."

They passed through the decontamination shield and into the city. An information square loomed ahead; Pas men and women were packed around it. Moving chutes and transport cars rumbled everywhere. Buildings and ramps and open-air machinery; the city was sealed in a protective dust-proof envelope. Tony unfastened his helmet and clipped it to his belt. The air was stale-smelling, artificial, but usable.

"Let me tell you something," the young female said carefully, as she strode along the foot-ramp beside Tony. "I wonder if this is a good day for you to come to Karnet. I know you've been coming here regularly to play with your friends. But perhaps today you ought to stay home, in your settlement."

"Why?"

"Because today everybody is upset."

"I know," Tony said. "My mother and father were upset. They were listening to the news from our base in the Rigel system."

"I don't mean your family. Other people are listening, too. These people here. My race."

"They're upset, all right," Tony admitted. "But I come here all the time. There's nobody to play with at the settlement, and anyhow we're working on a project."

"A model spaceport."

"That's right." Tony was envious. "I sure wish I was a telepath. It must be fun."

The female Pas-udeti was silent. She was deep in thought. "What would happen," she asked, "if your family left here and returned to Earth?"

"That couldn't happen. There's no room for us on Earth. C-bombs destroyed most of Asia and North America back in the Twentieth Century."

"Suppose you *had* to go back?"

Tony did not understand. "But we can't. Habitable portions of Earth are overcrowded. Our main problem is finding places for Terrans to live, in other systems." He added, "And anyhow, I don't particularly want to go to Terra. I'm used to it here. All my friends are here."

"I'll take my packages," the female said. "I go this other way, down this third-level ramp."

Tony nodded to his EEP and it lowered the bundles into the female's claws. She lingered a moment, trying to find the right words.

"Good luck," she said.

"With what?"

She smiled faintly, ironically. "With your model spaceport. I hope you and your friends get to finish it."

"Of course we'll finish it," Tony said, surprised. "It's almost done." What did she mean?

The Pas-udeti woman hurried off before he could ask her. Tony was troubled and uncertain; more doubts filled him. After a moment he headed slowly into the lane that took him toward the residential section of the city. Past the stores and factories, to the place where his friends lived.

The group of Pas-udeti children eyed him silently as he approached. They had been playing in the shade of an immense *bengelo*, whose ancient branches drooped and swayed with the air currents pumped through the city. Now they sat unmoving.

"I didn't expect you today," B'prith said, in an expressionless voice.

Tony halted awkwardly, and his EEP did the same. "How are things?" he murmured.

"Fine."

"I got a ride part way."

"Fine."

Tony squatted down in the shade. None of the Pas children stirred. They were small, not as large as Terran children. Their shells had not hardened, had not turned dark and opaque, like horn. It gave them a soft, unformed appearance, but at the same time it lightened their load. They moved more easily than their elders: they could hop and skip around, still. But they were not skipping right now.

"What's the matter?" Tony demanded. "What's wrong with everybody?"

No one answered.

"Where's the model?" he asked. "Have you fellows been working on it?"

After a moment Llyre nodded slightly.

Tony felt dull anger rise up inside him. "Say something! What's the matter? What're you all mad about?"

"Mad?" B'prith echoed. "We're not mad."

Tony scratched aimlessly in the dust. He knew what it was. The war, again. The battle going on near Orion. His anger burst up wildly. "Forget the war. Everything was fine yesterday, before the battle."

"Sure," Llyre said. "It was fine."

Tony caught the edge to his voice. "It happened a hundred years ago. It's not my fault."

"Sure," B'prith said.

"This is my home. Isn't it? Haven't I got as much right here as anybody else? I was born here."

"Sure," Llyre said, tonelessly.

Tony appealed to them helplessly. "Do you have to act this way? You didn't act this way yesterday. I was here yesterday—all of us were here yesterday. What's happened since yesterday?"

"The battle," B'prith said.

"What difference does *that* make? Why does that change everything? There's always war. There've been battles all the time, as long as I can remember. What's different about this?"

B'prith broke apart a clump of dirt with his strong claws. After a moment he tossed it away and got slowly to his feet. "Well," he said thoughtfully, "according to our audio relay, it looks as if our fleet is going to win, this time."

"Yes," Tony agreed, not understanding. "My father says we didn't build up adequate supply bases. We'll probably have to fall back to . . . " And then the impact hit him. 'You mean, for the first time in a hundred years—"

"Yes," Llyre said, also getting up. The others got up, too. They moved away from Tony, toward the nearby house. "We're winning. The Terran flank was turned, half an hour ago. Your right wing has folded completely."

Tony was stunned. "And it matters. It matters to all of you."

"Matters!" B'prith halted, suddenly blazing out in fury. "Sure it matters! For the first time—in a century. The first time in our lives we're beating you. We have you on the run, you—" He choked out the word, almost spat it out. "You white-grubs!"

They disappeared into the house. Tony sat gazing stupidly down at the ground, his hands still moving aimlessly. He had heard the word before, seen it scrawled on walls and in the dust near the settlement. *White-grubs.* The Pas term of derision for Terrans. Because of their softness, their whiteness. Lack of hard shells. Pulpy, doughy skin. But they had never dared say it out loud, before. To an Earthman's face.

Beside him, his EEP stirred restlessly. Its intricate radio mechanism sensed the hostile atmosphere. Automatic relays were sliding into place; circuits were opening and closing.

"It's all right," Tony murmured, getting slowly up. "Maybe we'd better go back."

He moved unsteadily toward the ramp, completely shaken. The EEP walked calmly ahead, its metal face blank and confident, feeling nothing, saying nothing. Tony's thoughts were a wild turmoil; he shook his head, but the crazy spinning kept up. He couldn't make his mind slow down, lock in place.

"Wait a minute," a voice said. B'prith's voice, from the open doorway. Cold and withdrawn, almost unfamiliar.

"What do you want?"

B'prith came toward him, claws behind his back in the formal Pas-udeti posture, used between total strangers. "You shouldn't have come here, today."

"I know," Tony said.

B'prith got out a bit of *tis* stalk and began to roll it into a tube. He pretended to concentrate on it. "Look," he said. "You said you have a right here. But you don't."

"I—" Tony murmured.

"Do you understand why not? You said it isn't your fault. I guess not. But it's not my fault, either. Maybe it's nobody's fault. I've known you a long time."

"Five years. Terran."

B'prith twisted the stalk up and tossed it away. "Yesterday we played together. We worked on the spaceport. But we can't play today. My family said to tell you not to come here any more." He hesitated, and did not look Tony in the face. "I was going to tell you, anyhow. Before they said anything."

"Oh," Tony said.

"Everything that's happened today—the battle, our fleet's stand. We didn't know. We didn't dare hope. You see? A century of running. First this system. Then the Rigel system, all the planets. Then the other Orion stars. We fought here and there—scattered fights. Those that got away joined up. We supplied the base at Orion—you people didn't know. But there was no hope; at least, nobody thought there was." He was silent a moment. "Funny," he said, "what happens when your back's to the wall, and there isn't any further place to go. Then you have to fight."

"If our supply bases—" Tony began thickly, but B'prith cut him off savagely.

"Your supply bases! Don't you understand? We're beating you! Now you'll have to get out! All you white-grubs. Out of our system!"

Tony's EEP moved forward ominously. B'prith saw it. He bent down, snatched up a rock, and hurled to straight at the EEP. The rock clanged off the metal hull and bounced harmlessly away. B'prith snatched up another rock. Llyre and the others came quickly out of the house. An adult Pas loomed up behind them. Everything was happening too fast. More rocks crashed against the EEP. One struck Tony on the arm.

"Get out!" B'prith screamed. "Don't come back! This is our planet!" His claws snatched at Tony. "We'll tear you to pieces if you—"

Tony smashed him in the chest. The soft shell gave like rubber, and the Pas stumbled back. He wobbled and fell over, gasping and screeching.

"Beetle," Tony breathed hoarsely. Suddenly he was terrified. A crowd of Pas-udeti was forming rapidly. They surged on all sides, hostile faces, dark and angry, a rising thunder of rage.

More stones showered. Some struck the EEP, others fell around Tony, near his boots. One whizzed past his face. Quickly he slid his helmet in place. He was scared. He knew his EEP's E-signal had already gone out, but it would be minutes before a ship could come. Besides, there were other Earthmen in the city to be taken care of; there were Earthmen all over the planet. In all the cities. On all the twenty-three Betelgeuse planets. On the fourteen Rigel planets. On the other Orion planets.

"We have to get out of here," he muttered to the EEP. "Do something!"

A stone hit him on the helmet. The plastic cracked; air leaked out, and then the autoseal filmed over. More stones were falling. The Pas swarmed close, a yelling, seething mass of black-sheathed creatures. He could smell them, the acrid body-odor of insects, hear their claws snap, feel their weight.

The EEP threw its heat beam on. The beam shifted in a wide band toward the crowd of Pas-udeti. Crude hand weapons appeared. A clatter of bullets burst around Tony; they were firing at the EEP. He was dimly aware of the metal body beside him. A shuddering crash—the EEP was toppled over. The crowd poured over it; the metal hull was lost from sight.

Like a demented animal, the crowd tore at the struggling EEP. A few of them smashed in its head; others tore off struts and shiny arm-sections. The EEP ceased struggling. The crowd moved away, panting and clutching jagged remains. They saw Tony.

As the first line of them reached for him, the protective envelope high above them shattered. A Terran scout ship thundered down, heat beam screaming. The crowd scattered in confusion, some firing, some throwing stones, others leaping for safety.

Tony picked himself up and made his way unsteadily toward the spot where the scout was landing.

❖ ❖ ❖

"I'm sorry," Joe Rossi said gently. He touched his son on the shoulder. "I shouldn't have let you go down there today. I should have known."

Tony sat hunched over in the big plastic easychair. He rocked back and forth, face pale with shock. The scout ship which had rescued him had immediately headed back toward Karnet; there were other Earthmen to bring out, besides this first load. The boy said nothing. His mind was blank. He still heard the roar of the crowd, felt its hate—a century of pent-up fury and resentment. The memory drove out everything else; it was all around him, even now. And the sight of the floundering EEP, the metallic ripping sound, as its arms and legs were torn off and carried away.

His mother dabbed at his cuts and scratches with antiseptic. Joe Rossi shakily lit a cigarette and said, "If your EEP hadn't been along they'd have killed you. Beetles." He shuddered. "I never should have let you go down there. All this time . . . They might have done it any time, any day. Knifed you. Cut you open with their filthy goddamn claws."

Below the settlement the reddish-yellow sunlight glinted on gunbarrels. Already, dull booms echoed against the crumbling hills. The defense ring was going into action. Black shapes darted and scurried up the side of the slope. Black patches moved out from Karnet, toward the Terran settlement, across the dividing line the Confederation surveyors had set up a century ago. Karnet was a bubbling pot of activity. The whole city rumbled with feverish excitement.

Tony raised his head. "They—they turned our flank."

"Yeah." Joe Rossi stubbed out his cigarette. "They sure did. That was at one o'clock. At two they drove a wedge right through the center of our line. Split the fleet in half. Broke it up—sent it running. Picked us off one by one as we fell back. Christ, they're like maniacs. Now that they've got the scent, the taste of our blood."

"But it's getting better," Leah fluttered. "Our main fleet units are beginning to appear."

"We'll get them," Joe muttered. "It'll take a while. But by God we'll wipe them out. Every last one of them. If it takes a thousand years.

We'll follow every last ship down—we'll get them all." His voice rose in frenzy. "Beetles! Goddamn insects! When I think of them, trying to hurt my kid, with their filthy black claws—"

"If you were younger, you'd be in the line," Leah said. "It's not your fault you're too old. The heart strain's too great. You did your job. They can't let an older person take chances. It's not your fault."

Joe clenched his fists. "I feel so—futile. If there was only something I could do."

"The fleet will take care of them," Leah said soothingly. "You said so yourself. They'll hunt every one of them down. Destroy them all. There's nothing to worry about."

Joe sagged miserably. "It's no use. Let's cut it out. Let's stop kidding ourselves."

"What do you mean?"

"Face it! We're not going to win, not this time. We went too far. Our time's come."

There was silence.

Tony sat up a little. "When did you know?"

"I've known a long time."

"I found out today. I didn't understand, at first. This is—stolen ground. I was born here, but it's stolen ground."

"Yes. It's stolen. It doesn't belong to us."

"We're here because we're stronger. But now we're not stronger. We're being beaten."

"They know Terrans can be licked. Like anybody else." Joe Rossi's face was gray and flabby. "We took their planets away from them. Now they're taking them back. It'll be a while, of course. We'll retreat slowly. It'll be another five centuries going back. There're a lot of systems between here and Sol."

Tony shook his head, still uncomprehending. "Even Llyre and B'prith. All of them. Waiting for their time to come. For us to lose and go away again. Where we came from."

Joe Rossi paced back and forth. "Yeah, we'll be retreating from now on. Giving ground, instead of taking it. It'll be like this today—losing fights, draws. Stalemates and worse."

He raised his feverish eyes toward the ceiling of the little metal housing unit, face wild with passion and misery.

"But, by God, we'll give them a run for their money. All the way back! Every inch!"

EXHIBIT PIECE

"That's a strange suit you have on," the robot pubtrans driver observed. It slid back its door and came to rest at the curb. "What are the little round things?"

"Those are buttons," George Miller explained. "They are partly functional, partly ornamental. This is an archaic suit of the twentieth century. I wear it because of the nature of my employment."

He paid the robot, grabbed up his briefcase, and hurried along the ramp to the History Agency. The main building was already open for the day; robed men and women wandered everywhere. Miller entered a PRIVATE lift, squeezed between two immense controllers from the pre-Christian division, and in a moment was on his way to his own level, the Middle Twentieth Century.

"Gorning," he murmured, as Controller Fleming met him at the atomic engine exhibit.

"Gorning," Fleming responded brusquely. "Look here, Miller. Let's have this out once and for all. What if everyone dressed like you? The Government sets up strict rules for dress. Can't you forget your damn anachronisms once in a while? What in God's name is that thing in your hand? It looks like a squashed Jurassic lizard."

"This is an alligator-hide briefcase," Miller explained. "I carry my study spools in it. The briefcase was an authority symbol of the managerial class of the later twentieth century." He unzipped the briefcase. "Try to understand, Fleming. By accustoming myself to everyday objects of my research period I transform my relation from mere intellectual curiosity to genuine empathy. You have frequently noticed I pronounce certain words oddly. The accent is that of an American businessman of the Eisenhower administration. Dig me?"

"Eh?" Fleming muttered.

"*Dig me* was a twentieth-century expression." Miller laid out his study spools on his desk. "Was there anything you wanted? If not I'll begin today's work. I've uncovered fascinating evidence to indicate that although twentieth-century Americans laid their own floor tiles, they did not weave their own clothing. I wish to alter my exhibits on this matter."

"There's no fanatic like an academician," Fleming grated. "You're two hundred years behind times. Immersed in your relics and artifacts. Your damn authentic replicas of discarded trivia."

"I love my work," Miller answered mildly.

"Nobody complains about your work. But there are other things than work. You're a political-social unit here in this society. Take warning, Miller! The Board has reports on your eccentricities. They approve devotion to work . . . " His eyes narrowed significantly. "But you go too far."

"My first loyalty is to my art," Miller said.

"Your what? What does that mean?"

"A twentieth-century term." There was undisguised superiority on Miller's face. "You're nothing but a minor bureaucrat in a vast machine. You're a function of an impersonal cultural totality. You have no standards of your own. In the twentieth century men had personal standards of workmanship. Artistic craft. Pride of accomplishment. These words mean nothing to you. You have no soul— another concept from the golden days of the twentieth century when men were free and could speak their minds."

"Beware, Miller!" Fleming blanched nervously and lowered his voice. "You damn scholars. Come up out of your tapes and face reality.

You'll get us all in trouble, talking this way. Idolize the past, if you want. But remember—it's gone and buried. Times change. Society progresses." He gestured impatiently at the exhibits that occupied the level. "That's only an imperfect replica."

"You impugn my research?" Miller was seething. "This exhibit is absolutely accurate! I correct it to all new data. There isn't anything I don't know about the twentieth century."

Fleming shook his head. "It's no use." He turned and stalked wearily off the level, onto the descent ramp.

Miller straightened his collar and bright hand-painted necktie. He smoothed down his blue pin stripe coat, expertly lit a pipeful of two-century-old tobacco, and returned to his spools.

Why didn't Fleming leave him alone? Fleming, the officious representative of the great hierarchy that spread like a sticky gray web over the whole planet. Into each industrial, professional, and residential unit. Ah, the freedom of the twentieth century! He slowed his tape scanner a moment, and a dreamy look slid over his features. The exciting age of virility and individuality, when men were men . . .

It was just about then, just as he was settling deep in the beauty of his research, that he heard the inexplicable sounds. They came from the center of his exhibit, from within the intricate, carefully regulated interior.

Somebody was in his exhibit.

He could hear them back there, back in the depths. Somebody or something had gone past the safety barrier set up to keep the public out. Miller snapped off his tape scanner and got slowly to his feet. He was shaking all over as he moved cautiously toward the exhibit. He killed the barrier and climbed the railing on to a concrete pavement. A few curious visitors blinked, as the small, oddly dressed man crept among the authentic replicas of the twentieth century that made up the exhibit and disappeared within.

Breathing hard, Miller advanced up the pavement and on to a carefully tended gravel path. Maybe it was one of the other theorists, a minion of the Board, snooping around looking for something with which to discredit him. An inaccuracy here—a trifling error of no consequence there. Sweat came out of his forehead; anger became terror. To his right was a flower bed. Paul Scarlet roses and low-growing pansies. Then the moist green lawn. The gleaming white garage, with its door half up. The sleek rear of a 1954 Buick—and then the house itself.

He'd have to be careful. If is *was* somebody from the Board he'd be up against official hierarchy. Maybe it was somebody big. Maybe even Edwin Carnap, President of the Board, the highest ranking official in the N'York branch of the World Directorate. Shakily, Miller climbed the three cement steps. Now he was on the porch of the twentieth-century house that made up the center of the exhibit.

It was a nice little house; if he had lived back in those days he would have wanted one of his own. Three bedrooms, a ranch style California bungalow. He pushed open the front door and entered the living room. Fireplace at one end. Dark wine-colored carpets. Modern couch and easy chair. Low hardwood glass-topped coffee table. Copper ashtrays. A cigarette lighter and a stack of magazines. Sleek plastic and steel floor lamps. A bookcase. Television set. Picture window overlooking the front garden. He crossed the room to the hall.

The house was amazingly complete. Below his feet the floor furnace radiated a faint aura of warmth. He peered into the first bedroom. A woman's boudoir. Silk bedcover. White starched sheets. Heavy drapes. A vanity table. Bottles and jars. Huge round mirror. Clothes visible within the closet. A dressing gown thrown over the back of a chair. Slippers. Nylon hose carefully placed at the foot of the bed.

Miller moved down the hall and peered into the next room. Brightly painted wallpaper: clowns and elephants and tight-rope walkers. The children's room. Two little beds for the two boys. Model airplanes. A dresser with a radio on it, pair of combs, school books, pennants, a No Parking sign, snapshots stuck in the mirror. A postage stamp album.

Nobody there, either.

Miller peered in the modern bathroom, even in the yellow-tiled shower. He passed through the dining room, glanced down the basement stairs where the washing machine and dryer were. Then he opened the back door and examined the back yard. A lawn, and the incinerator. A couple of small trees and then the three-dimensional projected backdrop of other houses receding off into incredibly convincing blue hills. And still no one. The yard was empty—deserted. He closed the door and started back.

From the kitchen came laughter.

A woman's laugh. The clink of spoons and dishes. And smells. It took him a moment to identify them, scholar that he was. Bacon and coffee. And hot cakes. Somebody was eating breakfast. A twentieth-century breakfast.

He made his way down the hall, past a man's bedroom, shoes and clothing strewn about, to the entrance of the kitchen.

A handsome late-thirtyish woman and two teenage boys were sitting around the little chrome and plastic breakfast table. They had finished eating; the two boys were fidgeting impatiently. Sunlight filtered through the window over the sink. The electric clock read half past eight. The radio was chirping merrily in the corner. A big pot of black coffee rested in the center of the table, surrounded by empty plates and milk glasses and silverware.

The woman had on a white blouse and checkered tweed skirt. Both boys wore faded blue jeans, sweatshirts, and tennis shoes. As yet they hadn't noticed him. Miller stood frozen at the doorway, while laughter and small talk bubbled around him.

"You'll have to ask your father," the woman was saying, with mock sternness. "Wait until he comes back."

"He already said we could," one of the boys protested.

"Well, ask him again."

"He's always grouchy in the morning."

"Not today. He had a good night's sleep. His hay fever didn't bother him. The new anti-hist the doctor gave him." She glanced up at the clock. "Go see what's keeping him, Don. He'll be late for work."

"He was looking for the newspaper." One of the boys pushed back his chair and got up. "It missed the porch again and fell in the flowers." He turned towards the door, and Miller found himself confronting him face to face. Briefly, the observation flashed through his mind that the boy looked familiar. Damn familiar—like somebody he knew, only younger. He tensed himself for the impact, as the boy abruptly halted.

"Gee," the boy said. "You scared me."

The woman glanced quickly up at Miller. "What are you doing out there, George?" she demanded. "Come on back in here and finish you coffee."

Miller came slowly into the kitchen. The woman was finishing her coffee; both boys were on their feet and beginning to press around him.

"Didn't you tell me I could go camping over the weekend up at Russian River with the group from school?" Don demanded. "You said I could borrow a sleeping bag from the gym because the one I had you gave to the Salvation Army because you were allergic to the kapok in it."

"Yeah," Miller muttered uncertainly. Don. That was the boy's name. And his brother, Ted. But how did he know that? At the table the woman had got up and was collecting the dirty dishes to carry over to the sink. "They said you already promised them," she said over her shoulder. The dishes clattered into the sink and she began sprinkling soap flakes over them. "But you remember that time they wanted to drive the car and the way they said it, you'd think they had got your okay. And they hadn't, of course."

Miller sank weakly down at the table. Aimlessly, he fooled with his pipe. He set it down in the copper ashtray and examined the cuff of his coat. What was happening? His head spun. He got up abruptly and hurried to the window, over the sink.

Houses, streets. The distant hills beyond the town. The sights and sounds of people. The three dimensional projected backdrop was utterly convincing; or was it the projected backdrop? How could he be sure. *What was happening?*

"George, what's the matter?" Marjorie asked, as she tied a pink plastic apron around her waist and began running hot water in the sink. "You better get the car out and get started to work. Weren't you saying last night old man Davidson was shouting about employees being late for work and standing around the water cooler talking and having a good time on company time?"

Davidson. The word stuck in Miller's mind. He knew it, of course. A clear picture leaped up; a tall, white-haired old man, thin and stern. Vest and pocket watch. And the whole office, United Electronic Supply. The twelve-story building in downtown San Francisco. The newspaper and cigar stand in the lobby. The honking cars. Jammed parking lots. The elevator, packed with bright-eyed secretaries, tight sweaters and perfume.

He wandered out of the kitchen, through the hall, past his own bedroom, his wife's, and into the living room. The front door was open and he stepped out on to the porch.

The air was cool and sweet. It was a bright April morning. The lawns were still wet. Cars moved down Virginia Street, towards Shattuck Avenue. Early morning commuting traffic, businessmen on their way to work. Across the street Earl Kelly cheerfully waved his Oakland Tribune as he hurried down the pavement towards the bus stop.

A long way off Miller could see the Bay Bridge, Yerba Buena Island, and Treasure Island. Beyond that was San Francisco itself. In a few minutes he'd be shooting across the bridge in his Buick, on his way to the office. Along with thousands of other businessmen in blue pinstripe suits.

Ted pushed past him and out on the porch. "Then it's okay? You don't care if we go camping?"

Miller licked his dry lips. "Ted, listen to me. There's something strange."

"Like what?"

"I don't know." Miller wandered nervously around on the porch. "This is Friday, isn't it?"

"Sure."

"I thought it was." But how did he know it was Friday? How did he know anything? But of course it was Friday. A long hard week—old man Davidson breathing down his neck. Wednesday, especially, when the General Electric order was slowed down because of a strike.

"Let me ask you something," Miller said to his son. "This morning—I left the kitchen to get the newspaper."

Ted nodded. "Yeah. So?"

"I got up and went out of the room. *How long was I gone?* Not long, was I?" He searched for words, but his mind was a maze of disjointed thoughts. "I was sitting at the breakfast table with you all, and then I got up and went to look for the paper. Right? And then I came back in. Right?" His voice rose desperately. "I got up and shaved and dressed this morning. I ate breakfast. Hot cakes and coffee. Bacon. *Right?*"

"Right," Ted agreed. "So?"

"Like I always do."

"We only have hot cakes on Friday."

Miller nodded slowly. "That's right. Hot cakes on Friday. Because your uncle Frank eats with us Saturday and Sunday and he can't stand hot cakes, so we stopped having them on weekends. Frank is Marjorie's brother. He was in the Marines in the First World War. He was a corporal."

"Good-bye," Ted said, as Don came out to join him. "We'll see you this evening."

School books clutched, the boys sauntered off towards the big modern high school in the center of Berkeley.

Miller re-entered the house and automatically began searching the closet for his briefcase. Where was it? Damn it, he needed it. The whole Throckmorton account was in it; Davidson would be yelling his head off if he left it anywhere, like in the True Blue Cafeteria that time they were all celebrating the Yankees' winning the series. Where the hell was it?

He straightened up slowly, as memory came. Of course. He had left it by his work desk, where he had tossed it after taking out the research tapes. While Fleming was talking to him. Back at the History Agency.

He joined his wife in the kitchen. "Look," he said huskily. "Marjorie, I think maybe I won't go down to the office this morning."

Marjorie spun in alarm. "George, is anything wrong?"

"I'm—completely confused."

"Your hay fever again?"

"No. My mind. What's the name of that psychiatrist the PTA recommended when Mrs. Bentley's kid had that fit?" He searched his disorganized brain. "Grunberg, I think. In the Medical-Dental building." He moved towards the door. "I'll drop by and see him. Something's wrong—really wrong. And I don't know what it is."

❖ ❖ ❖

Adam Grunberg was a large heavy-set man in his late forties, with curly brown hair and horn-rimmed glasses. After Miller had finished, Grunberg cleared his throat, brushed at the sleeve of his Brooks Bros. suit, and asked thoughtfully, "Did anything happen while you were out looking for the newspaper? Any sort of accident? You might try going over that part in detail. You got up from the breakfast table, went out on the porch, and started looking around in the bushes. And then what?"

Miller rubbed his forehead vaguely. "I don't know. It's all confused. I don't remember looking for any newspaper. I remember coming back in the house. Then it gets clear. But before that it's all tied up with the History Agency and my quarrel with Fleming."

"What was that again about your briefcase? Go over that."

"Fleming said it looked like a squashed Jurassic lizard. And I said—"

"No. I mean, about looking for it in the closet and not finding it."

"I looked in the closet and it wasn't there, of course. It's sitting beside my desk at the History Agency. On the Twentieth Century level. By my exhibits." A strange expression crossed Miller's face. "Good God, Grunberg. You realize this may be nothing but an *exhibit?* You and everybody else—maybe you're not real. Just pieces of this exhibit."

"That wouldn't be very pleasant for us, would it?" Grunberg said, with a faint smile.

"People in dreams are always secure until the dreamer wakes up," Miller retorted.

"So you're dreaming me," Grunberg laughed tolerantly. "I suppose I should thank you."

"I'm not here because I especially like you. I'm here because I can't stand Fleming and the whole History Agency."

Grunberg protested. "This Fleming. Are you aware of thinking about him before you went out looking for the newspaper?"

Miller got to his feet and paced around the luxurious office, between the leather-covered chairs and the huge mahogany desk. "I want to face this thing. I'm an exhibit. An artificial replica of the past. Fleming said something like this would happen to me."

"Sit down, Mr. Miller," Grunberg said, in a gentle but commanding voice. When Miller had taken his chair again, Grunberg continued, "I understand what you say. You have a general feeling that every-thing around you is unreal. A sort of stage."

"An exhibit."

"Yes, an exhibit in a museum."

"In the N'York History Agency. Level R, the Twentieth Century level."

"And in addition to this general feeling of—insubstantiality, there are specific projected memories of persons and places beyond this world. Another realm in which this one is contained. Perhaps I should say, the reality within which this is only a sort of shadow world."

"This world doesn't look shadowy to me." Miller struck the leather arm of the chair savagely. "This world is completely real. That's what's wrong. I came in to investigate the noises and now I can't get back out. Good God, do I have to wander around this replica the rest of my life?"

"You know, of course, that your feeling is common to most of mankind. Especially during periods of great tension. Where—by the way—was the newspaper? Did you find it?"

"As far as I'm concerned—"

"Is that a source of irritation with you? I see you react strongly to a mention of the newspaper."

Miller shook his head wearily. "Forget it."

"Yes, a trifle. The paperboy carelessly throws the newspaper in the bushes, not on the porch. It makes you angry. It happens again and again. Early in the day, just as you're starting to work. It seems to symbolize in a small way the whole petty frustrations and defeats of your job. Your whole life."

"Personally, I don't give a damn about the newspaper." Miller examined his wristwatch. "I'm going—it's almost noon. Old man Davidson will be yelling his head off if I'm not at the office by—" He broke off. "There it is again."

"There what is?"

"All this!" Miller gestured impatiently out the window. "This whole place. This damn world. This *exhibition*."

"I have a thought," Doctor Grunberg said slowly. "I'll put it to you for what it's worth. Feel free to reject it if it doesn't fit." He raised his shrewd, professional eyes. "Ever see kids playing with rocket ships?"

"Lord," Miller said wretchedly. "I've seen commercial rocket freighters hauling cargo between Earth and Jupiter, landing at La Guardia Spaceport."

Grunberg smiled slightly. "Follow me through on this. A question. Is it job tension?"

"What do you mean?"

"It would be nice," Grunberg said blandly, "to live in the world of tomorrow. With robots and rocket ships to do all the work. You could just sit back and take it easy. No worries, no cares. No frustrations."

"My position in the History Agency has plenty of cares and frustrations." Miller rose abruptly. "Look, Grunberg. Either this is an exhibit on R level of the History Agency, or I'm a middle-class businessman with an escape fantasy. Right now I can't decide which. One minute I think this is real, and the next minute—"

"We can decide easily," Grunberg said.

"How?"

"You were looking for the newspaper. Down the path, on to the lawn. *Where did it happen?* Was it on the path? On the porch? Try to remember."

"I don't have to try. I was still on the pavement. I had just jumped over the rail past the safety screens."

"On the pavement. Then go back there. Find the exact place."

"Why?"

"So you can prove to yourself there's nothing on the other side."

Miller took a deep slow breath. "Suppose there is?"

"There can't be. You said yourself: only one of the worlds can be real. This world is real—" Grunberg thumped his massive mahogany desk. "Ergo, you won't find anything on the other side."

"Yes," Miller said, after a moment's silence. A peculiar expression cut across his face and stayed there. "You've found the mistake."

"What mistake?" Grunberg was puzzled. "What—"

Miller moved towards the door of the office. "I'm beginning to get it. I've been putting up a false question. Trying to decide which world is real." He grinned humorlessly back at Doctor Grunberg. "They're both real, of course."

He grabbed a taxi and headed back to the house. No one was home. The boys were in school and Marjorie had gone downtown to shop. He waited indoors until he was sure nobody was watching along the street, and then started down the path to the pavement.

He found the spot without any trouble. There was a faint shimmer in the air, a weak place just at the edge of the parking strip. Through it he could see faint shapes.

He was right. There it was—complete and real. As real as the pavement under him.

A long metallic bar was cut off by the edges of the circle. He recognized it; the safety railing he had leaped over to enter the exhibit. Beyond it was the safety screen system. Turned off, of course. And beyond that, the rest of the level and the far walls of the History building.

He took a cautious step into the weak haze. It shimmered around him, misty and oblique. The shapes beyond became clearer. A moving figure in a dark blue robe. Some curious person examining the exhibits. The figure moved on and was lost. He could see his own work desk now. His tape scanner and heaps of study spools. Beside the desk was his briefcase, exactly where he had expected it.

While he was considering stepping over the railing to get the briefcase, Fleming appeared.

Some inner instinct made Miller step back through the weak spot, as Fleming approached. Maybe it was the expression on Fleming's face. In any case, Miller was back and standing firmly on the concrete pavement, when Fleming halted just beyond the juncture, face red, lips twisted with indignation.

"Miller," he said thickly. "Come out of there."

Miller laughed. "Be a good fellow, Fleming. Toss me my briefcase. It's that strange looking thing over by the desk. I showed it to you—remember?"

"Stop playing games and listen to me!" Fleming snapped. "This is serious. *Carnap knows*. I had to inform him."

"Good for you. The loyal bureaucrat."

Miller bent over to light his pipe. He inhaled and puffed a great cloud of gray tobacco smoke through the weak spot, out into the R level. Fleming coughed and retreated.

"What's that stuff?" he demanded.

"Tobacco. One of the things they have around here. Very common substance in the twentieth century. You wouldn't know about that—your period is the second century, B.C. The Hellenistic world. I don't know how well you'd like that. They didn't have very good plumbing back there. Life expectancy was damn short."

"What are you talking about?"

"In comparison, the life expectancy of *my* research period is quite high. And you should see the bathroom I've got. Yellow tile. And a shower. We don't have anything like that at the Agency leisure-quarters."

Fleming grunted sourly. "In other words, you're going to stay in there."

"It's a pleasant place," Miller said easily. "Of course, my position is better than average. Let me describe it for you. I have an attractive wife: marriage is permitted, even sanctioned in this era. I have two fine kids—both boys—who are going up to the Russian River this weekend. They live with me and my wife—we have complete custody of them. The State has no power of that, yet. I have a brand new Buick—"

"Illusions," Fleming spat. "Psychotic delusions."

"Are you sure?"

"You damn fool! I always knew you were too ego-recessive to face reality. You and your anachronistic retreats. Sometimes I'm ashamed I'm a theoretician. I wish I had gone into engineering." Fleming's lips twitched. "You're insane, you know. You're standing in the middle of an artificial exhibit, which is owned by the History Agency, a bundle of plastic and wire and struts. A replica of a past age. An imitation. And you'd rather be there than in the real world."

"Strange," Miller said thoughtfully. "Seems to me I've heard the same thing very recently. You don't know a Doctor Grunberg, do you? A psychiatrist."

Without formality, Director Carnap arrived with his company of assistants and experts. Fleming quickly retreated. Miller found himself facing one of the most powerful figures of the twenty-second century. He grinned and held out his hand.

"You insane imbecile," Carnap rumbled. "Get out of there before we drag you out. If we have to do that, you're through. You know what they do with advanced psychotics. It'll be euthanasia for you. I'll give you one last chance to come out of that fake exhibit—"

"Sorry," Miller said. "It's not an exhibit."

Carnap's heavy face registered sudden surprise. For a brief instant his massive pose vanished. "You still try to maintain—"

"This is a time gate," Miller said quietly. "You can't get me out, Carnap. You can't reach me. I'm in the past, two hundred years back. I've crossed back to a previous existence-coordinate. I found a bridge and escaped from your continuum to this. And there's nothing you can do about it."

Carnap and his experts huddled together in a quick technical conference. Miller waited patiently. He had plenty of time; he had decided not to show up at the office until Monday.

After a while Carnap approached the juncture again, being careful not to step over the safety rail. "An interesting theory, Miller. That's the strange part about psychotics. They rationalize their delusions into a logical system. *A priori*, your concept stands up well. It's internally consistent. Only—"

"Only what?"

"Only it doesn't happen to be true." Carnap had regained his confidence; he seemed to be enjoying the interchange. "You think you're really back in the past. Yes, this exhibit is extremely accurate. Your work has always been good. The authenticity of detail is unequalled by any of the other exhibits."

"I tried to do my work well," Miller murmured.

"You wore archaic clothing and affected archaic speech mannerisms. You did everything possible to throw yourself back. You devoted yourself to your work." Carnap tapped the safety railing with his fingernail. "It would be a shame, Miller. A terrible shame to demolish such an authentic replica."

"I see your point," Miller said, after a time. "I agree with you, certainly. I've been very proud of my work—I'd hate to see it all torn down. But that really won't do you any good. All you'll succeed in doing is closing the time gate."

"You're sure?"

"Of course. The exhibit is only a bridge, a link with the past. I passed *through* the exhibit, but I'm not there now. I'm beyond the exhibit." He grinned tightly. "Your demolition can't reach me. But seal me off, if you want. I don't think I'll be wanting to come back. I wish you could see this side, Carnap. It's a nice place here. Freedom, opportunity. Limited government, responsible to the people. If you don't like a job here you quit. There's no euthanasia, here. Come on over. I'll introduce you to my wife."

"We'll get you," Carnap said. "And all your psychotic figments along with you."

"I doubt if any of my 'psychotic figments' are worried. Grunberg wasn't. I don't think Marjorie is—"

"We've already begun demolition preparations," Carnap said calmly. "We'll do it piece by piece, not all at once. So you may have the opportunity to appreciate the scientific and—*artistic* way we take your imaginary world apart."

"You're wasting your time," Miller said. He turned and walked off, down the pavement, to the gravel path and up on to the front porch of the house.

In the living room he threw himself down in the easy chair and snapped on the television set. Then he went to the kitchen and got a can of ice cold beer. He carried it happily back into the safe, comfortable living room.

As he was seating himself in front of the television set he noticed something rolled up on the low coffee table.

He grinned wryly. It was the morning newspaper, which he had looked so hard for. Marjorie had brought it in with the milk, as usual. And of course forgotten to tell him. He yawned contentedly and reached over to pick it up. Confidently, he unfolded it—and read the big black headlines.

RUSSIA REVEALS COBALT BOMB
TOTAL WORLD DESTRUCTION AHEAD

THE CRAWLERS

He built, and the more he built the more he enjoyed building. Hot sunlight filtered down; summer breezes stirred around him as he toiled joyfully. When he ran out of material he paused awhile and rested. His edifice wasn't large; it was more a practice model than the real thing. One part of his brain told him that, and another part thrilled with excitement and pride. It was at least large enough to enter. He crawled down the entrance tunnel and curled up inside in a contented heap.

Through a rent in the roof a few bits of dirt rained down. He oozed binder fluid and reinforced the weak place. In his edifice the air was clean and cool, almost dust-free. He crawled over the inner walls one last time, leaving a quick-drying coat of binder over everything. What else was needed? He was beginning to feel drowsy; in a moment he'd be asleep.

He thought about it, and then he extended a part of himself up through the still-open entrance. That part watched and listened warily, as the rest of him dozed off in a grateful slumber. He was peaceful and content, conscious that from a distance all that was visible was a light mound of dark clay. No one would notice it: no one would guess what lay beneath.

And if they did notice, he had methods of taking care of them.

❖❖❖

The farmer halted his ancient Ford truck with a grinding shriek of brakes. He cursed and backed up a few yards. "There's one. Hop down and take a look at it. Watch the cars—they go pretty fast along here."

Ernest Gretry pushed the cabin door open and stepped down gingerly onto the hot mid-morning pavement. The air smelled of sun and drying grass. Insects buzzed around him as he advanced cautiously up the highway, hands in his trouser pockets, lean body bent forward. He stopped and peered down.

The thing was well mashed. Wheel marks crossed it in four places and its internal organs had ruptured and burst through. The whole thing was snaillike, a gummy elongated tube with sense organs at one end and a confusing mass of protoplasmic extensions at the other.

What got him most was the face. For a time he couldn't look directly at it: he had to contemplate the road, the hills, the big cedar trees, anything else. There was something in the little dead eyes, a glint that was rapidly fading. They weren't the lusterless eyes of a fish, stupid and vacant. The life he had seen haunted him, and he had got only a brief glimpse, as the truck bore down on it and crushed it flat.

"They crawl across here every once in a while," the farmer said quietly. "Sometimes they get as far as town. The first one I saw was heading down the middle of Grant Street, about fifty yards an hour. They go pretty slow. Some of the teenage kids like to run them down. Personally I avoid them, if I see them."

Gretry kicked aimlessly at the thing. He wondered vaguely how many more there were in the bushes and hills. He could see farmhouses set back from the road, white gleaming squares in the hot Tennessee sun. Horses and sleeping cattle. Dirty chickens scratching. A sleepy, peaceful countryside, basking in the late-summer sun.

"Where's the radiation lab from here?" he asked.

The farmer indicated. "Over there, on the other side of those hills. You want to collect the remains? They have one down at the Standard Oil Station in a big tank. Dead, of course. They filled the tank with kerosene to try to preserve it. That one's in pretty good shape, compared to this. Joe Jackson cracked its head with a two-by-four. He found it crawling across his property one night."

Gretry got shakily back into the truck. His stomach turned over and he had to take some long deep breaths. "I didn't realize there were so many. When they sent me out from Washington they just said a few had been seen."

"There's been quite a lot." The farmer started up the truck and carefully skirted the remains on the pavement. "We're trying to get used to them, but we can't. It's not nice stuff. A lot of people are moving away. You can feel it in the air, a sort of heaviness. We've got this problem and we have to meet it." He increased speed, leathery hands tight around the wheel. "It seems like there's more of *them* born all the time, and almost no normal children."

❖ ❖ ❖

Back in town, Gretry called Freeman long distance from the booth in the shabby hotel lobby. "We'll have to do something. They're all around here. I'm going out at three to see a colony of them. The fellow who runs the taxi stand knows where they are. He says there must be eleven or twelve of them together."

"How do the people around there feel?"

"How the hell do you expect? They think it's God's Judgment. Maybe they're right."

"We should have made them move earlier. We should have cleaned out the whole area for miles around. Then we wouldn't have this problem." Freeman paused. "What do you suggest?"

"That island we took over for the H-bomb tests."

"It's a damn big island. There was a whole group of natives we moved off and resettled." Freeman choked. "Good God, are there *that* many of them?"

"The staunch citizens exaggerate, of course. But I get the impression there must be at least a hundred."

Freeman was silent a long time. "I didn't realize," he said finally. "I'll have to put it through channels, of course. We were going to make further tests on that island. But I see your point."

"I'd like it," Gretry said. "This is a bad business. We can't have things like this. People can't live with this sort of thing. You ought to drop out here and take a look. It's something to remember."

"I'll—see what I can do. I'll talk to Gordon. Give me a ring tomorrow."

Gretry hung up and wandered out of the drab, dirty lobby onto the blazing sidewalk. Dingy stores and parked cars. A few old men hunched over on steps and sagging cane-bottom chairs. He lit a cigarette and shakily examined his watch. It was almost three. He moved slowly toward the taxi stand.

The town was dead. Nothing stirred. Only the motionless old men in their chairs and the out-of-town cars zipping along the highway. Dust and silence lay over everything. Age, like a gray spider web, covered all the houses and stores. No laughter. No sounds of any kind.

No children playing games.

A dirty blue taxicab pulled up silently beside him. "Okay, mister," the driver said, a rat-faced man in his thirties, toothpick hanging between his crooked teeth. He kicked the bent door open. "Here we go."

"How far is it?" Gretry asked, as he climbed in.

"Just outside town." The cab picked up speed and hurtled noisily along, bouncing and bucking. "You from the FBI?"

"No."

"I thought from your suit and hat you was." The driver eyed him curiously. "How'd you hear about the crawlers?"

"From the radiation lab."

"Yeah, it's that hot stuff they got there." The driver turned off the highway and onto a dirt side-road. "It's up here on the Higgins farm. The crazy damn things picked the bottom of old lady Higgins' place to build their houses."

"*Houses?*"

"They've got some sort of city, down under the ground. You'll see it—the entrances, at least. They work together, building and fussing." He twisted the cab off the dirt road, between two huge cedars, over a bumpy field, and finally brought it to rest at the edge of a rocky gully. "This is it."

It was the first time Gretry had seen one alive.

He got out of the cab awkwardly, his legs numb and unresponding. The things were moving slowly between the woods and the entrance tunnels in the center of the clearing. They were bringing building material, clay and weeds. Smearing it with some kind of ooze and plastering it in rough forms which were carefully carried beneath the ground. The crawlers were two or three feet long; some were older than others, darker and heavier. All of them moved with agonizing slowness, a silent flowing motion across the sun-baked ground. They were soft, shell-less, and looked harmless.

Again, he was fascinated and hypnotized by their faces. The weird parody of human faces. Wizened little baby features, tiny shoebutton eyes, slit of a mouth, twisted ears, and a few wisps of damp hair. What should have been arms were elongated pseudopods that grew and receded like soft dough. The crawlers seemed incredibly flexible; they extended themselves, then snapped their bodies back, as their feelers made contact with obstructions. They paid no attention to the two men; they didn't even seem to be aware of them.

"How dangerous are they?" Gretry asked finally.

"Well, they have some sort of stinger. They stung a dog, I know. Stung him pretty hard. He swelled up and his tongue turned black. He had fits and got hard. He died." The driver added half-apologetically, "He was nosing around. Interrupting their building. They work all the time. Keep busy."

"Is this most of them?"

"I guess so. They sort of congregate here. I see them crawling this way." The driver gestured. "See, they're born in different places. One or two at each farmhouse, near the radiation lab."

"Which way is Mrs. Higgins' farmhouse?" Gretry asked.

"Up there. See it through the trees? You want to—"

"I'll be right back," Gretry said, and started abruptly off. "Wait here."

❖ ❖ ❖

The old woman was watering the dark red geraniums that grew around her front porch, when Gretry approached. She looked up quickly, her ancient wrinkled face shrewd and suspicious, the sprinkling can poised like a blunt instrument.

"Afternoon," Gretry said. He tipped his hat and showed her his credentials. "I'm investigating the—crawlers. At the edge of your land."

"Why?" Her voice was empty, bleak, cold. Like her withered face and body.

"We're trying to find a solution." Gretry felt awkward and uncertain. "It's been suggested we transport them away from here, out to an island in the Gulf of Mexico. They shouldn't be here. It's too hard on people. It isn't right," he finished lamely.

"No. It isn't right."

"And we've already begun moving everybody away from the radiation lab. I guess we should have done that a long time ago."

The old woman's eyes flashed. "You people and your machines. See what you've done!" She jabbed a bony finger at him excitedly. "Now you have to fix it. You have to do something."

"We're taking them away to an island as soon as possible. But there's one problem. We have to be sure about the parents. They have complete custody of them. We can't just—" He broke off futilely. "How do they feel? Would they let us cart up their—children, and haul them away?"

Mrs. Higgins turned and headed into the house. Uncertainly,

Gretry followed her through the dim, dusty interior rooms. Musty chambers full of oil lamps and faded pictures, ancient sofas and tables She led him through a great kitchen of immense cast iron pots and pans down a flight of wooden stairs to a painted white door. She knocked sharply.

Flurry and movement on the other side. The sound of people whispering and moving things hurriedly.

"Open the door," Mrs. Higgins commanded. After an agonized pause the door opened slowly. Mrs. Higgins pushed it wide and motioned Gretry to follow her.

In the room stood a young man and woman. They backed away as Gretry came in. The woman hugged a long pasteboard carton which the man had suddenly passed to her.

"Who are you?" the man demanded. He abruptly grabbed the carton back; his wife's small hands were trembling under the shifting weight.

Gretry was seeing the parents of one of them. The young woman, brown-haired, not more than nineteen. Slender and small in a cheap green dress, a full-breasted girl with dark frightened eyes. The man was bigger and stronger, a handsome dark youth with massive arms and competent hands gripping the pasteboard carton tight.

Gretry couldn't stop looking at the carton. Holes had been punched in the top; the carton moved slightly in the man's arms, and there was a faint shudder that rocked it back and forth.

"This man," Mrs. Higgins said to the husband, "has come to take it away."

The couple accepted the information in silence. The husband made no move except to get a better grip on the box.

"He's going to take all of them to an island," Mrs. Higgins said. "It's all arranged. Nobody'll harm them. They'll be safe and they can do what they want. Build and crawl around where nobody has to look at them."

The young woman nodded blankly.

"Give it to him," Mrs. Higgins ordered impatiently. "Give him the box and let's get it over with once and for all."

After a moment the husband carried the box over to a table and put it down. "You know anything about them?" he demanded. "You know what they eat?"

"We—" Gretry began helplessly.

"They eat leaves. Nothing but leaves and grass. We've been bringing in the smallest leaves we could find."

"It's only a month old," the young woman said huskily. "It already wants to go down with the others, but we keep it here. We don't want it to go down here. Not yet. Later, maybe, we thought. We didn't know what to do. We weren't sure." Her large dark eyes flashed briefly in mute appeal, then faded out again. "It's a hard thing to know."

The husband untied the heavy brown twine and took the lid from the carton. "Here. You can see it."

❖ ❖ ❖

It was the smallest Gretry had seen. Pale and soft, less than a foot long. It had crawled in a corner of the box and was curled up in a messy web of chewed leaves and some kind of wax. A translucent covering spun clumsily around it, behind which it lay asleep. It paid no attention to them; they were out of its scope. Gretry felt a strange helpless horror rise up in him. He moved away, and the young man replaced the lid.

"We knew what it was," he said hoarsely. "Right away, as soon as it was born. Up the road, there was one we saw. One of the first. Bob Douglas made us come over and look at it. It was his and Julie's. That was before they started coming down and collecting together by the gully."

"Tell him what happened," Mrs. Higgins said.

"Douglas mashed its head with a rock. Then he poured gasoline on it and burned it up. Last week he and Julie packed and left."

"Have many of them been destroyed?" Gretry managed to ask.

"A few. A lot of men, they see something like that and they go sort of wild. You can't blame them." The man's dark eyes darted hopelessly. "I guess I almost did the same thing."

"Maybe we should have," his wife murmured. "Maybe I should have let you."

Gretry picked up the pasteboard carton and moved toward the door. "We'll get this done as quickly as we can. The trucks are on the way. It should be over in a day."

"Thank God for that," Mrs. Higgins exclaimed in a clipped, emotionless voice. She held the door open, and Gretry carried the carton through the dim, musty house, down the sagging front steps and out into the blazing midafternoon sun.

Mrs. Higgins stopped at the red geraniums and picked up her sprinkling can. "When you take them, take them all. Don't leave any behind. Understand?"

"Yes," Gretry muttered.

"Keep some of your men and trucks here. Keep checking. Don't let any stay where we have to look at them."

"When we get the people near the radiation lab moved away there shouldn't be any more of—"

He broke off. Mrs. Higgins had turned her back and was watering the geraniums. Bees buzzed around her. The flowers swayed dully with the hot wind. The old woman passed on around the side of the house, still watering and stooping over. In a few moments she was gone and Gretry was alone with his carton.

Embarrassed and ashamed, he carried the carton slowly down the hill and across the field to the ravine. The taxi driver was standing by his cab, smoking a cigarette and waiting patiently for him. The colony of crawlers was working steadily on its city. There were streets and passages. On some of the entrance-mounds he noticed intricate scratches that might have been words. Some of the crawlers were grouped together, setting up involved things he couldn't make out.

"Let's go," he said wearily to the driver.

The driver grinned and yanked the back door. "I left the meter running," he said, his ratty face bright with craft. "You guys all have a swindle sheet—you don't care."

❖ ❖ ❖

He built, and the more he built the more he enjoyed building. By now the city was over eighty miles deep and five miles in diameter. The whole island had been converted into a single vast city that honeycombed and interlaced farther each day. Eventually it would reach the land beyond the ocean; then the work would begin in earnest.

To his right, a thousand methodically moving companions toiled silently on the structural support that was to reinforce the main breeding chamber. As soon as it was in place everyone would feel better; the mothers were just now beginning to bring forth their young.

That was what worried him. It took some of the joy out of building. He had seen one of the first born—before it was quickly hidden and the thing hushed up. A brief glimpse of a bulbous head, foreshortened body, incredibly rigid extensions. It shrieked and wailed and turned red in the face. Gurgled and plucked aimlessly and kicked its *feet.*

In horror, somebody had finally mashed the throwback with a rock. And hoped there wouldn't be any more.

SALES PITCH

Commute ships roared on all sides, as Ed Morris made his way wearily home to Earth at the end of a long hard day at the office. The Ganymede-Terra lanes were choked with exhausted, grim-faced businessmen; Jupiter was in opposition to Earth and the trip was a good two hours. Every few million miles the great flow slowed to a grinding, agonized halt; signal-lights flashed as streams from Mars and Saturn fed into the main traffic-arteries.

"Lord," Morris muttered. "How tired can you *get?*" He locked the autopilot and momentarily turned from the control-board to light a much-needed cigarette. His hands shook. His head swam. It was past six; Sally would be fuming; dinner would be spoiled. The same old thing. Nerve-wracking driving, honking horns and irate drivers zooming past his little ship, furious gesturing, shouting, cursing . . .

And the ads. That was what really did it. He could have stood everything else—but the ads, the whole long way from Ganymede to Earth. And on Earth, the swarms of sales robots; it was too much. And they were everywhere.

He slowed to avoid a fifty-ship smashup. Repair-ships were scurrying around trying to get the debris out of the lane. His audio-speaker wailed as police rockets hurried up. Expertly, Morris raised his ship, cut between two slow-moving commercial transports, zipped momentarily into the unused left lane, and then sped on, the wreck left behind. Horns honked furiously at him; he ignored them.

"Trans-Solar Products greets you!" an immense voice boomed in his ear. Morris groaned and hunched down in his seat. He was getting near Terra; the barrage was increasing. "Is your tension-index pushed over the safety-margin by the ordinary frustrations of the day? Then you need an Id-Persona Unit. So small it can be worn behind the ear, close to the frontal lobe—"

Thank God, he was past it. The ad dimmed and receded behind, as his fast-moving ship hurtled forward. But another was right ahead.

"Drivers! Thousands of unnecessary deaths each year from inter-planet driving. Hypno-Motor Control from an expert source-point insures your safety. Surrender your body and save your life!" The voice roared louder. "Industrial experts say—"

Both audio ads, the easiest to ignore. But now a visual ad was forming; he winced, closed his eyes, but it did no good.

"Men!" an unctuous voice thundered on all sides of him. "Banish internally-caused obnoxious odors *forever*. Removal by modern pain-less methods of the gastrointestinal tract and substitution system will relieve you of the most acute cause of social rejection." The visual image locked; a vast nude girl, blonde hair disarranged, blue eyes half shut, lips parted, head tilted back in sleep-drugged ecstasy. The features ballooned as the lips approached his own. Abruptly the orgi-astic expression on the girl's face vanished. Disgust and revulsion swept across, and then the image faded out.

"Does this happen to you?" the voice boomed. "During erotic sex-play do you offend your love-partner by the presence of gastric processes which—"

The voice died, and he was past. His mind his own again, Morris kicked savagely at the throttle and sent the little ship leaping. The pressure, applied directly to the audio-visual regions of his brain, had faded below spark point. He groaned and shook his head to clear it. All around him the vague half-defined echoes of ads glittered and gibbered, like ghosts of distant video-stations. Ads waited on all sides; he steered a careful course, dexterity born of animal desperation, but not all could be avoided. Despair seized him. The outline of a new visual-audio ad was already coming into being.

"You, mister wage-earner!" it shouted into the eyes and ears, noses and throats, of a thousand weary commuters. "Tired of the same old job? Wonder Circuits Inc. has perfected a marvelous long-range thoughtwave scanner. Know what others are thinking and saying. Get the edge on fellow employees. Learn facts, figures about your employer's personal existence. Banish uncertainty!"

Morris' despair swept up wildly. He threw the throttle on full blast; the little ship bucked and rolled as it climbed from the traffic-lane into the dead zone beyond. A shrieking roar, as his fender whipped through the protective wall—and then the ad faded behind him.

He slowed down, trembling with misery and fatigue. Earth lay ahead. He'd be home, soon. Maybe he could get a good night's sleep. He shakily dropped the nose of the ship and prepared to hook onto the tractor beam of the Chicago commute field.

"The best metabolism adjuster on the market," the salesrobot shrilled. "Guaranteed to maintain a perfect endocrine-balance, or your money refunded in full."

Morris pushed wearily past the salesrobot, up the sidewalk toward the residential-block that contained his living-unit. The robot followed a few steps, then forgot him and hurried after another grim-faced commuter.

"All the news while it's news," a metallic voice dinned at him. "Have a retinal vidscreen installed in your least-used eye. Keep in touch with the world; don't wait for out-of-date hourly summaries."

"*Get out of the way*," Morris muttered. The robot stepped aside for him and he crossed the street with a pack of hunched-over men and women.

❖ ❖ ❖

Robot-salesmen were everywhere, gesturing, pleading, shrilling. One started after him and he quickened his pace. It scurried along, chanting its pitch and trying to attract his attention, all the way up the hill to his living-unit. It didn't give up until he stooped over, snatched up a rock, and hurled it futilely. He scrambled in the house and slammed the doorlock after him. The robot hesitated, then turned and raced after a woman with an armload of packages toiling up the hill. She tried vainly to elude it, without success.

"Darling!" Sally cried. She hurried from the kitchen, drying her hands on her plastic shorts, bright-eyed and excited. "Oh, you poor thing! You look so tired!"

Morris peeled off his hat and coat and kissed his wife briefly on her bare shoulder. "What's for dinner?"

Sally gave his hat and coat to the closet. "We're having Uranian wild pheasant; your favorite dish."

Morris' mouth watered, and a tiny surge of energy crawled back into his exhausted body. "No kidding? What the hell's the occasion?"

His wife's brown eyes moistened with compassion. "Darling, it's your birthday; you're thirty-seven years old today. Had you forgotten?"

"Yeah," Morris grinned a little. "I sure had." He wandered into the kitchen. The table was set; coffee was steaming in the cups and there was butter and white bread, mashed potatoes and green peas. "My golly. A real occasion."

Sally punched the stove controls and the container of smoking pheasant was slid onto the table and neatly sliced open. "Go wash your hands and we're ready to eat. Hurry—before it gets cold."

Morris presented his hands to the wash slot and then sat down gratefully at the table. Sally served the tender, fragrant pheasant, and the two of them began eating.

"Sally," Morris said, when his plate was empty and he was leaning back and sipping slowly at his coffee. "I can't go on like this. Something's got to be done."

1

2

3

194   PHILIP K. DICK

"You mean the drive? I wish you could get a position on Mars like Bob Young. Maybe if you talked to the Employment Commission and explained to them how all the strain—"

"It's not just the drive. *They're right out front*. Everywhere. Waiting for me. All day and night."

"Who are, dear?"

"Robots selling things. As soon as I set down the ship. Robots and visual-audio ads. They dig right into a man's brain. They follow people around until they die."

"I know." Sally patted his hand sympathetically. "When I go shopping they follow me in clusters. All talking at once. It's really a panic—you can't understand half what they're saying."

"We've got to break out."

"Break out?" Sally faltered. "What do you mean?"

"We've got to get away from them. They're destroying us."

Morris fumbled in his pocket and carefully got out a tiny fragment of metal-foil. He unrolled it with painstaking care and smoothed it out on the table. "Look at this. It was circulated in the office, among the men; it got to me and I kept it."

"What does it mean?" Sally's brow wrinkled as she made out the words. "Dear, I don't think you got all of it. There must be more than this."

"A new world," Morris said softly. "Where they haven't got to, yet. It's a long way off, out beyond the solar system. Out in the stars."

"Proxima?"

"Twenty planets. Half of them habitable. Only a few thousand people out there. Families, workmen, scientists, some industrial survey teams. Land free for the asking."

"But it's so—" Sally made a face. "Dear, isn't it sort of under-developed? They say it's like living back in the twentieth century. Flush toilets, bathtubs, gasoline driven cars—"

"That's right." Morris rolled up the bit of crumpled metal, his face grim and dead-serious. "It's a hundred years behind times. None of this." He indicated the stove and the furnishings in the living room. "We'll have to do without. We'll have to get used to a simpler life. The way our ancestors lived." He tried to smile but his face wouldn't cooperate. "You think you'd like it? No ads, no salesrobots, traffic moving at sixty miles an hour instead of sixty million. We could raise passage on one of the big trans-system liners. I could sell my commute rocket . . . "

There was a hesitant, doubtful silence.

"Ed," Sally began. "I think we should think it over more. What about your job? What would you do out there?"

"I'd find something."

"But *what*? Haven't you got that part figured out?" A shrill tinge of annoyance crept into her voice. "It seems to me we should consider that part just a little more before we throw away everything and just—take off."

"If we don't go," Morris said slowly, trying to keep his voice steady, "they'll get us. There isn't much time left. I don't know how much longer I can hold them off."

"Really, Ed! You make it sound so melodramatic. If you feel that bad why don't you take some time off and have a complete inhibition check? I was watching a vidprogram and I saw them going over a man whose psychosomatic system was much worse than yours. A much older man."

She leaped to her feet. "Let's go out tonight and celebrate. Okay?" Her slim fingers fumbled at the zipper of her shorts. "I'll put on my new plastirobe, the one I've never had nerve enough to wear."

Her eyes sparkled with excitement as she hurried into the bedroom. "You know the one I mean? When you're up close it's translucent but as you get farther off it becomes more and more sheer until—"

"I know the one," Morris said wearily. "I've seen them advertised on my way home from work." He got slowly to his feet and wandered into the living room. At the door of the bedroom he halted. "Sally—"

"Yes?"

Morris opened his mouth to speak. He was going to ask her again, talk to her about the metal-foil fragment he had carefully wadded up and carried home. He was going to talk to her about the frontier. About Proxima Centauri. Going away and never coming back. But he never had a chance.

The doorchimes sounded.

"Somebody's at the door!" Sally cried excitedly. "Hurry up and see who it is!"

❖ ❖ ❖

In the evening darkness the robot was a silent, unmoving figure. A cold wind blew around it and into the house. Morris shivered and moved back from the door. "What do you want?" he demanded. A strange fear licked at him. "What is it?"

The robot was larger than any he had seen. Tall and broad, with heavy metallic grippers and elongated eye-lenses. Its upper trunk was a square tank instead of the usual cone. It rested on four treads, not the customary two. It towered over Morris, almost seven feet high. Massive and solid.

"Good evening," it said calmly. Its voice was whipped around by the night wind; it mixed with the dismal noises of evening, the echoes of traffic and the clang of distant street signals. A few vague shapes hurried through the gloom. The world was black and hostile.

"Evening," Morris responded automatically. He found himself trembling. "What are you selling?"

"I would like to show you a fasrad," the robot said.

Morris' mind was numb; it refused to respond. What was a *fasrad*? There was something dreamlike and nightmarish going on. He struggled to get his mind and body together. "A what?" he croaked.

"A fasrad." The robot made no effort to explain. It regarded him without emotion, as if it was not its responsibility to explain anything. "It will take only a moment."

"I—" Morris began. He moved back, out of the wind. And the robot, without change of expression, glided past him and into the house.

"Thank you," it said. It halted in the middle of the living room. "Would you call your wife, please? I would like to show her the fasrad, also."

"Sally," Morris muttered helplessly. "Come here."

Sally swept breathlessly into the living room, her breasts quivering with excitement. "What is it? Oh!" She saw the robot and halted uncertainly. "Ed, did you order something? Are we buying something?"

"Good evening," the robot said to her. "I am going to show you the fasrad. Please be seated. On the couch, if you will. Both together."

Sally sat down expectantly, her cheeks flushed, eyes bright with wonder and bewilderment. Numbly, Ed seated himself beside her. "Look," he muttered thickly. "What the hell is a fasrad? *What's going on?* I don't want to buy anything!"

"What is your name?" the robot asked him.

"Morris." He almost choked. "Ed Morris."

The robot turned to Sally. "Mrs. Morris." It bowed slightly. "I'm glad to meet you, Mr. and Mrs. Morris. You are the first persons in your neighborhood to see the fasrad. This is the initial demonstration in this area." Its cold eyes swept the room. "Mr. Morris, you are employed, I assume. Where are you employed?"

"He works on Ganymede," Sally said dutifully, like a little girl in school. "For the Terran Metals Development Co."

The robot digested this information. "A fasrad will be of value to you." It eyed Sally. "What do you do?"

"I'm a tape transcriber at Histo-Research."

"A fasrad will be of no value in your professional work, but it will be helpful here in the home." It picked up a table in its powerful steel grippers. "For example, sometimes an attractive piece of furniture is damaged by a clumsy guest." The robot smashed the table to bits; fragments of wood and plastic rained down. "A fasrad is needed."

Morris leaped helplessly to his feet. He was powerless to halt events; a numbing weight hung over him, as the robot tossed the fragments of table away and selected a heavy floor lamp.

"Oh dear," Sally gasped. "That's my best lamp."

"When a fasrad is possessed, there is nothing to fear." The robot seized the lamp and twisted it grotesquely. It ripped the shade, smashed the bulbs, then threw away the remnants. "A situation of this kind can occur from some violent explosion, such as an H-Bomb."

"For God's sake," Morris muttered. "We—"

"An H-Bomb attack may never occur," the robot continued, "but in such an event a fasrad is indispensable." It knelt down and pulled an intricate tube from its waist. Aiming the tube at the floor it atomized a hole five feet in diameter. It stepped back from the yawning pocket. "I have not extended this tunnel, but you can see a fasrad would save your life in case of attack."

The word *attack* seemed to set off a new train of reactions in its metal brain.

"Sometimes a thug or hood will attack a person at night," it continued. Without warning it whirled and drove its fist through the wall. A section of the wall collapsed in a heap of powder and debris. "That takes care of the thug." The robot straightened out and peered around the room. "Often you are too tired in the evening to manipulate the buttons on the stove." It strode into the kitchen and began punching the stove controls; immense quantities of food spilled in all directions.

"Stop!" Sally cried. "Get away from my stove!"

"You may be too weary to run water for your bath." The robot tripped the controls of the tub and water poured down. "Or you may wish to go right to bed." It yanked the bed from its concealment and threw it flat. Sally retreated in fright as the robot advanced toward her. "Sometimes after a hard day at work you are too tired to remove your clothing. In that event—"

"Get out of here!" Morris shouted at it. "Sally, run and get the cops. The thing's gone crazy. *Hurry.*"

"The fasrad is a necessity in all modern homes," the robot continued. "For example, an appliance may break down. The fasrad repairs it instantly." It seized the automatic humidity control and tore the wiring and replaced it on the wall. "Sometimes you would prefer not to go to work. The fasrad is permitted by law to occupy your position for a consecutive period not to exceed ten days. If, after that period—"

"Good God," Morris said, as understanding finally came. "You're the fasrad."

"That's right," the robot agreed. "Fully Automatic Self-Regulating Android (Domestic). There is also the fasrac (Construction), the fasram (Managerial), the fasras (Soldier), and the fasrab (Bureaucrat). I am designed for home use."

"You—" Sally gasped. "You're for sale. You're selling yourself."

"I am demonstrating myself," the fasrad, the robot, answered. Its impassive metal eyes were fixed intently on Morris as it continued, "I am sure, Mr. Morris, you would like to own me. I am reasonably priced and fully guaranteed. A full book of instructions is included. I cannot conceive of taking *no* for an answer."

❖ ❖ ❖

At half past twelve, Ed Morris still sat at the foot of the bed, one shoe on, the other in his hand. He gazed vacantly ahead. He said nothing.

"For heaven's sake," Sally complained. "Finish untying that knot and get into bed; you have to be up at five-thirty."

Morris fooled aimlessly with the shoelace. After a while he dropped the shoe and tugged at the other one. The house was cold and silent. Outside, the dismal night-wind whipped and lashed at the cedars that grew along the side of the building. Sally lay curled up beneath the radiant-lens, a cigarette between her lips, enjoying the warmth and half-dozing.

In the living room stood the fasrad. It hadn't left. It was still there, was waiting for Morris to buy it.

"Come on!" Sally said sharply. "What's wrong with you? It fixed all the things it broke; it was just demonstrating itself." She sighed drowsily. "It certainly gave me a scare. I thought something had gone wrong with it. They certainly had an inspiration, sending it around to sell itself to people."

Morris said nothing.

Sally rolled over on her stomach and languidly stubbed out her cigarette. "That's not so much, is it? Ten thousand gold units, and if we get our friends to buy one we get a five per cent commission. All we have to do is show it. It isn't as if we had to *sell* it. It sells itself." She giggled. "They always wanted a product that sold itself, didn't they?"

Morris untied the knot in his shoelace. He slid his shoe back on and tied it tight.

"What are you doing?" Sally demanded angrily. "You come to bed!" She sat up furiously, as Morris left the room and moved slowly down the hall. "Where are you going?"

In the living room, Morris switched on the light and sat down facing the fasrad. "Can you hear me?" he said.

"Certainly," the fasrad answered. "I'm never inoperative. Sometimes an emergency occurs at night: a child is sick or an accident takes place. You have no children as yet, but in the event—"

"Shut up," Morris said, "I don't want to hear you."

"You asked me a question. Self-regulating androids are plugged in to a central information exchange. Sometimes a person wishes immediate information; the fasrad is always ready to answer any theoretical or factual inquiry. Anything not metaphysical."

Morris picked up the book of instructions and thumbed it. The fasrad did thousands of things; it never wore out; it was never at a loss; it couldn't make a mistake. He threw the book away. "I'm not going to buy you," he said to it. "Never. Not in a million years."

"Oh, yes you are," the fasrad corrected. "This is an opportunity you can't afford to miss." There was calm, metallic confidence in its voice. "You can't turn me down, Mr. Morris. A fasrad is an indispensable necessity in the modern home."

"Get out of here," Morris said evenly. "Get out of my house and don't come back."

"I'm not your fasrad to order around. Until you've purchased me at the regular list price, I'm responsible only to Self-Regulating Android Inc. Their instructions were to the contrary; I'm to remain with you until you buy me."

"Suppose I never buy you?" Morris demanded, but in his heart ice formed even as he asked. Already he felt the cold terror of the answer that was coming; there could be no other.

"I'll continue to remain with you," the fasrad said, "eventually you'll buy me." It plucked some withered roses from a vase on the mantel and dropped them into its disposal slot. "You will see more and more situations in which a fasrad is indispensable. Eventually you'll wonder how you ever existed without one."

"Is there anything you can't do?"

"Oh, yes; there's a great deal I can't do. But I can do anything *you* can do—and considerably better."

Morris let out his breath slowly. "I'd be insane to buy you."

"You've got to buy me," the impassive voice answered. The fasrad extended a hollow pipe and began cleaning the carpet. "I am useful in all situations. Notice how fluffy and free of dust this rug is." It withdrew the pipe and extended another. Morris coughed and staggered quickly away; clouds of white particles billowed out and filled every part of the room.

"I am spraying for moths," the fasrad explained.

The white cloud turned to an ugly blue-black. The room faded into ominous darkness; the fasrad was a dim shape moving methodically about in the center. Presently the cloud lifted and the furniture emerged.

"I sprayed for harmful bacteria," the fasrad said.

It painted the walls of the room and constructed new furniture to go with them. It reinforced the ceiling in the bathroom. It increased the number of heat-vents from the furnace. It put in new electrical wiring. It tore out all the fixtures in the kitchen and assembled more modern ones. It examined Morris' financial accounts and computed his income tax for the following year. It sharpened all the pencils; it caught hold of his wrist and quickly diagnosed his high blood-pressure as psychosomatic.

"You'll feel better after you've turned responsibility over to me," it explained. It threw out some old soup Sally had been saving. "Danger of botulism," it told him. "Your wife is sexually attractive, but not capable of a high order of intellectualization."

Morris went to the closet and got his coat.

"Where are you going?" the fasrad asked.

"To the office."

"At this time of night?"

Morris glanced briefly into the bedroom. Sally was sound asleep under the soothing radiant-lens. Her slim body was rosy pink and healthy, her face free of worry. He closed the front door and hurried down the steps into the darkness. Cold night wind slashed at him as he approached the parking lot. His little commute ship was parked with hundreds of others; a quarter sent the attendant robot obediently after it.

In ten minutes he was on his way to Ganymede.

❖ ❖ ❖

The fasrad boarded his ship when he stopped at Mars to refuel.

"Apparently you don't understand," the fasrad said. "My instructions are to demonstrate myself until you're satisfied. As yet, you're not wholly convinced; further demonstration is necessary." It passed an intricate web over the controls of the ship until all the dials and meters were in adjustment. "You should have more frequent servicing."

It retired to the rear to examine the drive jets. Morris numbly signalled the attendant, and the ship was released from the fuel pumps. He gained speed and the small sandy planet fell behind. Ahead, Jupiter loomed.

"Your jets aren't in good repair," the fasrad said, emerging from the rear. "I don't like that knock to the main brake drive. As soon as you land I'll make extensive repair."

"The Company doesn't mind your doing favors for me?" Morris asked, with bitter sarcasm.

"The Company considers me your fasrad. An invoice will be mailed to you at the end of the month." The robot whipped out a pen and a pad of forms. "I'll explain the four easy-payment plans. Ten thousand gold units cash means a three per cent discount. In addition, a number of household items may be traded in—items you won't have further need for. If you wish to divide the purchase in four parts, the first is due at once, and the last in ninety days."

"I always pay cash," Morris muttered. He was carefully resetting the route positions on the control board.

"There's no carrying charge for the ninety day plan. For the six month plan there's a six per cent per annum charge which will amount to approximately—" It broke off. "We've changed course."

❖ ❖ ❖

"We've left the official traffic lane." The fasrad stuck its pen and pad away and hurried to the control board. "What are you doing? There's a two unit fine for this."

Morris ignored it. He hung on grimly to the controls and kept his eyes on the viewscreen. The ship was gaining speed rapidly. Warning buoys sounded angrily as he shot past them and into the bleak darkness of space beyond. In a few seconds they had left all traffic behind.

They were alone, shooting rapidly away from Jupiter, out into deep space.

The fasrad computed the trajectory. "We're moving out of the solar system. Toward Centaurus."

"You guessed it."

"Hadn't you better call your wife?"

Morris grunted and notched the drive bar farther up. The ship bucked and pitched, then managed to right itself. The jets began to whine ominously. Indicators showed the main turbines were beginning to heat. He ignored them and threw on the emergency fuel supply.

"I'll call Mrs. Morris," the fasrad offered. "We'll be beyond range in a short while."

"Don't bother."

"She'll worry." The fasrad hurried to the back and examined the jets again. It popped back into the cabin buzzing with alarm. "Mr. Morris, this ship is not equipped for inter-system travel. It's a Class D four-shaft domestic model for home consumption only. It was never made to stand this velocity."

"To get to Proxima," Morris answered, "we need this velocity."

The fasrad connected its power cables to the control board. "I can take some of the strain off the wiring system. But unless you rev her back to normal I can't be responsible for the deterioration of the jets."

"The hell with the jets."

The fasrad was silent. It was listening intently to the growing whine under them. The whole ship shuddered violently. Bits of paint drifted down. The floor was hot from the grinding shafts. Morris' foot stayed on the throttle. The ship gained more velocity as Sol fell behind. They were out of the charted area. Sol receded rapidly.

"It's too late to vid your wife," the fasrad said. "There are three emergency-rockets in the stern; if you want, I'll fire them off in the hope of attracting a passing military transport."

"Why?"

"They can take us in tow and return us to the Sol system. There's a six hundred gold unit fine, but under the circumstances it seems to me the best policy."

Morris turned his back to the fasrad and jammed down the throttle with all his weight. The whine had grown to a violent roar. Instruments smashed and cracked. Fuses blew up and down the board. The lights dimmed, faded, then reluctantly came back.

"Mr. Morris," the fasrad said, "you must prepare for death. The statistical probabilities of turbine explosion are seventy-thirty. I'll do what I can, but the danger-point has already passed."

Morris returned to the viewscreen. For a time he gazed hungrily up at the growing dot that was the twin star Centaurus. "They look all right, don't they? Prox is the important one. Twenty planets." He examined the wildly fluttering instruments. "How are the jets holding up? I can't tell from these; most of them are burned out."

The fasrad hesitated. It started to speak, then changed its mind. "I'll go back and examine them," it said. It moved to the rear of the ship and disappeared down the short ramp into the thundering, vibrating engine chamber.

Morris leaned over and put out his cigarette. He waited a moment longer, then reached out and yanked the drives full up, the last possible notch on the board.

The explosion tore the ship in half. Sections of hull hurtled around him. He was lifted weightless and slammed into the control board. Metal and plastic rained down on him. Flashing incandescent points winked, faded, and finally died into silence, and there was nothing but cold ash.

❖❖❖

The dull *swish-swish* of emergency air-pumps brought consciousness back. He was pinned under the wreckage of the control board; one arm was broken and bent under him. He tried to move his legs but there was no sensation below his waist.

The splintered debris that had been his ship was still hurling toward Centaurus. Hull-sealing equipment was feebly trying to patch the gaping holes. Automatic temperature and grav feeds were thumping spasmodically from self-contained batteries. In the viewscreen the vast flaming bulk of the twin suns grew quietly, inexorably.

He was glad. In the silence of the ruined ship he lay buried beneath the debris, gratefully watching the growing bulk. It was a beautiful sight. He had wanted to see it for a long time. There it was, coming closer each moment. In a day or two the ship would plunge into the fiery mass and be consumed. But he could enjoy this interval; there was nothing to disturb his happiness..

He thought about Sally, sound asleep under the radiant-lens. Would Sally have liked Proxima? Probably not. Probably she would have wanted to go back home as soon as possible. This was something he had to enjoy alone. This was for him only. A vast peace descended over him. He could lie here without stirring, and the flaming magnificence would come nearer and nearer . . .

A sound. From the heaps of fused wreckage something was rising. A twisted, dented shape dimly visible in the flickering glare of the viewscreen. Morris managed to turn his head.

The fasrad staggered to a standing position. Most of its trunk was gone, smashed and broken away. It tottered, then pitched forward on its face with a grinding crash. Slowly it inched its way toward him, then settled to a dismal halt a few feet off. Gears whirred creakily. Relays popped open and shut. Vague, aimless life animated its devastated hulk.

"Good evening," its shrill, metallic voice grated.

Morris screamed. He tried to move his body but the ruined beams held him tight. He shrieked and shouted and tried to crawl away from it. He spat and wailed and wept.

"I would like to show you a fasrad," the metallic voice continued.

"Would you call your wife, please? I would like to show her a fasrad, too."

"Get away!" Morris screamed. "Get away from me!"

"Good evening," the fasrad continued, like a broken tape. "Good evening. Please be seated. I am happy to meet you. What is your name? Thank you. You are the first persons in your neighborhood to see the fasrad. Where are you employed?"

Its dead eye-lenses gaped at him empty and vacant.

"Please be seated," it said again. "This will take only a second. Only a second. This demonstration will take only a—"

UPON THE DULL EARTH

Silvia ran laughing through the night brightness, between the roses and cosmos and Shasta daisies, down the gravel path and beyond the heaps of sweet-tasting grass swept from the lawns. Stars, caught in pools of water, glittered everywhere, as she brushed through them to the slope beyond the brick wall. Cedars supported the sky and ignored the slim shape squeezing past, her brown hair flying, her eyes flashing.

"Wait for me," Rick complained, as he cautiously threaded his way after her, along the half familiar path. Silvia danced on without stopping. "Slow down!" he shouted angrily.

"Can't—we're late." Without warning, Silvia appeared in front of him, blocking the path. "Empty your pockets," she gasped, her gray eyes sparkling. "Throw away all metal. You know they can't stand metal."

Rick searched his pockets. In his overcoat were two dimes and a fifty-cent piece. "Do these count?"

"*Yes!*" Silvia snatched the coins and threw them into the dark heaps of calla lilies. The bits of metal hissed into the moist depths and were gone. "Anything else?" She caught hold of his arm anxiously. "They're already on their way. Anything else, Rick?"

"Just my watch." Rick pulled his wrist away as Silvia's wild fingers snatched for the watch. "*That's* not going in the bushes."

"Then lay it on the sundial—or the wall. Or in a hollow tree." Silvia raced off again. Her excited, rapturous voice danced back to him. "Throw away your cigarette case. And your keys, your belt buckle—everything metal. You know how they hate metal. Hurry, we're late!"

Rick followed sullenly after her. "All right, *witch*."

Silvia snapped at him furiously from the darkness. "Don't *say* that! It isn't true. You've been listening to my sisters and my mother and—"

Her words were drowned out by the sound. Distant flapping, a long way off, like vast leaves rustling in a winter storm. The night sky was alive with the frantic poundings; they were coming very quickly this time. They were too greedy, too desperately eager to wait. Flickers of fear touched the man and he ran to catch up with Silvia.

Silvia was a tiny column of green skirt and blouse in the center of the thrashing mass. She was pushing them away with one arm and trying to manage the faucet with the other. The churning activity of wings and bodies twisted her like a reed. For a time she was lost from sight.

"Rick!" she called faintly. "Come here and help!" She pushed them away and struggled up. "They're suffocating me!"

Rick fought his way through the wall of flashing white to the edge of the trough. They were drinking greedily at the blood that spilled from the wooden faucet. He pulled Silvia close against him; she was terrified and trembling. He held her tight until some of the violence and fury around them had died down.

"They're hungry," Silvia gasped feebly.

"You're a little cretin for coming ahead. They can sear you to ash!"

"I know. They can do anything." She shuddered, excited and frightened. "Look at them," she whispered, her voice husky with awe. "Look at the size of them—their wing-spread. And they're *white*, Rick. Spotless—perfect. There's nothing in our world as spotless as that. Great and clean and wonderful."

"They certainly wanted the lamb's blood."

Silvia's soft hair blew against his face as the wings fluttered on all sides. They were leaving now, roaring up into the sky. Not up, really—away. Back to their own world whence they had scented the blood. But it was not only the blood—they had come because of Silvia. *She* had attracted them.

The girl's gray eyes were wide. She reached up towards the rising white creatures. One of them swooped close. Grass and flowers sizzled as blinding white flames roared in a brief fountain. Rick scrambled away. The flaming figure hovered momentarily over Silvia and then there was a hollow *pop*. The last of the white-winged giants was gone. The air, the ground, gradually cooled into darkness and silence.

"I'm sorry," Silvia whispered.

"Don't do it again," Rick managed. He was numb with shock. "It isn't safe."

"Sometimes I forget. I'm sorry, Rick. I didn't mean to draw them so close." She tried to smile. "I haven't been that careless in months. Not since that other time, when I first brought you out here." The avid, wild look slid across her face. "Did you *see* him? Power and flames! And he didn't even touch us. He just—looked at us. That was all. And everything's burned up, all around."

Rick grabbed hold of her. "Listen," he grated. "You mustn't call them again. It's wrong. This isn't their world."

"It's not wrong—it's beautiful."

"It's not safe!" His fingers dug into her flesh until she gasped. "Stop tempting them down here!"

Silvia laughed hysterically. She pulled away from him, out into the blasted circle that the horde of angels had seared behind them as they rose into the sky. "I can't *help* it," she cried. "I belong with them. They're my family, my people. Generations of them, back into the past."

"What do you mean?"

"They're my ancestors. And some day I'll join them."

"You are a little witch!" Rick shouted furiously.

"No," Silvia answered. "Not a witch, Rick. Don't you see? I'm a saint."

❖ ❖ ❖

The kitchen was warm and bright. Silvia plugged in the Silex and got a big red can of coffee down from the cupboards over the sink. "You mustn't listen to them," she said, as she set out plates and cups and got cream from the refrigerator. "You know they don't understand. Look at them in there."

Silvia's mother and her sisters, Betty Lou and Jean, stood huddled together in the living room, fearful and alert, watching the young couple in the kitchen. Walter Everett was standing by the fireplace, his face blank, remote.

"Listen to *me*," Rick said. "You have this power to attract them. You mean you're not—isn't Walter your real father?"

"Oh, yes—of course he is. I'm completely human. Don't I look human?"

"But you're the only one who has the power."

"I'm not physically different," Silvia said thoughtfully. "I have the ability to see, that's all. Others have had it before me—saints, martyrs. When I was a child, my mother read to me about St. Bernadette. Remember where her cave was? Near a hospital. They were hovering there and she saw one of them."

"But the blood! It's grotesque. There never was anything like that."

"Oh, yes. The blood draws them, lamb's blood especially. They hover over battlefields. Valkyries—carrying off the dead to Valhalla. That's why saints and martyrs cut and mutilate themselves. You know where I got the idea?"

Silvia fastened a little apron around her waist and filled the Silex with coffee. "When I was nine years old, I read of it in Homer, in the

Odyssey. Ulysses dug a trench in the ground and filled it with blood to attract the spirits. The shades from the nether world."

"That's right," Rick admitted reluctantly. "I remember."

"The ghosts of people who died. They had lived once. Everybody lives here, then dies and goes there." Her face glowed. "We're all going to have wings! We're all going to fly. We'll all be filled with fire and power. We won't be worms any more."

"Worms! That's what you always call me."

"Of course you're a worm. We're all worms—grubby worms creeping over the crust of the Earth, through dust and dirt."

"Why should blood bring them?"

"Because it's life and they're attracted by life. Blood is *uisge beatha*—the water of life."

"Blood means death! A trough of spilled blood . . . "

"It's *not* death. When you see a caterpillar crawl into its cocoon, do you think it's dying?"

Walter Everett was standing in the doorway. He stood listening to his daughter, his face dark. "One day," he said hoarsely, "they're going to grab her and carry her off. She wants to go with them. She's waiting for that day."

"You see?" Silvia said to Rick. "He doesn't understand either." She shut off the Silex and poured coffee. "Coffee for you?" she asked her father.

"No," Everett said.

"Silvia," Rick said, as if speaking to a child, "if you went away with them, you know you couldn't come back to us."

"We all have to cross sooner or later. It's all part of our life."

"But you're only nineteen," Rick pleaded. "You're young and healthy and beautiful. And our marriage—what about our marriage?" He half rose from the table. "Silvia, you've got to stop this!"

"I *can't* stop it. I was seven when I saw them first." Silvia stood by the sink, gripping the Silex, a faraway look in her eyes. "Remember, Daddy? We were living back in Chicago. It was winter. I fell, walking home from school." She held up a slim arm. "See the scar? I fell and cut myself on the gravel and slush. I came home crying—it was sleeting and the wind was howling around me. My arm was bleeding and my mitten was soaked with blood. And then I looked up and saw them."

There was silence.

"They want you," Everett said wretchedly. "They're flies—bluebottles, hovering around, waiting for you. Calling you to come along with them."

"Why not?" Silvia's gray eyes were shining and her cheeks radiated joy and anticipation. "You've seen them, Daddy. You know what it means. Transfiguration—from clay into gods!"

Rick left the kitchen. In the living-room, the two sisters stood together, curious and uneasy. Mrs. Everett stood by herself, her face granite-hard, eyes bleak behind her steel-rimmed glasses. She turned away as Rick passed them.

"What happened out there?" Betty Lou asked him in a taut whisper. She was fifteen, skinny and plain, hollow cheeked, with mousy, sand-colored hair. "Silvia never lets us come out with her."

"Nothing happened," Rick answered.

Anger stirred the girl's barren face. "That's not true. You were both out in the garden, in the dark, and—"

"Don't talk to him!" her mother snapped. She yanked the two girls away and shot Rick a glare of hatred and misery. Then she turned quickly from him.

❖ ❖ ❖

Rick opened the door to the basement and switched on the light. He descended slowly into the cold, damp room of concrete and dirt, with its unwinking yellow light hanging from the dust-covered wires overhead.

In one corner loomed the big floor furnace with its mammoth hot air pipes. Beside it stood the water heater and discarded bundles, boxes of books, newspapers and old furniture, thick with dust, encrusted with strings of spider webs.

At the far end were the washing machine and spin dryer. And Silvia's pump and refrigeration system.

From the work bench Rick selected a hammer and two heavy pipe wrenches. He was moving towards the elaborate tanks and pipes when Silvia appeared abruptly at the top of the stairs, her coffee cup in one hand.

She hurried quickly down to him. "What are you doing down here?" she asked, studying him intently. "Why that hammer and those two wrenches?"

Rick dropped the tools back onto the bench. "I thought maybe this could be solved on the spot."

Silvia moved between him and the tanks. "I thought you understood. They've always been a part of my life. When I brought you with me the first time, you seemed to see what—"

"I don't want to lose you," Rick said harshly, "to anybody or anything—in this world or any other. *I'm not going to give you up.*"

"It's not giving me up!" Her eyes narrowed. "You came down here to destroy and break everything. The moment I'm not looking you'll smash all this, won't you?"

"That's right."

Fear replaced anger on the girl's face. "Do you want me to be chained here? I have to go on—I'm through with this part of the journey. I've stayed here long enough."

"Can't you wait?" Rick demanded furiously. He couldn't keep the ragged edge of despair out of his voice. "Doesn't it come soon enough anyhow?"

Silvia shrugged and turned away, her arms folded, her red lips tight together. "You want to be a worm always. A fuzzy, little creeping caterpillar."

"I want *you*."

"You can't *have* me!" She whirled angrily. "I don't have any time to waste with this."

"You have higher things in mind," Rick said savagely.

"Of course." She softened a little. "I'm sorry, Rick. Remember Icarus? You want to fly, too. I know it."

"In my time."

"Why not now? Why wait? You're afraid." She slid lithely away from him, cunning twisting her red lips. "Rick, I want to show you something. Promise me first—you won't tell anybody."

"What is it?"

"Promise?" She put her hand to his mouth. "I have to be careful. It cost a lot of money. Nobody knows about it. It's what they do in China—everything goes towards it."

"I'm curious," Rick said. Uneasiness flicked at him. "Show it to me."

Trembling with excitement, Silvia disappeared behind the huge lumbering refrigerator, back into the darkness behind the web of frost-hard freezing coils. He could hear her tugging and pulling at something. Scraping sounds, sounds of something large being dragged out.

"See?" Silvia gasped. "Give me a hand, Rick. It's heavy. Hardwood and brass—and metal lined. It's hand-stained and polished. And the carving—see the carving! Isn't it beautiful?"

"What is it?" Rick demanded huskily.

"It's my cocoon," Silvia said simply. She settled down in a contented heap on the floor, and rested her head happily against the polished oak coffin.

Rick grabbed her by the arm and dragged her to her feet. "You can't sit with that coffin, down here in the basement with—" He broke off. "What's the matter?"

Silvia's face was twisting with pain. She backed away from him and put her finger quickly to her mouth. "I cut myself—when you pulled me up—on a nail or something." A thin trickle of blood oozed down her fingers. She groped in her pocket for a handkerchief.

"Let me see it." He moved towards her, but she avoided him. "Is it bad?" he demanded.

"Stay away from me," Silvia whispered.

"What's wrong? Let me see it!"

"Rick," Silvia said in a low intense voice, "get some water and adhesive tape. As quickly as possible!" She was trying to keep down her rising terror. "I have to stop the bleeding."

"Upstairs?" He moved awkwardly away. "It doesn't look too bad. Why don't you . . . "

"Hurry." The girl's voice was suddenly bleak with fear. "Rick, *hurry!*"

Confused, he ran a few steps.

Silvia's terror poured after him. "No, it's too late," she called thinly. "Don't come back—keep away from me. It's my own fault. I trained them to come. *Keep away!* I'm sorry, Rick. *Oh—*" Her voice was lost to him, as the wall of the basement burst and shattered. A cloud of luminous white forced its way through and blazed out into the basement.

It was Silvia they were after. She ran a few hesitant steps towards Rick, halted uncertainly, then the white mass of bodies and wings settled around her. She shrieked once. Then a violent explosion blasted the basement into a shimmering dance of furnace heat.

He was thrown to the floor. The cement was hot and dry—the whole basement crackled with heat. Windows shattered as pulsing white shapes pushed out again. Smoke and flames licked up the walls. The ceiling sagged and rained plaster down.

Rick struggled to his feet. The furious activity was dying away. The basement was a littered chaos. All surfaces were scorched black, seared and crusted with smoking ash. Splintered wood, torn cloth and broken concrete were strewn everywhere. The furnace and washing machine were in ruins. The elaborate pumping and refrigeration system—now were a glittering mass of slag. One whole wall had been twisted aside. Plaster was rubbled over everything.

Silvia was a twisted heap, arms and legs doubled grotesquely.

Shriveled, carbonized remains of fire-scorched ash, settling in a vague mound. What had been left were charred fragments, a brittle burned-out husk.

❖ ❖ ❖

It was a dark night, cold and intense. A few stars glittered like ice from above his head. A faint, dank wind stirred through the dripping calla lilies and whipped gravel up in a frigid mist along the path between the black roses.

He crouched for a long time, listening and watching. Behind the cedars, the big house loomed against the sky. At the bottom of the slope a few cars slithered along the highway. Otherwise, there was no sound. Ahead of him jutted the squat outline of the porcelain trough and the pipe that had carried blood from the refrigerator in the basement. The trough was empty and dry, except for a few leaves that had fallen in it.

Rick took a deep breath of thin night air and held it. Then he got stiffly to his feet. He scanned the sky, but saw no movement. They were there, though, watching and waiting—dim shadows, echoing into the legendary past, a line of god-figures.

He picked up the heavy gallon drums, dragged them to the trough and poured blood from a New Jersey abattoir, cheap-grade steer refuse, thick and clotted. It splashed against his clothes and he backed away nervously. But nothing stirred in the air above. The garden was silent, drenched with night fog and darkness.

He stood beside the trough, waiting and wondering if they were coming. They had come for Silvia, not merely for the blood. Without her there was no attraction but the raw food. He carried the empty metal cans over to the bushes and kicked them down the slope. He searched his pockets carefully, to make sure there was no metal in them.

Over the years, Silvia had nourished their habit of coming. Now she was on the other side. Did that mean they wouldn't come? Somewhere in the damp bushes something rustled. An animal or a bird?

In the trough the blood glistened, heavy and dull, like old lead. It was their time to come, but nothing stirred the great trees above. He picked out the rows of nodding black roses, the gravel path down which he and Silvia had run—violently he shut out the recent memory of her flashing eyes and deep red lips. The highway beyond the slope—the empty, deserted garden—the silent house in which her family huddled and waited. After a time, there was a dull, swishing sound. He tensed, but it was only a diesel truck lumbering along the highway, headlights blazing.

He stood grimly, his feet apart, his heels dug into the soft black ground. He wasn't leaving. He was staying there until they came. He wanted her back—at any cost.

Overhead, foggy webs of moisture drifted across the moon. The sky was a vast barren plain, without life or warmth. The deathly cold of deep space, away from suns and living things. He gazed up until his neck ached. Cold stars, sliding in and out of the matted layer of fog. Was there anything else? Didn't they want to come, or weren't they interested in him? It had been Silvia who had interested them—now they had her.

Behind him there was a movement without sound. He sensed it and started to turn, but suddenly, on all sides, the trees and undergrowth shifted. Like cardboard props they wavered and ran together, blending dully in the night shadows. Something moved through them, rapidly, silently, then was gone.

They had come. He could feel them. They had shut off their power and flame. Cold, indifferent statues, rising among the trees, dwarfing the cedars—remote from him and his world, attracted by curiosity and mild habit.

"Silvia," he said clearly. "Which are you?"

There was no response. Perhaps she wasn't among them. He felt foolish. A vague flicker of white drifted past the trough, hovered momentarily and then went on without stopping. The air above the trough vibrated, then died into immobility, as another giant inspected briefly and withdrew.

Panic breathed through him. They were leaving again, receding back into their own world. The trough had been rejected; they weren't interested.

"Wait," he muttered thickly.

Some of the white shadows lingered. He approached them slowly, wary of their flickering immensity. If one of them touched him, he would sizzle briefly and puff into a dark heap of ash. A few feet away he halted.

"You know what I want," he said. "I want her back. She shouldn't have been taken yet."

Silence.

"You were too greedy," he said. "You did the wrong thing. She was going to come over to you, eventually. She had it all worked out."

The dark fog rustled. Among the trees the flickering shapes stirred and pulsed, responsive to his voice. "*True*," came a detached impersonal sound. The sound drifted around him, from tree to tree, without location or direction. It was swept off by the night wind to die into dim echoes.

Relief settled over him. They had paused—they were aware of him—listening to what he had to say.

"You think it's right?" he demanded. "She had a long life here. We were to marry, have children."

There was no answer, but he was conscious of a growing tension. He listened intently, but he couldn't make out anything. Presently he realized a struggle was taking place, a conflict among them. The tension grew—more shapes flickered—the clouds, the icy stars, were obscured by the vast presence swelling around him.

"Rick!" A voice spoke close by. Wavering, drifting back into the dim regions of the trees and dripping plants. He could hardly hear it—the words were gone as soon as they were spoken. "Rick—help me get back."

"Where are you?" He couldn't locate her. "What can I do?"

"I don't know." Her voice was wild with bewilderment and pain. "I don't understand. Something went wrong. They must have thought I—wanted to come right away. I *didn't*!"

"I know," Rick said. "It was an accident."

"They were waiting. The cocoon, the trough—but it was too soon." Her terror came across to him, from the vague distances of another universe. "Rick, I've changed my mind. I want to come back."

"It's not as simple as that."

"I know. Rick, time is different on this side. I've been gone so long—your world seems to creep along. It's been years, hasn't it?"

"One week," Rick said.

"It was their fault. You don't blame me, do you? They know they did the wrong thing. Those who did it have been punished, but that doesn't help me." Misery and panic distorted her voice so he could hardly understand her. "How can I come back?"

"Don't they know?"

"They say it can't be done." Her voice trembled. "They say they destroyed the clay part—it was incinerated. There's nothing for me to go back to."

Rick took a deep breath. "Make them find some other way. It's up to them. Don't they have the power? They took you over too soon—they must send you back. It's *their* responsibility."

The white shapes shifted uneasily. The conflict rose sharply; they couldn't agree. Rick warily moved back a few paces.

"They say it's dangerous," Silvia's voice came from no particular spot. "They say it was attempted once." She tried to control her voice. "The nexus between this world and yours is unstable. There are vast amounts of free-floating energy. The power we—on this side—have isn't really our own. It's a universal energy, tapped and controlled."

"Why can't they . . . "

"This is a higher continuum. There's a natural process of energy from lower to higher regions. But the reverse process is risky. The blood—it's a sort of guide to follow—a bright marker."

"Like moths around a light bulb," Rick said bitterly.

"If they send me back and something goes wrong—" She broke off and then continued, "If they make a mistake, I might be lost between the two regions. I might be absorbed by the free energy. It seems to be partly alive. It's not understood. Remember Prometheus and the fire . . . "

"I see," Rick said, as calmly as he could.

"Darling, if they try to send me back, I'll have to find some shape to enter. You see, I don't exactly have a shape any more. There's no real material form on this side. What you see, the wings and the whiteness, are not really there. If I succeeded in making the trip back to your side . . . "

"You'd have to mold something," Rick said.

"I'd have to take something there—something of clay. I'd have to enter it and reshape it. As He did a long time ago, when the original form was put on your world."

"If they did it once, they can do it again."

"The One who did that is gone. He passed on upward." There was unhappy irony in her voice. "There are regions beyond this. The ladder doesn't stop here. Nobody knows where it ends, it just seems to keep on going up and up. World after world."

"Who decides about you?" Rick demanded.

"It's up to me," Silvia said faintly. "They say, if I want to take the chance, they'll try it."

"What do you think you'll do?" he asked.

"I'm afraid. What if something goes wrong? You haven't seen it, the region between. The possibilities there are incredible—they terrify me. He was the only one with enough courage. Everyone else has been afraid."

"It was their fault. They have to take responsibility."

"They know that." Silvia hesitated miserably. "Rick, darling, please tell me what to do."

"Come back!"

Silence. Then her voice, thin and pathetic. "All right, Rick. If you think that's the right thing."

"It is," he said firmly. He forced his mind not to think, not to picture or imagine anything. *He had to have her back.* "Tell them to get started now. Tell them—"

A deafening crack of heat burst in front of him. He was lifted up and tossed into a flaming sea of pure energy. They were leaving and the scalding lake of sheer power bellowed and thundered around him. For a split second he thought he glimpsed Silvia, her hands reaching imploringly towards him.

Then the fire cooled and he lay blinded in dripping, night-moistened darkness. Alone in the silence.

Walter Everett was helping him up. "You damn fool!" he was saying, again and again. "You shouldn't have brought them back. They've got enough from us."

Then he was in the big, warm living room. Mrs. Everett stood silently in front of him, her face hard and expressionless. The two daughters hovered anxiously around him, fluttering and curious, eyes wide with morbid fascination.

"I'll be all right," Rick muttered. His clothing was charred and blacked. He rubbed black ash from his face. Bits of dried grass stuck to his hair—they had seared a circle around him as they'd ascended. He lay back against the couch and closed his eyes. When he opened them, Betty Lou Everett was forcing a glass of water into his hands.

"Thanks," he muttered.

"You should never have gone out there," Walter Everett repeated. "Why? Why'd you do it? You know what happened to her. You want the same thing to happen to you?"

"I want her back," Rick said quietly.

"Are you mad? You can't get her back. She's gone." His lips twitched convulsively. "You saw her."

Betty Lou was gazing at Rick intently. "What happened out there?" she demanded. "You saw her."

Rick got heavily to his feet and left the living room. In the kitchen he emptied the water in the sink and poured himself a drink. While he was leaning wearily against the sink, Betty Lou appeared in the doorway.

"What do you want?" Rick demanded.

The girl's face was flushed an unhealthy red. "I know something happened out there. You were feeding them, weren't you?" She advanced towards him. "You're trying to get her back?"

"That's right," Rick said.

Betty Lou giggled nervously. "But you can't. She's dead—her body's been cremated—I saw it." Her face worked excitedly. "Daddy always said that something bad would happen to her, and it did." She leaned close to Rick. "She was a witch! She got what she deserved!"

"She's coming back," Rick said.

"*No!*" Panic stirred the girl's drab features. "She *can't* come back. She's dead—like she always said—worm into butterfly—she's a butterfly!"

"Go inside," Rick said.

"You can't order me around," Betty Lou answered. Her voice rose hysterically. "This is *my* house. We don't want you around here any more. Daddy's going to tell you. He doesn't want you and I don't want you and my mother and sister . . . "

The change came without warning. Like a film gone dead, Betty Lou froze, her mouth half open, one arm raised, her words dead on her tongue. She was suspended, an instantly lifeless thing raised off the floor, as if caught between two slides of glass. A vacant insect, without speech or sound, inert and hollow. Not dead, but abruptly thinned back to primordial inanimacy.

Into the captured shell filtered new potency and being. It settled over her, a rainbow of life that poured into place eagerly—like hot fluid—into every part of her. The girl stumbled and moaned; her body jerked violently and pitched against the wall. A china teacup tumbled from an overhead shelf and smashed on the floor. The girl retreated numbly, one hand to her mouth, her eyes wide with pain and shock.

"Oh!" she gasped. "I cut myself." She shook her head and gazed up mutely at him, appealing to him. "On a nail or something."

"*Silvia!*" He caught hold of her and dragged her to her feet, away from the wall. It was *her* arm he gripped, warm and full and mature. Stunned gray eyes, brown hair, quivering breasts—she was now as she had been those last moments in the basement.

"Let's see it," he said. He tore her hand from her mouth and shakily examined her finger. There was no cut, only a thin white line rapidly dimming. "It's all right, honey. You're all right. There's nothing wrong with you!"

"Rick, I was over *there*." Her voice was husky and faint. "They came and dragged me across with them." She shuddered violently. "Rick, am I actually *back*?"

He crushed her tight. "Completely back."

"It was so long. I was over there a century. Endless ages. I thought—" Suddenly she pulled away. "Rick . . . "

"What is it?"

Silvia's face was wild with fear. "There's something wrong."

"There's nothing wrong. You've come back home and that's all that matters."

Silvia retreated from him. "But they took a living form, didn't they? Not discarded clay. They don't have the power, Rick. They altered His work instead." Her voice rose in panic. "A mistake—they should have known better than to alter the balance. It's unstable and none of them can control the . . . "

Rick blocked the doorway. "Stop talking like that!" he said fiercely. "It's worth it—*anything's* worth it. If they set things out of balance, it's their own fault."

"We can't turn it back!" Her voice rose shrilly, thin and hard, like drawn wire. "We've set it in motion, started the waves lapping out. The balance He set up is *altered*."

"Come on, darling," Rick said. "Let's go and sit in the living room with your family. You'll feel better. You'll have to try to recover from this."

They approached the three seated figures, two on the couch, one in the straight chair by the fireplace. The figures sat motionless, their faces blank, their bodies limp and waxen, dulled forms that did not respond as the couple entered the room.

Rick halted, uncomprehending. Walter Everett was slumped forward, newspaper in one hand, slippers on his feet; his pipe was still smoking in the deep ashtray on the arm of his chair. Mrs. Everett sat with a lapful of sewing, her face grim and stern, but strangely vague. An unformed face, as if the material were melting and running together. Jean sat huddled in a shapeless heap, a ball of clay wadded up, more formless each moment.

Abruptly Jean collapsed. Her arms fell loose beside her. Her head sagged. Her body, her arms and legs filled out. Her features altered rapidly. Her clothing changed. Colors flowed in her hair, her eyes, her skin. The waxen pallor was gone.

Pressing her fingers to her lips she gazed up at Rick mutely. She blinked and her eyes focused. "Oh," she gasped. Her lips moved awkwardly; the voice was faint and uneven, like a poor sound-track. She struggled up jerkily, with uncoordinated movements that propelled her stiffly to her feet and towards him—one awkward step at a time—like a wire dummy.

"Rick, I cut myself," she said. "On a nail or something."

What had been Mrs. Everett stirred. Shapeless and vague, it made dull sounds and flopped grotesquely. Gradually it hardened and shaped itself. "My finger," its voice gasped feebly. Like mirror echoes dimming off into darkness, the third figure in the easy chair took up the words. Soon, they were all of them repeating the phrase, four fingers, their lips moving in unison.

"My finger. I cut myself, Rick."

Parrot reflections, receding mimicries of words and movement. And the settling shapes were familiar in every detail. Again and again, repeated around him, twice on the couch, in the easy chair, close beside him—so close he could hear her breath and see her trembling lips.

"What is it?" the Silvia beside him asked.

On the couch one Silvia resumed its sewing—she was sewing methodically, absorbed in her work. In the deep chair another took up its newspapers, its pipe and continued reading. One huddled, nervous and afraid. The one beside him followed as he retreated to the door. She was panting with uncertainty, her gray eyes wide, her nostrils flaring.

"Rick . . ."

He pulled the door open and made his way out onto the dark porch. Machine-like, he felt his way down the steps, through the pools of night collected everywhere, toward the driveway. In the yellow square of light behind him, Silvia was outlined, peering unhappily after him. And behind her, the other figures, identical, pure repetitions, nodding over their tasks.

He found his coupe and pulled out onto the road.

Gloomy trees and houses flashed past. He wondered how far it would go. Lapping waves spreading out—a widening circle as the imbalance spread.

He turned onto the main highway; there were soon more cars around him. He tried to see into them, but they moved too swiftly. The car ahead was a red Plymouth. A heavyset man in a blue business suit was driving, laughing merrily with the woman beside him. He pulled his own coupe up close behind the Plymouth and followed it. The man flashed gold teeth, grinned, waved his plump hands. The girl was dark-haired, pretty. She smiled at the man, adjusted her white gloves, smoothed down her hair, then rolled up the window on her side.

He lost the Plymouth. A heavy diesel truck cut in between them. Desperately he swerved around the truck and nosed in beyond the swift-moving red sedan. Presently it passed him and, for a moment, the two occupants were clearly framed. The girl resembled Silvia. The same delicate line of her small chin—the same deep lips, parting slightly when she smiled—the same slender arms and hands. It was Silvia. The Plymouth turned off and there was no other car ahead of him.

He drove for hours through the heavy night darkness. The gas gauge dropped lower and lower. Ahead of him dismal rolling countryside spread out, blank fields between towns and unwinking stars suspended in the bleak sky. Once, a cluster of red and yellow lights gleamed. An intersection—filling stations and a big neon sign. He drove on past it.

At a single-pump stand, he pulled the car off the highway, onto the oil-soaked gravel. He climbed out, his shoes crunching the stone underfoot, as he grabbed the gas hose and unscrewed the cap of his car's tank. He had the tank almost full when the door of the drab station building opened and a slim woman in white overalls and navy shirt, with a little cap lost in her brown curls, stepped out.

"Good evening, Rick," she said quietly.

He put back the gas hose. Then he was driving out onto the highway. Had he screwed the cap back on again? He didn't remember. He gained speed. He had gone over a hundred miles. He was nearing the state line.

At a little roadside cafe, warm, yellow light glowed in the chill gloom of early morning. He slowed the car down and parked at the edge of the highway in the deserted parking lot. Bleary-eyed he pushed the door open and entered.

Hot, thick smells of cooking ham and black coffee surrounded him, the comfortable sight of people eating. A jukebox blared in the corner. He threw himself onto a stool and hunched over, his head in his hands. A thin farmer next to him glanced at him curiously and then returned to his newspaper. Two hard-faced women across from him gazed at him momentarily. A handsome youth in denim jacket and jeans was eating red beans and rice, washing it down with steaming coffee from a heavy mug.

"What'll it be?" the pert blonde waitress asked, a pencil behind her ear, her hair tied back in a tight bun. "Looks like you've got some hangover, mister."

He ordered coffee and vegetable soup. Soon he was eating, his hands working automatically. He found himself devouring a ham and cheese sandwich; had he ordered it? The jukebox blared and people came and went. There was a little town sprawled beside the road, set back in some gradual hills. Gray sunlight, cold and sterile, filtered down as morning came. He ate hot apple pie and sat wiping dully at his mouth with a napkin.

The cafe was silent. Outside nothing stirred. An uneasy calm hung over everything. The jukebox had ceased. None of the people at the counter stirred or spoke. An occasional truck roared past, damp and lumbering, windows rolled up tight.

When he looked up, Silvia was standing in front of him. Her arms were folded and she gazed vacantly past him. A bright yellow pencil was behind her ear. Her brown hair was tied back in a hard bun. At the corner others were sitting, other Silvias, dishes in front of them, half dozing or eating, some of them reading. Each the same as the next, except for their clothing.

He made his way back to his parked car. In half an hour he had crossed the state line. Cold, bright sunlight sparkled off dew-moist roofs and pavements as he sped through tiny unfamiliar towns.

Along the shiny morning streets he saw them moving—early risers, on their way to work. In twos and threes they walked, their heels echoing in sharp silence. At bus stops he saw groups of them collected together. In the houses, rising from their beds, eating breakfast, bathing, dressing, were more of them—hundreds of them, legions without number. A town of them preparing for the day, resuming their regular tasks, as the circle widened and spread.

He left the town behind. The car slowed under him as his foot slid heavily from the gas pedal. Two of them walked across a level field together. They carried books—children on their way to school. Repetition, unvarying and identical. A dog circled excitedly after them, unconcerned, his joy untainted.

He drove on. Ahead a city loomed, its stern columns of office buildings sharply outlined against the sky. The streets swarmed with noise and activity as he passed through the main business section. Somewhere, near the center of the city, he overtook the expanding periphery of the circle and emerged beyond. Diversity took the place of the endless figures of Silvia. Gray eyes and brown hair gave way to countless varieties of men and women, children and adults, of all ages and appearances. He increased his speed and raced out on the far side, onto the wide four-lane highway.

He finally slowed down. He was exhausted. He had driven for hours; his body was shaking with fatigue.

Ahead of him a carrot-haired youth was cheerfully thumbing a ride, a thin bean-pole in brown slacks and light camel's-hair sweater. Rick pulled to a halt and opened the front door. "Hop in," he said.

"Thanks, buddy." The youth hurried to the car and climbed in as Rick gathered speed. He slammed the door and settled gratefully back against the seat. "It was getting hot, standing there."

"How far are you going?" Rick demanded.

"All the way to Chicago." The youth grinned shyly. "Of course, I don't expect you to drive me that far. Anything at all is appreciated." He eyed Rick curiously. "Which way you going?"

"Anywhere," Rick said. "I'll drive you to Chicago."

"It's two hundred miles!"

"Fine," Rick said. He steered over into the left lane and gained speed. "If you want to go to New York, I'll drive you there."

"You feel all right?" The youth moved away uneasily. "I sure appreciate a lift, but . . . " He hesitated. "I mean, I don't want to take you out of your way."

Rick concentrated on the road ahead, his hands gripping hard around the rim of the wheel. "I'm going fast. I'm not slowing down or stopping."

"You better be careful," the youth warned, in a troubled voice. "I don't want to get in an accident."

"I'll do the worrying."

"But it's dangerous. What if something happens? It's too risky."

"You're wrong," Rick muttered grimly, eyes on the road. "It's worth the risk."

"But if something goes wrong—" The voice broke off uncertainly and then continued, "I might be lost. It would be so easy. It's all so unstable." The voice trembled with worry and fear. "Rick, please . . . "

Rick whirled. "How do you know my name?"

The youth was crouched in a heap against the door. His face had a soft, molten look, as if it were losing its shape and sliding together in an unformed mass. "I want to come back," he was saying, from within himself, "but I'm afraid. You haven't seen it—the region between. It's nothing but energy, Rick. He tapped it a long time ago, but nobody else knows how."

The voice lightened, became clear and treble. The hair faded to a rich brown. Gray, frightened eyes flickered up at Rick. Hands frozen, he hunched over the wheel and forced himself not to move. Gradually he decreased speed and brought the car over into the right-hand lane.

"Are we stopping?" the shape beside him asked. It was Silvia's voice now. Like a new insect, drying in the sun, the shape hardened and locked into firm reality. Silvia struggled up on the seat and peered out. "Where are we? We're between towns."

He jammed on the brakes, reached past her and threw open the door. "Get out!"

Silvia gazed at him uncomprehendingly. "What do you mean?" she faltered. "Rick, what is it? What's wrong?"

"*Get out!*"

"Rick, I don't understand." She slid over a little. Her toes touched the pavement. "Is there something wrong with the car? I thought everything was all right."

He gently shoved her out and slammed the door. The car leaped ahead, out into the stream of mid-morning traffic. Behind him the small, dazed figure was pulling itself up, bewildered and injured. He forced his eyes from the rearview mirror and crushed down the gas pedal with all his weight.

The radio buzzed and clicked in vague static when he snapped it briefly on. He turned the dial and, after a time, a big network station came in. A faint, puzzled voice, a woman's voice. For a time he couldn't make out the words. Then he recognized it and, with a pang of panic, switched the thing off.

Her voice. Murmuring plaintively. Where was the station? Chicago. The circle had already spread that far.

He slowed down. There was no point hurrying. It had already passed him by and gone on. Kansas farms—sagging stores in little old Mississippi towns—along the bleak streets of New England manu-facturing cities swarms of brown-haired gray-eyed women would be hurrying.

It would cross the ocean. Soon it would take in the whole world. Africa would be strange—kraals of white-skinned young women, all exactly alike, going about the primitive chores of hunting and fruit-gathering, mashing grain, skinning animals. Building fires and weaving cloth and carefully shaping razor-sharp knives.

In China . . . he grinned inanely. She'd look strange there, too. In the austere high-collar suit, the almost monastic robe of the young communist cadres. Parade marching up the main streets of Peiping. Row after row of slim-legged full-breasted girls, with heavy Russian-made rifles. Carrying spades, picks, shovels. Columns of cloth-booted soldiers. Fast-moving workers with their precious tools. Reviewed by an identical figure on the elaborate stand overlooking the street, one slender arm raised, her gentle, pretty face expressionless and wooden.

He turned off the highway onto a side road. A moment later he was on his way back, driving slowly, listlessly, the way he had come.

At an intersection a traffic cop waded out through traffic to his car. He sat rigid, hands on the wheel, waiting numbly.

"Rick" she whispered pleadingly as she reached the window. "Isn't everything all right?"

"Sure," he answered dully.

She reached in through the open window and touched him imploringly on the arm. Familiar fingers, red nails, the hand he knew so well. "I want to be with you so badly. Aren't we together again? Aren't I back?"

"Sure."

She shook her head miserably. "I don't understand," she repeated. "I thought it was all right again."

Savagely he put the car into motion and hurtled ahead. The intersection was left behind.

It was afternoon. He was exhausted, riddled with fatigue. He guided the car towards his own town automatically. Along the streets she hurried everywhere, on all sides. She was omnipresent. He came to his apartment building and parked.

The janitor greeted him in the empty hall. Rick identified him by the greasy rag clutched in one hand, the big push-broom, the bucket of wood shavings. "Please," she implored, "tell me what it is, Rick. Please tell me."

He pushed past her, but she caught at him desperately. "Rick, *I'm back.* Don't you understand? They took me too soon and then they sent me back again. It was a mistake. I won't ever call them again—that's all in the past." She followed after him, down the hall to the stairs. "I'm never going to call them again."

He climbed the stairs. Silvia hesitated, then settled down on the bottom step in a wretched, unhappy heap, a tiny figure in thick workman's clothing and huge cleated boots.

He unlocked his apartment door and entered.

The late afternoon sky was a deep blue beyond the windows. The roofs of nearby apartment buildings sparkled white in the sun.

His body ached. He wandered clumsily into the bathroom—it seemed alien and unfamiliar, a difficult place to find. He filled the bowl with hot water, rolled up his sleeves and washed his face and hands in the swirling hot stream. Briefly, he glanced up.

It was a terrified reflection that showed out of the mirror above the bowl, a face, tear-stained and frantic. The face was difficult to catch—it seemed to waver and slide. Gray eyes, bright with terror. Trembling red mouth, pulse-fluttering throat, soft brown hair. The face gazed out pathetically—and then the girl at the bowl bent to dry herself.

She turned and moved wearily out of the bathroom into the living room.

Confused, she hesitated, then threw herself onto a chair and closed her eyes, sick with misery and fatigue.

"Rick," she murmured pleadingly. "Try to help me. I'm back, aren't I?" She shook her head, bewildered. "Please, Rick, I thought everything was all right."

A WORLD OF TALENT

I

When he entered the apartment, a great number of people were making noises and flashing colors. The sudden cacophony confused him. Aware of the surge of shapes, sounds, smells, three-dimensional oblique patches, but trying to peer through and beyond, he halted at the door. With an act of will, he was able to clear the blur somewhat; the meaningless frenzy of human activity settled gradually into a quasi-orderly pattern.

"What's the matter?" his father asked sharply.

"This is what we previewed a half-hour ago," his mother said when the eight-year-old boy failed to answer. "I wish you'd let me get a Corpsman to probe him."

"I don't fully trust the Corps. And we have twelve years to handle this ourselves. If we haven't cracked it by then—"

"Later." She bent down and ordered in a crisp tone, "Go on in, Tim. Say hello to people."

"Try to hold an objective orientation," his father added gently. "At least for this evening, to the end of the party."

Tim passed silently through the crowded living room ignoring the various oblique shapes, his body tilted forward, head turned to one side. Neither of his parents followed him; they were intercepted by the host and then surrounded by Norm and Psi guests.

In the melee, the boy was forgotten. He made a brief circuit of the living room, satisfied himself that nothing existed there, and then sought a side hall. A mechanical attendant opened a bedroom door for him and he entered.

The bedroom was deserted; the party had only begun. He allowed the voices and movement behind him to fade into an indiscriminate blur. Faint perfumes of women drifted through the swank apartment, carried by the warm, Terran-like, artificial air pumped from the central ducts of the city. He raised himself up and inhaled the sweet scents, flowers, fruits, spices—and something more.

He had to go all the way into the bedroom to isolate it. There it was—sour, like spoiled milk—the warming he counted on. And it *was* in the bedroom.

Cautiously, he opened a closet. The mechanical selector tried to present him with clothing, but he ignored it. With the closet open, the scent was stronger. The Other was somewhere near the closet, if not actually in it.

Under the bed?

He crouched down and peered. Not there. He lay outstretched and stared under Fairchild's metal workdesk, typical furniture of a Colonial official's quarters. Here, the scent was stronger. Fear and excitement touched him. He jumped to his feet and pushed the desk away from the smooth plastic surface of the wall.

The Other clung against the wall in the dark shadow where the desk had rested.

It was a Right Other, of course. He had only identified one Left and that for no more than a split second. The Other hadn't managed to phase totally. He retreated warily from it, conscious that, without his cooperation, it had come as far as it could. The Other watched him calmly, aware of his negative actions, but there was little it could do. It made no attempt to communicate, for that had always failed.

❖ ❖ ❖

Tim was safe. He halted and spent a long moment scrutinizing the Other. This was his chance to learn more about it. A space separated the two of them, across which only the visual image and odor—small vaporized particles—of the Other crossed.

It was not possible to identify this Other; many were so similar, they appeared to be multiples of the same unit. But sometimes the Other was radically different. Was it possible that various selections were being tried, alternate attempts to get across?

Again the thought struck him. The people in the living room, both Norm and Psi classes—and even the Mute-class of which he was a part—seemed to have reached a workable stalemate with their own Others. It was strange, since their Lefts would be advanced over his own . . . unless the procession of Rights diminished as the Left group increased.

Was there a finite total of Others?

He went back to the frenetic living room. People murmured and swirled on all sides, gaudy opaque shapes everywhere, warm smells overpowering him with their closeness. It was clear that he would have to get information from his mother and father. He had already spun the research indices hooked to the Sol System educational transmission—spun them without results, since the circuit was not working.

"Where did you wander off to?" his mother asked him, pausing in the animated conversation that had grown up among a group of Norm-class officials blocking one side of the room. She caught the expression on his face.

"Oh," she said. "Even here?"

He was surprised at her question. Location made no difference. Didn't she know that? Floundering, he withdrew into himself to consider. He needed help; he couldn't understand without outside assistance. But a staggering verbal block existed. Was it only a problem of terminology or was it more?

As he wandered around the living room, the vague musty odor filtered to him through the heavy curtain of people-smells. The Other was still there, crouched in the darkness where the desk had been, in the shadows of the deserted bedroom. Waiting to come over. Waiting for him to take two more steps.

❖ ❖ ❖

Julie watched her eight-year-old son move away, an expression of concern on her petite face. "We'll have to keep our eyes on him," she said to her husband. "I preview a mounting situation built around this thing of his."

Curt had caught it, too, but he kept on talking to the Norm-class officials grouped around the two Precogs. "What would you do," he demanded, "if they really opened up on us? You know Big Noodle can't handle a stepped-up shower of robot projectiles. The handful now and then are in the nature of experiments . . . and he has the half-hour warnings from Julie and me."

"True." Fairchild scratched his gray nose, rubbed the stubble of beard showing below his lip. "But I don't think they'll swing to overt war operations. It would be an admission that we're getting somewhere. It would legalize us and open things up. We might collect you Psi-class people together and—" he grinned wearily—"and think the Sol System far out past the Andromache Nebula."

Curt listened without resentment, since the man's words were no surprise. As he and Julie had driven over, they had both previewed the party, its unfruitful discussions, the growing aberrations of their son. His wife's precog span was somewhat greater than his own. She was seeing, at this moment, ahead of his own vision. He wondered what the worried expression on her face indicated.

"I'm afraid," Julie said tightly, "that we're going to have a little quarrel before we get home tonight."

Well, he had also seen that. "It's the situation," he said, rejecting the topic. "Everybody here is on edge. It isn't only you and I who're going to be fighting."

Fairchild listened sympathetically. "I can see some drawbacks to being a Precog. But knowing you're going to have a spat, can't you alter things before it begins?"

"Sure," Curtis answered, "the way we give you pre-information and you use it to alter the situation with Terra. But neither Julie nor I particularly care. It takes a huge mental effort to stave off something like this . . . and neither of us has that much energy."

"I just wish you'd let me turn him over to the Corps," Julie said in a low voice. "I can't stand him wandering around, peering under things, looking in closets for God knows what!"

"For Others," Curt said.

"Whatever that might be."

Fairchild, a natural-born moderator, tried intercession. "You've got twelve years," he began. "It's no disgrace to have Tim stay in the Mute-class; every one of you starts out that way. If he has Psi powers, he'll show."

"You talk like an infinite Precog," Julie said, amused. "How do you know they'll show?"

Fairchild's good-natured face twisted with effort. Curt felt sorry for him. Fairchild had too much responsibility, too many decisions to make, too many lives on his hands. Before the Separation with Terra, he had been an appointed official, a bureaucrat with a job and clearly defined routine. Now there was nobody to tap out an inter-system memo to him early Monday morning. Fairchild was working without instructions.

"Let's see that doodad of yours," Curt said. "I'm curious about how it works."

Fairchild was astonished. "How the hell—" Then he remembered. "Sure, you must have already previewed it." He dug around in his coat. "I was going to make it the surprise of the party, but we can't have surprises with you two Precogs around."

The other Norm-class officials crowded around as their boss unwrapped a square of tissue paper and from it lifted a small glittering stone. An interested silence settled over the room as Fairchild examined the stone, his eyes close to it, like a jeweler studying a precious gem.

"An ingenious thing," Curt admitted.

"Thanks," Fairchild said. "They should start arriving any day, now. The glitter is to attract children and lower-class people who would go out for a bauble—possible wealth, you know. And women, of course. Anybody who would stop and pick up what they thought was a diamond, everybody but the Tech-classes. I'll show you."

He glanced around the hushed living room at the guests in their gay party clothes. Off to one side, Tim stood with his head turned at an angle. Fairchild hesitated, then tossed the stone across the carpet in front of the boy, almost at his feet. The boy's eyes didn't flicker. He was gazing absently through the people, unaware of the bright object at his feet.

Curt moved forward, ready to take up the social slack. "You'd have to produce something the size of a jet transport." He bent down and retrieved the stone. "It's not your fault that Tim doesn't respond to such mundane things as fifty-carat diamonds."

Fairchild was crestfallen at the collapse of his demonstration. "I forgot." He brightened. "But there aren't any Mutes on Terra any more. Listen and see what you think of the spiel. I had a hand at writing it."

In Curt's hand, the stone rested coldly. In his ears, a tiny gnatlike buzz sounded, a controlled, modulated cadence that caused a stir of murmurs around the room.

"My friends," the canned voice stated, "the causes of the conflict between Terra and the Centaurian colonies have been grossly misstated in the press."

"Is this seriously aimed at children?" Julie asked.

"Maybe he thinks Terran children are advanced over our own," a Psi-class official said as a rustle of amusement drifted through the room.

The tiny whine droned on, turning out its mixture of legalistic arguments, idealism and an almost pathetic pleading. The begging quality grated on Curt. Why did Fairchild have to get down on his knees and plead with the Terrans? As he listened, Fairchild puffed confidently on his pipe, arms folded, heavy face thick with satisfaction. Evidently Fairchild wasn't aware of the precarious *thinness* of his canned words.

It occurred to Curt that none of them—including himself—was facing how really fragile their Separation movement was. There was no use blaming the weak words wheezing from the pseudogem. Any description of their position was bound to reflect the querulous half-fear that dominated the Colonies.

"It has long been established," the stone asserted, "that freedom is the natural condition of Man. Servitude, the bondage of one man or one group of men to another, is a remnant of the past, a vicious anachronism. Men must govern themselves."

"Strange to hear a stone saying that," Julie said, half amused. "An inert lump of rock."

"You have been told that the Colonial Secessionist movement will jeopardize your lives and your standard of living. *This is not true.* The standard of living of all mankind will be raised if the colony planets are allowed to govern themselves and find their own economic markets. The mercantile system practiced by the Terran government on Terrans living outside the Sol group—"

"The children will bring this thing home," Fairchild said. "The parents will pick it up from them."

The stone droned on. "The Colonies could not remain mere supply bases for Terra, sources of raw materials and cheap labor. The Colonists could not remain second-class citizens. Colonists have as much right to determine their own society as those remaining in the Sol group. Thus, the Colonial Government has petitioned the Terran Government for a severance of those bonds to keep us from realizing our manifest destinies."

Curt and Julie exchanged glances. The academic text-book dissertation hung like a dead weight in the room. Was this the man the Colony had elected to manage the resistance movement? A pedant, a salaried official, a bureaucrat and—Curt couldn't help thinking—a man without Psi powers. A Normal.

Fairchild had probably been moved to break with Terra over some trivial miswording of a routine directive. Nobody, except perhaps the telepathic Corps, knew his motives or how long he could keep going.

"What do you think of it?" Fairchild asked when the stone had finished its monologue and had started over. "Millions of them showering down all over the Sol group. You know what the Terran press is saying about us—vicious lies—that we want to take over Sol, that we're hideous invaders from outer space, monsters, mutants, freaks. We have to counter such propaganda."

"Well," Julie said, "a third of us are freaks, so why not face it? I know my son is a useless freak."

Curt took her arm. "Nobody's calling Tim a freak, not even you!"

"But it's true!" She pulled away. "If we were back in the Sol System—if we hadn't separated—you and I would be in detention camps, waiting to be—you know." She fiercely jabbed in the direction of their son. "There wouldn't be any Tim."

From the corner a sharp-faced man spoke up. "We wouldn't be in the Sol System. We'd have broken out on our own without anybody's help. Fairchild had nothing to do with it; we brought him along. Don't ever forget that!"

Curt eyed the man hostilely. Reynolds, chief of the telepathic Corps, was drunk again. Drunk and spilling over his load of vitriolic hate for Norms.

"Possibly," Curt agreed, "but we would have had a hell of a time doing it."

"You and I know what keeps this Colony alive," Reynolds answered, his flushed face arrogant and sneering. "How long could these bureaucrats keep on going without Big Noodle and Sally, you two Precogs, the Corps and all the rest of us? Face facts—we don't need this legalistic window-dressing. We're not going to win because of any pious appeals for freedom and equality. We're going to win because there are no Psis on Terra."

The geniality of the room dwindled. Angry murmur rose from the Norm-class guests.

"Look here," Fairchild said to Reynolds, "you're still a human being, even if you can read minds. Having a talent doesn't—"

"Don't lecture me," Reynolds said. "No numbskull is going to tell me what to do."

"You're going too far," Curt told Reynolds. "Somebody's going to smack you down some day. If Fairchild doesn't do it, maybe I will."

"You and your meddling Corps," a Psi-class Resurrector said to Reynolds, grabbing hold of his collar. "You think you're above us because you can merge your minds. You think—"

"Take your hands off me," Reynolds said in an ugly voice. A glass crashed to the floor; one of the women became hysterical. Two men struggled; a third joined and, in a flash, a wild turmoil of resentment was boiling in the center of the room.

Fairchild shouted for order. "For God's sake, if we fight each other, we're finished. Don't you understand—*we have to work together!*"

It took a while before the uproar subsided. Reynolds pushed past Curt, white-faced and muttering under his breath. "I'm getting out of here." The other Telepaths trailed belligerently after him.

❖ ❖ ❖

As he and Julie drove slowly home through the bluish darkness, one section of Fairchild's propaganda repeated itself in Curt's brain over and over again.

"You've been told a victory by the Colonist means a victory of Psis over Normal human beings. This is not true! The Separation was not planned and is not conducted by either Psis or Mutants. The revolt was a spontaneous reaction by Colonists of all classes."

"I wonder," Curt mused. "Maybe Fairchild's wrong. Maybe he's being operated by Psis without knowing it. Personally, I like him, stupid as he is."

"Yes, he's stupid," Julie agreed. In the darkness of the car's cabin, her cigarette was a bright burning coal of wrath. In the back seat, Tim lay curled up asleep, warmed by the heat from the motor. The barren, rocky landscape of Proxima III rolled out ahead of the small surface-car, a dim expanse, hostile and alien. A few Man-made roads and buildings lay here and there among crop-tanks and fields.

"I don't trust Reynolds," Curt continued, knowing he was opening the previewed scene between them, yet not willing to sidestep it. "Reynolds is smart, unscrupulous and ambitious. What he wants is prestige and status. But Fairchild is thinking of the welfare of the Colony. He means all that stuff he dictated into his stones."

"That drivel," Julie was scornful. "The Terrans will laugh their heads off. Listening to it with a straight face was more than I could manage, and God knows our lives depend on this business."

"Well," Curt said carefully, knowing what he was getting into, "there may be Terrans with more sense of justice than you and Reynolds." He turned toward her. "I can see what you're going to do and so can you. Maybe you're right, maybe we ought to get it over with. Ten years is a long time when there's no feeling. And it wasn't our idea in the first place."

"No," Julie agreed. She crushed her cigarette out and shakily lit another. "If there had been another male Precog besides you, just *one*. That's something I can't forgive Reynolds for. It was his idea, you know. I never should have agreed. For the glory of the race! Onward and upward with the Psi banner! The mystical mating of the first real Precogs in history . . . and look what came of it!"

"Shut up," Curt said. "He's not asleep and he can hear you."

Julie's voice was bitter. 'Hear me, yes. Understand, no. We wanted to know what the second generation would be like—well, now we know. Precog plus Precog equals freak. Useless mutant. Monster—let's face it, the M on his card stands for monster."

Curt's hands tightened on the wheel. "That's a word neither you nor anybody else is going to use."

"Monster!" She leaned close to him, teeth white in the light from the dashboard, eyes glowing. "Maybe the Terrans are right—maybe we Precogs ought to be sterilized and put to death. Erased. I think..." She broke off abruptly, unwilling to finish.

"Go ahead," Curt said. "You think perhaps when the revolt is successful and we're in control of the Colonies, we should go down the line selectively. With the Corps on top naturally."

"Separate the wheat from the chaff," Julie said. "First the Colonies from Terra. Then us from them. And when he comes up, even if he is my son..."

"What you're doing," Curt interrupted, "is passing judgment on people according to their use. Tim isn't useful, so there's no point in letting him live, right?" His blood pressure was on the way up, but he was past caring. "Breeding people like cattle. A human hasn't a right to live; that's a privilege we dole out according to our whim."

Curt raced the car down the deserted highway. "You heard Fairchild prattle about freedom and equality. He believes it and so do I. And I believe Tim—or anybody else—has a right to exist whether we can make use of his talent or whether he even has a talent."

"He has a right to live," Julie said, "but remember he's not one of us. He's an oddity. He doesn't have our ability, our—" she ground out the words triumphantly—"superior ability."

Curt pulled the car over to the edge of the highway. He brought it to a halt and pushed open the door. Dismal, arid air billowed into the car.

"You drive on home." He leaned over the back seat and prodded Tim into wakefulness. "Come on, kid. We're getting out."

Julie reached over to get the wheel. "When will you be home? Or have you got it completely set up now? Better make sure. She might be the kind that has a few others on the string."

Curt stepped from the car and the door slammed behind him. He took his son's hand and led him down the roadway to the black square of a ramp that rose darkly in the night gloom. As they started up the steps, he heard the car roar off down the highway through the darkness toward home.

"Where are we?" Tim asked.

"You know this place. I bring you here every week. This is the school where they train people like you and me—where we Psis get our education."

II

Lights came on around them. Corridors branched off the main entrance ramp like metal vines.

"You may stay here for a few days," Curt said to his son. "Can you stand not seeing your mother for a while?"

Tim didn't answer. He had lapsed back into his usual silence as he followed along beside his father. Curt again wondered how the boy could be so withdrawn—as he obviously was—and yet be so terribly alert. The answer was written over each inch of the taut, young body. Tim was only withdrawn from contact with human beings. He maintained an almost compulsive tangency with the outside world—or, rather, an outside world. Whatever it was, it didn't include humans, although it was made up of real, external objects.

As he had already previewed, his son suddenly broke away from him. Curt let the boy hurry down a side corridor. He watched as Tim stood tugging anxiously at a supply locker, trying to get it open.

"Okay," Curt said resignedly. He followed after him and unlocked the locker with his pass key. "See? There's nothing in it."

How completely the boy lacked precog could be seen by the flood of relief that swept his face. Curt's heart sank at the sight. The precious talent that both he and Julie possessed simply hadn't been passed on. Whatever the boy was, he was not a Precog.

It was past two in the morning, but the interior departments of the School Building were alight with activity. Curt moodily greeted a couple of Corpsmen lounging around the bar, surrounded by beers and ashtrays.

"Where's Sally?" he demanded. "I want to go in and see Big Noodle."

One of the Telepaths lazily jerked a thumb. "She's around somewhere. Over that way, in the kids' quarters, probably asleep. It's late." He eyed Curt, whose thoughts were on Julie. "You ought to get rid of a wife like that. She's too old and thin, anyhow. What you'd really like is a plump young dish—"

Curt lashed a blast of mental dislike and was satisfied to see the grinning young face go hard with antagonism. The other Telepath pulled himself upright and shouted after Curt. "When you're through with your wife, send her around to us."

"I'd say you're after a girl of about twenty," another Telepath said as he admitted Curt to the sleeping quarters of the children's wing. "Dark hair—correct me if I'm wrong—and dark eyes. You have a fully formed image. Maybe there's a specific girl. Let's see, she's short, fairly pretty and her name is—"

Curt cursed at the situation that required them to turn their minds over to the Corps. Telepaths were interlaced throughout the Colonies and, in particular, throughout the School and the offices of the Colonial Government. He tightened his grip around Tim's hand and led him through the doorway.

"This kid of yours," the Telepath said as Tim passed close to him, "sure probes queer. Mind if I go down a little?"

"Keep out of his mind." Curt ordered sharply. He slammed the door shut after Tim, knowing it made no difference, but enjoying the feel of the heavy metal sliding in place. He pushed Tim down a narrow corridor and into a small room. Tim pulled away, intent on a side door; Curt savagely yanked him back. "There's nothing in there!" he reprimanded harshly. "That's only a bathroom."

Tim continued to tug away. He was still tugging when Sally appeared, fastening a robe around her, face puffy with sleep. "Hello, Mr. Purcell," she greeted Curt. "Hello, Tim." Yawning, she turned on a floor lamp and tossed herself down on a chair. "What can I do for you this time of night?"

She was thirteen, tall and gangling, with yellow cornsilk hair and freckled skin. She picked sleepily at her thumbnail and yawned again as the boy sat down across from her. To amuse him, she animated a pair of gloves lying on a sidetable. Tim laughed with delight as the gloves groped their way to the edge of the table, waved their fingers blindly and began a cautious descent to the floor.

"Fine," Curt said. "You're getting good. I'd say you're not cutting any classes."

Sally shrugged. "Mr. Purcell, the School can't teach me anything. You know I'm the most advanced Psi with the power of animation. They just let me work alone. In fact, I'm instructing a bunch of little kids, still Mutes, who might have something. I think a couple of them could work out, with practice. All they can give me is encouragement; you know, psychological stuff and lots of vitamins and fresh air. But they can't teach me anything."

"They can teach you how important you are," Curt said. He had previewed this, of course. During the last half hour, he had selected a number of possible approaches, discarded one after another, finally ended with this. "I came over to see Big Noodle. That meant I had to wake you. Do you know why?"

"Sure," Sally answered. "You're afraid of him. And since Big Noodle is afraid of me, you need me to come along." She allowed the gloves to sag into immobility as she got to her feet. "Well, let's go."

He had seen Big Noodle many times in his life, but he had never got used to the sight. Awed, in spite of his preview of this scene, Curt stood in the open space before the platform, gazing up, silent and impressed as always.

"He's fat," Sally said practically. "If he doesn't get thinner, he won't live long."

Big Noodle slumped like a gray, sickly pudding in the immense chair the Tech Department had built for him. His eyes were half-closed; his pulpy arms lay slack and inert at his sides. Wads of oozing dough hung in folds over the arms and sides of the chair. Big Noodle's egglike skull was fringed with damp, stringy hair, matted like decayed seaweed. His nails were lost in the sausage fingers. His teeth were rotting and black. His tiny plate-blue eyes flickered dully as he identified Curt and Sally, but the obese body did not stir.

"He's resting," Sally explained. "He just ate."

"Hello," Curt said.

From the swollen mouth, between rolls of pink flesh lips, a grumbled response came.

"He doesn't like to be bothered this late," Sally said yawning. "I don't blame him."

She wandered around the room, amusing herself by animating light brackets along the wall. The brackets struggled to pull free from the hot-pour plastic in which they were set.

"This seems so dumb, if you don't mind my saying so, Mr. Purcell. The Telepaths keep Terran infiltrators from coming in here, and all this business of yours is against them. That means you're helping Terra, doesn't it? If we didn't have the Corps to watch out for us—"

"I keep out Terrans," Big Noodle mumbled. "I have my wall and I turn back everything."

"You turn back projectiles," Sally said, "but you can't keep out infiltrators. A Terran infiltrator could come in here this minute and you wouldn't know. You're just a big stupid lump of lard."

Her description was accurate. But the vast mound of fat was the nexus of the Colony's defense, the most talented of the Psis. Big

Noodle was the core of the Separation movement . . . and the living symbol of its problem.

Big Noodle had almost infinite parakinetic power and the mind of a moronic three-year-old. He was, specifically, an idiot savant. His legendary powers had absorbed his whole personality, withered and degenerated it, rather than expanded it. He could have swept the Colony aside years ago if his bodily lusts and fears had been accompanied by cunning. But Big Noodle was helpless and inert, totally dependent on the instructions of the Colonial Government, reduced to sullen passivity by his terror of Sally.

"I ate a whole pig." Big Noodle struggled to a quasi-position, belched, wiped feebly at his chin. "Two pigs, in fact. Right here in this room, just a little while ago. I could get more if I wanted."

The diet of the colonist consisted mainly of tank-grown artificial protein. Big Noodle was amusing himself at their expense.

"The pig," Big Noodle continued grandly, "came from Terra. The night before, I had a flock of wild ducks. And before that, I brought over some kind of animal from Betelgeuse IV. It doesn't have any name; it just runs around and eats."

"Like you," Sally said, "Only you don't run around."

Big Noodle giggled. Pride momentarily overcame his fear of the girl. "Have some candy," he offered. A shower of chocolate rattled down like hail. Curt and Sally retreated as the floor of the chamber disappeared under the deluge. With the chocolate came fragments of machinery, cardboard boxes, sections of display counter, a jagged chunk of concrete floor. "Candy factory on Terra," Big Noodle explained happily. "I've got it pinpointed pretty good."

Tim had awakened from his contemplation. He bent down and eagerly picked up a handful of chocolates.

"Go ahead," Curt said to him. "You might as well take them"

"I'm the only one that gets the candy," Big Noodle thundered, outraged. The chocolate vanished. "I sent it back," he explained peevishly. "It's mine."

There was nothing malevolent in Big Noodle, only an infinite childish selfishness. Through his power, every object in the Universe had become his possession. There was nothing outside the reach of his bloated arms; he could reach for the Moon and get it. Fortunately, most things were outside his span of comprehension. He was uninterested.

"Let's cut out these games," Curt said. "Can you say if any Telepaths are within probe range of us?"

Big Noodle made a begrudging search. He had a consciousness of objects wherever they were. Through his talent, he was in contact with the physical contents of the Universe.

"None near here," he declared after a time. "One about a hundred feet off . . . I'll move him back. I hate Teeps getting into my privacy."

"Everybody hates Teeps," Sally said. "It's a nasty, dirty talent. Looking into other people's minds is like watching them when they're bathing or dressing or eating. It isn't natural."

Curt grinned. "Is it any different from Precog? You wouldn't call that natural."

"Precog has to do with events, not people," Sally said. "Knowing what's going to happen isn't any worse than knowing what's already happened."

"It might even be better," Curt pointed out.

"No," Sally said emphatically. "It's got us into this trouble. I have to watch what I think all the time because of you. Every time I see a Teep, I get goose bumps, and no matter how hard I try, I can't keep from thinking about *her*, just because I know I'm not supposed to."

"My precog faculty has nothing to do with Pat," Curt said. "Precog doesn't introduce fatality. Locating Pat was an intricate job. It was a deliberate choice I made."

"Aren't you sorry?" Sally demanded.

"No."

"If it wasn't for me," Big Noodle interrupted, "you never would have got across to Pat."

"I wish we hadn't," Sally said fervently. "If it wasn't for Pat, we wouldn't be mixed up in all this business." She shot a hostile glance at Curt. "And I don't think she's pretty."

"What would you suggest?" Curt asked the child with more patience than he felt. He had previewed the futility of making a child and an idiot understand about Pat. "You know we can't pretend we never found her."

"I know," Sally admitted. "And the Teeps have got something from our minds already. That's why there're so many of them hanging around here. It's a good thing we don't know where she is."

"I know where she is," Big Noodle said. "I know exactly where."

"No, you don't," Sally answered. "You just know how to get to her and that's not the same thing. You can't explain it; you just send us over there and back."

"It's a planet," Big Noodle said angrily, "with funny plants and a lot of green things. And the air's thin. She lives in a camp. People go out and farm all day. There's only a few people there. A lot of dopey animals live there. It's cold."

"Where is it?" Curt asked.

Big Noodle sputtered. "It's . . . " His pulpy arms waved. "It's some place near . . . " He gave up, wheezed resentfully at Sally and then brought a tank of filthy water into being above the girl's head. As the water flowed toward her, the child made a few brief motions with her hands.

Big Noodle shrieked in terror and the water vanished. He lay panting with fright, body quivering, as Sally mopped at a wet spot on her robe. She had animated the fingers of his left hand.

"Better not do that again," Curt said to her. "His heart might give out."

"The big slob." Sally rummaged around in a supply closet. "Well, if you've made up your mind, we might as well get it over with. Only let's not stay so long. You get to talking with Pat and then the two of you go off, and you don't come back for hours. At night, it's freezing and they don't have any heating plants." She pulled down a coat from the closet. "I'll take this with me."

"We're not going," Curt told her. "This time is going to be different."

Sally blinked. "Different? How?"

Even Big Noodle was surprised. "I was just getting ready to move you across," he complained.

"I know," Curt said firmly. "But this time I want you to bring Pat here. Bring her to this room, understand? This is the time we've been talking about. The big moment's arrived."

There was only one person with Curt as he entered Fairchild's office. Sally was now in bed, back at the school. Big Noodle never stirred from his chamber. Tim was still at the School, in the hands of Psi-class authorities, not Telepaths.

Pat followed hesitantly, frightened and nervous as the men sitting around the office glanced up in annoyance.

She was perhaps nineteen, slim and copper-skinned, with large dark eyes. She wore a canvas workshirt and jeans, heavy shoes caked with mud. Her tangle of black curls was tied back and knotted with a red bandana. Her rolled-up sleeves showed tanned, competent arms. At her leather belt she carried a knife, a field telephone and an emergency pack of rations and water.

"This is the girl," Curt said. "Take a good look at her."

"Where are you from?" Fairchild asked Pat. He pushed aside a heap of directives and memotapes to find his pipe.

Pat hesitated. "I—" she began. She turned uncertainly to Curt. "You told me never to say, even to you."

"It's okay," Cut said gently. "You can tell us now." He explained to Fairchild, "I can preview what she's going to say, but I never knew before. I didn't want to get it probed out of me by the Corps."

"I was born on Proxima VI," Pat said in a low voice. "I grew up there. This is the first time I've left the planet."

Fairchild's eyes widened. "That's a wild place. In fact, about our most primitive region."

Around the office, his group of Norm and Psi consultants moved closer to watch. One wide-shouldered old man, face weathered as stone, eyes shrewd and alert, raised his hand. "Are we to understand that Big Noodle brought you here?"

Pat nodded. "I didn't know. I mean it was unexpected." She tapped her belt. "I was working, clearing the brush . . . we've been trying to expand, develop more usable land."

"What's your name?" Fairchild asked her.

"Patricia Ann Connley."

"What class?"

The girl's sun-cracked lips moved. "Mute class."

A stir moved through the officials. "You're a Mutant," the old man asked her, "without Psi powers? Exactly how do you differ from the Norm?"

Pat glanced at Curt and he moved forward to answer for her. "This girl will be twenty-one in two years. You know what that means. If she's still in the Mute-class, she'll be sterilized and put in a camp. That's our Colonial policy. And if Terra whips us, she'll be sterilized in any case, as will all of us Psis and Mutants."

"Are you trying to say she has a talent?" Fairchild asked. "You want us to lift her from Mute to Psi?" His hands fumbled at the papers on the table. "We get a thousand petitions a day like this. You came down here at four in the morning just for this? There's a routine form you can fill out, a common office procedure."

The old man cleared his throat and blurted, "This girl is close to you?"

"That's right," Curt said. "I have a personal interest."

"How did you meet her?" the old man asked. "If she's never been off Proxima VI . . . "

"Big Noodle shuttled me there and back," Curt answered. "I've made the trip about twenty times. I didn't know it was Prox VI, of course. I only knew it was a Colony planet, primitive, still wild. Originally, I came across an analysis of her personality and neural characteristics in our Mute-class files. As soon as I understood, I gave Big Noodle the identifying brain pattern and had him send me across."

"What is that pattern?" Fairchild asked. "What's different about her?"

"Pat's talent has never been acknowledged as Psi," Curt said. "In a way, it isn't, but it's going to be one of the most useful talents we've discovered. We should have known it would arise. Wherever some organism develops, so does another to prey on it."

"Get to the point," Fairchild said. He rubbed the blue stubble on his chin. "When you called me, all you said was that—"

"Consider the various Psi talents as survival weapons," Curt said. "Consider telepathic ability as evolving for the defense of an organism. It puts the Telepath head and shoulders above his enemies. Is this going to continue? Don't these things usually balance out?"

It was the old man who understood. "I see," he said with a grin of wry admiration. "This girl is opaque to telepathic probes."

"That's right," Curt said. "The first, but there'll likely be others. And not only defenses to telepathic probes. There are going to be organisms resistant to Parakineticists, to Precogs like myself, to Resurrectors, to Animators, to every and all Psi powers. Now we have a fourth class. The Anti-Psi class. It was bound to come into existence."

III

The coffee was artificial, but hot and satisfying. Like the eggs and bacon it was synthetically compounded from tank-grown meals and proteins, with a carefully regulated mix of native-grown plant fiber. As they ate, the morning sun rose outside. The barren gray landscape of Proxima III was touched with a faint tint of red.

"It looks nice," Pat said shyly, glancing out the kitchen window. "Maybe I can examine your farming equipment. You have a lot we don't have."

"We've had more time," Curt reminded her. "This planet was settled a century before your own. You'll catch up with us. In many ways Prox VI is richer and more fertile."

Julie wasn't sitting at the table. She stood leaning against the refrigerator, arms folded, her face hard and frigid. "Is she really staying here?" she demanded in a thin, clipped voice. "In this house with us?"

"That's right," Curt answered.

"How long?"

"A few days. A week. Until I can get Fairchild moving."

Faint sounds stirred beyond the house. Here and there in the residential syndrome people were waking up and preparing for the day. The kitchen was warm and cheerful; a window of clear plastic separated it from the landscape of tumbled rocks, thin trees and plants that stretched to a few hundred miles off. Cold morning wind whipped around the rubbish that littered the deserted inter-system field at the rim of the syndrome.

"That field was the link between us and the Sol System," Curt said. "The umbilical cord. Gone now, for a while at least."

"It's beautiful," Pat stated.

"The field?"

She gestured at the towers of an elaborate mining and smelting combine partly visible beyond the rows of houses. "Those, I mean. The landscape is like ours; bleak and awful. It's all the installations that mean something . . . where you've pushed the landscape back." She shivered. "We've been fighting trees and rocks all my life, trying to get the soil usable, trying to make a place to live. We don't have any heavy equipment on Prox VI, just hand tools and our own backs. You know, you've seen our villages."

Curt sipped his coffee. "Are there many Psis on Prox VI?"

"A few. Mostly minor. A few Resurrectors, a handful of Animators. No one even as good as Sally." She laughed, showing her teeth. "We're rustic hicks, compared to this urban metropolis. You saw how we live. Villages stuck here and there, farms, a few isolated supply centers, one miserable field. You saw my family, my brothers and my father, our home life, if you can call that log shack a home. Three centuries behind Terra."

"They taught you about Terra?"

"Oh, yes. Tapes came direct from the Sol System until the Separation. Not that I'm sorry we separated. We should have been out working anyhow, instead of watching the tapes. But it was interesting to see the mother world, the big cities, all the billions of people. And the earlier colonies on Venus and Mars. It was amazing." Her voice throbbed with excitement. "Those colonies were like ours, once. They had to clear Mars the same way we're clearing Prox VI. We'll get Prox VI cleared, cities built up and fields laid out. And we'll all go on doing our part."

Julie detached herself from the refrigerator and began gathering dishes from the table without looking at Pat. "Maybe I'm being naive," she said to Curt, "but where's she going to sleep?"

"You know the answer," Curt answered patiently. "You've previewed all this. Tim's at the School so she can have his room."

"What am I supposed to do? Feed her, wait on her, be her maid? What am I supposed to tell people when they see her?" Julie's voice rose to a shrill. "Am I supposed to say she's my sister?"

Pat smiled across at Curt, toying with a button on her shirt. It was apparent that she was untouched, remote from Julie's harsh voice. Probably that was why the Corps couldn't probe her. Detached, almost aloof, she seemed unaffected by rancor and violence.

"She won't need any supervision," Curt said to his wife. "Leave her alone."

Julie lit a cigarette with rapid, jerky fingers. "I'll be glad to leave her alone. But she can't go around in those work clothes looking like a convict."

"Find her something of yours," Curt suggested.

Julie's face twisted. "She couldn't wear my things; she's too heavy." To Pat she said with deliberate cruelty, "What are you, about a size 30 waist? My God, what have you been doing, dragging a plow? Look at her neck and shoulders . . . she looks like a fieldhorse."

Curt got abruptly to his feet and pushed his chair back from the table. "Come on," he said to Pat. It was vital to show her something besides this undercurrent of resentment. "I'll show you around."

Pat leaped up, her cheeks flushed. "I want to see everything. This is all so new." She hurried after him as he grabbed his coat and headed for the front door. "Can we see the School where you train the Psis? I want to see how you develop their abilities. And can we see how the Colonial Government is organized? I want to see how Fairchild works with the Psis."

Julie followed the two of them out onto the front porch. Cool, chill morning air billowed around them, mixed with the sounds of cars heading from the residential syndrome toward the city. "In my room you'll find skirts and blouses," she said to Pat. "Pick out something light. It's warmer here than on Prox VI."

"Thank you," Pat said. She hurried back into the house.

"She's pretty," Julie said to Curt. "When I get her washed and dressed, I guess she'll look all right. She's got a figure—in a healthy sort of way. But is there anything to her mind? To her personality?"

"Sure," Curt answered.

Julie shrugged. "Well, she's young. A lot younger than I am." She smiled wanly. "Remember when we first met? Ten years ago . . . I was so curious to see you, talk to you. The only other Precog besides myself. I had so many dreams and hopes about both of us. I was her age, perhaps a little younger."

"It was hard to see how it would work out," Curt said. "Even for us. A half-hour preview isn't much, in a thing like this."

"How long has it been?" Julie asked.

"Not long."

"Have there been other girls?"

"No. Only Pat."

"When I realized there was somebody else, I hoped she was good enough for you. If I could be sure this girl had something to offer. I suppose it's her remoteness that gives an impression of emptiness. And you have more rapport with her than I do. Probably you don't feel the lack, if it is a lack. And it may be tied in with her talent, her opaqueness."

Curt fastened the cuffs of his coat. "I think it's a kind of innocence. She's not touched by a lot of things we have here in our urban, industrial society. When you were talking about her it didn't seem to reach her."

Julie touched his arm lightly. "Then take care of her. She's going to need it around here. I wonder what Reynolds' reaction is going to be."

"Do you see anything?"

"Nothing about her. You're going off . . . I'm by myself for the next interval, as far as I can preview, working around the house. As for now, I'm going into town to do some shopping, to pick up some new clothes. Maybe I can get something for her to wear."

"We'll get her things," Curt said. "She should get her clothes first-hand."

Pat appeared in a cream-colored blouse and ankle-length yellow skirt, black eyes sparkling, hair moist with morning mist. "I'm ready! Can we go now?"

Sunlight glittered down on them as they stepped eagerly onto the level ground. "We'll go over to the School first and pick up my son."

❖ ❖ ❖

The three of them walked slowly along the gravel path that led by the white concrete School Building, by the faint sheen of wet lawn that was carefully maintained against the hostile weather of the planet. Tim scampered on ahead of Pat and Curt, listening and peering intently past the objects around him, body tensed forward, lithe and alert.

"He doesn't speak much," Pat observed.

"He's too busy to pay any attention to us."

Tim halted to gaze behind a shrub. Pat followed a little after him, curious. "What's he looking for? He's a beautiful child . . . he has Julie's hair. She has nice hair."

"Look over there," Curt said to his son. "There are plenty of children to sort over. Go play with them."

At the entrance to the main School Building, parents and their children swarmed in restless, anxious groups. Uniformed School Officials moved among them, sorting, checking, dividing the children into various sub-groups. Now and then a small sub-group was admitted through the check-system into the School Building. Apprehensive, pathetically hopeful, the mothers waited outside.

Pat said, "It's like that on Prox VI, when the School Teams come to make their census and inspection. Everybody wants to get the unclassified children put up into the Psi-class. My father tried for years to get me out of Mute. He finally gave up. That report you saw was one of his periodic requests. It was filed away somewhere, wasn't it? Gathering dust in a drawer."

"If this works out," Curt said, "many more children will have a chance to get out of the Mute-class. You won't be the only one. You're the first of many, we hope."

Pat kicked at a pebble. "I don't feel so new, so astonishingly different. I don't feel anything at all. You say I'm opaque to telepathic invasion, but I've only been scanned one or two times in my life." She touched her head with her copper-colored fingers and smiled. "If no Corpsman is scanning me, I'm just like anybody else."

"You ability is a counter-talent," Curt pointed out. "It takes the original talent to call it into being. Naturally, you're not conscious of it during your ordinary routine of living."

"A counter-talent. It seems so—so negative. I don't do anything, like you do . . . I don't move objects or turn stones into bread or give birth without impregnation or bring dead people back to life. I just negate somebody else's ability. It seems like a hostile, stultifying sort of ability—to cancel out the telepathic factor."

"That could be as useful as the telepathic factor itself. Especially for all of us non-teeps."

"Suppose somebody comes along who balances your ability, Curt." She had turned dead serious, sounding discouraged and unhappy. "People will arise who balance out *all* Psi talents. We'll be back where we started from. It'll be like not having Psi at all."

"I don't think so," Curt answered. "The Anti-Psi factor is a natural restoration of balance. One insect learns to fly, so another learns to build a web to trap him. Is that the same as no flight? Clams developed hard shells to protect them; therefore birds learn to fly the clam up high in the air and drop him on a rock. In a sense you're a life-form preying on the Psis and the Psis are life-forms that prey on the Norms. That makes you a friend of the Norm-class. Balance, the full circle, predator and prey. It's an eternal system and frankly I can't see how it could be improved."

"You might be considered a traitor."

"Yes," Curt agreed. "I suppose so."

"Doesn't it bother you?"

"It bothers me that people will feel hostile toward me. But you can't live very long without arousing hostility. Julie feels hostility toward you. Reynolds feels hostility for me already. You can't please everybody, because people want different things. Please one and you displease another. In this life you have to decide which of them you want to please. I'd prefer to please Fairchild."

"He should be glad."

"If he's aware of what's going on. Fairchild's an overworked bureaucrat. He may decide I exceeded my authority in acting on your father's petition. He may want it filed back where it was, and you returned to Prox VI. He may even fine me a penalty."

❖ ❖ ❖

They left the School and drove down the long highway to the shore of the ocean. Tim shouted with happiness at the vast stretch of deserted beach as he raced off, arms waving, his yells lost in the ceaseless lapping of the ocean waves. The red-tinted sky warmed above them. The three of them were completely isolated by the bowl of ocean and sky and beach. No other humans were visible, only a flock of indigenous birds strolling around in search of sand crustaceans.

"It's wonderful," Pat said, awed. "I guess the oceans of Terra are like this, big and bright and red."

"Blue," Curt corrected. He lay sprawled out on the warm sand, smoking his pipe and gazing moodily at the probing waves that oozed up on the beach a few yards away. The waves left heaps of steaming seaplants stranded.

Tim came hurrying back with his arms full of the dripping, slimy weeds. He dumped the coils of still quivering vegetable life in front of Pat and his father.

"He likes the ocean," Pat said.

"No hiding places for Others," Curt answered. "He can see for miles, so he knows they can't creep up on him."

"Others?" She was curious. "He's such a strange boy. So worried and busy. He takes his alternate world so seriously. Not a pleasant world, I guess. Too many responsibilities."

The sky turned hot. Tim began building an intricate structure out of wet sand lugged from the water's edge.

Pat scampered barefooted to join Tim. The two of them labored, adding infinite walls and side-buildings and towers. In the hot glare of the water, the girl's bare shoulders and back dripped perspiration. She sat up finally, gasping and exhausted, pushed her hair from her eyes and struggled to her feet.

"It's too hot," she gasped, throwing herself down beside Curt. "The weather's so different here. I'm sleepy."

Tim continued building the structure. The two of them watched him languidly, crumbling bits of dry sand between their fingers.

"I guess," Pat said after a while, "there isn't much left to your marriage. I've made it impossible for you and Julie to live together."

"It's not your fault. We were never really together. All we had in common was our talent and that has nothing to do with over-all personality. The total individual."

Pat slid off her skirt and waded down to the ocean's edge. She curled up in the swirling pink foam and began washing her hair. Half-buried in the piles of foam and seakelp, her sleek, tanned body glowed wet and healthy in the overhead sun.

"Come on!" she called to Curt. "It's so cool."

Curt knocked the ashes from his pipe into the dry sand. "We have to get back. Sooner or later I've got to have it out with Fairchild. We need a decision."

Pat strode from the water, body streaming, head tossed back, hair dripping down her shoulders. Tim attracted her attention and she halted to study his sand building.

"You're right," she said to Curt. "We shouldn't be here wading and dozing and building sand castles. Fairchild's trying to keep the Separation working, and we have real things to build up in the backward Colonies."

As she dried herself with Curt's coat she told him about Proxima VI.

"It's like the Middle Ages back on Terra. Most of our people think Psi powers are miracles. They think the Psis are saints."

"I suppose that's what the saints were," Curt agreed. "They raised the dead, turned inorganic material into organic and moved objects around. The Psi ability has probably always been present in the human race. The Psi-class individual isn't new; he's always been with us, helping here and there, sometimes doing harm when he exploited his talent against mankind."

Pat tugged on her sandals. "There's an old woman near our village, a first-rate Resurrector. She won't leave Prox VI; she won't go with the Government Teams or get mixed up with the School. She wants to stay where she is, being a witch and wise woman. People come to her and she heals the sick."

Pat fastened her blouse and started toward the car. "When I was seven I broke my arm. She put her old withered hands on it and the break repaired itself. Apparently her hands radiate some kind of generative field that affects the growth-rate of the cells. And I remember one time when a boy was drowned and she brought him back to life."

"Get an old woman who can heal, another who can precog the future, and your village is set up. We Psis have been helping longer than we realize."

"Come on, Tim!" Pat called, tanned hands to her lips. "Time to go back!"

The boy bent down one last time to peer into the depths of his structure, the elaborate inner sections and his sand building.

Suddenly he screamed, leaped back and came racing frantically toward the car.

Pat caught hold of him and he clung to her, face distorted with terror. "What is it?" Pat was frightened. "Curt, *what was it?*"

Curt came over and squatted down beside the boy. "What was in there?" he asked gently. "You built it."

The boy's lips moved. "A *Left*," he muttered almost inaudibly. "There was a Left, I know it. The first real Left. And it hung on."

Pat and Curt glanced at each other uneasily. "What's he talking about?" Pat asked.

Curt got behind the wheel of the car and pushed open the doors for the two of them. "I don't know. But I think we'd better get back to town. I'll talk to Fairchild and get this business of Anti-Psi cleared up. Once that's out of the way, you and I can devote ourselves to Tim for the rest of our lives."

❖❖❖

Fairchild was pale and tired as he sat behind his desk in his office, hands folded in front of him, a few Norm-class advisors here and there, listening intently. Dark circles mooned under his eyes. As he listened to Curt he sipped at a glass of tomato juice.

"In other words," Fairchild muttered, "you're saying we can't really trust you Psis. It's a paradox." His voice broke with despair. "A Psi comes here and says *all Psis lie*. What the hell am I supposed to do?"

"Not all Psis." Being able to preview the scene gave Curt remarkable calmness. "I'm saying that in a way Terra is right . . . the existence of super-talented humans poses a problem for those without super-talents. But Terra's answer is wrong; sterilization is vicious and senseless. But cooperation isn't as easy as you imagine. You're dependent on our talents for survival and that means we have you where we want you. We can dictate to you because, without us, Terra would come in and clap you all into military prison."

"And destroy you Psis," the old man standing behind Fairchild reminded him. "Don't forget that."

Curt eyed the old man. It was the same wide-shouldered, gray-faced individual of the night before. There was something familiar about him. Curt peered closer and gasped, in spite of his preview.

"You're a Psi," he said.

The old man bowed slightly. "Evidently."

"Come on," Fairchild said. "All right, we've seen this girl and we'll accept your theory of Anti-Psi. *What do you want us to do?*" He wiped his forehead miserably. "I know Reynolds is a menace. But damn it, Terran infiltrators would be running all around here without the Corps!"

"I want you to create a legal fourth class," Curt stated. "The Anti-Psi class. I want you to give it status-immunity from sterilization. I want you to publicize it. Women come in here with their children from all parts of the Colonies, trying to convince you they've got Psis to offer, not Mutes. I want you to set up the Anti-Psi talents out where we can utilize them."

Fairchild licked his dry lips. "You think more exist already?"

"Very possibly. I came on Pat by accident. But get the flow started! Get the mothers hovering anxiously over their cribs for Anti-Psis . . . We'll need all we can get."

There was silence.

"Consider what Mr. Purcell is doing," the old man said at last. "An Anti-Precog may arise, a person whose actions in the future can't be previewed. A sort of Heisenberg's indeterminate particle . . . a man who throws off all precog prediction. And yet Mr. Purcell has come here to make his suggestions. He's thinking of Separation, not himself."

Fairchild's fingers twitched. "Reynolds is going to be mad as hell."

"He's already mad," Curt said. "He undoubtedly knows about this right now."

"He'll protest!"

Curt laughed; some of the officials smiled. "Of course he'll protest. Don't you understand? *You're being eliminated.* You think Norms are going to be around much longer? Charity is damn scarce in this universe. You Norms gape at Psis like rustics at a carnival. Wonderful . . . magical. You encouraged Psis, built the School, gave us our chance here in the Colonies. In fifty years you'll be slave laborers for us. You'll be doing our manual labor—unless you have sense enough to create the fourth class, the Anti-Psi class. You've got to stand up to Reynolds."

"I hate to alienate him," Fairchild muttered. "Why the hell can't we all work together?" He appealed to the others around the room. "Why can't we all be brothers?"

"Because," Curt answered, "we're not. Face facts. Brotherhood is a fine idea, but it'll come into existence sooner if we achieve a balance of social forces."

"Is it possible," the old man suggested, "that once the concept of Anti-Psi reaches Terra the sterilization program will be modified?

This idea may erase the irrational terror the non-mutants have, their phobia that we're monsters about to invade and take over their world. Sit next to them in theaters. Marry their sisters."

"All right," Fairchild agreed. "I'll construct an official directive. Give me an hour to word it—I want to get all the loopholes out."

Curt got to his feet. It was over. As he had previewed, Fairchild had agreed. "We should start getting reports almost at once," he said. "As soon as routine checking of the files begins."

Fairchild nodded. "Yes, almost at once."

"I assume you'll keep me informed." Apprehension moved through Curt. He had succeeded . . . or had he? He scanned the next half hour. There was nothing negative he could preview. He caught a quick scene of himself and Pat, himself and Julie and Tim. But still his uneasiness remained, an intuition deeper than his precog.

Everything looked fine, but he knew better. Something basic and chilling had gone wrong.

IV

He met Pat in a small out-of-the-way bar at the rim of the city. Darkness flickered around their table. The air was thick and pungent with the presence of people. Bursts of muted laughter broke out, muffled by the steady blur of conversation.

"How'd it go?" she asked, eyes large and dark, as he seated himself across from her. "Did Fairchild agree?"

Curt ordered a Tom Collins for her and bourbon and water for himself. Then he outlined what had taken place.

"So everything's all right." Pat reached across the table to touch his hand. "Isn't it?"

Curt sipped at his drink. "I guess so. The Anti-Psi class is being formed. But it was too easy. Too simple."

"You can see ahead, can't you? Is anything going to happen?"

Across the dark room the music machine was creating vague patterns of sound, random harmonics and rhythms in a procession of soft clusters that drifted through the room. A few couples moved languidly together in response to the shifting patterns.

Curt offered her a cigarette and the two of them lit up from the candle in the center of the table. "Now you have your status."

Pat's dark eyes flickered. "Yes, that's so. The new Anti-Psi class. I don't have to worry now. That's all over."

"We're waiting for others. If no others show, you're a member of a unique class. The only Anti-Psi in the Universe."

For a moment Pat was silent. Then she asked, "What do you see after that?" She sipped her drink. "I mean, I'm going to stay here, aren't I? Or will I be going back?"

"You'll stay here."

"With you?"

"With me. And with Tim."

"What about Julie?"

"The two of us signed mutual releases a year ago. They're on file, somewhere. Never processed. It was an agreement we made, so neither of us could block the other later on."

"I think Tim likes me. He won't mind, will he?"

"Not at all," Curt said.

"It ought to be nice, don't you think? The three of us. We can work with Tim, try to find out about his talent, what he is and what he's thinking. I'd enjoy that . . . he responds to me. And we have a long time; there's no hurry."

Her fingers clasped around his. In the shifting darkness of the bar her features swam close to his own. Curt leaned forward, hesitated a moment as her warm breath stained his lips and then kissed her.

Pat smiled up at him. "There're so many things for us to do. Here, and perhaps later on Prox VI. I want to go back there, sometime. Could we? Just for a while; we wouldn't have to stay. So I can see that it's still going on, all the things I worked at all my life. So I could see my world."

"Sure," Curt said. "Yes, we'll go back there."

Across from them a nervous little man had finished his garlic bread and wine. He wiped his mouth, glanced at his wristwatch and got to his feet. As he squeezed past Curt he reached into his pocket, jangled change and jerkily brought out his hand. Gripping a slender tube, he turned around, bent over Pat, and depressed the tube.

A single pellet dribbled from the tube, clung for a split second to the shiny surface of her hair, and then was gone. A dull echo of vibration rolled up toward the nearby tables. The nervous little man continued on.

Curt was on his feet, numb with shock. He was still gazing down, paralyzed, when Reynolds appeared beside him and firmly pulled him away.

"She's dead," Reynolds was saying. "Try to understand. She died instantly; there was no pain. It goes directly to the central nervous system. She wasn't even aware of it."

Nobody in the bar had stirred. They sat at their tables, faces impassive, watching as Reynolds signaled for more light. The darkness faded and the objects of the room leaped into clarity.

"Stop that machine," Reynolds ordered sharply. The music machine stumbled into silence. "These people here are Corpsmen," he explained to Curt. "We probed your thoughts about this place as you entered Fairchild's office."

"But I didn't catch it," Curt muttered. "There was no warning. No preview."

"The man who killed her is an Anti-Psi," Reynolds said. "We've known of the category for a number of years; remember, it took an initial probe to uncover Patricia Connley's shield."

"Yes," Curt agreed. "She was probed years ago. By one of you."

"We don't like the Anti-Psi idea. We wanted to keep the class out of existence, but we were interested. We've uncovered and neutralized fourteen Anti-Psis over the past decade. On this, we have virtually the whole Psi-class behind us—except you. The problem, of course, is that no Anti-Psi talent can be brought out unless matched against the Psionic talent it negates."

Curt understood. "You had to match this man against a Precog. And there's only one Precog other than myself."

"Julie was cooperative. We brought the problem to her a few months ago. We had definite proof to give her concerning your affair with this girl. I don't understand how you expected to keep Telepaths from knowing your plans, but apparently you did. In any case, the girl is dead. And there won't be any Anti-Psi class. We waited as long as possible, for we don't like to destroy talented individuals. But Fairchild was on the verge of signing the enabling legislation, so we couldn't hold off any longer."

Curt hit out frantically, knowing even as he did so that it was futile. Reynolds slid back; his foot tangled with the table and he staggered. Curt leaped on him, smashed the tall cold glass that had held Pat's drink and lifted the jagged edges over Reynolds' face.

Corpsmen pulled him off.

Curt broke away. He reached down and gathered up Pat's body. She was still warm; her face was calm, expressionless, an empty burned-out shell that mirrored nothing. He carried her from the bar and out into the frigid night-dark street. A moment later he lowered her into his car and crept behind the wheel.

He drove to the School, parked the car, and carried her into the main building. Pushing past astonished officials, he reached the children's quarters and forced open the door to Sally's rooms with his shoulder.

She was wide-awake and fully dressed. Seated on a straight-back chair the child faced him defiantly. "You see?" she shrilled. "See what you did?"

He was too dazed to answer.

"It's all your fault! You made Reynolds do it. He *had* to kill her." She leaped to her feet and ran toward him screaming hysterically. "You're an enemy! You're against us! You want to make trouble for all of us. I told Reynolds what you were doing and he—"

Her voice trailed off as he moved out of the room with his heavy armload. As he lumbered up the corridor the hysterical girl followed him.

"You want to go across—you want me to get Big Noodle to take you across!" She ran in front of him, darting here and there like a maniacal insect. Tears ran down her cheeks; her face was distorted beyond recognition. She followed him all the way to Big Noodle's chamber. "I'm not going to help you! You're against all of us and I'm never going to help you again! I'm *glad* she's dead. I wish you were dead, too. And you're going to be dead when Reynolds catches you. He told me so. He said there wasn't going to be any more like you and we would have things the way they ought to be, and nobody, not you nor any of those *numbskulls* can stop us!"

He lowered Pat's body onto the floor and moved out of the chamber. Sally raced after him.

"You know what he did to Fairchild? He had him fixed so he can't do anything ever again."

Curt tripped a locked door and entered his son's room. The door closed after him and the girl's frenzied screams died to a muffled vibration. Tim sat up in bed, surprised and half-stupefied by sleep.

"Come on," Curt said. He dragged the boy from his bed, dressed him, and hurried him outside into the hall.

Sally stopped them as they re-entered Big Noodle's chamber. "He won't do it," she screamed. "He's afraid of me and I told him not to. You understand?"

❖❖❖

Big Noodle lay slumped in his massive chair. He lifted his great hand as Curt approached him. "What do you want?" he muttered. "What's the matter with her?" He indicated Pat's inert body. "She pass out or something?"

"Reynolds killed her!" Sally shrilled, dancing around Curt and his son. "And he's going to kill Mr. Purcell! He's going to kill everybody that tries to stop us!"

Big Noodle's thick features darkened. The wattles of bristly flesh turned a flushed, mottled crimson. "What's going on, Curt?" he muttered.

"The Corps is taking over," Curt answered.

"They killed your girl?"

"Yes."

Big Noodle strained to a sitting position and leaned forward. "Reynolds is after you?"

"Yes."

Big Noodle licked his thick lips hesitantly. "Where do you want to go?" he asked hoarsely. "I can move you out of here, to Terra, maybe. Or—"

Sally made frantic motions with her hands. Part of Big Noodle's chair writhed and became animate. The arms twisted around him, cut viciously into his puddinglike paunch. He retched and closed his eyes.

"I'll make you sorry!" Sally chanted. "I can do terrible things to you!"

"I don't want to go to Terra," Curt said. He gathered up Pat's body and motioned Tim over beside him. "I want to go to Proxima VI."

Big Noodle struggled to make up his mind. Outside the room officials and Corpsmen were in cautious motion. A bedlam of sound and uncertainty rang up and down the corridors.

Sally's shrill voice rose over the rumble of sound as she tried to attract Big Noodle's attention. "You know what I'll do! You know what will happen to you!"

Big Noodle made his decision. He tried an abortive stab at Sally before turning to Curt; a ton of molten plastic transported from some Terran factory cascaded down on her in a hissing torrent. Sally's body dissolved, one arm raised and twitching, the echo of her voice still hanging in the air.

Big Noodle had acted, but the warp directed at him from the dying girl was already in existence. As Curt felt the air of space-transformation all around him, he caught a final glimpse of Big Noodle's torment. He had never known precisely what it was Sally dangled over the big idiot's head. Now he saw it and understood Big Noodle's hesitation. A high-pitched scream rattled from Big Noodle's throat and around Curt as the chamber ebbed away. Big Noodle altered and flowed as Sally's change engulfed him.

Curt realized, then, the amount of courage buried in the vegetable rolls of fat. Big Noodle had known the risk, taken it, and accepted—more or less—the consequences.

The vast body had become a mass of crawling spiders. What had been Big Noodle was now a mound of hairy, quivering beings, thousands of them, spiders without number, dropping off and clinging again, clustering and separating and reclustering.

And then the chamber was gone. He was across.

❖ ❖ ❖

It was early afternoon. He lay for a time, half-buried in tangled vines. Insects hummed around him, seeking moisture from the stalks of foul-smelling flowers. The red-tinted sky baked in the mounting sunlight. Far off, an animal of some kind called mournfully.

Nearby, his son stirred. The boy got to his feet, wandered about aimlessly and finally approached his father.

Curt pulled himself up. His clothes were torn. Blood oozed down his cheek, into his mouth. He shook his head, shuddered, and looked around.

Pat's body lay a few feet off. A crumpled and broken thing, it was without life of any kind. A hollow husk, abandoned and deserted.

He made his way over to her. For a time he squatted on his haunches, gazing vacantly down at her. Then he leaned over, picked her up, and struggled to his feet.

"Come on," he said to Tim. "Let's get started."

They walked a long time. Big Noodle had dropped them between villages, in the turgid chaos of the Proxima VI forests. Once he stopped in an open field and rested. Against the line of drooping trees a waver of blue smoke drifted. A kiln, perhaps. Or somebody clearing away the brush. He lifted Pat up in his arms again and continued on.

When he crashed from the underbrush and out into the road, the villagers were paralyzed with fright. Some of them raced off, a few remained, staring blankly at the man and the boy beside him.

"Who are you?" one of them demanded as he fumbled for a hack-knife. "What have you got there?"

They got a work-truck for him, allowed him to dump Pat in with the rough-cut lumber and then drove him and his son to the nearest village. He wasn't far off, only a hundred miles. From the common store of the village he was given heavy work clothes and fed. Tim was bathed and cared for, and a general conference was called.

He sat at a huge, rough table, littered with remains of the midday meal. He knew their decision; he could preview it without trouble.

"She can't fix up anybody that far gone," the leader of the village explained to him. "The girl's whole upper ganglia and brain are gone, and most of the spinal column."

He listened, but didn't speak. Afterwards, he wangled a battered truck, loaded Pat and Tim in, and started on.

❖ ❖ ❖

Her village had been notified by short-wave radio. He was pulled from the truck by savage hands; a pandemonium of noise and fury boiled around him, excited faces distorted by grief and horror. Shouts, outraged shoves, questions, a blur of men and women milling and pushing until finally her brothers cleared a path for him to their home.

"It's useless," her father was saying to him. "And the old woman's gone, I think. That was years ago." The man gestured toward the mountains. "She lived up there—used to come down. Not for years." He grabbed Curt roughly. "It's too late, God damn it! She's dead! You can't bring her back!"

He listened to the words, still said nothing. He had no interest in predictions of any kind. When they had finished talking to him, he gathered up Pat's body, carried it back to the truck, called his son and continued on.

It grew cold and silent as the truck wheezily climbed the road into the mountains. Frigid air plucked at him; the road was obscured by dense clouds of mist that billowed up from the chalky soil. At one point a lumbering animal barred his way until he drove it off by throwing rocks at it. Finally the truck ran out of fuel and stopped. He got out, stood for a time, then woke up his son and continued on foot.

It was almost dark when he found the hut perched on a lip of rock. A fetid stench of offal and drying hides stung his nose as he staggered past heaps of discarded rubble, tin cans and boxes, rotting fabric and vermin-infested lumber.

The old woman was watering a patch of wretched vegetables. As he approached, she lowered her sprinkling can and turned toward him, wrinkled face tight with suspicion and wonder.

"I can't do it," she said flatly as she crouched over Pat's inert body. She ran her dry, leathery hands over the dead face, pulled aside the girl's shirt and kneaded the cold flesh at the base of the neck. She pushed aside the tangle of black hair and gripped the skull with her strong fingers. "No, I can't do a thing." Her voice was rusty and harsh in the night fog that billowed around them. "She's burned out. No tissue left to repair."

Curt made his cracked lips move. "Is there another?" he grated. "Any more Resurrectors here?"

The old woman struggled to her feet. "Nobody can help you, don't you understand? She's dead!"

He remained. He asked the woman again and again. Finally there was a begrudging answer. Somewhere on the other side of the planet there was supposed to be a competitor. He gave the old woman his cigarettes and lighter and fountain pen, picked up the cold body and started back. Tim trailed after him, head drooping, body bent with fatigue.

"Come on," Curt ordered harshly. The old woman watched silently as they threaded their way down by the light of Proxima VI's two sullen, yellowed moons.

❖ ❖ ❖

He got only a quarter mile. In some way, without warning, her body was gone. He had lost her, dropped her along the way. Somewhere among the rubbish-littered rocks and weeds that fingered their way over the trail. Probably into one of the deep gorges that cut into the jagged side of the mountain.

He sat down on the ground and rested. There was nothing left. Fairchild had dwindled into the hands of the Corps. Big Noodle was destroyed by Sally. Sally was gone, too. The colonies were open to the Terrans; their wall against projectiles had dissolved when Big Noodle died. And Pat.

There was a sound behind him. Panting with despair and fatigue, he turned only slightly. For a brief second he thought it was Tim catching up with him. He strained to see; the shape that emerged from the half-light was too tall, too sure-footed. A familiar shape.

"You're right," the old man said, the ancient Psi who had stood beside Fairchild. He came up, vast and awesome in the aged yellow moonlight. "There's no use trying to bring her back. It could be done, but it's too difficult. And there are other things for you and me to think about."

Curt scrambled off. Falling, sliding, slashed by the stones under him, he made his way blindly down the trail. Dirt rattled after him while, choking, he struggled onto the level ground.

When he halted again, it was Tim who came after him. For an

instant he thought it had been an illusion, a figment of his imagination. The old man was gone; he hadn't been there.

He didn't fully understand until he saw the change take place in front of him. And this time it went the other way. He realized that this one was a *Left*. And it was a familiar figure, but in a different way. A figure he remembered from the past.

Where the boy of eight had stood, a wailing, fretful baby of sixteen months struggled and groped. Now the substitution had gone in the other direction . . . and he couldn't deny what his eyes saw.

"All right," he said, when the eight-year-old Tim reappeared and the baby was gone. But the boy remained only a moment. He vanished almost at once, and this time a new shape stood on the trail. A man in his middle thirties, a man Curt had never seen before.

A familiar man.

"*You're my son*," Curt said.

"That's right." The man appraised him in the dim light. "You realize that she can't be brought back, don't you? We have to get that out of the way before we can proceed."

Curt nodded wearily. "I know."

"Fine." Tim advanced toward him, hand out. "Then let's get back down. We have a lot to do. We middle and extreme Rights have been trying to get through for some time. It's been difficult to come back without the approval of the Center one. And in these cases the Center is too young to understand."

"So that's what he meant," Curt murmured as the two of them made their way along the road, toward the village. "The Others are himself, along his time-track."

"Left is previous Others," Tim answered. "Right, of course, is the future. You said that Precog and Precog made nothing. Now you know. They make the ultimate Precog—the ability to move through time."

"You Others were trying to get over. He'd see you and be frightened."

"It was very hard, but we knew eventually he'd grow old enough to comprehend. He built up an elaborate mythology. That is, we did. I did." Tim laughed. "You see, there still isn't an adequate terminology. There never is for a unique happening."

"I could change the future," Curt said, "because I could see into it. But I couldn't change the present. You can change the present by going back into the past. That's why that extreme Right Other, the old man, hung around Fairchild."

"That was our first successful crossing. We were finally able to induce the Center to take his two steps Right. That switched the two, but it took time."

"What's going to happen now?" Curt asked. "The war? The Separation? All this about Reynolds?"

"As you realized before, we can alter it by going back. It's dangerous. A simple change in the past may completely alter the present. The time-traveling talent is the most critical—and the most Promethean. Every other talent, without exception, can change only what's going to happen. I could wipe out everything that stands. I precede everyone and everything. Nothing can be used against me. I am always there first. I have always been there."

Curt was silent as they passed the abandoned, rusting truck. Finally he asked. "What is Anti-Psi? What did you have to do with that?"

"Not much," his son said. "You can take credit for bringing it out into the open, since we didn't begin operating until the last few hours. We came along in time to aid it—you saw us with Fairchild. We're *sponsoring* Anti-Psi. You'd be surprised to see some of the alternate time-paths on which Anti-Psi fails to get pushed forward. Your precog was right—they're not very pleasant."

"So I've had help lately."

"We're behind you, yes. And from now on, our help will increase. Always, we try to introduce balances. Stalemates, such as Anti-Psi. Right now, Reynolds is a little out of balance, but he can easily be checked. Steps are being taken. We're not infinite in power, of course. We're limited by our life-span, about seventy years. It's a strange feeling to be outside of time. You're outside of change, subject to no laws.

"It's like suddenly being lifted off the chess board and seeing everybody as pieces—seeing the whole Universe as a game of black and white squares—with everybody and every object stuck on his space-time spot. We're off the board; we can reach down from above. Adjust, alter the position of the men, change the game without the pieces knowing. From outside."

"And you won't bring her back?" Curt appealed.

"You can't expect me to be too sympathetic toward the girl," his son said. "After all, Julie is my mother. I know now what they used to mean by *mill of the gods*. I wish we could grind less small . . . I wish we could spare some of those who get caught in the gears. But if you could see it as we do, you'd understand. We have a universe hanging in the balance; it's an awfully big board."

"A board so big that one person doesn't count?" Curt asked, agonized.

His son looked concerned. Curt remembered looking like that himself when trying to explain something to the boy that was beyond the child's comprehension. He hoped Tim would do a better job than he'd been able to do.

"Not that," Tim said. "To us, she isn't gone. She's still there, on another part of the board that you can't see. She always was there. She always will be. No piece ever falls off the board . . . no matter how small."

"For you," said Curt.

"Yes. We're outside the board. It may be that our talent will be shared by everybody. When that happens, there will be no misunderstanding of tragedy and death."

"And meanwhile?" Curt ached with the tension of *willing* Tim to agree. "I don't have the talent. To me, she's dead. The place she occupied on the board is empty. Julie can't fill it. Nobody can."

Tim considered. It looked like deep thought, but Curt could sense that his son was moving restlessly along the timepaths, seeking a rebuttal. His eyes focused again on his father and he nodded sadly.

"I can't show you where she is on the board," he said. "And your life is vacant along every path except one."

Curt heard someone coming through the brush. He turned—and then Pat was in his arms.

"This one," Tim said.

STORY NOTES

BREAKFAST AT TWILIGHT
Reached the Scott Meredith Literary Agency (hereinafter, SMLA) on January 17, 1953, published in *Amazing*, July 1954. "There you are in your home," he wrote in a story note for this tale's republication in *The Best of Philip K. Dick* (Ballantine, 1977), "and the soldiers smash down the door and tell you you're in the middle of World War III. Something's gone wrong with time. I love to fiddle with the idea of basic categories of reality, such as space and time, breaking down. It's my love of chaos, I suppose." *Amazing Stories* had been the first magazine dedicated to science fiction, its founding by Hugo Gernsback in 1926 a pivotal event in the field's history. In 1953 its editor was Howard Browne, sometime author of tales of the prehistoric warrior Tharn, who supposedly hated science fiction himself. "Breakfast at Twilight" was the fourth Dick's story Browne purchased for the magazine, following "The Commuter," "The Builder," and "Small Town," all of them, like this one, stories expressing a yearning for escape from intolerable worlds. Overtly anti-McCarthyite—in its open discussion of how a war with communism destroys personal freedoms—it would be Dick's last story for *Amazing* until 1963.

SURVEY TEAM
Reached SMLA on April 3, 1953, published in *Fantastic Universe*, May 1954. *Fantastic Universe*, published and at the time this issue went to press edited as well by 1930s pulp veteran Leo Margulies, lasted from 1953 to

1960 and was precisely the sort of penny a word, "bottom market" outlet Dick's agents at SMLA found for most of his early stories. The story's grim realism comes not so much in the space explorers' discovery but in their determination to ignore it and proceed with their plans anyway. It's the flip side of Dick's (or the genre's) indefatigable heroes who in this author's more popular stories—see for example this volume's "The Turning Wheel" or "The Last of the Masters"—crawl out of the rubble and get back to work. This particular story was tossed away and never reprinted during Dick's lifetime. Too bad, for as the unfolding nightmare of the 21st century threatens to make our planet uninhabitable "Survey Team" may wind up being the most prophetic story Philip K. Dick ever wrote.

THE HANGING STRANGER

Reached SMLA on May 4, 1953, published in *Science Fiction Adventures*, September 1953. This powerful story appeared in the last issue of this ambitious magazine edited by its founder, veteran writer and editor Lester del Rey. Del Rey (1915-93) had first made his mark with the sentimental man-robot love story "Helen O'Loy" (1938)—which the human-android love story of *Do Androids Dream of Electric Sheep?* (1968) is indebted to, if only as a counterexample—and with "Nerves" (1942), which anticipates an accident in a nuclear power plant. Much later, in 1977, he would co-found Del Rey Books, a popular science fiction and fantasy imprint. In 1952-53, before falling out with his publisher, he edited this highly literate, well-paying journal, stating in a manifesto in its first issue

> (T)he problems of the people in the stories must be stressed more than the gadgets they use. Fiction is concerned with the reactions of human believable characters in unusual predicaments. The fact that the character is a robot or a man from Sirius, and the predicament is one which can only exist in the future or on another world, doesn't change that; it only gives a freshness or gives added punch to a story.

"The Hanging Stranger" utilizes the same idea, that of alien possession of the good people of a small town, employed by Jack Finney in his *The Body Snatchers* (1954), filmed as *Invasion of the Body Snatchers* in 1956 (and three times since). Both tales were anticipated by Robert Heinlein in his overtly anti-Communist allegory *The Puppet Masters* (1951). Dick's short story "The Father-Thing" (written two months after "The Hanging Stranger") uses the same idea of pods being used to replicate humans that Finney uses in his tale. In both of his stories Dick is less interested in the possession itself (as with Heinlein and Finney) than on the psychological toll the possession wrecks on its witnesses. As such it was a perfect story for Del Rey's *Science Fiction Adventures*, which only lasted a year after its founding editor resigned in protest over an order to reduce payments to its authors.

THE EYES HAVE IT

Reached SMLA March 13, 1953, published in *Science Fiction Stories* No. 1, 1953. This journal enjoyed several incarnations, both during the prewar science fiction boom (1939-41) and again intermittently from 1953-60, of which this issue was the first of its revival, a one-shot digest-sized experiment to see if it would sell. It did, and Dick's agents placed another story, "The Turning Wheel," in issue No. 2 the following year. This amusing story satirizes both the paranoia story (a popular subgenre in science fiction, as in L. Ron Hubbard's 1940 classic "Fear"—a favorite of Dick's), and bad writing generally. There's such a thing as being too literal.

THE TURNING WHEEL

Reached SMLA July 8, 1953, published in *Science Fiction Stories* No. 2, 1954. "The Turning Wheel" glancingly satirizes another science fiction writer, L. Ron Hubbard, who had first promulgated his self-improvement technique, Dianetics, by publicizing it in *Astounding Science Fiction* in 1950, and later in a best-selling book. Branch offices offering Dianetics treatment opened across the U.S. in 1950-51; Philip Dick's mother Dorothy Dick Hudner was deeply involved for a while. Dick was well aware of Hubbard, if only for his prolific authorship of fantasy and science fiction stories from the late 1930s onward. Hubbard began expanding Dianetics into an "applied religious philosophy" in 1952; the first Church of Scientology followed officially in December 1953. Dick's story refers to the governing religion's founder as "Elron Hu" and parodies one of Scientology's goals, "clearness" in the salutation "Clearness be with you." Much of the story is based however not on Scientology but on Eastern concepts of reincarnation. It rejects its fatalism in favor of rebuilding one's way out of the rubble, in what would be a defining characteristic of his later work.

THE LAST OF THE MASTERS
Submitted as "Protection Agency." Reached SMLA July 8, 1953, published in *Orbit Science Fiction*, November-December 1954. *Orbit* was edited by Donald Wollheim in all but name; Wollheim was just at the time this story appeared preparing to publish Dick's first science fiction novel, *Solar Lottery* (1955). Late in his life Dick contributed this story note to its reprinting in the Mark Hurst-edited anthology *The Golden Man* (Berkley, 1980): "Now I show trust of robot as leader, a robot who is the suffering servant, which is to say a form of Christ. Leader as servant of man; leader who should be dispensed with—perhaps. An ambiguity hangs over the morality of this story. Should we have a leader or should we think for ourselves? Obviously the latter, in principle. But—sometimes there lies a gulf between what is theoretically right and that which is practical. It's interesting that I could trust a robot and not an android. Perhaps it's because a robot does not try to deceive you as to what it is."

STRANGE EDEN
Submitted as "Immolation." Reached SMLA Aug. 4, 1953, published in *Imagination*, December 1954. The chatty, informal "Madge," as its fans called it, was edited by William Hamling, its only editor over its eight year run (1950-58). "The little lady is the love of my life," proclaimed Hamling in its June 1954 issue. One letter writer wrote in approvingly

in the November issue that while some magazines were A, "waste of time," others like *Imagination* were in his category B, "pleasant reading." (*Astounding* and *Galaxy* qualified as C, "true science fiction.") Joe Sanders, in his entry on the journal in the outstanding reference book on the field (Marshall B. Tymn and Mike Ashley's *Science Fiction, Fantasy, and Weird Fiction Magazines*), puts the letter writer's comments another way by likening the experience of reading *Imagination* to "passing time effortlessly, like a routine TV adventure show." It's hard to imagine, however, any routine TV adventure with such a fate in store for its aggressive, James T. Kirk-like hero. "Brent only wanted to look around the planet," went this story's description in this issue's table of contents. "The trouble was, he looked too far!"

TONY AND THE BEETLES

Reached SMLA Aug. 31, 1953, published in *Orbit Science Fiction* No. 2, 1953. Scott Meredith had many sub-agents in his employ, who commented on their authors' properties as they reached them. This story's reader, perhaps subliminally put off by its anti-triumphalist tone (so out of tune with Eisenhower America), found it "pedestrian . . . Rather corny stuff pretending to be impressive." It was designated for the "lower markets." It wound up in the second issue of Donald Wollheim's *Orbit*, where it appears to have been sent immediately, given its unusual speed of publication. Wollheim and Dick had a long history together, for it was another magazine Wollheim edited, *Stirring Science Stories*, that was the very first science fiction magazine the young Philip K. Dick ever found and read. "One thing I'm proud of," Wollheim told this writer, "is that Philip K. Dick never saw a science fiction magazine until he saw *Stirring Science Stories*—if you throw a thousand seeds out, one sprouts! I've always been happy about that."

EXHIBIT PIECE

Reached SMLA Oct. 21, 1953, published in *If*, August 1954. *If* was at the time this story was published edited by its publisher, James L. Quinn, and Assistant Editor Eve Wulff. Neither one of the field's most prestigious journals, like Anthony Boucher's *The Magazine of Fantasy and Science Fiction*, John W. Campbell's *Astounding*, or Horace Gold's *Galaxy*, nor a "bottom market" like *Imagination*, *If* featured the whole run of 1950s science fiction writers, from Isaac Asimov to Walter M. Miller, from Arthur C. Clarke to William Tenn, and newcomers like Harlan Ellison and Robert Silverberg as well. Dick stands out even among these very talented men for the realism of his contributions—note the detailing in his description of George Miller's Berkeley home. Even the street directions are accurate—Virginia Street towards Shattuck Avenue is still the way to the Bay Bridge.

THE CRAWLERS

Submitted as "Foundling Home." Reached SMLA October 29, 1953, published in *Imagination*, July 1954. The Meredith sub-agent who commented on this property in the SMLA files liked this one, calling it "one of his better stories." It still wound up at the low-paying "Madge," perhaps because of its extremely disturbing nature. A surprising number of Dick's stories deal with infanticide, and his 1974 story "The Pre-Persons" can be considered a logical extension of this tale. Dick was a fan of Franz Kafka's—his friend Ray Nelson said that he could quote passages from memory—but it's unknown if he ever read Kafka's story "The Burrow" which in some way this story resembles. Like it, we start in the mind of the burrower itself. Kafka, however, keeps you inside that mind. Dick's story, unlike Kafka's, was accompanied in its first magazine appearance by an illustration of a farmer about to crush the viewpoint character of its opening lines with a stick. W. E. Terry, the magazine's competent draftsman, depicted the character as a kind of a seal with a baby's face, and the story's tagline ("Radiation labs were causing terrible human mutations. Was this the end of mankind?") left nothing for granted either. Interestingly, while *Imagination*'s letter columns were full of commentary on its published stories—and Dick's were sometimes singled out—not a word of comment was published on this one.

SALES PITCH

Reached SMLA November 19, 1953, published in *Future*, June 1954. *Future* began in 1939, shut down in 1943, and then restarted in 1950, lasting in various formats until 1960. Its editor for most of its lifespan was Robert W. Lowndes. The issue "Sales Pitch" appeared in was its first as a digest (as opposed to the larger "pulp" size). In his notes for this story's appearance in *The Golden Man*, Dick wrote: "When this story first appeared, the fans detested it. I read it over, perplexed by their hostility, and could see why: it is a superdowner story, and relentlessly so. Could I rewrite it I would have it end differently, I would have the man and the robot, i.e., the fasrad, form a partnership at the end and become friends. The logic of paranoia of this story should be deconstructed into its opposite; Y, the human-against-robot theme, should have been resolved into null-Y, human-and-robot-against-the-universe. I really deplore the ending. So when you read the story, try and imagine it as it ought to have been written. The fasrad says 'Sir, I am here to help you. The hell with my sales pitch. Let's be together forever.' Yes, but then I would have been criticized for a false upbeat ending, I guess. Still, this ending is not good. The fans were right."

UPON THE DULL EARTH

Reached SMLA December 30, 1953, published in *Beyond Fantasy Fiction*, November 1954. *Beyond* was launched by Horace Gold (1914-96) as a fantasy companion to his successful science fiction magazine *Galaxy*. Its run was brief, July 1953 to January 1955, but in that time it published work by names like Ray Bradbury, Theodore Sturgeon, Frederik Pohl, Philip Jose Farmer and many more. This particular issue featured "The Green Magician" by L. Sprague de Camp and Fletcher Pratt on its cover, and like every story in the magazine Dick's story ended with a copy of the author's signature. Gold defined fantasy in his editorial accompanying the first issue as "the unconscious interpretation of reality," which is one reading possible of this masterpiece. One of Dick's most significant early stories, "Upon the Dull Earth" anticipates the many "possession state" tales Dick would write over the next thirty years. Many other authors have also depicted these experiences in their fiction, including two of Dick's known favorites, Guy de Maupassant in "The Horla" and Fyodor Dostoyevsky in "The Double." In this case, however, when Rick looks in the mirror and sees his dead wife, he is not seeing "himself" but someone else. Thus this story anticipates that dark masterpiece *The Three Stigmata of Palmer Eldritch*: The bug-like alien Palmer Eldritch "looks into our eyes and out of our eyes."

A WORLD OF TALENT
Submitted as "Two Steps Right." Reached SMLA June 4, 1954, published in *Galaxy*, October 1954. Horace Gold's *Galaxy* was one of the great names in science fiction publishing in its thirty year run, 1950-1980. Gold himself edited the magazine from 1950 until 1961, when ill health forced his retirement. Gold's editorial policy emphasized wit, intelligence, and science fiction as sociological commentary, and produced such classics as Fritz Leiber's "Coming Attraction" (1950), Robert Heinlein's *The Puppet Masters* (1951), Cyril Kornbluth and Frederik Pohl's "Gravy Planet" (1952), novelized as *The Space Merchants*, and Ray Bradbury's "The Fireman" (1951), expanded into *Fahrenheit 451*. Other key authors—Robert Sheckley, Theodore Sturgeon, Kurt Vonnegut—also flourished there. Philip K. Dick's relations with Gold were more contentious. They had much in common. Thanks to his traumatic battlefield experiences during World War II, Gold was an agoraphobe who never ventured out of his New York City apartment. The two men exchanged a mutually sympathetic correspondence in 1952-54, Gold inviting communication on any topic. Dick placed some substantial work there: "The Defenders" (1953), "Colony" (1953), "Shell Game" (1954), this story, "Autofac" (1955)—and then nothing until "War Game" in 1959. The problem was Gold's tendency to rewrite his authors without their permission. Many other writers put up with this—*Galaxy* was prestigious, and did pay a munificent three cents a word. Dick however preferred silence, and to name a cat "Horace Gold" in the 1960s. He named a companion cat "John W. Campbell," but that's another story.